TITAN BLOOD

TITAN BLOOD

1

COLOSS

Victor watched the horizon, wondering if the great horn-plated serpent would make another appearance, but all he saw were the occasional swirls of desert sand, lifting on hot currents of air. Motion to his left brought his attention back to Valla, and he looked at her as she slowly walked in a circle on the top of the low, sandy rise. She avoided stepping in the blood trail left by Boaegh's head as it had bounced down the slope, and Victor noted her frown as she passed by the wizard's body.

"How'd he chain you up, anyway?" he asked.

"My own foolishness. I grew so heated in the chase that I threw caution aside. I charged through the door into his portal room, and the chains wrapped me in their grip—he'd set them up with some sort of warding magic."

"Then he tossed you through the portal?" Victor frowned.

"Exactly, though 'tossed' is the wrong word. He gestured with his hands, and the damnable bindings dragged me through. They're rather advanced magical items . . ." She trailed off, looking at Boaegh's corpse, then added, "Have you searched him? I dropped my sword when the chains wrapped me."

"No, let's check it out before we have to run away from a big damn snake or something." Victor knelt by the gray-robed, headless body. The robes were quite saturated with blood from when he'd buried Lifedrinker between the Pyromancer's shoulders, so he grabbed the dry part near the dead wizard's waist and flopped him over.

The robes concealed most of the body, seeming to have multiple layers that clung to his legs and arms. Still, Boaegh's fingers and hands were exposed below the wide cuffs, and Victor sucked in a breath. He'd never gotten a good look at the mage, and now that he reached to pull the rings from his fingers, he felt morbid curiosity about what his face looked like—the fingers were lightly scaled and orange with long black, pointy nails tipping each of them.

"What kinda dude was this asshole?" Victor muttered as he pulled a ring from each of his hands. He handed them to Valla then walked down the slope toward the head that had come to rest against a dry scrub bush.

"Do you want me to bond with these?" Valla called after him.

"Yeah, but we're sharing the goods. Find your sword now, though." Victor knelt by the head; the face had come to rest facing the dusty ground, and the back only showed layers of black cloth that the wizard had wrapped around himself. Victor grabbed the sides of the head and turned it to study the face of his former tormentor. "Ugly, weren't you?" he grunted when he saw the strange, orange, reptilian visage.

Orange was an oversimplification—Boaegh had scales that varied in shades, darker along his snout and brow and lighter on his cheeks and neck. Still, overall it was orange. "Lizard or snake?" Victor wondered aloud.

"Seems more like a snake to me, but I guess the limbs make a sort of counterargument," Valla said, looking down at him. Victor was glad to see she already had her sword in her hand. "The ring's loaded with stuff—Energy beads, jewelry, furniture, clothing, food, scrolls, books, and on and on and on. We should get somewhere safe before we really go through it. The other ring is some kind of Pyromancer charm—it increases the damage of flame-related spells."

Valla's words reminded Victor of the rings he'd taken from ap'Horrin, and he nodded, saying, "Yeah. Let's figure some shit out, and then we can go through our loot from the oubliette."

"Figure 'shit' out sounds about right. If we can't find our way back to Fanwath, Rellia's either going to have to go into hiding or die." She pointed in a direction that Victor figured was south because the heavy, glowering, yellow-orange sun was off to her right, and it had slowly been inching toward the horizon. "I think I can make out a road or track in that direction. It's hard to say for sure." She shrugged and added, "It could be the path of a giant snake."

"Hang on," Victor said as she started to trudge in that direction. "What about the Far Scribe books?"

"Oh!" Valla said, suddenly holding a book easily as thick as the one Victor had bought to communicate with Lam. He thought about trying to send Lam a message but figured he'd let Valla see if the magic worked first. While she was busy scratching out a message, Victor reached up and pressed his fingers against the familiar lump of Gorz's amulet.

"Hey, you there, Gorz?"

"Victor, how are you? I'm sensing a break in continuity from when we last spoke; did we teleport?"

"You really that out of it? Didn't you notice the conversations I've been having? The oubliette? The portal?"

"I'm sorry, Victor, but I find it harder and harder to remain cognizant of my surroundings between our conversations. I wonder . . ." For the first time that Victor could remember, Gorz trailed off mid-sentence.

"You wonder what, Gorz?"

"I wonder if my spirit shard is losing its anchoring to this plane of existence. I don't know how that could be, unless . . ." Again, his voice faded out, and Victor was about to prompt him, but then he continued, *"Unless the bindings on this amulet are growing weaker and my greater spirit has moved farther away from the material plane. Could it be? Am I being called to rejoin it?"*

"I don't know, buddy. Is that something that can happen?" Victor was skeptical—hadn't Gorz been trapped for thousands of years already?

"I'll . . . think on it."

"Right . . ."

"Victor, I'm not seeing a response," Valla announced, interrupting Victor's commune with Gorz.

"Well, shit. Let's give it some time; it's not like we're in the same neighborhood anymore."

Valla frowned but nodded, and her book disappeared back into her ring. She turned and, back straight as a board, started marching to the very thin, very faint line of brown near the horizon. She still held her sword, naked blade resting on her shoulder, and Victor followed, Lifedrinker held crossways in his two hands.

He took a good look at his axe and grinned ferociously. She'd done him proud back in the oubliette. He'd even say she'd guided herself through the air to smash into Boaegh's back perfectly. The veins of Heart Silver ran in jagged, thick rivulets from her gleaming edge through the darker, denser metal of her axe-head, and he could feel the potential in her, the vibrating eagerness for battle. It felt as if she were on the threshold of "leveling up" as she'd done back in the dungeon so long ago.

"Your axe looks different," Valla said, slowing down and watching him as he walked toward her. Victor glanced up from his study of Lifedrinker and smiled.

"Yeah, I think she's getting ready to evolve, or whatever it's called when she advances. She's done it before," he said. "When I first got her, she was smaller—didn't have this pointy bit at the back of her axe-head."

"A truly wondrous weapon," Valla said, nodding. "I love my sword, but it's not alive."

"Maybe we'll figure a way to wake it up. You think that's possible?"

"I don't know. I don't know what it's made of or what goes into creating a living artifact like your axe. I thought it was the Heart Silver that made it intelligent?"

"Well, yeah, but not all intelligent artifacts are Heart Silver, right?"

"No, but most are like your amulet—spirits trapped to serve a purpose." Valla was looking at her sword while she walked and almost tripped into a small cactus with pencillike pads covered in dark red spines, and Victor grabbed onto her elbow.

"Careful. Who knows what kinda nastiness is lurking on those pokers."

"They blend in with the landscape! I thought it was a scrub brush in my peripheral vision; I was going to stomp through it!" Valla said, hopping around the little cactus.

"Yeah, keep your eyes peeled," Victor laughed. As the sun continued to set and the glare on the desert landscape faded, he looked around, admiring the bright red- and orange-streaked clouds hanging high in the sky. "Quite a sunset."

"Yes, it's lovely," Valla replied, though she barely glanced at the sky. Her eyes were trained on the southern horizon, and she added, "It's definitely a road! I see posts—little markers evenly spaced."

"Shit!" Victor said, shading his eyes and staring in the direction she pointed. Sure enough, he saw little wooden posts evenly spaced along the brown ribbon of, presumably, the roadway. "You're right! Let's pick up the pace, eh?" He didn't wait for a response, breaking into an easy jog he knew he could maintain for hours, eating up the miles. Valla kept pace behind him without comment, and Victor grinned. That was his favorite quality about her as a travel companion: she never complained and rarely second-guessed him.

Fifteen minutes later, they were standing on a wide, flat dirt road next to one of the regular posts on its southern shoulder. The post was square, about four inches by four, and around five feet high. Brass letters stamped vertically into the wood read "COLOSS." Underneath the letters were similar brass numerals that said "37."

"Like, mile markers?" Victor mused.

"Mile markers? Oh, you mean it's saying that Coloss, whatever that is, is thirty-seven miles?"

"Not exactly," Victor said, pointing down the road to the next marker. "That one's not a mile away, maybe more like a quarter mile. Let's go see if it says thirty-six or thirty-eight." He started jogging down the road, and Valla gamely ran behind him. A couple of minutes later, he came to a halt before the next marker, and sure enough, it said "COLOSS" and "36."

"You think it's a town?" Valla asked.

"That would be my guess." Victor shrugged, then he snapped his fingers and said, "Check your Far Scribe book."

Valla nodded and produced the book, flipping to the most recent page, and her face lit up with delight. "There's a response!"

"Oh, sweet!" Victor clapped his hands together, then added, "Did you tell her about our, uh, trip?"

"Not yet, but I said we were out of reach. We still have fourteen weeks until the campaign is officially supposed to begin; Lam's planning a parade through Persi Gables to kick off the march. I think we can find a way back before then, don't you?" She raised her seafoam green eyebrows, and Victor couldn't help chuckling at the mischief in her eyes.

"Hell yeah, I think we can!" Victor said, always game to poke the eye of authority. "Let's not tell her until we know for sure one way or the other. If shit looks terrible, like we'll never make it, you can warn her. Is that cool?"

"Yes," Valla said, nodding.

"Well? Let's start jogging toward whatever Coloss is, and if we see a place to rest before we get there, we can chill for the night and go through our loot."

"Yes." Valla nodded again. "Let's chill." Then she started jogging as Victor's mouth fell open.

"You . . ." he started, running to catch up. "You almost used that right!"

They ran as the sun descended behind them, and by the time the orange-streaked sky turned dark—revealing a brilliant starfield and a huge, crater-pocked moon, distinctly green in tone—they were at marker seventeen. All the while they were running, Victor could hear the sounds of distant wild-life—coughing roars, weird howls and barks, yowling, and even screeching. They never laid eyes on any more monsters, big or small, though they saw quite a few airborne birds and creatures in the distance.

"The place seems quite alive; I wonder if the denizens would view us as prey should we linger in place."

"Yeah, I don't know. Rather get to a town and ask than do some experiments, you know?"

"Agreed," Valla huffed. She hadn't had much trouble keeping up with him, and he had to admit he admired the way she could keep up a fast jog while holding her big sword at the ready.

"You think you could go faster? We have seventeen more markers, so something like four miles. I bet we could make it pretty quick if we wanted to." Rather than answer him, Valla grinned and started to really run. Victor whooped and ran after her. As he began to gain on her, Valla's hands were suddenly empty, and she kicked it into another gear, sprinting down the road. "Cheater!" Victor laughed, shaking Lifedrinker over his head as he ran. "I can't put her in storage!"

"Your . . . problem!" Valla laughed between breaths. Victor grinned and boosted his agility with Sovereign Will, then he veritably flew down the road, madly laughing as he passed by Valla. She wasn't one to be outdone, though; as he worked on lengthening his lead, he felt a rush of wind, and then Valla charged past him, gusts and miniature gales throwing dirt and pebbles up around her feet.

Victor laughed in dismay, pumping his legs for all he was worth, but suddenly Valla slid to a stop ahead of him, kicking up dust that he inhaled as he thundered up to her, trying to slow down. Coughing and heaving for breath, he leaned forward, hands on his knees, and tried to see why Valla had stopped.

The road continued down a gradual decline, but in the distance, where the star-speckled black sky met the dark horizon of the desert, the lights of a walled city glittered like a pile of jewels in the darkness. "That's something else," Victor said; even his limited experience told him that the city was much larger than Persi Gables or Gelica.

"Coloss, I suppose," Valla said, stretching her arms over her head as she got her wind back.

"Kinda weird we didn't see any traffic. That place looks enormous."

"Well, it was late afternoon when we got here. Maybe people don't like this desert at night." Valla glanced around meaningfully, and Victor nodded, well aware of all the creature sounds in the night.

"Let's keep moving," he said, starting back into a jog. "Let's hope they take beads here—I could use a bath and a good night's sleep."

"If the System exists here, they'll take beads. I think," Valla replied, running beside him.

"Have you ever been to another world?"

"No. Rellia has, but only to a linked city where she was trying to make a trade deal."

"Linked city?"

"She went through the System Stone in Gelica to a city in a nearby world. One that had already been traveled through in both directions—people call that a 'linked city' because we've, well, we've established a link."

"How do you know it's close to Fanwath?"

"The cost. The System charges exorbitant fees to facilitate transport between worlds, and the more distant the world, the more absurd the price."

"So," Victor said, smiling at how easy it was to carry on a conversation while running—no way he'd have done that back in wrestling practice—"we better hope this world isn't distant from Fanwath."

"Yeah, I suppose that is a concern. There were quite a few beads in Boaegh's ring, though."

"Yeah, I saw some bags of 'em in ap'Horrin's ring, too. Hopefully, we're good."

They both got lost in their thoughts for a while after that, and the enormous, light-bedecked walls of the city were soon looming above them, forestalling any other topic of conversation. Victor wasn't a stone expert, but he thought the massive tan-colored blocks of the wall looked like what the Egyptians used on their pyramids. Each one was the size of a car, and the walls were higher than apartment buildings, at least the ones Victor had experience with. "How tall do you figure that wall is? A hundred feet?"

"Easily. Maybe two hundred. It's much bigger and thicker than the one around Persi Gables. Look at that gate!" Victor followed her pointing finger, and his mouth fell open—the only reason he hadn't noticed the enormous black iron gate was that it looked small inside the great wall. As they approached, though, he could see it was at least thirty feet high and twenty wide. And it was closed.

Great glow lamps illuminated the space around the walls; each was rectangular, about five feet by two, and poured out massive arcs of bright yellow light. The gate had two such lamps on each side, and as Victor and Valla approached, they had to squint against the bright glare. No guards stood outside, and no voices drifted down from the high walls to challenge them. Victor looked around at the dark, moonlit desert behind them, then back at the gate and shrugged.

"Hello?" he called, cupping his hands to his mouth. Valla jumped at his shout and whirled to stare daggers at him. "What?" he asked.

"You startled me. Look, though," she said, pointing to the left-hand corner of the enormous gate. Victor saw a smaller rectangle in the rust-flecked black iron and realized it was a person-sized door.

"Oh! So they don't have to open the gate to let a person through." He nodded, walked up to the smaller door, and lifted a hand to knock. Before his knuckles fell on the hard surface, though, an even smaller rectangle at eye level slid open, and big yellow eyes stared out at him.

"Who calls?" a gruff, scratchy voice asked.

"Hello," Valla said, striding up next to Victor, "We're travelers seeking shelter."

"That right? At the east gate in the night? You have a desire for death?" the voice asked, but Victor heard the clank and scrape of a large bolt being slid aside, and the door was pushed open. "Come through, then, 'fore a terror grabs ya up."

"Thanks," Victor said, stepping through the iron threshold and into a dim stone tunnel that would have looked about right passing through the Hoover Dam. Before he could take in the scene, though, his eyes were drawn to the six large guards with spears leveled at him and Valla. They looked like burlier versions of Boaegh—tall yellow-, green-, and orange-scaled serpent people clad in all sorts of exotic armor. Many wore helms, most had other weapons bristling from their belts, and some had four arms rather than two.

"Declare your names and your intentions in Coloss," the first scratchy voice said, and Victor followed the sound to the green-scaled serpent man on the right, the only guard leaning on his spear rather than pointing it.

"Hey, we're honestly just trying to get home," Victor said, and Valla stepped forward, clearing her throat.

"We mistakenly took a portal from our world to the desert nearby. We don't know where we are and would like access to your City Stone."

"You're lucky, then. The Garsh Wastes"—the guard flicked one of his four hands toward the gates, indicating the area outside—"aren't friendly. It's good that you made your way to Coloss, but you won't so easily access the City Stone."

"What do you mean, sir?" Valla asked, making the assumption of a lifetime, as far as Victor was concerned. He winced and waited to see if she'd guessed right.

"Simply that the stone isn't open to the public. Warlord Thoargh only grants access to people willing to pay." He looked at the other five guards and motioned with his top right arm for them to lower their spears. They complied and then disbursed around the tunnel, standing here and there near the gate, clearly still trying to listen to the spokesman's conversation with Victor and Valla.

"We can pay," Victor said, perhaps too quickly.

The guard grinned, though, and shook his head. "I doubt that. You're new to this world, yes? Warlord Thoargh only grants access to people with Coloss prize tokens."

"I can guess the rest," Valla said, shaking her head. "This Warlord—he's the one that hands out the tokens?"

"Well, not personally," the guard said, and Victor caught a glimpse of his long, forked tongue flicking lightning fast between his scaled lips. "There are prize committees." He yawned and leaned against the metal doors. "I don't really get paid enough to educate every runt that wanders in here, though. Why not head into the city and see if you can get someone with a less important job to explain things further." He gestured with his spear down the enormous tunnel, and Victor, his jaw hanging open at the guard's choice of words, allowed Valla to pull him away.

"He called me a runt?" Victor said, looking around at the tunnel—it had to be three hundred feet long, and the walls and ceiling were composed of those enormous stone blocks that made up the city wall. "Is the wall this damn thick?" he asked, finally registering the absurd proportions.

"This wall puts the one around the noble district in Tharcray to shame," Valla said, echoing his sentiments.

"I'm sure it's thicker here at the bottom than at the top," Victor said, trying to wrap his head around the amount of stone it would take to build a wall this size around an entire city. "What kind of Energy user can cut and move stones like this? It seems impossible that this was done by hand."

"Earth affinity," Valla quickly replied. "Someone much more powerful than I."

Victor nodded and turned his gaze away from the massive stone blocks to the end of the tunnel. People, in large numbers, were moving along what appeared to be a busy street. Something seemed strange about the crowd of people, and it took Victor a minute to put his finger on it; he'd grown so used to the predominance of Ardeni and Shadeni people in Persi Gables and Gelica that the lack of red and blue skin was throwing him off.

As they drew closer, details about the city's people became more evident. Victor had thought he was looking at adults and children, but he realized that nearly half of the people walking around out there were giants—eight, ten, even twelve feet tall. Many of the others looked human enough, but some had extra limbs, others had horns, and one guy walking by had a big cyclops-like eye.

Then there were the snake people and—surprising only to Valla—brightly carapaced insect people. The insects weren't all green like Ksajik; some were pale orange, others were sandy brown, and still others were golden yellow. The people that looked the most like humans were the giants, and Victor began to understand why the guard had called him a runt.

"Victor," Valla said, reaching to grab his wrist and slow their walk, "do you feel their auras?"

"Now you mention it," Victor said, finally consciously acknowledging what his gut had been telling him since he'd first been confronted by the guards at the gate. It wasn't just his suddenly less-than-impressive stature; many of these people were exuding a level of Energy, of power, that made him feel small. "Yeah, we're not in Kansas anymore."

"Kansas?" Valla looked at him as though he'd lost his mind.

"It's a figure of speech from my world—some kinda old movie or something."

"Movie?" Valla shook her head and continued, "Never mind. The point I was trying to make was that many of these people feel like you; they have a huge presence. Let's be careful with our words."

"This is what I feel like?"

"Maybe to a lesser degree," Valla said, narrowing her eyes at him.

"You're just afraid to compliment me." Victor laughed, and then they stepped out of the tunnel onto a busy cobbled road. Energy lamps on tall iron posts drove back the night's shadows, and it was clear that Coloss didn't go to bed with the sun. Victor stood there, mouth agape, staring at the crowds of strange and enormous people, at the tall stone buildings and floating magical carts.

He'd just begun to take in the smells of spicy food and strange incense when a hand gently nudged him aside, pushing him to the edge of the cobbled path. "Hey," Victor started, but then choked off the word as the hand's owner stomped past him—an armor-clad man nearly twice his height. He wasn't thin, either, and judging by the effortless way he'd brushed Victor aside, he wasn't lacking muscle.

"Victor!" Valla hissed, again grabbing his arm and pulling him along. "Don't stand in the middle of traffic!"

"Yeah," Victor said, still unable to wrap his head around the size and strength of the guy that had nudged him aside. He watched the man's mighty frame as he strode away down the street and couldn't help wondering how he'd stack up to him in his Quinametzin form. He walked along next to Valla, trying to avoid the big guys, and that's when he realized that the people in the city seemed to walk in lanes; the big people were on the left, toward the center of the street, and the more "normal-sized" people were on the right.

As he and Valla walked along with the traffic, Victor looked at the buildings and the signs and began noticing new details. Many of the businesses had high, massive doors, and he figured that was to accommodate the giant people, but perhaps more strange were the occasional shops that didn't have big doors—were they intentionally excluding the giants?

They passed by grocers, tailors, cobblers, butchers, bakeries, furniture makers, and restaurants. At the first intersection, they came to a gigantic building with a sign that read "Weary Travelers, Welcome! The Basilisk Inn and Tavern." The structure had a huge door, which Victor took to mean giants were welcome. A stable stood next door, filling the air with the scents of straw and animal dung, but over that was the smell of roasting meats, and Victor's mouth began to water. "Let's go in here," he said.

"The first inn we see?" Valla asked, wrinkling her nose.

"Hey, we can always look for something else, but right now, I'd like to get off the street and learn more about this place before we go exploring. What do you think?"

"Makes sense." Valla nodded and started up the giant steps to the door. Victor laughed, watching her; she looked like a person trying to take regular steps three at a time. He took them in springing bounds and pulled the heavy wooden door open, gesturing for Valla to lead the way inside.

She smirked as she took the last big step, then stepped past, and he followed. The common room of the inn looked much like any other, but mixed in with the normal-sized furniture were huge tables and chairs, and the crowd was a mixture of people; many were the human-like people with their strange—to Victor—features, from horns to tusks to an odd number of eyes. Here and there, Victor saw some of the serpent people, and, of course, some giants occupied the oversized furniture.

"Come in," a thin, dark-haired man with ruddy skin said, gesturing Victor and Valla over to his counter. Victor approached him, noting how the bar was staggered—half was about five feet high and the other half a few feet taller, clearly meant to accommodate the larger people. "New to town?" the man asked, absently wiping dry a mug with a white towel. He turned his head slightly, and Victor saw a long, curved black horn poking out the right side of it.

"Hey," Victor replied, nodding. "Yeah, we just got here. You have a room available?"

"Sure! Have a seat here, and I'll give you something to wash the dust out of your throats."

"Thank you," Valla replied, climbing atop one of the open stools. Victor nodded and sat next to her.

"Where do you hail from?"

"A world called Fanwath," Valla replied.

"Oh, new to the world, not just Coloss, hmm?"

"Yeah, that's right. We really weren't meaning to come here and want to get home as soon as possible. The guard at the gate was telling us something about how there's a warlord or something that doesn't allow access to the City Stone?" Victor had decided to get right to the point, hoping this inn-keeper was as friendly as all the others he'd met.

"Oh, that's true. Warlord Thoargh capitalizes on his City Stone, what with Coloss being the only city for a few thousand miles in any direction. Do you have the means to travel great distances through perilous territory?" He turned to fill a couple of mugs from one of the taps behind him, and Valla looked at Victor with a raised eyebrow. He took her expression to mean she was leaving it to him to decide how much to say.

"I guess it depends on how hard it is to get these, um, tokens they give out to access the Stone," he said as the horned man set the two frothy mugs of pale beer in front of him and Valla.

"Oh, not too hard, I'd think. You can earn them by turning in monster trophies or for winning arena battles." He paused and glanced from Victor to Valla. "Now, don't let that discourage you two! Even low-tier people like you can earn monster trophies—just get with one of the monster hunting expeditions and help out; they pay helpers in scraps."

2

FIRST IMPRESSIONS

So, four major groups of people originate from this world?" Victor asked, his words slurred by the potent ale he and Valla had been drinking.

"Aye," replied Livag, their innkeeper and bartender. "You've got those like me, the Vesh." He reached up and touched the long black horn curving out the side of his head. "Then you've got our cousins, the big folk, the Degh." He paused, nodding to himself, then pointed behind Victor and to the left, where some of the bright green insect people were sharing a loaf of bread at a nearby table. "There's the Tong-pan, and if you look behind them"—he pointed to a corner table where some hooded serpent people were sipping drinks—"you can see some Yazzians."

"No offense," Victor said, glancing around the room and wiping his tingling cheeks and nose, "but I don't think I'll remember all that. I was just starting to wrap my head around the different people from Fanwath, er, Valla's world." Victor pointed to Valla, who watched him coolly, sipping at her beer. "Don't mind her," Victor said, leaning closer to Livag. "She's not a big conversationalist."

"Ha!" Livag shook his head and turned to fill a mug for another patron.

"Careful, Victor," Valla said, "The alcohol is strong here; they must brew it with alchemy to have a greater effect on people with high vitality scores."

"Yeah." Victor nodded. It was true—he hadn't felt a buzz like this since he and Thayla had put away half a dozen pitchers at the Red Roladii Inn. With a slight frown, he boosted his vitality with Sovereign Will and pushed his mug back on the bar top. "Give me a few to sober up, I guess."

Valla nodded and spoke softly. "Probably best to keep our wits until we know more about this place."

"Yep." Victor cleared his throat and said, "Livag, how much for a room?"

"Ten beads per night."

"Ten?" Victor could easily afford it, especially considering the yet uncounted treasures lying within ap'Horrin's and Boaegh's rings. Still, ten beads for a night was a lot more than they'd pay in Persi Gables.

"Aye, pup. Ten." Livag's easy grin didn't falter as he pushed a mug of ale toward another member of his species, a woman with enormous tusks jutting up from her oversized jaw.

"Hey, another thing. You assumed me and Valla were 'low tier'—what does that mean in these parts?"

"Low tier? Anyone who has yet to reach level fifty."

"Hey!" Valla said, speaking up to Livag for the first time since he'd poured her ale. "I'm level fifty-two."

"Oh, well, no offense, but your aura isn't even as heavy as Victor's here, and I can tell he ain't out of the lower tiers."

"Really?" Valla frowned.

"Aye, but don't fret. You're from a newer world, aren't you?" Livag reached for Valla's cup, but she pulled it back, holding her hand over the top.

"Yes. I believe Fanwath is a relatively new world. The System crafted it a bit more than four hundred years ago."

"There you have it! You all haven't had thousands and thousands of years to stockpile natural treasures and learn the best way to gain certain classes, skills, or Cores. The monsters that roam the wastes out there"—he gestured broadly with one arm—"would probably pose quite a threat to a city in your world. While we grow stronger, so do they."

"Is that why the Warlord offers prize tokens for killing them? So they don't threaten the city?" Victor asked, already starting to feel the edge of his buzz fading away.

"Nah! Even an adult wyrm would break itself on our great wall. No, the Warlord wants monster trophies because they're natural treasures—he can use them to improve his or his people's strength."

"So if we're low tier, what's high tier?" Victor asked, still annoyed at being considered a runt.

"Well, here in Coloss, if you're between levels fifty and eighty, you're considered mid-tier. People over that are high tier. There aren't so many of them."

"Seems like really broad categories. If I fought in the arena you mentioned, is it separated by tiers?"

"Oh, aye, lad. I wouldn't go in there, though. The prizes are great, but so's the risk; mercy is encouraged but not guaranteed, and if you lose, there's a good chance of being maimed or slain." He moved off to fill another drink request, and Victor studied Valla's face; she looked troubled, almost annoyed, her pale green eyebrows drawn together, creasing her forehead as her eyes stared into the void of introspection.

"Something wrong?"

"Several things," she replied, shoving her mug back on the bar with a look of disgust. "Us being weaklings certainly doesn't bode well for our chances to get back to Fanwath; that's one. Two, I just learned that because I come from a backwater, ignorant world, I've ruined my potential—I've spent fifty levels with subpar skills, classes, even my Core."

"Hold up," Victor said, turning to look at Valla more directly. "Livag didn't say you were ruined, just that it wasn't surprising you were from a newish world. Right, Livag?" Victor asked, getting the barkeep's attention.

"What's that, Victor?"

"Do you think Valla's chances for being strong are ruined cause she came from a low-tier world?"

"Ruined? No, I wouldn't say that. You're at a deficit, but I've met many people from many worlds, and you aren't the worst I've seen. Maybe you can get some treasures to improve your Core while you're here. Why, there might be a mentor here for you! What affinity do you channel?"

"I . . ." Valla glanced at Victor, clearly uncomfortable talking about herself. Victor nodded, and she continued. "I have elemental affinities: iron and air."

"Oh? That's a strong combination! What about your class? Is it advanced, at least?"

"Yes, I've had an advanced class since Tier Two."

"There you go! A little work with a master and a few natural treasures, and you'll be up to snuff. With the right master, I'd be shocked if your next refinement didn't pull you an epic class option."

Victor watched Valla while Livag spoke, and he saw her scowl smooth out as she nodded along. "You're a good bartender, Livag," Victor said, slapping the counter. "Hey, we could use some rest, but in the morning, I'm going to want to do some research. Will you be working? I want to get directions from you."

"Yes, and can you point me in the direction of a 'master' for my affinities?" Valla added, suddenly more talkative.

"I'll be here. Never a day off for an old tavern commander. Talk to me over breakfast, and I'll point you where you need to go. Here," he said, pulling a smooth crystal disc about the size of a drink coaster from his belt. "Touch your finger to this stone, both of you." Victor and Valla reached out together and placed their fingers on the stone, hers thin and pale blue, Victor's swarthy and enormous next to it. Livag nodded and pressed his own calloused, hairy digit on the smooth surface. It flashed with mauve Energy, and he nodded, scooping it up and slipping it into his belt.

"What was that supposed to do?" Valla asked belatedly.

"Hand me ten beads, please—I just assigned you to room twelve. The door will open for you when you head up."

"Hey! Pretty cool," Victor said as he dug a handful of beads from his storage ring. He glanced to his right, where the staircase climbed the back wall of the common room, and said, "So, no giant rooms upstairs?"

Valla frowned, following his glance, but Livag spoke. "Nope. All the Degh rooms are on the first floor. It saves a lot on construction costs."

"I noticed quite a few businesses on the way in that didn't have giant-sized doors. Do the Degh not get upset?"

"Upset?" Livag frowned, "Why would they? This isn't a Degh city." He shrugged and added, "Most Degh are grateful for those of us willing to go to the expense of building to accommodate them. It pays off, though, between you and me. Degh pay well."

"Huh, I guess I just pictured the Warlord as one of them," Victor said, scooting out his stool, "I mean one of the Degh."

"Nah, he's a proud Vesh like me!" Livag thumped his chest. "Though he's as strong as any Degh, you can believe that!"

"Okay, cool. C'mon, Valla." Victor wound his way between tables, standard and giant sized, and started up the steps, keeping to the right to avoid bumping into a group of the serpent people coming down. He shook his head ruefully—he'd already forgotten what they were called. Two of the four had passed by him, but the third gave him a shoulder check that sent him reeling into the banister.

"Watch your step, scaleless," the tall, wiry, orange-scaled . . . person hissed.

Victor felt his heart start to thud, felt his rage-attuned Energy begin to bleed into his pathways, and he stood up straight and stared into the serpent person's weird yellow eyes. "Excuse you."

"Leave the scaleless runt in peace, Cheggra. It doesn't even have a horn or tusk to collect," a more yellow-toned, slightly smaller serpent person said.

"Sure," Victor replied, then he pulled a large black felt sack out of ap'Horrin's ring and set it on the bed. It was heavy and clicked with the telltale sound of Energy beads. "He's got five sacks like this, and I think they each have more than a thousand beads." Valla had stood up and was carefully examining the blade of one of the rapiers—it was thin and appeared fragile compared to her broadsword, but Victor could see there was something special about it; the blade looked like crystal, not metal.

"I won't use this rapier, but it'll fetch an enormous sum at auction. Its blade is a single blood crystal; I imagine ap'Horrin used it in conjunction with his affinity. Rumors around Persi Gables were that he had a blood affinity."

"Yeah, he sure did." Victor shook his head, remembering the creepy spells ap'Horrin had used while he'd pursued him around the oubliette. "He was sucking the Energy out of one of those insect guys when I found him—it looked like he was pulling his blood through the air."

"Ancestors!" Valla shuddered, then said, "This other blade is also valuable, but not so much as the first one." She pulled the second sword free of its scabbard to show Victor. It had a shiny, silvery blade with golden runes etched into it. "It's an enchanted steel alloy. I'm not sure what metals went into it, but they must have been rich because it has strong effects, more than an Artificer could impart on simple steel."

"All right. Well? What about Boaegh's ring?"

"Nearly twenty thousand beads," Valla said, walking over to the foot of her bed and proceeding to unload leather sacks of Energy beads, one after another, until she'd set down nearly thirty bags. "Put them into one of your rings, please."

"We should split 'em up, don't you think?"

"No! I have my own wealth. You made these kills despite my failings, not with my aid, so no, I'll not be taking a share. Hurry now, pick these up before we're robbed. There are a couple of items in Boaegh's ring that you might be interested in; the rest are mundane objects—food, clothing, furniture, and books."

"All right, but let me know if you need some money while we're here." Victor moved among the leather sacks, touching each one to transfer it into one of his rings. He wasn't going to argue with Valla—for all he knew, she had a million beads in her dimensional containers. He wondered how many beads the adopted daughter of one of the most powerful families in an empire would consider a fortune.

Valla had moved back to her bed and was setting some objects on the thin gray blanket, so Victor spent a minute gathering and organizing the beads from several containers into one area. With the money from Boaegh and ap'Horrin added to his own pile of beads, he knew he had nearly forty thousand, and that was without selling many of the potentially precious items he'd been hoarding. "What have we got here?" he asked, looking over Valla's shoulder.

"Four items we should probably sell," Valla said, gesturing her hand over her bedspread. "A Diadem of Concentration, used for spell casting during combat—I think it speeds up the process of gathering Energy and focusing it into a complicated spell pattern." She pointed to a weird silver and ruby-studded headband with long metal points that would hang down over the wearer's cheekbones.

"Huh." Victor shrugged. "What else?"

"This rod." Valla picked up a thick, rune-etched, dull, black metal wand. "Another focus item for fire-attuned Energy.

"'Kay. What about that cloak?" Victor pointed to a folded, hooded red cloak.

"Cloak of the Flame Walker. It allows 'brief immunity to scorching flames.'" She picked it up and shook it out, showing Victor its rich fabric and crimson, silky lining. "I don't know how hot 'scorching' is or how long 'brief immunity' is, but it seems like it could be useful."

"Well, that's pretty awesome. I think it's kind of wasted on me with my new feat, but why don't you keep it? We might meet more Pyromancers or maybe fire-breathing monsters." He'd expected Valla to object, saying they should sell it or something, but she just nodded briefly and swung the cloak up to fasten at her shoulders. The garment seemed to contract on itself, shrinking to fit her perfectly. "Looks good," Victor said, reaching out to feel the silky fabric between his thumb and forefinger.

"I like it; it's brighter than I would have bought for myself." Valla pulled the finely stitched lapels closer together and fastened the ornate brass button near her throat. "I didn't mention that it's supposed to reduce the discomfort of a hot environment." She looked up at Victor and grinned, perhaps some-what guiltily.

"Oh, you 'didn't mention' that, huh?" Victor laughed. "No wonder you didn't argue about keeping it!"

"Yes, well." She cleared her throat, and Victor saw her blue cheeks had grown a bit darker and that she was struggling with words. Was she really feeling guilty about snagging up that cloak? He laughed and reached out, jostling her shoulder.

"Relax. I'm glad you took it—not my style." He looked at the bed and saw the last item was a dagger in a shiny black scabbard. It had an ornate basket hilt and a red gem at its pommel. "What about the dagger?"

"It's been charged with a spell, something called Lava Blood. It has one use—a person stabbed with that knife will have the spell discharged upon them, and the weapon will be destroyed in the process. According to the description, anyway."

Victor picked up the dagger and nodded. "Might come in handy, huh? We can always sell it later if not, but for now, I'll hold onto this, okay?"

"Of course. Do you want me to hold the other items until I've had a chance to sell them?"

"Yes, please. I have too much to keep track of in these rings already." Victor looked down at himself—most of his armor and clothes were clean, thanks to their enchantments, but the backs of his hands had bits of dried, caked blood on them, and he knew his hair and neck and the rest of him needed cleaning. "I'm going to check out the baths. What about you?"

"We should stay together, or at least close," Valla said, moving to the door. "We don't know what people are like here other than powerful. Would they break in here and kill us for our belongings? For your axe or my sword?"

"All right, heading to the baths together, then." Victor moved through the door and then turned left down the hallway. At the far end were three doors with bathtub-shaped images carved into the wood. Faded blue paint depicted overflowing water, and Victor smiled at the artistic touch.

Two of the doors were locked, but one was open. Victor pushed open the unlocked door, revealing a small room with a bench, clothing pegs, and a simple brass tub, big enough to accommodate people larger even than he.

"At least they're private," Valla said, and she might have tried to disguise it, but Victor heard the relief in her voice.

"Yeah, you go first." Victor nudged her into the opening and said as he pulled the door, "I'll wait for another to open up. Just holler if someone messes with you." Valla didn't protest, and he heard the lock click home after he pulled the door shut. Sighing, he leaned his back against the doorjamb and watched the other two doors, waiting for one to open.

He let his mind wander, thinking about what he'd already learned about this world. He pictured giant, powerful monsters, and then he thought about a different kind of monster; it didn't have a face, more an amorphous mob consisting of the thousands of people in Coloss that would make Polo Vosh seem like a novice. He felt a gentle nudge at his shoulder and nearly jumped out of his skin—had he been that out of it, or had this person moved like a ghost to stand next to him?

"Excuse me, sir," said a dry, wispy voice from within the deep blue hood.

"Yeah?" Victor asked, turning to face the tall, slender, robed figure. He tried to hide his irritation at being surprised but doubted he did a good job of it.

The hooded figure reached up with long blue-gloved fingers to pull the hood back, and Victor was startled to see a very human-looking woman standing before him. He supposed she was one of the Vesh—like the innkeeper—but he couldn't see any horns or tusks or extra eyes. Maybe she had a tail or something, he mused during the three seconds it took for the woman to lower her hood from her curled blonde hair and say, "Is that your mate within?" She gestured to the door where Victor leaned his shoulder.

"My mate? That's my friend."

"We've not seen one such as she in Coloss. My employer, War Captain Forl, would enjoy the opportunity to meet her." Her bright pink lips curled up, brandishing a brilliant, white-toothed smile at Victor, her hazel eyes twinkling in the glow lamps. She held out, between gloved fingers, a simple white piece of card stock. "He's invited her to dinner, and you are welcome to escort her."

"Oh?" Victor reached out and took the card, noting the pale orange runes painted on one side.

"Yes, just activate this card, and it will guide you to his estate."

"Sorry, but I'm new here; is a War Captain, like, an official title?"

"Yes, he's one of four War Captains that serve under the Warlord."

"Well, I'll pass on the invitation, but I don't speak for Valla. If she's not into it, we won't be coming."

"There are no expectations attached to the invitation, sir. We'll hope to see you." She bowed then and began to turn, but Victor's impulsive mouth wouldn't let her slip away that easily.

"Hey, are you one of the, um, Vesh people?"

"Me? Oh no," she said, and then her skin darkened from pale flesh to glimmering blue scales, and her body elongated and thickened with a surge of Energy that was palpable to Victor. "I'm a dragon, manling," said the woman's pleasant voice from the extended snout that now loomed before him, thick white fangs poking up around the scaly lips that still somehow curved into a smile. "I'd take on my full shape to show you, but it would ruin this building."

"Holy shit," Victor managed to utter as the dragon's aura pressed him back into the door, his body's urge to flee threatening to destroy the puny wooden barrier. He inhaled a shaky breath, and then, with another surge of Energy, the lovely, normal-sized woman was standing before him again, still grinning like a cat with a mouse.

"I, too, am a visitor to this world. It's been an age or more since I laid eyes on a human. If the War Captain knew you weren't just a runty Deshi, he'd be more interested in you than your companion, I'd wager. Worry not, human. I'm just here for my own amusement, traveling and learning from a few talents I've yet to meet in this part of the universe. Still, I do hope you and your friend will attend the War Captain's dinner tomorrow. It could also prove fruitful for you—connections are important in this city."

She smiled again, stunning Victor with her radiance, and pulled her hood back over her head, turning to leave. "Wait," Victor finally choked out. "Does he know? The War Captain?"

She glanced back over her shoulder at Victor and asked, "That I'm a dragon?" At his nod, she continued, "No. You're the only one in this world I've shown. Strange, don't you think?"

"I . . ." Victor started to say, but she was gone. A faint misty blue haze lingered near the floorboards, the only evidence that she'd ever been there. "Fucking hell. I didn't know dragons were *chicas bonitas* on the inside."

3

✦

MONSTER HUNTERS

So, this War Captain invited us to dinner simply because he thought I looked interesting?" Valla didn't look directly into Victor's eyes while she spoke, and he realized she was embarrassed.

"He's probably just a rich asshole who's used to getting what he wants. Forget it—we don't need to go."

"No . . ." Valla said, holding up a hand and shifting under her blanket. Victor had found her nearly asleep after he'd finished his time in the bath. He was standing at the foot of her bed, having just handed her the invitation card the dragon lady had given him. While he'd soaked in the tub, it had dawned on him that he hadn't even gotten the woman's name, so dumbstruck had he been. "I think we should go," Valla finished. "If only because we need to learn the politics of this place if we hope to return to Fanwath in a timely manner."

"Okay, but if the guy gets too creepy, we can bail. Just let me know." Victor wanted to say more, wanted to assure Valla that he had her back or that her feelings mattered to him, but despite their time together, she still had a sort of default chill toward him, especially when her feelings were the topic of conversation.

"Well, that's for tomorrow. Tonight we should get some sleep. We can get an early start; I'd like to learn more about the prize tokens. I wonder if it's difficult to join a monster-hunting 'crew' as the innkeeper suggested." She turned to her side, back toward him and his bed, and fluffed her pillow, tucking it up under her head.

"Yeah, me too. Also, we can try to find someone to help you with your Core." Victor moved to the far side of his bed and sat down to pull off his boots; he hadn't wanted to walk back from the baths barefooted. He heard Valla yawn as he slipped his belt, boots, and shirt into his storage ring, then he leaned Lifedrinker against the wall next to the little maple-colored headboard.

He ducked under his blanket, stretching his legs, and was somewhat surprised that the bed didn't creak alarmingly and that his feet didn't hit the footboard. "Kinda weird not to be the biggest guy around," he said with a loud yawn of his own.

"I can imagine. Back home, you were starting to loom large in size and reputation."

"Home . . ." Victor said softly, wondering at how strange it seemed to think of Fanwath that way.

"I suppose you don't feel that way yet," Valla said, shifting under her covers so that she lay on her other side, facing him. Victor also turned from his back to his side and frowned, staring across the little gap between their beds into her otherworldly green eyes that reminded him of mint ice cream.

"I don't know. I feel like the Victor that came here from Tucson is dead. Damn, that's depressing to say out loud. Anyway, yeah, I almost feel like I don't have a home. There's no place I fit in." Valla's eyes narrowed, and he saw her mouth open as if she wanted to say something, but she closed it again, apparently lost for words. Victor cleared his throat and added, "Eh, that was overdramatic. Don't mind me; I just need some sleep."

"I . . ." Valla tried again, then she sighed and said, "Good night, Victor."

"Night," he replied, closing his eyes and forcefully slowing his breathing. He heard Valla touch the glow lamp on the little table between their beds, then the red glow of his eyelids turned black. Though he was only pretending to sleep, he soon found his mind drifting. He tried to think about what he would do the next day or wonder what Thayla and Deyni were up to, but soon, true sleep captured him, and he didn't stir again until warm sunlight was falling on his face through the window they'd neglected to pull the curtains on.

He stretched, pressing his arms against the headboard and pointing his toes as the movement became involuntary and his muscles strained against the bonds of his flesh. As the little waves of pleasure and relief ran through him, he inhaled deeply and grinned, realizing the bed had creaked and groaned from his efforts. "See, I still have what it takes," he whispered, stealing a glance at Valla's bed, happy to see she was still sleeping, her blanket pulled up over her head.

Victor sat up on the side of his bed and got himself dressed. He pulled an old notebook out of his storage ring and wrote a note for Valla, letting her know he'd gone to get breakfast. Truthfully, he wanted to give her some space to get dressed; when they'd traveled together to Persi Gables, she'd had her own tent, and he'd never felt as though he was awkwardly looming over her while she handled her personal business. This room felt too small, as far as he was concerned.

As he pulled the door closed, carefully depressing the latch so it wouldn't make noise, he resolved to find better accommodations. He was a damn successful adventurer; why should he share a tiny room with twin beds? He walked down the hallway to the stairs, his nose informing him that breakfast was definitely up for grabs.

Livag saw him coming down the steps and motioned him over to the bar. "Morning, traveler. Was your bed acceptable?"

"Well, I'll be honest; I was going to complain about it, but I slept like the dead, so, yeah—it was good." Victor pulled out a stool and sat down, glancing over his shoulder at a pair of the giant Degh who sat a short way behind him at one of the oversized tables.

"You were going to complain?" Livag asked, turning to pour steaming black liquid into a mug.

"Well, yeah. I mean, for ten beads, I thought we'd have a bit more space, you know?"

"Ten beads is cheap in this town, lad. I thought I sort of made that clear last night." He set the steaming drink before Victor and smiled. "If you've the means, I have an acquaintance with much finer accommodations. I could send you her way."

"What's this?" Victor asked, lifting the mug and wondering if his nose was playing tricks; it smelled like coffee.

"Coffee. They don't have it in your homeworld?"

"Are you shitting me? They have it in my homeworld, but not Fanwath, the world I've been living in recently. I thought I'd lost it forever. I mean, don't get me wrong; I didn't drink a ton of this stuff—too easy to pop open an energy drink, you know?" Livag just nodded as if he understood precisely what Victor meant, so he pushed on. "I'd get some now and then, though, and my *abuela* drank it every morning."

"Well, you should be pleased to know that many worlds have coffee.

So many, in fact, that once some interworld trade becomes established, it's uncommon not to find it."

Victor lifted the mug and took a tentative sip. It was bitter, but the smell was so nostalgic that he smiled, thinking of his *abuela* at the kitchen table sipping her coffee while he hoovered down some eggs and tortillas. "Thanks, Livag. I didn't know Fanwath was so backward. Shit, man, I should buy a boatload of this stuff before I head back." He took another sip, then grinned and asked, "So, when you say 'if we have the means,' what kinda price are we talking about?"

"Well, my cousin, Brecia, runs a fine establishment in the Arena District—suites only. I think she's got some available for ninety."

"Ninety beads a night?"

"Right." Livag nodded, then asked, "Porridge and toast all right for breakfast?"

"Porridge, huh? Yeah, why not?" As Livag turned to holler through the swinging door behind the bar, presumably at someone in the kitchen, Victor added, "Will you give me directions to your cousin's inn? I wanted to check out the arena, anyway."

"Of course. I've the name of a few powerful Elementalists in the city, as well. I think your friend would do well to speak to one or more of them."

"I was about to ask you about that. Thanks, Livag." Victor took another sip of his coffee and then set it down; some of his nostalgia had worn off, and it wasn't exactly delicious to him anymore. "You have some cream I could put into that?"

"Oh, sure. I should've offered," Livag said, then turned back to the kitchen door and stepped through, leaving Victor alone at the bar.

"You going to the arena, Deshi?" one of the giants behind him rumbled. Victor didn't know the word, so he didn't think the guy was talking to him at first. Still, no one answered, so he turned over his shoulder. Both the giants were looking at him, and the nearer one, a hugely muscled man with black hair cut as if someone had put a bowl on top of his head, raised a thick, wiry eyebrow in question.

"Oh, me?"

"See any other Deshi around here?" the man rumbled.

"Sorry, I'm not from here. What's a Deshi?"

"Deshi? Half Degh, half Vesh runt," the huge man replied, pointing at Victor as if to illustrate.

"Oh, right. I didn't know that was even possible; I'm not from this world. I'm actually called a . . ." he started to say, but then he remembered the dragon lady's words and hurriedly changed the topic. "It's not important. I was thinking of going to the arena, yeah."

"Low tier?" The giant thumped his palm on his table, and Victor wasn't sure if he was asking or declaring.

"Yeah, I'm low tier."

"Best time to fight in the arena; people are more vicious, more in need of wins and fame. I love watching low-tier fights."

"Oh, cool. Good to know, thanks," Victor said, turning back to the counter, not really enjoying the attention the enormous man was giving him.

"Will you win?" This time the voice was different, and Victor turned back to see the other Degh had joined in. He was lankier than his stocky friend, though he probably outweighed Victor by three hundred pounds. He had long, curly red hair and bright green eyes. His thick, rosy lips twisted into a grin, and he repeated the question as Victor made eye contact with him. "Will you win?"

"I wasn't really sure I'd fight in the arena; I just wanted to check it out."

"Huh," the dark-haired Degh said, shaking his head as though disappointed.

"I mean, I might! I've been in plenty of pit fights in my day." Victor silently cussed at himself. Why did he say that? Was he really going to let the disappointment of a couple of strangers pressure him into signing up for a life-or-death battle?

"Hmm. Experienced, eh? What's your name, then, stranger?"

"Victor," he said before his brain could tell his mouth to shut up.

"Mmm," the red-haired Degh said, nodding. "I like the way it echoes through the ether. We'll wager on you, Deshi. Good luck." With that, Victor felt dismissed because the two giants turned away from him and tucked into their rather enormous bowls of porridge. Victor turned to the counter to find his own bowl with two buttery slabs of bread stacked on the side. His coffee had turned from black to creamy brown, and he grinned, getting to work on the food.

"Good; eat up, Victor," Livag said, straightening up from where he'd been stacking some dishes under the bar. "You need your strength if you're going to the arena."

"Arena?" Valla asked, climbing onto the stool next to him.

"Good morning! I'm just going to check it out . . ."

"Good idea," she said, surprising him. "I'll just take toast, Livag," she added, eyeing Victor's bowl of porridge with pursed lips and a raised eyebrow.

When they left Livag's inn, they had a list of places to go and directions to get there. Victor had, somewhat guiltily, roused Gorz to pay attention to the directions, so they didn't have to write them down. The amulet spirit had seemed a little groggy but otherwise happy to oblige. While they walked to their first stop—a place called Hunter's Hall where, according to Livag, people could join monster-hunting expeditions—he tried to engage the amulet in some conversation, thinking his words to him as he'd done back in the mine.

"Gorz, how are things? Have you noticed any other strange . . . feelings, I guess?"

"Yes, Victor. I feel more and more detached. My grasp on this reality feels strained. While you engage me and I focus on the impression of your surroundings, I can stay present, but it feels like I've been gone a hundred years since you last spoke to me."

"Really? It's only been a day."

"I wonder if leaving Fanwath, traveling to wherever this world exists in the universe, has somehow weakened the bonds holding me to this plane."

"But you weren't from Fanwath . . ."

"Yes, I'm aware of the flaw in my logic, but there might be other factors. Perhaps drifting through the ether as we did, my larger soul felt me. I feel a pull, a tugging sensation. I feel more and more incomplete as the decades slip by."

"Gorz, let me remind you; it's only been a day."

"Odd. Turn left, Victor. Your destination lies in the square ahead."

"Up here," Victor said, carefully looking left and right before he crossed the street to follow Gorz's directions. Valla jogged along with him as he hurried between a barge-like floating wagon and a group of Degh riding atop mammoth-sized, maroon-colored lizards. The animals had leather blinders over their eyes, and their bridles were heavy-looking metal affairs that doubled as muzzles. As they crossed the smooth brown cobbles behind the great animals, Victor almost stepped into a ripe, steaming pile of black dung.

"Ugh! What do those things eat?" Valla asked, skirting around the stinking pile.

"People!" laughed one of the Degh, glancing over the rump of his animal and winking.

"C'mon," Victor said, eyeing the huge floating wagon coming their way. It had high, fence-like sides, and he could see some sort of livestock milling around within. It didn't appear to be slowing. He grabbed Valla's arm and hurried to the opposite corner of the intersection. He didn't slow until they were up on the pedestrian cobbles. Even then, they had to hustle to the far right side of the path to walk at a normal pace; Degh strode along on the left faster than Victor would typically jog.

"This city is busy!" Valla said, her eyes alight and pale blue cheeks sort of rosy with excitement.

"You like it!" Victor chuckled, continuing toward the upcoming square.

"Yes! I've not seen so many wondrous sights in all my time on Fanwath!"

"You just say that because you were born on Fanwath. None of this seems more 'wondrous' to me than the things I've seen in Persi Gables."

"I suppose it does have a lot to do with everything here being new to me," Valla replied, nodding. "Still, it's exciting, isn't it?"

"Yeah, I guess so," Victor replied, quickly looking away from a scowling, tusked Vesh with one eye that glowed as though the socket were full of roiling lava. "Just a little nerve-racking, maybe," he muttered. When they stepped into the square and more space opened up, allowing them to walk more sedately with less fear of being trampled, he exhaled a breath he hadn't realized he'd been holding and tried to relax a little.

The square was enormous compared to those in Gelica and Persi Gables. A vast expanse of dun-colored cobbles spread out before them, with one structure dominating the center: a great open-air building with a high-peaked roof held up by massive marble or stone columns. Food stands and merchant carts dotted the rest of the space, but plenty of wide, open area remained; traffic was directed around the edges of the square with a high curb discouraging mounts or vehicles from traversing the central portion.

"That must be the Hunter Hall or whatever it's called," Victor said, striding through the square directly toward the big structure. Valla followed along in his wake, eyes wide as she took in the sights.

"Did you see that man with the wings?" she asked, pointing toward the edge of the square off to their right where a tall man, probably a kind of Vesh, had launched himself into the air and was rapidly beating his bright turquoise wings to gain elevation, streaking off to the south.

Victor nodded. "Pretty badass."

"Faster than I've ever seen a Ghelli fly," Valla breathed, her voice hushed and full of wonder.

"You seem different today," Victor said, skirting to his left to avoid a big group of the insect people—he'd forgotten what they were called.

"Oh? I slept well!" Valla said, hurrying to match his long stride. "Why are you walking so fast?"

"I . . ." Victor started but then stopped to really think about it. Why *was* he hurrying? "I feel vulnerable, I guess." He shrugged and kept walking; the truth was that he was worried about Valla and didn't want to say as much. She'd already had one apparently powerful guy take an interest in her. What would he do if one of these high-level assholes decided to "ask" her on a date or some other bullshit?

"You really are feeling your change in stature, aren't you?" Valla's voice held a hint of amusement.

"Look," Victor said, slowing to a stop so he could turn and face her, "I spent a lot of time on Fanwath being a punk that got pushed around and nearly killed a few dozen times. I was starting to get over that, starting to feel like I could walk around with my head up, and now I'm here, with everyone and their *pinche abuela* stronger than me!"

"Victor," Valla said, shaking her head, "think about your life, about people you've known. What sorts of people get picked on?" She reached a hand up to his shoulder and gave him a nudge to start walking again while they spoke.

"I dunno, weaklings?"

"Come, even I, with my poor social skills and lack of friends, know that the people who act timid, afraid, weak—they attract abuse."

"It's not me . . ." He shook his head. He wasn't Valla's father. He wasn't her brother. Why was he feeling responsible for her? Shit, she had a lot of levels on him! "Never mind; you're right. Fuck these assholes."

"It's not you?" Valla asked, and Victor sighed. Why couldn't he have shut his mouth a fraction of a second faster?

"C'mon, Valla. Do you see how these dudes are looking at you? You're the only person with blue skin I've seen, and you're not exactly ugly!"

Valla pressed her lips together, and her eyebrows drew down into an alarmingly sharp V. She let go of Victor's shoulder and said, "You aren't my chaperone."

"Right. Uh . . . sorry," Victor said, knowing there was nothing else he could say.

"I'm a Captain of the Imperial Legion. I'm a Tier Five Sword Dancer," Valla growled, still glowering at him as they walked.

Victor avoided her eye contact, quickly glanced at her, and said, "Yeah, sorry." He wasn't going to get into an argument with her about this; he'd seen too many women in his life get that expression on their faces, and he knew there was nothing he could say to make her realize his intentions were in the right place, even if it was offensive or whatever. No, the only solution he knew of was to apologize and let her cool off on her own.

To his surprise, Valla said, "Well, I appreciate the thought, anyway. You're right, now that you mention it; I'm suddenly quite aware of the stares some of those Vesh are giving me."

"Yeah," Victor nodded, vindication loosening his vocal cords. "Those are the guys I was talking about! The snakes and bugs aren't giving us a second glance."

"Victor!" Valla hissed, reaching up to grab his shoulder again. "Don't describe them like that! You know, some people gain exceptional hearing as they advance in power! Not to mention, it's rude!"

"Right," Victor said, ruefully running his hands through his hair, grabbing the sides of his head, and looking around the square. No one seemed particularly irritated with him. "Guess I got lucky. Um, what are they called again?"

Very softly, Valla said, "Tong-pan and Yazzians."

"I'm sure I'll forget that again, but I'll be more careful with my . . . descriptions." They'd come to a flight of marble steps that led up to the open structure. As they climbed, cresting the top, they saw that the soaring roof of the building provided shade to a concave depression underneath. A big crowd milled about in the central area, moving from table to table where, apparently, monster-hunting groups were recruiting.

"Have you noticed guards like that anywhere else?" Valla asked, drawing Victor's attention to the men and women in silver cloaks standing around the building at regular intervals.

"Now you mention it, I don't think so," Victor replied. Some of the guards were Degh, but most were the human-monster-looking Vesh.

"None of them are, uh, Tongpin or Yozzians," he said, wincing at his butchery of the names.

"Almost," Valla said, smiling, again surprising him with her good humor. "Tong-pan and Yazzians, and you're right! That's interesting, isn't it? I wonder if they're culturally distinct. Maybe they're seen as visitors to this part of the world."

"Well, let's check out one of these, uh, booths," Victor said, climbing down the short flight of steps to the central arena-like depression under the vaulted stone canopy. Valla walked beside him, and after they'd carefully worked their way through the milling crowd to the first table on that side of the space, Victor approached the Vesh woman sitting behind it. "Hello."

"Hey there, traveler! Interested in joining an expedition to Vagrant's Oasis? We're chasing down rumors of a blood wyrm sighting!" She was thin, with limbs that seemed too long for her body, and looked very human, with a tan complexion and coppery red hair; but as with most Vesh Victor had seen, there were a few things that ended the comparison—she had a single thick white horn sprouting from the center of her forehead, and what looked like folded black leathery wings on her back. What really stood out about her, though, was her aura; Victor could feel the weight of it more so than anyone else he'd spoken to on this new world, save the dragon woman.

"I'm Victor, and"—Victor turned to include Valla in the conversation—"we're new here if that isn't obvious. How does this all work?" He gestured around the hall.

"New to Coloss, hmm? Low tier?" She frowned but pressed on, "We've room for the likes of you on the expedition. I'm the hunt master, so it'll be me that determines your pay; it's based on contribution. Most of the hunting companies operate the same way." She paused, pointed to the table to her right, and continued, "Some are like Royne there; they'll offer you a fixed payout, and as long as the hunting company returns intact, you'll be paid that amount, no matter what."

"So, there are two kinds of contracts? Contribution and fixed pay?" Valla asked.

"Since you're new and low tier, I'll give you a tip," the woman said, leaning forward. Victor saw the way her yellow-green eyes glimmered with Energy, and he wondered how far she'd advanced her race; she exuded power. "Most companies that give fixed payments won't be worth the time for a low-tier unless you're a real lazybones. You'll be out for days or weeks and come back to be paid with a few handfuls of scales or a piece of bone—nothing great."

"But your way is better?" Valla prompted.

"Sure! If you work hard or get lucky. As long as you have a fair hunt master, that is." She grinned and thumped her silky blue blouse at the center of her chest with her fist. "I'm very fair!"

"So, if I do a lot of damage in the battle with whatever monster we find, I'll get a bigger piece of the prize?" Victor asked, trying to demonstrate his understanding.

"Exactly! Don't forget about the Energy, too! We're hunting monsters that require a real team to take down; if you do a lot of the work, the System will give you a big portion of the prize. I've seen a low-tier gain three levels from one kill. Sure, she had high Energy affinity, but still." She shrugged and smiled, then pointed to a gray slate on the table before her. "Should I sign you up?"

"How long do we have to decide?" Valla asked.

"I'm hiring twelve hunters today; you've got however long that takes." She grinned and drummed her fingers on the slate.

"Um, when does your hunt start, and how long do you think it will take?" Victor asked.

"We leave in three days, and the journey to the oasis will take another three. After that, it depends on how long it takes us to find our quarry."

"Sign us up," Victor said and was immediately rewarded with an elbow in the ribs from Valla.

"Shouldn't we talk about this? Maybe check some of the other tables?"

"We can if you want, but I get a good feeling from this lady. Uh, sorry, I didn't get your name." Victor shrugged sheepishly.

"I'm Cayle, and my hunting company is called Spears of the Copper Sunset!" She smiled hugely as she said the name of her company, and Victor looked from her to Valla, watching as his companion's purplish lips pressed together as if fighting the urge to smile.

"I like that name, Cayle," Valla said, nodding.

"It paints a pretty picture," Victor agreed, hoping this meant that Valla was going to agree to sign up for the hunt.

"What if we don't make it for some reason? To wherever your hunting company meets up in three days?" Valla asked.

"Then never come asking me for a job again," Cayle replied, shrugging. "I might also spread word to some of the other companies; reputation is important for a monster hunter."

"Sounds fair," Victor said. "So, yeah, let's sign up. We've got a few other places to get today."

"Right! Welcome to the company, at least temporarily. Though, if you do well and you like the way things go, you might sign on for a longer commission; you'll earn more as a regular member. Of course, it all depends on how your first hunt goes. We might decide you're not a good fit." She pushed the gray slate over the tabletop toward them and said, "Put your hands on the slate, and we'll make it official."

4

ARENA

Victor and Valla caught glimpses of the arena long before it came into direct view. It was an enormous building that loomed over the surrounding architecture, a dozen stories high and wide enough to require a square several times larger than the other markets they'd passed through on their way to it. When Victor stepped out of the flow of traffic, up the steps to the arena square, he paused to take it all in.

Just like the expansive cobbled area outside Hunter's Hall, the arena was surrounded by smooth, tan pavers, gardens, and little sectioned-off, L-shaped avenues where booths—currently closed—would presumably sell goods to arena patrons. The arena was made of pale stone, and great columns stretched from the ground all the way up to the highest tiers. Gargoyles, dragons, things that looked like birds and dinosaurs, and even people dressed like gladiators were carved into gigantic statues standing around the building on shelves at various tiers, and all along the top edge, high in the sky.

"Pretty cool," Victor said, pointing at a statue of a warrior wearing armor that looked distinctly Roman, holding two swords over his head and looming over the dark, barricaded entrance of the arena. "That statue must be thirty feet high."

"The place looks deserted," Valla said, pointing at the closed gates under the giant statue's swords.

"There's someone moving around in there; let's go ask." Victor started walking, happy not to have to contend with a crowd. When he came to the closed, wrought iron gate, he peered through into the wide stone breezeway that led up to a row of ticket booths. A man with two short horns poking out of his white hair was on his knees, scrubbing the cobbles with a thick rag and a steaming bucket of soapy water. "Hello," Victor called through the bars.

The man looked up, his blue eyes bright in the sunlight coming from behind Victor, and said, "Hello yourself."

"Where do you go to see who's fighting? Or, I guess, to sign up for fights?"

"Fighters' gate 'round the north end," the man said, gesturing with his thumb to Victor's left.

"Right, thanks." Victor turned to Valla, and she shrugged, walking in the indicated direction. Victor walked along with her and cleared his throat.

"So, when are you going to, you know, tell me I shouldn't fight in the arena?"

"Hmm?" Valla glanced at him and narrowed her eyes slightly. "Seems like your decision. Do you want my opinion?"

"I guess; I'm kinda used to Thayla telling me what I should and shouldn't do. Shit, that's not fair to Thayla; there's Lam and Edeya and Rellia and Oynalla—you get the idea."

"I know how that feels. Let's see what we can find out, and if you want my opinion after that, simply ask." Valla quickened her pace, and Victor whistled and grinned, matching her stride.

When they came around the curve of the monumental oval-shaped building, they saw more activity near another smaller gate. A few people—human-sized and giant—milled about, talking with each other, looking at bulletin boards, and standing in line at a walk-up window where an arena employee stood behind a counter.

As they approached, Valla slowed to look at the bulletin boards, so Victor joined her. There were boards plastered with advertisements for local businesses, boards promoting certain fighters, and boards promoting fights, upcoming and old—it didn't look as though the arena spent many resources clearing off old flyers. "I don't recognize this date," Valla said, pointing to a poster advertising an upcoming tournament. "I expected the System to translate the days and months into something I understood. It usually works that way, I think. Odd . . ."

"Why's that odd? I thought it was damn weird that you all have a seven-day week with Fridays, Saturdays, and all the other days we have in my homeworld."

"Yes, I suppose it's all very 'odd' depending on how you look at it," an old-looking, stooped, but still very tall Degh said, leaning close to Victor and

Valla. "I've heard that most System worlds share similar measurements for time, from seconds to years, and that it has something to do with elder races and the marks of civilization they left on the worlds they visited. Of course, it could be the System manipulating things from the shadows . . ." He trailed off when he saw Victor's wide eyes and how he and Valla had turned to him with surprise.

"Excuse my interruption; I heard your conversation, and it's a topic that's always fascinated me." He reached out a huge hand to Victor and added, "I'm Lorce; I was just here hoping to get an idea about the lineup for tomorrow's matches. Nothing's posted yet, though."

Victor reached out to accept the handshake, almost embarrassed by the way the other man's palm engulfed his entire hand. Still, Lorce didn't squeeze hard, and he had a very unassuming posture, leaning with one hand on a large, gnarled cane. "Good to meet you; I'm Victor, and this is Valla. We're new around here, but what you were saying is interesting. How many days are in your week, if you don't mind me asking?"

"Why, seven!" he responded enthusiastically, his deep, resonant voice tainted by a slight lisp as his tongue found a significant gap in his teeth. It looked as if Lorce might have been a fighter once, judging by his scars, missing fingers, and absent teeth.

"Oh, there goes my theory," Valla said. "I thought maybe the names were different because you had a different system. What day is today?"

"Sunday; no fights on Sunday or Thursday," the old giant said, gesturing to the arena.

"Wait," Valla said and pointed to the poster she'd been reading. "This says the next fight is on Horc's Day."

"Ha! Now I see the confusion! That's not a day of the week; that's a holiday. Horc is one of the founders of Coloss." The man seemed nice, and Victor appreciated the info, but as he spoke, the scent of something rotten wafted toward Victor on his breath, and he had to fight to keep his expression neutral as he battled down the urge to gag. He wondered if Lorce had a rotten tooth or something.

"Hey, um, nice to meet you. Lorce, right? I'm gonna go get in line." He glanced at Valla and jerked his chin toward the line of people waiting to speak to the employee at the window.

"Oh, of course, youngster," the old giant said, nodding his gray head and rubbing at his rough, stubbled chin. "Will you be fighting tomorrow? Prizes will be special on a holiday!"

"Um, maybe!" Victor replied, stepping away and waving. Valla hurried with him, but as they put a dozen feet or so between them and the older man, she frowned and spoke.

"Was something wrong?"

"Didn't you smell that guy's breath? I almost lost my breakfast," Victor said, whispering hoarsely.

"No . . ." She frowned and shrugged. "Interesting about the days, though, isn't it?"

"Yeah, and I've noticed a few things like that on Fanwath. You guys have some different month names, though." He paused and added, "I mean different from my world, Earth. Like, what's the date we're supposed to meet Rellia?"

"The tenth of Tanewik."

"See?" Victor grinned, stepping into line behind a man with red spines poking out through stitched holes in his armor, running up and down the center of his back, all the way to the top of his skull. "There's no Tanewik on Earth, but we have other months I've heard mentioned on Fanwath, like December."

"Strange . . . How many months are there in a year on Earth?

"Twelve."

"Same as Fanwath; maybe the different names for some of the months are due to tradition. They may have something to do with the names of historical events or people that the System doesn't translate as easily as other terms."

"Yeah," Victor said with a shrug. "Makes sense, I guess."

The line moved slowly at first, with the people near the front apparently having a lot to say to the clerk working at the window. As they got closer and closer to the front of the line, Victor tried to eavesdrop on the conversations and found that most of the people were signing up to fight on one date or another. It became apparent that the person at the window had some means of evaluating people and verifying they were trying to compete in the correct tier. It was this evaluation process that slowed down the queue.

Valla stood beside him patiently, her eyes ever roving the shaded area they stood in near the gate, taking in the people, the signs, and the architecture in the distance. Occasionally, she'd remark about something that stood out to her—a tall clock tower, or a group of giant Degh tussling over a perceived insult by the nearby road, or a poster illustrating a monstrous-looking Vesh with a crown of horns and proclaiming him "Karnice: Undefeated Champion of the Arena."

They were next in line to step up to the window when a snarling voice said from behind them, "Whelps signing up together? The crowd won't like it if you go easy on each other."

Victor turned to see a Vesh woman with high, dog-like ears covered in short, velvety black fur. She was tall, wiry, and had deep-set, pale brown eyes. Her dark hair was wavy and hung to her coppery, tanned shoulders, and if it weren't for the mean twist to her lips and the angry glint in her eyes, Victor might have called her pretty. She grinned when he looked her way, exposing enormous canines. As he opened his mouth to answer her question, Valla beat him to it.

"I'm not interested in the arena."

"Oh? The pretty blue one isn't interested, men, sorry," she snarled, turning back toward a few other Vesh lined up behind her. Some of them chuckled, but most snorted or completely ignored her words. "What about you, big Deshi?"

Victor frowned, contemplating the value of debating his ancestral origins with this woman. He decided it didn't matter; if it helped people to think of him as a Deshi, why did he care? Something stirred in his gut, though, and he felt the urge to straighten his back, and, almost unbidden, words came to his tongue.

He looked down his nose at the Vesh woman; she was nearly as tall as he, and he could feel her aura, dark and crushing; he had the impression she was quite a few levels above him. Still, he grinned, pushed some rage into his pathways, and said, "The blood of titans pumps through my veins; don't call me Deshi."

"Oh?" Her voice rose in instant amusement. "Did you hear that, lads? We've got a titan on our hands!" She laughed, and to Victor, it sounded like something that should be coming from a hyena's throat. Her words had a greater effect on the Vesh lined up behind her this time—many of them broke into laughter, and one of them walked forward and grabbed Victor's shoulder, pointing toward a Degh giant nearby.

"There's a titan, boy. If you get confused again, just go stand next to him or one of his kin; you're just a runt, Deshi."

Victor eyed the Vesh, a burly man with curly brown hair and the complexion and facial features of a pig—literally. He had bright pink flesh, soft, fuzzy white-and-brown spotted facial hair, and a flat nose with long tusks protruding from his lower lip. Victor's eyes traveled from the man's face to his thickly muscled arm and the black-nailed fingers that gripped his shoulder.

An unreasonable surge of anger boiled in his gut, and he felt his Core flare to life and feed red-hot Energy into his pathways.

As his vision started to shade toward crimson and everything other than the man before him faded into blurry, inconsequential background noise, Victor reached up to the thick hairy wrist and grabbed the meat of the man's thumb, just milliseconds away from twisting it into a vicious armlock. Before he acted, though, he felt Valla's cool hand on his other wrist, and some of the redness bled from his vision as he realized what he was doing; he didn't want to get into a fight right there in the middle of the arena square—who was to say what the guards might do, or if the other Vesh nearby would join in against him.

With an effort of will, he suppressed his rage and said, "Hey, please keep your hands to yourself." He carefully pulled the man's hand off his shoulder and then released it.

"Whoa, watch out, Reege!" the woman said, "Did you see his eyes? The pup was angry enough to bite!" That got some laughter out of the surrounding crowd, and Victor was sorely tempted to say something snarky back or to cuss her out, but Valla tugged at his wrist again and spoke.

"It's our turn," she said, pointing to the window, and something in her tone indicated that this wasn't the first time she'd said as much.

"Right," Victor grunted, inhaling deeply and further cooling his rage. He turned away from the group of Vesh, but he couldn't tune out the woman's sharp voice chasing him to the window.

"Maybe we'll see you in the arena, whelp! You can show us what a titan you are!" Again, the woman's hyena-like laughter followed her words, and when he swallowed his reaction, it felt like a lump of hot magma sliding down his throat. Valla didn't react, didn't say anything, but she kept her grip on his wrist as they stepped up to the window.

"Yes?" the thin, nearly human-looking man asked. He wore a uniform of sorts—a black bowler-style hat and a striped black-and-white vest over a white collared shirt. He was pleasant looking and trim for a Vesh, and the only things that stood out, marking him as such, were the long, strange tufts of wiry whiskers that sprouted from the centers of his cheeks.

Victor cleared his throat, trying to push the mocking laughter from his mind. Though it echoed in his perceived reality, he knew it was all in his head at that point; the Vesh had quieted down as he and Valla stepped up to the window. "Hey, I need some info on the arena."

"Right, what kind of info, mate? I'm the only one here, and I haven't got time to pull all your questions out of you, okay?"

"What sorts of prizes can a low-tier win? I'm trying to get access to the City Stone."

"Well, first, I'd need to confirm you are low tier. After that, I can sign you up to compete, and there are a few options as far as that's concerned. For instance, if you're interested in prizes, you should consider signing up for tomorrow's festival matches. We have sixteen slots for low-tier fighters, and so far, we've had thirty sign-ups, so there's a good chance the arena master will choose you."

"Festival matches?" Victor asked.

"Yes, for Horc's Day! We have an open bracket tournament for low-tiers in the morning and then seeded brackets for mid-tiers in the afternoon. We'll wrap things up in the evening with two matches between high-tier champions!"

"And the prizes? For low-tiers, I mean," Victor prompted, leaning forward, resting his elbows on the little counter outside the window.

"Well, there's a prize for winning in each bracket. Eight fights, then four, then two, then the championship, all fought before midday. Here," the clerk said, handing Victor a flyer. "The prizes are all listed here, but if you're interested, you should sign up and wait around; the arena master will make his selections within the hour."

"How does he decide who will fight?" Valla asked.

"That's his secret; only arena masters know how the selections are made." While the clerk answered Valla's question, Victor was perusing the list of prizes on the flyer, and his eyes bugged out as he read through them.

Low-Tier Prizes

Round 1: Coloss Prize Token

*Round 2: Coloss Prize Token & Crypt Drake Gall Bladder**

*Semifinal Match: Coloss Prize Token & Rock Wyrm Magma Horn***

*Championship: Coloss Prize Token, wildcard seed in Gazra's Day Tournament, and Red Spinefiend Heart****

**Known to enhance (permanently) the strength and vitality of those who consume it in a properly prepared alchemical mixture.*

***When ground and consumed in a distilled tincture, known to provide breakthroughs in Core development.*

****Known to pull forth threads of the consumer's bloodline or racial ancestry when eaten whole and raw.*

"So, if I win all four matches, I walk away with four prize tokens plus all the other prizes?" he asked, interrupting the clerk's response to something Valla had asked.

"Sure, but there will be some heavy competition . . ."

"And why would I need more than one? Don't they just allow access to the City Stone?"

"Uh, no," the clerk replied with a chuckle. "You need a token to get to the City Stone, sure, but once there, you can turn them in for, you know, prizes."

"Oh, what if we just want to use the Stone to teleport home?"

"Mmhmm, sure, that's one of the rewards in the prize store, but I think you need more than one token for that; I've never looked into it myself, so I'm not completely sure."

"Hey, are you shit stains about done?" the Vesh woman called out from behind Victor. He felt his shoulders tense, and he almost turned around, but he took a breath and ignored the insult.

"Sign me up; might as well see if the arena master chooses me."

"Fights are known to be quite vicious in holiday tournaments . . ." the clerk said, but trailed off as he saw the anger in Victor's eyes; he didn't know the fury wasn't directed his way. "I'm sure you'll be all right, though."

Victor glanced at Valla, but she had a vacant, distant look in her eyes and didn't offer him any objections. The clerk cleared his throat, and Victor looked back to see he was holding out a gray stone orb. "What's this?"

"It tests whether you're trying to fight in the correct tier. Hold it in your hand, and I'll do the rest. The orb is a non-invasive way for us to measure potential fighters that doesn't expose any of your exact abilities, affinities, or otherwise compromise any secrets you might have about your fighting prowess." He held it out a bit farther, and Victor shrugged, taking the heavy, smooth, perfectly round rock. It was cool to the touch, and Victor struggled to hold it above the counter; it felt very much like the stone was trying to pull itself to the ground and him along with it.

The clerk reached out one finger to touch the stone, and then it began to grow warm. Victor watched, his forearm muscles straining to keep the orb aloft and his elbow painfully grinding into the wooden countertop. "You can rest your hand against the counter, sir," the clerk said as he studied the orb, waiting for something to happen.

"Thanks," Victor said, happily letting his knuckles rest against the counter as the orb continued to grow warmer. As he watched, the gray surface started to lighten and glow with a steady orange-yellow luminescence. Eventually, the stone resembled a lightbulb, and Victor had to squint to look directly at it. The clerk nodded, but that wasn't the end; the orb began to pulse, slowly at first but then more rapidly, and it looked to Victor as if the clerk was timing the pulses.

After a minute or two, the clerk reached out and took the orb, and as he touched it, it seemed as though someone had taken a hundred pounds off Victor's hand. "Very good. You're definitely in the low tier, but your potency is nearly off the chart. The arena master will be happy with your ticket, I think." With that, the clerk scribbled some notes on an official gold-leaf piece of decorative card stock and handed it to Victor. "Present this to the arena master when they open the gates."

"Thanks," Victor said, taking the ticket and moving to the side, consciously refusing to glance at the line behind him.

"That was interesting," Valla said, reaching out a hand. "Could I see the ticket?"

"Sure," Victor handed it to her, and she read the notes the clerk had written: *T-3, ****, 54 ppm*. She shrugged and handed it back. "So?" he asked, watching her face closely, "Any objections?"

"I'll admit to some stress," Valla replied, leaning a shoulder against the stone of the arena. Her back was to the clerk's window, and the people lined up, waiting to speak to him, making it easy for Victor to see what the hostile Vesh woman was doing, but he ignored her and her friends and focused on Valla.

"Stress about me dying in an arena on some distant planet before I can return to Fanwath and perform my duties for Rellia?" Victor grinned sardonically, trying to lighten the tone of his words.

"Well, sure. I'm not going to berate you with things you already know—Rellia's campaign, the thousands of people dependent on it being successful, what might happen to me in this strange world if you were to die . . . Shall I go on?"

Victor opened his mouth to reply, scrambling for a response, but she held up a hand. "I also know that we'll never get back to Fanwath without some risk. It sounds like we'll need more than one prize token to teleport, so we should explore many avenues. There are also the mitigating factors—it doesn't sound like the arena fights have to be to the death, and I know you're strong for your level, freakishly so. Even that little clerk seemed impressed by his test."

"Speaking of teleporting, I had a thought earlier," Victor said. "What are the odds we could find a wizard or something who can open a portal for us? Do we really need to go through the City Stone?"

"I don't know, Victor. Nobody I know on Fanwath has the ability to do what Boaegh did; I'm not sure he made that portal, but I know such things are possible. I just don't know how it works or who to speak to about it. I suppose that's another avenue we should pursue, though! Perhaps at our dinner party tonight, we could ask around."

"Shit, I almost forgot about that . . ." Victor started to say, but then he heard the sound of metal clanking and a shout from the small gate near the clerk's booth.

"Anyone with a fight ticket, get in here!"

Victor glanced at Valla, and she nodded to him. "I'll watch from here; it doesn't look like he's taking you anywhere, just in that hallway."

"Right." Victor nodded and walked toward the little gate where an enormous, heavily muscled Degh stood. He wore very fine-looking clothing—shiny polished boots, silky black slacks, and a perfectly pressed, fitted white buttoned shirt with a richly embroidered silver and black cape hanging from his shoulders. He had neatly trimmed red hair and a matching beard, and if it weren't for his size, Victor would have thought he was just a very handsome, very fit human.

"Line up along the passage wall there! I've got sixteen slots and, according to my list, thirty-seven fighters. Have your fight ticket ready when I get to you!" He strode away from the gate and into the long, arched corridor that presumably led into the arena's sections where fighters were meant to prepare for their bouts.

Victor stood against the stone block wall next to the Vesh he'd seen earlier, the one with the red spines poking out of his armor. He thought he'd claimed an end spot, but a Degh woman wearing bone-plated leather armor and smelling as if she'd been sweating for a few days without a bath stood on his other side. "Hey," she said, surprising him with a friendly smile. She had long, curly blonde hair, and her face, though crisscrossed with faint white scars, was young and open. Still, she made Victor feel like a runt as she glanced down at him and said, "I'm Kreecia—hope I don't have to fight you."

"Uh, Victor. Same here," Victor replied, wondering if that was a standard way to greet other contenders. The Vesh next to him completely ignored him, so he doubted it.

"All right! Keep quiet! I have a hard enough time making these decisions without any laughing and bickering." The arena master started at the other end of the line, pausing by each fighter, looking at their ticket, and seemingly staring into their eyes before moving on. He spoke softly to each fighter, but it wasn't until he was talking to the Vesh next to Victor that he heard some of the questions.

"Been in the arena before?"

"Nar," said the Vesh.

"Scared of dying?"

"Er, nah," the Vesh said, but even Victor could hear the hesitation. The arena master just grunted, then stared for a long minute at the Vesh, his gaze wandering from his feet to his eyes and lingering there for a long while. Then he stepped over in front of Victor.

"Ticket," he said, and Victor held it out. He looked at it for a couple of seconds then said, "Name?"

"Victor."

"Deshi?"

"No, I'm from another world." Victor shrugged at the man's upraised eyebrow.

"Ever fought in the arena before?"

"Not this one."

"Fought in others?"

"Lots of 'em."

"Scared of dying?"

"More scared of dying alone," Victor replied, having thought about the question when he heard it asked of his neighbor.

"Interesting," the man said, leaning down to look closely into Victor's eyes. It was hard for Victor to maintain that gaze; the arena master exuded a powerful aura, and though Victor could feel him restraining it, it weighed on him, pressing him back toward the stone wall. His instinct was to look down, to avoid the stare of this powerful being. With an effort of will, he stiffened his spine and looked into the man's deep, pale blue eyes.

It felt like hours that he fought to hold that gaze, but he knew it was only seconds before the arena master nodded and stepped away, moving in front of Kreecia to evaluate her. While he waited for the arena master to finish and make his decisions, Victor was struck with an urge to look at his status sheet, so he pulled it up:

Status			
Name:	Victor Sandoval		
Race:	Human (Quinametzin Bloodline): Improved 4		
Class:	Spirit Carver: Epic		
Level:	35		
Core:	Spirit Class: Improved 1		
Energy Affinity:	3.1, Fear 9.4, Rage 9.1, Inspiration 7.4	Energy:	3236/3236
Strength:	135	Vitality:	140
Dexterity:	40	Agility:	63
Intelligence:	32	Will:	315
Points Available:	8		
Titles & Feats:	Titanic Rage, Flame-Touched		

As usual, he was struggling with what to do with his free points. His will had grown monstrous in comparison to his other attributes, and he wondered if he should be building up something else. He knew Oynalla would tell him to keep working on his will, but wouldn't it be wise to get a second opinion? Maybe from a master from another world, someone impossibly powerful by Fanwath's standards? He decided to hold on to those points and see what he could learn, starting with Valla's dinner party.

"Listen for your names!" the arena master hollered. "The fighters for tomorrow's low-tier tournament are Kreecia, Victor, Harf, Necla, Krafe, Ronno, Porist of Coloss." He paused and looked at a Degh that had started to pump his fist in the air and shouted, "Not Porist of Domrak!" The huge Degh lowered his fist and, with a crestfallen slump of his huge shoulders, started to walk away. "Garl, Rekka, Jast of Thubia, Yarge, Krista, Jojar, Durg, Leena, and Sanima."

Lots of cheering, back thumping, and exclamations of rage and frustration echoed around the tunnel. The arena master held up his clipboard and shouted, "Don't try to change any of this or bargain with me! It's set in the master book! If your name wasn't called, clear out and don't start trouble, or

I'll settle you myself!" With that, he unleashed his aura, and the crushing weight of it silenced the rabble.

After most of the people had cleared out, and Victor turned to make his way back toward Valla, a familiar, sharp, sneering voice caught Victor's attention. "Congratulations. I hope we're matched up tomorrow. Know my name—Krista." The woman with the German shepherd ears was standing next to him and grinning, exposing those sharp canines.

"Here's hoping," Victor replied, matching her grin.

5

THE ELEMENTALIST GUILD

W e don't have to visit the Elementalist Guild today," Valla said as they walked away from the arena. "We're due to go to the War Captain's dinner in a couple of hours."

"What else are we gonna do? No, I think this is important, and you've been patient with me while I messed around here. Come on, aren't you excited? It's a whole guild dedicated to your kind of magic! Do they even have those on Fanwath?"

"There are guilds of practitioners, but none that specialize in elemental magic, at least none that I know of. I suppose there might be private groups in some of the academies . . ." She trailed off, her eyes going kind of vacant as she searched her memory.

"You see? Tomorrow you'll be busy cheering for me in the arena, and who knows what'll happen after that. Let's at least stop by." Victor dashed across the busy street that ran alongside the arena, trying to follow Gorz's instructions to the guild house Livag had told them about.

"This way, Gorz?" he asked, turning up a less crowded, upward-sloping lane. Gorz didn't reply at first, so he repeated the question.

"Yes, that's correct, Victor."

"You okay, buddy?"

"I feel the same as when we last spoke. When was that? It feels like years . . ."

"Gorz, I asked you for directions about ten minutes ago."

"My apologies. How strange . . ."

"Something wrong?" Valla asked, and Victor realized he'd been scowling while he spoke to the amulet.

"Yeah, actually. The spirit in my amulet—you know, the one that memorizes maps and documents and, well, everything—he's kind of losing it. He feels like he's being pulled, like his bindings to the amulet are fading, and every time I speak to him, he acts like it's been years."

"I'm no Artificer, but maybe we could visit one here that might be able to help."

"Not a bad idea at all. We should do some shopping here, anyway—I imagine, in a world with so many high-tier Energy users, shops like that are going to have some good magical items for sale."

The road they were walking along was less busy than the other streets they'd visited, and Victor noted that the architecture was starting to look a little more refined. Tall, more delicate structures with towers capped with colorful tile became more and more common, and Victor noted that none of them were sized for the Degh giants.

"Seems like a wealthier part of the city," Valla said, echoing his thoughts.

"Yeah, and maybe older? Livag said this wasn't a Degh city, so maybe that's why this section doesn't have buildings sized for them."

"Perhaps. We're climbing upward, so you would presume the city started up this way, and as it expanded, it stretched down the hill and into the surrounding country." Valla turned back and gestured the way they'd come, and it was evident they'd gained a lot of altitude, more than Victor had realized. The tops of buildings and tightly packed streets stretched out below them for miles, right up to the edge of the enormous walls that surrounded the city.

"How many streets have we passed since we started up this one?"

"Four, I think. No, five," Valla said, looking back the way they'd come again.

"Okay, the guild's supposed to be up around the next corner on the left." Victor led the way, turning past a storefront displaying beautifully woven rugs, then down a broad avenue with very light traffic. The pedestrians in the area were almost all Vesh, though a few of the snake people, the Yazzians, walked here and there in their typical hooded robes woven from muted earth-toned fabrics. "Gorz? The Elementalist Guild's on this street, right?"

"Victor! Are you still seeking that guild? My instructions must have been unclear; my apologies. From the corner, it's supposed to be the seventh building on the left."

"Thanks, Gorz, and your instructions are fine." Victor wanted to tell him it had only been a few minutes since he last spoke to him, but he was starting to feel like a broken record. It didn't seem to do any good to remind the amulet of the correct passage of time.

He continued walking, looking back to count the buildings he'd passed, and when he came to the seventh structure, he stopped and looked at the tall brick wall with wrought iron arches and gates. The central gate was open on one side, so he started forward, hoping to get a better look at the building.

A gust of air rushed up before him, creating a sort of swirling curtain of air that reminded Victor of a dust devil, though with less dirt. Unlike a dust devil, it didn't move, hanging in the air before him. A crackling, electric voice said, "Hold, stranger! I detect no elemental Energy at your Core."

"Uh . . ." Victor grunted, backing up a step, not sure what to say.

"I seek entry," Valla said, stepping forward, and again the voice crackled out of the swirling wind.

"You may pass, Elementalist."

"May I bring my companion?"

"You are permitted a guest. Hostilities will not be tolerated within," the voice said, its weird, static-like nature giving Victor goosebumps at the nape of his neck.

"Understood," Valla replied, and the wind suddenly died away, leaving a clear passage through the arched gateway to the stone paved walkway that led to the tall, narrow brick structure within. Victor counted the stories as he followed Valla through the courtyard, coming up with six distinct sets of windows. The peaked gables at the top were capped in brilliant turquoise tiles.

Victor allowed his eyes to drift down and noticed that all the shrubs and flower bushes in the garden were manicured into the shapes of wild creatures. Fountains burbled welcomingly, and to his amazement, Victor saw one fountain's water rise up from the placid pool in its base and take the shapes of a pair of dancing, translucent people. "Pretty cool," he said, jostling Valla's shoulder and pointing.

"Beautiful," she breathed, a rare smile touching her lips. Then she turned and climbed the short flight of stairs to the canopy-covered front doors of the building, and when she reached for the handle, they opened inward, seemingly at their own impetus. Victor followed her into the foyer of the building, where a broad, gleaming hardwood floor led into a vaulted round room with hallways leading off in every direction. An intricately carved spiral staircase led up to the exposed landings of the upper levels, its wood made to look like flowering vines, branches, and roots.

A young woman wearing pale yellow robes approached them from one of the side passages, and though she was clearly a Vesh with a pair of short ivory horns, she reminded Victor of one of his old classmates—Sierra Harwick. She looked so much like her that Victor felt struck by déjà vu, and for a heartbeat, his mind skipped back to the last time he'd been in school, and he felt perplexed and lost—as when a person wakes up in a strange bed, momentarily forgetting how they got there.

"Welcome," the woman said, pressing her hands together and bowing slightly as she walked toward them. Her attention was wholly on Valla.

"Thank you," Valla replied.

"How can we help you today, mistress? Are you seeking to join the ranks of the Elementalist Guild?"

"Perhaps, though I primarily came here for advice. I'm new to this world and understand that there's much I could learn from the masters here." Valla's diction never failed to impress Victor, and he stood quietly, sure he'd say the wrong thing or be kicked out if he interrupted.

"Advice is freely given by many of the masters that make their home here. What topic, if I may ask, do you seek elucidation upon? I'll more easily take you to the correct person if you can share such information." The woman spoke in a sort of singsong that felt both pleasant and forced to Victor, and he wasn't sure what to think of her. Was she a servant? Was she an Elementalist herself? She didn't give him the impression of a powerful aura like the one he'd felt from the arena master or even some of the potential competitors.

"I seek advice to better my Core, my abilities, and my potential for my next class refinement. My world is less practiced in these areas than this one. I don't know how long I'll be here, but our hope"—she indicated Victor with a tilt of her head—"is to leave fairly soon."

"You don't wish to remain on Zaafor?" The woman frowned, pursing her bright red lips almost in a pout.

"No, we have obligations we must see to back home," Valla replied, ever stoic in the face of feigned emotion. Victor found himself opening his mouth, about to step into the conversation, and he realized he was going to say something flirty. He clamped his mouth shut and carefully arranged his face in a neutral expression—they were here for Valla, and he needed to let her handle things.

"Well, I believe I feel a hint of an air affinity about you. Is there something more?"

Valla shifted uncomfortably and stole a glance at Victor. He broke his determination to stay out of things and gave her a brief nod. She nodded back and said, "I also have an affinity for iron."

"Iron? Oh, intriguing! I know just the Elementalist to bring you to. Follow me, please." the woman reached up to tuck a curly strand of blonde hair behind an ear, and as she walked toward the spiral staircase, she gave Victor a look and said, "Will you be bringing your . . . companion? I could show him to the parlor."

"He'll attend me." Valla's tone didn't brook any argument, and the woman nodded, continuing on her way. Victor's mouth fell open again, and he wanted to ask Valla what the fuck she meant by "attend," but again he clamped it shut and followed along.

As they walked, the woman said, "My name is Camia. Might I ask yours, mistress?"

"Valla," she said, and nothing more. Victor wasn't surprised. They climbed the stairs past two landings, and then their guide led them down a long, broad, wood-paneled hallway past several doors, stopping at a lovely set of double doors made from some sort of cherry-colored wood. Camia straightened up, cleared her throat, and knocked politely.

"Elementalist Troft is a master of iron and fire. Hopefully, he isn't engaged in anything that cannot be interrupted . . ." Camia began to say but was stopped as the door opened slightly.

"Hello, Camia," said a young man in an orange robe, much like Camia's yellow one.

"Ry, hello yourself! This is Mistress Valla, and she seeks an audience with Master Troft."

"Oh? Something important?" Ry asked, still holding the door partially closed, only exposing his rather mousy face. Victor couldn't really have described him, though; his attention was focused on the fact that Ry had sharp quills all over his head rather than hair.

"Important to Mistress Valla, yes. Nothing that should trouble your master, though. Is he available?"

"I believe so. Please come in," Ry replied, stepping back and pulling the door wide. The room beyond was a simple but spacious sitting area lined with couches, bookshelves, and a pair of desks occupying one corner. "Please have a seat," Ry said, gesturing toward a couch. "I'll tell Master Troft that you're waiting."

"Very well," Camia said, then stepped to the side. As Ry walked through a doorway in the opposite wall, Camia said, "You should be in good hands with Elementalist Troft. Please come down to the foyer if you need anything else, and I'll be glad to assist you."

"Thank you, Camia." Valla nodded her head and then walked over to the flower-patterned couch. Victor followed, offering Camia a smile, perhaps because he felt Valla should have done so, but the woman ignored him, slipping back through the door and closing it behind her. Victor sat down next to Valla, and she said, "So far, everyone's been very polite. I'm worried there's something coming—a binding contract, an exorbitant fee, or some such."

"Well, try to stay positive," Victor said, enjoying not being in the driver's seat for a change.

Valla looked ready to say something more, but the door opened, and a man wearing many-layered, brilliant red robes stepped through. He was tall and lean, his cheek and skull bones evident on his clean-shaven head and face. He was a Vesh, Victor was sure, because he had great, green-scaled wings folded at his back, and his eyes were bright yellow with vertical pupils. "Hello," he said, walking toward the couch. His voice was warm and mellow, and his eyes squinted as he smiled and reached a hand out to Valla.

Valla stood up and took his hand. "Pleased to meet you. I'm Valla ap'Yensha from the world of Fanwath." She glanced at Victor, still sitting down, and added, "This is my companion, Victor."

Troft had eyes only for Valla, completely ignoring Victor as he scratched his chin and said, "Fanwath. Hmm, I don't think I've heard of that one. What brings you to Coloss?"

"An accident," Valla said truthfully. "We were battling a mage in our world who'd created a portal to this world. He forced me through the portal, and Victor came through to aid me." Troft finally gave Victor a solid glance as she explained, and his eyes narrowed in momentary confusion.

"Ah! At first glance, I thought your companion was a Deshi. I see I was mistaken. Good of you to chase your mistress into the unknown that way, lad."

"My . . ." Victor started to say, then sighed and said, "Thanks."

"While we're stranded here, I thought I should take advantage of the greater knowledge of elemental magic in this world. It's become apparent to me that my power is rather lacking for my level."

"Mmhmm," Troft said, rubbing his chin and looking closely at Valla. He looked around, and his gaze settled on a nearby chair that he pulled over so he could sit directly in front of her. He stared at her for a long minute, enough that Victor was starting to feel uncomfortable, but Valla sat there stoically, staring directly back at the Elementalist. "Let's see," he said after a long while, "air and an earth affinity, aha, iron. Just like me! Well, as far as the iron goes."

"You have a good eye," Valla said, nodding.

"What level are you, Valla? I'd guess something like thirty?"

"Fifty-two," Valla replied, frowning.

"Oh dear," he said frowning, "Yes, I see how that's a problem. Your aura lacks the appropriate weight. Have you not been building your will and intelligence attributes?"

"I was raised in a martial family and have taken classes that primarily boosted my physical attributes."

"Ahh." Troft nodded. "A pity, but nothing a dozen levels focused on the right things won't fix. You've got your work cut out for you during this tier, though—you'll want to ensure you get the right kind of refinement at Tier Six."

"I've heard similar from others I've spoken to, but I don't know how to proceed."

"Does your current class give you any unbound attribute points at each level?"

"I'm a Sword Dancer, and no, my agility, dexterity, and vitality are each improved with my levels."

"Then you'll need to seek alchemical mixtures and natural treasures to improve your mental attributes as much as possible until level sixty. You'll want to focus your time on improving your Core. What's your Core's current level?"

"Improved Nine." Her answer surprised Victor. He'd thought she was miles ahead of him, but he was already nearing Improved Two.

"Ah! So low? By Tier Five, your Core should be in the advanced stages." Those words caused Valla's eyes to widen, and Victor felt his own heart start to beat as a bit of panic touched his mind—he felt as if he were listening to a teacher explaining how he should have mastered college algebra a long time ago. "You'll want to really work on that. Buy Core enhancements, spend time cultivating." He paused and then continued, his voice stern and emphasizing his words, "Much more time than you spend on sword work!"

"Aren't weapon skills important . . ."

"Of course, but with your affinities, you'll be able to enhance your weapon skills far beyond what you can do with natural skills."

"Really? The impression I got from Elementalists back home was that iron and air were a terrible pair, that they conflict."

Troft looked at Valla, raising his eyebrows, and then he laughed, a deep, rich belly laugh. He leaned back in his chair and seemed to give in to it, literally holding his sides and laughing until tears sprang from his eyes. Victor couldn't help smiling with him, and though he didn't know what was funny, a chuckle of his own escaped his lips, breaking his silent streak.

Valla didn't laugh. She didn't even smile. She frowned at Victor, then at Troft, and said, "I wish I knew what was funny."

"Oh dear," Troft said, wiping at his cheeks and finally calming enough to speak, "I'm sorry, but that was the first good laugh I've had in years, and I wanted to embrace it."

Valla stared at him until he continued, "The Elementalists on your world are either lying to you, or you've only spoken to abject idiots."

"Oh?" Valla's frown began to fade.

"Yes! Iron and air are a powerful combination of affinities. I've a dozen spells I could teach you that use both elements to great effect. Do you not know how to weave your air affinity into electricity?"

"Weave it into . . ." Valla said softly, absently scratching at one pale green eyebrow. "I've been taught that if I wanted to weave my Energies, I would have to weave iron with air and that it was impossible because they are opposing elements."

"Gods! Is that true? Are they really so backward?" Troft leaned forward and took Valla's hand, "Iron is an excellent match for an air affinity, but first, you must convert the form of your air energy into electricity. It's really not hard, Valla. I know a spell that will grant your sword tremendous speed and enhance its damage. There's a spell that will let you warp from one part of a battlefield to another. Both use air-attuned Energy but in the form of electricity. Just as a water affinity can take the form of ice or mist, and earth can take the shape of stone or soil, so too can air take the shape of electricity. You didn't know this?"

"I . . ." Valla started to say, then shook her head and continued, "I'm a fool. I know there are mages that cast lightning spells and that they have air affinities. I never learned them, and I never thought to try changing the shape of my Energy to mix it with my iron affinity. I was warned off mixing air with iron, but I should have pursued it further. I should have spoken to more experts."

"Tut, don't be hard on yourself, youngster. It sounds to me that the people in your life who had an influence over you were steering you away from such things, no? I'm sure you'd have figured things out eventually; I'm just glad I could help you avoid some painful mistakes going forward." He watched as Valla's frown deepened, but she nodded, and Victor knew what she was thinking—for all her help and guidance, Rellia had messed Valla up by pushing her to master the sword and forego the other aspects of her affinities.

"What must I do to learn some of your spells, Master Troft?" Valla asked, her voice quiet but determined.

"I'll give you two things for free, Valla. I'll show you the weave to turn air into electricity, and I'll give you one spell. After that, if you want more teaching, I'll need something from you."

"What do . . ." Valla started to ask, but Master Troft held up a hand, and she stopped speaking.

"Don't worry about what my fee might be, not yet. Master what I give you; if you want more, we can speak. I think this will keep you busy for a long while because just knowing how to make electricity from your air affinity will allow you to alter the skills and spells you already know. Oh, dear! I said I was only going to give you two things, and here I am giving you clues to pursue so many more . . ." He chuckled as Valla's eyes widened. Victor couldn't help himself and bumped an elbow into Valla's shoulder, grinning like a fool at her good news.

Valla ignored Victor and stood, bowing before the Elementalist and saying, "Thank you very much, Master Troft."

"You're quite welcome, Valla. How would it look if I didn't help a young Elementalist, the first visitor I know of from a new world? Wait here, won't you? I'll have one of my assistants write out the weave and the spell pattern. Come back and let me know when you've mastered them." With that, he stood, patted Valla in a comradely fashion on the shoulder, and exited the way he'd come.

"That's some pretty cool shit," Victor said when they were alone. "You never knew you could make electricity from air?"

"I knew it, but I thought it had to do with the spells you cast; all the spells I learned used simple air-attuned Energy." She looked at Victor and said, "What about you? Are there other forms of your affinities?"

"Yeah, I think so. I mean, I know so—I can twist my inspiration-attuned Energy into discouragement." Victor's eyes squinted as his thoughts began to race. "I never thought about it, but I wonder if I can twist rage into the opposite form like that? What the fuck would it be anyway? What's the opposite of rage? Peace?"

"I don't know . . . happiness?" Valla shrugged. "I think you should do some experimenting when we have some time. I'll have plenty to keep me busy, it sounds like." Victor nodded, still deep in thought and only half registering her words.

He thought about how he'd used his inspiration-attuned Energy when he cast Project Spirit; Victor had never been taught any sort of pattern to twist it the way he did. In a way, it was instinctual. Something told him twisting rage in a similar way wouldn't be so easy. When he projected rage, he stripped out aspects of it, taking away the benefits to strength and healing, but it was still rage.

They both sat quietly, lost in their own thoughts, until the door opened and Ry stepped through, holding two tightly bound paper scrolls. "Mistress, the master sends these with his compliments. I'm instructed to let you know that you're welcome here any time and that he wishes you great success."

"Thank you," Valla said, standing up and accepting the two scrolls.

"Now, allow me to show you out," Ry said, moving to the exit and pulling open the door. "The stairway is just down the hallway to the right."

When Victor and Valla descended the grand staircase, Valla was deep in thought, and Victor spent time ogling the architecture—the high arched windows, the beautifully carved wood, from the balustrade to the lintels to the doors themselves, and the way the space just seemed so grand, so vast. He wondered if the building was larger inside than outside, and he chuckled. "Of course it is," he said, remembering that it was the home of a guild of powerful wizards.

Camia greeted them at the bottom of the stairs and asked, "Was Master Troft able to help you?"

"Very much so," Valla said, nodding. "Thank you, Camia."

"You're quite welcome! You should know I've earned several merits with the guild for my assistance to you. So it's you I should be thanking for the opportunity." Camia smiled broadly as she spoke and opened the front door for them.

"Oh?" Valla said as they exited. "An intriguing system."

Victor couldn't help himself and said, "Nice to meet you, Camia," on his way out. The woman smiled and nodded at him, and that was that; they were outside, and Camia had closed the door behind them.

Valla didn't linger but walked straight down the path, out the gate, and then finally turned to Victor. "That was nerve-racking. Thank you for accompanying me."

"It was? I thought it was pretty relaxing. I didn't know you were stressing out."

"Well, I was. I've avoided seeking help from mages in the past. I think the news I've gotten through Rellia's 'experts' dissuaded me on the subject. I've focused on sword work because that's where my talent seemed to be, but I've worried it was a great mistake, which made me fear I'd hear some bad news in there." She gestured toward the Elementalist Guild. "I was afraid they'd say something that would destroy any hopes I've been harboring in here." She touched her chest over her heart.

"Well, I'm glad it was good news," Victor said, surprising himself with a yawn and stretching. "Guess we're about out of time." He pointed to the orange sky in the west where the sun was setting. "Dinnertime soon. What do you think we should wear?"

6

BLUE

I didn't realize you wanted to change inns," Valla said as they made their way back to the Arena District.

"Yeah, don't you think we could stand to have a little more space? Maybe a bath inside our rooms? Anyway, Livag told me how to find his cousin's inn. Wait . . . maybe it was his sister, I can't remember. Anyway, her name was Brecia, and her inn is called the Sunset Songbird." Victor hopped over a fallen, partially full sack of grain some wagon or cart had let fall on the side of the road.

"A pretty name. It seems the people of Coloss enjoy poetic titles."

"That or they really like sunsets," Victor replied, thinking of the name of the monster-hunting company they'd signed on with. He glanced at Valla and changed the subject. "Are you nervous?"

She jerked her head his way and narrowed her eyes. "About?"

"Your big dinner tonight." He chuckled and grinned, letting her know he was just messing around.

"Ancestors! I know you're teasing me, but yes, I'm a bit nervous. I hate formal affairs, and though Rellia dragged me to many, I often found myself slipping away early. Promise me something—if I look to be having a terrible time, will you make an excuse for us to leave? I'm not good at such things."

"Oh?" Victor was surprised by her admission. "Yeah, I can do that. I mean, I've got an arena fight tomorrow morning. I can't very well be out late, can I?"

"That's an excellent point, Victor," Valla laughed, reaching out to delicately pat him on the shoulder as though granting him a point.

"The square's just up here, and I saw the inn on our way out earlier. It's right around this corner." He quickened his pace, and Valla easily matched it. The arena square had grown busier since their earlier visit, but they didn't have to fight the crowd much; they rounded the corner, walked for half a block, and then stood before a burnt-orange brick building that rose several stories over the cobbles of the square.

A stable building took up the lot next to the inn, but having no mounts of their own, Victor and Valla walked past the waiting stablehands and approached the liveried doorman. He was a Vesh with black horns and wore a fancy brass-buttoned maroon coat over black velvety trousers. As they walked up, he said, "Welcome to the Sunset Songbird," and opened the human-sized door wide for them.

"No Degh allowed, I guess," Victor said quietly to Valla as they walked into the bustling lobby. Vesh and Yazzian people moved about, some chatting noisily and others walking here and there, toward the stairs or through the arched opening that led to the common room. A long counter stood off to one side, and behind it, Victor saw several people that must serve as the innkeepers on duty.

Stringed instruments could be heard playing in the common room, and the music drifted through the air. That, combined with the hanging plants and the bright light filtered through stained glass, lent a peaceful atmosphere to the room. Spices hung heavy in the air, the scent of good cooking if Victor were any judge, and his mouth began to salivate. "I haven't eaten since breakfast," he announced, and Valla snorted.

"Save your appetite. We're going to dinner soon, remember?"

"Right," Victor grunted, approaching one of the Vesh ladies behind the counter. The floor was tiled in pale brown stone, and the walls were coated in something like stucco, and Victor felt like the place had a very Mediterranean vibe. He could even hear a fountain trickling from one of the nearby interior courtyards. "Hello," he said, thumping one of his heavy hands onto the counter.

"Hello, sir. Welcome to the Sunset Songbird! Are you seeking accommodation or information?"

"Yeah, we're looking for a room or two." Victor gestured to Valla as she stepped forward beside him.

"Very good; we have limited availability due to the festival starting on the morrow, but I can offer you a suite with a courtyard terrace." The young woman had, to Victor's sensibilities, a rather unsightly tusk jutting up from a prominent lower jaw, but he figured Vesh had different ideas of beauty.

"Sounds nice. We'll take it."

"Thank you, sir. Might I ask your name?" she asked, sliding a gray slate toward him. "Please touch this with your Energy."

"I'm Victor," he said, pressing a finger to the slate and trickling a bit of Energy into it. It pulsed with orange light and then resumed its flat gray appearance.

"How should the staff address you, sir? Do you have a particular honorific?"

"Just Victor. This is Captain Valla, though," Victor said, enjoying putting the spotlight on his reticent friend.

"Oh! I'm pleased to meet you, Captain. I'm sorry, I didn't realize this was your attendant; I assumed you were a couple."

"He's not my attendant. At the very least, we are of equal status on our world. Don't let his modesty fool you; he's a champion fighter and will be displaying his prowess in your arena on the morrow." Valla narrowed her eyes at him as she spoke, and Victor realized he shouldn't have been messing with her.

"Oh? You're fighting in the Horc's Day tournament? I can offer you a discount in that case! Only one hundred and forty beads per night for your suite." Victor had figured the price would be higher than the ninety Livag had quoted him; if the inn only had a few rooms available, he doubted they were the least expensive ones. Still, it was more than he'd expected, and that was with a discount. He took some pleasure in the way Valla's lips parted and how she seemed a bit lost for words.

"Sounds good. We'll need the room for a couple of nights." He pulled a heavy sack of beads from his ring and started counting them out. The woman smiled and lifted a wooden stick that looked very much like a wand to Victor and held it toward him.

"I have a counting rod, if you'll allow me?"

"Uh, sure," Victor said, moving his hand away from the bag. She smiled and adjusted a couple of tiny knobs at the rod's base. Then she tapped the bag. A neat pile of beads appeared next to it, and the cloth deflated a little. "Oh, cool." Victor nodded and scooped up the slightly lighter bag, and the inn attendant waved the rod at the pile of beads; they disappeared, presumably to some hidden container.

"Very good, Captain Valla and Victor—you're paid in full for two nights. The room has been attuned to you, Victor, so the door will open at your touch. If the Captain would like similar access, there's a slate inside the door where you can grant it to her."

"Okay, can you show us how to get to it? The room, I mean," Victor said.

"The most direct route is through the courtyard there." She pointed through an arched opening in the wall opposite the inn's main entrance. "Your rooms are on the other side of the fountain—the Sand Drake Suite." She paused, then said more loudly, "Tral, I'm going to show our new guests to their suite."

"Very good, Jatta," the woman further down the counter replied, and Jatta stepped out from around the counter and gestured for Victor and Valla to follow her.

"Nice service," Valla muttered.

"Yeah, this is more like it," Victor said, grinning as he followed a few feet behind Jatta. The courtyard wasn't very large, and he realized there were only three rooms that opened onto it on the first floor. Balconies on the upper levels hung over the flowering plants and burbling fountains, though, and he could hear people's murmured conversations drifting through the air. Jatta showed them to a little patio with glass-paneled doors and waited for Victor to reach out and touch the handle. It clicked, and he pulled it open.

"You know where to find me, should you need anything else. Once again, welcome to the Sunset Songbird."

"Thank you," Valla said, but Victor was already walking into the room, barely registering the woman's words. The suite's main room was decorated in a similar fashion to the lobby. It boasted a table and chairs, comfortable couches, a small kitchen complete with a stove and a cold cabinet, and bookcases lined with knickknacks and books, mostly filled with poetry. There were two bedrooms with large, comfortable beds, and each had an adjoining bathroom. Victor was pleased.

"This is definitely more like it, Valla," he called from his bathroom after sampling the hot water flowing from the spigot in the big bronze tub.

"Yes, it's lovely. Thank you, Victor," she replied after a few seconds, speaking from the doorway into his room. "We should get ready for the War Captain's dinner."

"About that," Victor said, stepping from his bathroom and into his room to look at her. "What should I wear?"

"I'm going to wear my dress uniform. I suggest you wear your armor—the shimmersteel is lovely and finer than any of your shirts. Do you have some black pants?"

Victor looked down at his pants, more khaki than brown if he had to put a label on them. "Yeah, I have black ones—a few pairs."

"Good, and polish your boots." She scowled at his boots, the same ones he'd bought all the way back in Steampool Vale. They were holding up all right and fit his feet like a second skin. Thanks to their enchantments, they weren't scuffed, but they were definitely not shiny; a thick layer of dust coated the dark leather, and the steel toes were dull—far from the gleaming shine they'd had when he bought them.

"Okay, this is embarrassing, but I don't have any, like, shoe-shining stuff."

Valla smiled and stepped forward, a small tin and a soft cloth appearing in her hands. "Rub some of this on the boots and buff them vigorously with the cloth." She looked him up and down as he reached for the offered items and added, "Do the same for your belt. Keep it, by the way; I have a dozen different leather conditioners I've bought over the years."

"Somehow, that doesn't surprise me," Victor chuckled, pointedly eyeing Valla's gleaming black boots.

"A shave wouldn't hurt, either," Valla said over her shoulder as she walked out of the room. "I'm going to bathe and get dressed. Meet you in half an hour in the sitting room?"

"Yep," Victor said, unscrewing the little tin and sniffing the yellowish, creamy contents—it smelled like wax with a hint of something else, like sandalwood, maybe, but he couldn't place it for sure.

Twenty minutes later, Victor exited his bedroom, cleaner than he had been in quite a while. His boots shone, especially the gleaming metal-clad toes. He'd rubbed the road and battle stains from the leather of his belt, and Lifedrinker hung from it proudly. Victor's armor hadn't needed any attention; the enchantments and the magical metal kept it lustrous, shimmering from copper to green depending on the angle from which a person viewed it. He'd given himself a shave, combed his hair, and wore his best pair of black, self-cleaning pants. All in all, he felt he'd made plenty of effort for some military dinner.

Valla was waiting for him, pacing in a tight circle by the terrace doors. She wore a uniform similar to the one Victor was accustomed to seeing her in but far finer. Her boots reflected the glow lamps like dark mirrors, and she'd tucked her tight white pants into them.

She'd donned a short, fitted, brocaded coat with shiny brass buttons. Dozens of gleaming pins crafted from precious metals covered the left breast, and its high collar framed her head dramatically. The shirt she wore beneath it, white with pearlescent buttons, was tied at the neck with a red, scarf-like tie that matched the stripes on her pants and coat.

Valla always looked neat, so her perfectly coiffed, short green hair didn't surprise Victor, but the makeup did; she'd painted her lips and the pale blue flesh around her eyes in a shimmering turquoise that highlighted her hair and eyes. "You look nice," Victor said, noting that she wore a sword at her waist—not her usual blade, something fancier and probably a lot less deadly. It looked like a saber of some sort, though it was ornate and decorative, and Victor doubted she'd use it in a fight.

"Thank you." She nodded and then added, "You look . . . better."

"Heh," Victor snorted, producing the invitation the dragon lady had given him. "This is supposed to guide us to the correct address. You ready?"

"I am; the sooner, the better."

"Okay," Victor said, channeling some Energy into the card. As soon as his Energy touched the card, it burst into a shower of blue sparks, and a brilliant, glimmering blue butterfly hovered in the afterglow. The butterfly flitted in a circle around Victor and then, trailing a shower of blue sparkles, flew to the doors and waited.

"Looks like we have a guide!" Victor laughed, hurrying after the butterfly to open the doors. It flew into the courtyard, and Victor and Valla followed it.

"It's beautiful," Valla said, and for the second time that day, she smiled.

"Yeah, it is," Victor replied, following the butterfly through the inn's lobby. "Hey, what's with the chest full of gold and platinum? Are those medals?"

"Yes, I earned them during my time in the legion. Duels, victories, academic achievements, rank insignias—I could bore you for an hour telling you about each one."

"I don't think it would be boring. They're pretty badass, if you ask me."

"Maybe when we start the campaign of the Untamed Marches, we should institute some achievement criteria, and you can earn your own 'chest full of gold and platinum,'" she said, and though she was at least half-joking, Victor rather liked the idea.

They followed the flitting, spark-trailing, blue butterfly through the night-cloaked streets of Coloss. It didn't move quickly but rather in spurts, always pausing to wait for Victor and Valla. It seemed to know when a part of the road was too crowded to pass and would wait until a break in traffic allowed easy passage, and Victor had time to take in the sights, sounds, and smells of Coloss at night.

People seemed more cheerful, elegant, and colorful than they did in the daytime. He saw representatives of all the local peoples wearing bright, fine clothing. He saw Yazzians in robes limned with light and reflective metallic threads; he saw a giant Degh wearing plate armor that shone in the darkness, leaving a silvery trail as she jogged down the street as fast as most horses could run. The crowds in the squares were denser, there was music playing everywhere, and the scents of food that hung in the air had Victor's mouth salivating and his stomach rumbling.

Victor was close to breaking down and buying something from a vendor to tide him over when the butterfly turned up a steep road that climbed into a part of the city that reminded him of where they'd visited the Elementalist Guild. The crowds thinned out, the street vendors faded away, and soon they were walking among finely dressed Vesh, clearly on their way to gatherings of their own.

"I believe this city was founded by Vesh," Valla surprised him by saying. "In these noble districts, you don't see many of the other peoples."

"Yeah, I noticed that." Victor nodded toward a pair of large gate guards wearing black plate armor. The butterfly flew past them, continuing down the cobbled walkway toward another gate, this one brightly illuminated by blue-tinted glow lamps. The guards outside this gate also wore plate armor, but it followed the blue theme. When the butterfly reached it, it spun into a tight spiral and exploded in a shower of blue sparkles. "I think our host likes blue."

"Yes," Valla said, frowning and walking toward the guards. "I begin to understand why he has an interest in me."

"Welcome," the guard to the left said, his voice echoing strangely from his heavy metal helmet. Neither of the guards' faces were visible through their thick plate visors. He gestured toward the open gateway and the cobbled path beyond. Blue glow lamps lined the pathway, illuminating the way, though dimly, allowing the darkness beyond to cling like a shadowy blanket. "The War Captain and his guests await; follow the pathway to the manor."

As they walked up the path, Victor tried to match Valla's pace, trying to remind himself that this was her event; he was here only because she'd been invited. The walk to the manor wasn't long; how could it be in a city so crowded with structures? When they rounded the first bend, following the dim blue lights, they saw it ahead; a palace that matched Lam's estate in elegance, though it was easily twice the size.

What stood out, what bothered Victor, was the predominance of the color blue everywhere. Blue stained glass windows, more blue glow lamps, guards in blue armor, servants in blue livery, carpets and rugs all in shades of blue, and even many of the walls were plastered or painted blue. As they followed one of the servants that had waited near the door, guiding them through the corridors toward the "great hall," Victor couldn't hold his tongue any longer, and he asked, "What's the deal with all the blue?"

"Sir?" the Vesh woman asked, pausing to face him.

"The blue? Everywhere? The, um, War Captain's favorite color?"

"I'm not sure of his personal preference, but each War Captain is assigned a color. This is the home of War Captain Blue, and he has three peers—Black, Red, and Green."

"Ah!" Valla said, smiling at the woman. "Thank you for clearing that up; we're new to Coloss."

"Of course, Lady." The woman curtsied delicately in her blue skirts, then turned and continued guiding them through the manor. When they came to a set of enormous blue-stained wooden doors, she presented them to the two uniformed guards, each wearing gleaming plate helmets with high feathered plumes—naturally, they were blue.

The guard on the left turned, pulled open one of the doors, and announced, loud enough that his voice cut through the din beyond, "The Lady Captain Valla of Fanwath and her escort, Victor!" He turned, bowed, and gestured for them to proceed into the suddenly quiet hall. Valla reached up to grab Victor's elbow, and he felt himself stand up straighter, suddenly feeling nervous for the first time.

Of course, the great hall was carpeted in blue, patterned with flowers, and the lights were, thankfully, more white than blue, but still, the chandeliers dangled strands of blue crystals that threw dazzling patterns on the walls. Victor couldn't take in any more of the decor because he became aware of the hundreds of Vesh guests, finely dressed, standing around in groups or sitting at tables along the perimeter, all seemingly stopping whatever they'd been doing to stare at him and Valla.

After a moment of standing transfixed, never having had such a silent crowd observe him, Victor shrugged and started walking over the carpet toward the high table at the far end of the room. He felt Valla's grip tighten on his elbow, but she walked with him, head high. Victor had an absurd urge to ham it up for all the staring weirdos; he wanted to wave and shout something like "How's it going?" into the silence, but he didn't want to embarrass Valla, so he just walked with her toward the group of elegant, beastly Vesh that sat around a man in a massive, blue stone, throne-like chair.

When they were just a few feet away, and the man who had to be the War Captain Blue was just a bit farther away than the width of his table, Victor stopped and waited for him, or anyone, to say something. The War Captain was big, easily a head taller than any Vesh Victor had seen. He wore a beautifully tailored blue suit cut in a fashion that highlighted his massively muscled physique. He had fine, handsome features, only spoiled—to Victor's human sensibilities—by a pair of long, straight, black horns that stood up from the top of his forehead.

The War Captain reached up, smoothed his neat black hair back, tucking some stray strands behind an ear, and spread his lips in a smile, revealing brilliant white fangs. He squinted his pale yellow eyes and said, "It's true what I heard, Lady Valla—you're more beautiful than I could have imagined." His voice was rich and deep, and despite his desire to be irritated, Victor couldn't help but admire the man. "Please, come sit." He gestured to an empty chair on his left-hand side.

"And my escort, War Captain?" Valla asked before Victor even registered that there was only one empty seat at the table.

"Please call me Blue. This large fellow? We've a spot for him just over there." The War Captain pointed to one of the tables that ran perpendicular to his along the side of the hall.

"I'd prefer . . ." Valla started to say, but Victor interrupted her.

"It's fine, Valla." He knew he was being a little selfish; he had no desire to sit at the high table and watch this guy try to flirt with Valla, and he'd noticed that the dragon lady was seated at the table where the War Captain had pointed. "Come on, I'll walk you to your seat," he said, turning to walk around the Captain's table.

"What happened to the music?" Blue shouted, and suddenly the room was filled with the lilting tunes of a group of stringed instrument players that occupied the far corner of the chamber. Victor tried to keep his face impassive as he walked with Valla around the table, but he couldn't help frowning when he saw the dirty looks many of the Vesh sitting at the table were throwing their way.

He leaned toward Valla's ear to whisper, and he noticed, for the first time, that she'd worn silver and diamond earrings in a half-moon pattern from her ear's top curve all the way down to her lobe, seven of them. How had he missed that? Shaking his head, he hissed, "Be careful; these people are mad jealous of you."

"I'm not happy about this," she whispered back. "Please watch me; if I stand up, it means I want to leave."

"You got it, *chica*," Victor said, pulling out her seat so she could sit down.

"Thank you, warrior," Blue said, dismissing Victor. Victor was surprised that Blue had called him "warrior," but then he realized he was the only person in the room, at least sitting at a table, wearing armor. He shrugged, gave Valla's shoulder a squeeze, and then made his way around the back of the Captain's table, down one tier, and to the lower table where his seat waited.

The empty chair was second from the head, and the dragon lady sat at that top seat. She smiled at him as he approached, then said to the Vesh woman beside her, "Krae, would you mind moving down so I can speak to this off-worlder?"

"Of course, Tes," the woman said, standing to curtsy. To his surprise, she glanced at Victor and pleasantly smiled as she moved down to his formerly assigned seat.

Victor sat in her seat, still warm from her presence, and said, "Thanks," nodding to her. Then he turned to the dragon lady and said, "Tes, is it?"

"Tesia'liveen'ashalah, actually, but I find people I meet prefer my short name." She smiled, her perfectly human-looking cheeks dimpling at the gesture.

"Well, yeah, I think I'll stick with Tes if it's all right," Victor replied, though his eyes were on Valla, studying her face, and he felt himself relax when she laughed at something the War Captain said.

"You're worried about your friend?" Tes asked, following his gaze.

"I mean, yeah. I think this dude's interested in her because she has blue skin. It's kinda fucked up, don't you think?"

"What an interesting way to speak . . ." Tes started to say, but then a commotion from the head table erupted, and she stopped to look where Victor was already staring. A Vesh woman wearing a beautiful blue silky gown had stood up from her seat two spaces down on the War Captain's right, throwing her chair back, so it clattered against the wall. Her cheeks were red, her eyes like blazing embers, and she strode behind Blue to stare at Valla, who'd also risen from her seat, her hand reaching for her ornamental sword.

The Vesh woman opened her black-scaled wings with a resounding *crack* and loomed over Valla, easily half a foot taller. The room had grown quiet again, and everyone heard what she said, her words thick with emotion, "Enough of this farce! I challenge you to a duel, off-worlder! If the Blue likes your skin so much, I'll have it made into a cloak and present it to him as a Horc's Day gift." The War Captain, to Victor's horror, didn't object; he glanced from Valla to the Vesh woman, and his eyes squinted in amusement, a deep chuckle emerging from his lips.

"Fucking hell," Victor said.

7

A DINNER CONVERSATION

Victor stood up, his chair toppling behind him in his haste, but he felt a grip on his wrist that might as well have been a steel shackle for how little it moved when he tugged at it. "Wait," said Tes. "See how things play out before you throw your dice on the table."

Valla's voice rang out through the room. "You wish to duel? I don't even know you." Her back was straight as a post, face betraying no emotion as she stared the taller, threatening woman in the eyes.

"Reis, restrain yourself," War Captain Forl—Blue—finally said, still chuckling. Victor started to relax, assuming the man would put a stop to the situation, but Blue kept speaking. "We have too many events taking place today and tomorrow. If you insist on a duel, it will have to be overmorrow."

"Very well," said the Vesh lady, Reis. "Overmorrow, it is. Gird yourself well, blue-skin; I won't stop at first blood."

Valla looked from Reis to the War Captain and, unflinching, said, "Is that how things are done in this world, then? Duels without cause, regardless of level or tier? How backward." That got a reaction from the crowd—gasps and murmured outrage at her audacity. Victor had seen enough; he tugged again at Tes's grip on his arm, but she held fast.

"Victor, no violence will occur tonight; don't make things worse by inserting yourself. I promise you—it's the wrong move." Tes seemed to speak softly, but her voice rang in Victor's ears, and he took another breath, willing his rage to calm.

"We care about fairness, lovely," the War Captain said, chuckling. "Were you not just telling me that you've recently joined the ranks of the mid-tier? Darling Reis is, herself, in the same category."

Valla looked at Reis coolly, assessing her stature, her glittering black-scaled wings, the fire in her eyes, and the way her hair, long and plaited, gleamed like polished obsidian. Victor knew she was sizing the woman up and measuring the strength of her aura. Finally, Valla said, "And if I refuse?"

"Then you are disgraced," Reis answered for Blue.

"Sadly, it's true, beautiful," Blue said, turning his chair so he could look at the two women more easily. "You're free to avoid the duel, but I'll have to ask you to leave. Such disgraceful behavior won't stand among us—the highborn Vesh. Why, you'd have to forego any access to the finer things in Coloss: the arena, sanctioned monster hunts, even the protection of the Warlord, and access to his City Stone."

Victor couldn't contain himself any longer. "This is bullshit," he growled.

"Oh, dear!" Blue said, glancing his way. "Your barbarian seems to have slipped his muzzle."

Valla jerked her head toward Victor, saw him standing there, eyes blazing in anger, with Tes firmly gripping his wrist, and she stared hard at him until their eyes locked. She narrowed them slightly and gave her head a quick shake, making it clear to Victor, even in his burgeoning rage, that she wanted him to stand down. When she saw some tension leave his posture, she turned back to Reis and said with a firm, steady voice, "Very well, Reis. I will accept your duel."

Reis grinned savagely, her dark eyes blazing with sparkling Energy. Before the challenger could speak, though, Valla turned to Blue and said, "I understand it's to be the day after tomorrow. Are there any other rules of which I should be aware? The time of day and location, for instance?"

"Wonderful question!" The War Captain stood up and turned to address the entire room. "We have cause to celebrate! Our guest, the beautiful lady from off-world, Valla, will be dueling our very own Reis, the Lady of Tuul. I shall host the event right here, in my grand hall, overmorrow at noon. Each combatant will use their preferred weapon, and no abilities shall be barred, save those that might damage my property!"

To Victor's surprise, as the crowd cheered, Valla straightened her chair and sat down, turning her back to Reis, who looked angrier than ever. Blue chuckled and said, "Reis, you've made your point; please take your seat so that we may enjoy the feast."

Victor stared at Valla until she met his eyes, and she gave him a nod; she was okay. He sighed and turned to pick up his chair, and that's when he realized Tes had released his wrist. The conversation around the room resumed, somewhat more animated than before the challenge, and Victor's muttered "Fuck these stuck-up assholes" was lost in the buzz as he retook his seat.

"You have an amusing vernacular," Tes said, sipping from a blue crystal wine glass.

"I can't tell if I should be pissed or thankful about you holding onto me like that."

"Oh, thankful, I should think. There are those in this hall that could smite you rather easily." She smiled and licked at a droplet of wine at the corner of her mouth and said, "Tell me, Victor, are there many humans in the world from which you hail? I believe my network told me it's called Fanwath, yes?"

"Just like that?" Victor said, looking around the room. "My friend was just challenged by some racist bitch to fight to the death, and we're all going to act like nothing happened?"

The woman to his left shifted uncomfortably, turning to speak with her neighbor, and Tes frowned, shaking her head slightly. Softly, she said, "Victor, the people here fancy themselves above such concerns. If you continue to speak so vulgarly, the wrong person may hear you and decide to administer a lesson."

Victor didn't speak; he just glowered and reached for the wine glass in front of him. He sipped at the dark red vintage, and though he didn't consider himself a wine drinker, it tasted good in that moment, and its potency was not in question. Finally, more calmly, he said, "What about you? Could anyone here teach you 'a lesson'?"

Tes smiled, reaching up to twirl a blonde curl with her long, frightfully strong fingers, and said, "I should think not. Consider that for a moment and think about the implications of having me for a friend." She glanced pointedly in Valla's direction.

"Is there something you can do to help her?" Victor asked again, leaning closer so he could speak even more quietly. "She's underpowered for her level and just barely in the mid-tier."

"Two things, Victor. One, duels aren't always about the participants' maximum power, though it's certainly a factor. And two, of course I'll help your friend; I love an underdog. Perhaps tomorrow, while you're playing in the arena, I'll spend some time with her."

"They say underdog where you come from? Are there dogs in your world?"

"I'll answer that question if you answer mine." She smiled coyly and took another sip of wine. It took Victor a minute to remember what her question had been, then he answered.

"Fanwath? No, I think I'm the only human there. Well, that used to be there."

"Truly? How is that possible? You don't have parents?"

"I was summoned to that world from mine."

"Ah! Now the picture grows more clear. Would you mind telling me of your homeworld?"

"Yeah, but first, tell me how you spending a day with Valla is going to help her enough to survive. What level is that Reis woman? Also, you owe me an answer about dogs."

Tes looked to the head table, eyes on Reis, who'd retaken her seat, and after a moment, she looked back at Victor and said, "Tier Seven, I'd wager."

"Fuck me!" Victor sighed, putting his head in his hands. Tes looked at him for a moment, then frowned and stood. Lifting her glass, she cleared her throat, and then her voice, clear as a crystal, rang out through the great hall, cutting through the conversations as though she stood next to every person there. "Great War Captain Blue, I would endeavor to thank you for this fine occasion by offering a toast and a prophecy." Victor jerked his head up from his hands, and she offered him a quick wink.

Blue stood up immediately, eyes flaring with excitement, and bellowed, "Silence! Let the Lady Tes speak!" His shout was superfluous—everyone had grown quiet as Tes's clarion voice rang through the hall.

"My Lord Blue," Tes said again, her voice echoing off the walls of the hall, though she spoke as if to a person right next to her, "I've had a vision. Should you host the duel between the Ladies Valla and Reis, not overmorrow, but in a month and a day, you will draw the Warlord's interest, and he will attend the event." She paused as her words sank in and then added, "Here's to the elevation of War Captain Blue!" She held her wine glass aloft, and the crowd thundered their enthusiastic echo of the toast.

"You heard her!" Blue roared, throwing his empty glass over his shoulder to shatter on the wall. "My apologies, Lady Reis, but your duel will be postponed for one month and one day!"

Victor watched Valla while he spoke, how she stared impassively at Tes, and though she didn't look angry or pleased, he thought he saw some tension leave her posture. Tes, for her part, hammed it up, curtsying to Blue, lifting her lovely multilayered blue and yellow skirts daintily. When she retook her seat, she sighed, smiling at Victor, and snapped her fingers. Victor heard a popping noise in his ears, and then she said, "You may speak freely. Interloping ears will find our words strangely garbled."

"Why now?" Victor asked, thinking back to their prior, hushed conversation.

"Because I fear you're about to ask me about my false prophecy, etcetera." She smirked and drank some more wine.

"Well?"

"Very well, I'll give you some answers, and then you'll owe me a few. Fair?" When Victor nodded, she continued, "Yes, there are dogs on Aradnue. Dragons quite enjoy their company, though a few savages will eat them. No, I didn't have a vision regarding your friend's duel. I can tell you with great confidence, though, that the duel will generate tremendous excitement around the city, thanks to my words, and the Warlord will surely attend—a self-fulfilling prophecy, if you will. Blue believes me because I have shared some auguries with him in recent history that came true; it's a gift of mine and allowed me to gain status in Coloss quite rapidly."

"So, we have a month to get out of town?" Victor said.

"Well, that, or prepare your friend in a manner that allows her to win. I intend to keep my earlier promise to help her; I find the prospect intriguing." She took another drink, and Victor mimicked her, draining his glass. After she'd swallowed and gestured for a waiting attendant to bring more, she said, "Now it's your turn. Tell me of your homeworld."

"I'm from Earth. We don't have Energy there, and I was Base Zero when I got summoned to Fanwath. The guys who summoned me threw me into a pit fighting circuit, kind of like throwing out the garbage, I guess."

"Earth?" A slow smile had spread on her face while she listened to him. "I'm familiar with this world, and though it may be a dead world now, it was once so rich in Energy that mighty armies of elder races fought over it. There are texts on Aradnue written by legendary dragons that spent time there. I'd give much to visit, even in its current state. Might I have a sample of your blood, Victor?"

"What?" Victor raised an eyebrow and shifted back in his seat.

"With your blood, there are those on Aradnue who could open a gateway to your homeworld. I'd enjoy visiting, though it would be difficult, and I'd need to bring an enormous store of Energy to avoid fading."

"Fading?"

"Dead worlds cannot sustain creatures of any significant Energy. You would grow weak and die should you try to return. How sad and frustrating that must be!"

Victor frowned, some of his darkest fears suddenly made real. His mind wanted to mull over the blunt news this dragon woman had just dropped on him, but he forced himself to remain present, to push those feelings into a corner of his mind, and said, "I'd wondered about that. There aren't people with superhuman abilities on Earth, and I worried I'd lose my strength and abilities if I returned."

"No, it would be worse than that, I'm afraid. Your body has changed significantly as you have gained power on Fanwath. You require Energy to function. It isn't a simple matter of undoing all of your growth; you'd quite literally starve, and it would be a horrible sensation as it happened."

"But you want to visit? Couldn't I bring Energy home with me?"

"Yes, I imagine you could make a quick visit; the Energy required to keep you alive and comfortable for more than a few days is likely beyond your means, but that much is possible. It might afford you a chance to say farewell to your loved ones."

"Would you help me if I gave you my blood?"

"Or I could simply take it," she said, grinning, and suddenly Victor had a vision of her true form—her enormous blue-scaled body filling his vision and her scythe-like teeth gleaming with saliva. He blinked his eyes and shook his head, and she sat before him again, simply a beautiful, petite, human-looking woman. "I jest." Her eyes twinkled in amusement, and she continued, "I will help you, but not now, Victor. You'd be rather difficult to protect on Aradnue in your current state. Speak to me when you've gained the strength to fend off those such as me, and then I'll see that you visit your home."

"When I can 'fend off' people like you?" Victor scoffed, her dragon form looming large in his mind. "My *abuela* might not live that long!" He leaned forward earnestly, his eyes watery, his sudden new hope just as suddenly dashed.

"Tut, Victor. There's no telling if your grandmother is still alive as it is. Before we spoke, you had no hope; now you have some. Look at this as another reason to gain power. By the way, I'm not being cruel or arbitrary in my demand. I'm far from the most potent of dragons, and when some of the ancients of my kind smell your presence, you'll need great strength to make your petition."

"Are there others that could do it? Someone here, maybe? Open a gateway to Earth, I mean?"

"There are those on Zaafor that can open portals between worlds, but none that could do so with a dead world. It takes an order of magnitude more power and expertise to reach the worlds deprived of the rivers and oceans of Energy."

"But some asshole from this world went to Fanwath and summoned me there."

"Summoning someone, given the proper key, is far easier than opening a gateway onto another world. If someone with the requisite skill had a sample of your blood and the strength of will to crush yours, they could summon you from nearly anywhere; reaching out and snatching hold of someone is different than establishing a portal, an opening through space. Tell me, did the wizard have some connection to you, some way to tie his magic to you?"

"Now that you mention it, Rellia—" He paused when Tes frowned, unfamiliar with the name, then clarified, "A noblewoman who helped me with some information. She said something about some biological material . . ."

"There you have it! With a biological connection to you, they could reach out and snatch you through the ether. That's something you should look into, Victor. How did they get such material?" As she spoke, servants began to deliver the food, and Victor sat back, mulling over everything she'd told him.

He'd learned that he couldn't return home to live, not ever. He'd already sort of resigned himself to that, but feeling a certain way and knowing it was true were two different things, and he suddenly felt very morose, very moody. He struggled even to acknowledge the food placed before him. He'd also, in the same conversation, learned that he might be able to visit home, but the hurdles to do so seemed insurmountable, at least in the near term. How many more years did his *abuelita* have? She was in her seventies.

"I've ruined your dinner," Tes said, having just inhaled the aromas on her plate. Her smile turned into a pout as she saw Victor sitting there, brooding. "Victor, I'll give you the means to contact me. When you're ready, I'll help you. I have no obligation to, you know, but I find the prospect—and you— amusing. Don't ruin that with a sour mood."

Victor shook his head, trying to throw off the dour thoughts running through his mind, and said, "All right. One thing at a time, huh? For now, let's make sure Valla survives this duel, hmm?"

"That's the spirit! It's always best to devour your meal one bite at a time. Let me worry about your friend; I believe you have your own challenges to overcome, starting with an arena tournament on the morrow."

"Yeah, but, to be honest, I'm looking forward to it. I've felt like getting into a fight all damn day." Victor took a bite of the rare, bloody meat on his plate, admiring how nicely the silver knife from his place setting cut through it. The coppery, salty tang was good, and it woke up his hunger. As he wolfishly began to attack his serving, he listened to Tes.

"It's good to have a release, no doubt. Might I make a suggestion, though?" Victor grunted assent, and she continued, "Don't put all your abilities on display until you have to. If you struggle but still win, it will make your later fights much more glorious; don't give your opponents a chance to devise strategies around your greatest strengths. I can see more thoroughly into you than the people of Coloss, and I'm certain you're being greatly underestimated. Make them pay for it."

"Underestimated?" Victor asked between mouthfuls, eating a pile of sweet purple mash that reminded him of yams.

"If they knew anything of humans, they'd give you a closer look, approach you with more caution."

That caught Victor's attention, and he looked at Tes with a raised eyebrow, swallowed his food, and said, "I guess that brings to mind some other questions I had for you. What is it about Earth and humanity that interests you? I get that there are books about Earth on your world, but what in those books makes it seem special?"

"Earth was teeming with elder races once upon a time—dragons, various species of titan, the fae, demonkind, and celestial beings. I could go on if I had one of my grandmatron's texts, but those are the ones I can think of off the top of my head. Among those great, powerful species, a younger race was born. Humans were excellent adapters, and many of the elder races grew fond of them, spawning hybrids who were left behind as the currents of Energy were pulled away, leaving Earth to wither."

"Seriously? Demons?" Victor shook his head and said, "Forget it. Tell me why the Energy left Earth."

"War between the fae is the most likely culprit. The Winter Court makes something of a habit of stealing Energy from worlds in the physical plane, redirecting it into the Faewild, specifically into their territories." She paused, took a drink of her wine and a bite of meat, and, still chewing, continued speaking.

"Well, that's a possibility, but there are others. With so many powerful beings vying for territory, any number of cataclysms could have occurred that pulled your world out of the flow. It's also possible the System, younger and more clumsy in those days, disrupted the current further upstream. I think I'll research this topic if I can use your blood to open a gateway." Tes stared into space, almost dreamily, tapping one perfectly manicured nail against her chin while she swallowed her bite.

"So humans are special somehow because we grew up around powerful beings?" Victor prompted.

"Oh, silly man, it's not just that you 'grew up' around them; did you not hear me mention spawning hybrids? Your kind lay with them—sex! It's not a coincidence that my bipedal form looks human! Your bloodlines are rich with the strength of beings as great as I. More than that, you have an affinity for Energy that generally rivals that of any elder race. Given time and training, humans have immense potential."

"Damn . . ." Victor felt like a little kid that had caught his mom sleeping with an alien.

"Indeed! Do you see why these people of Coloss are foolish to underestimate you? Wait until they get a look at your inner titan." She grinned wickedly and winked at Victor. "These Degh are a pale shadow."

"You know . . ."

"I told you." She touched a finger just under her eye. "I see more than anyone in this city."

"Well, on that topic, maybe you could give me some advice?" Victor asked.

"Oh? Matters of the heart?" She glanced over at the head table.

"No, shit, no," Victor laughed and quickly added, "I mean about my attributes. I've been dumping a lot of points into will because it seems to benefit me in lots of ways, thanks to my Spirit Core and the classes I've had. Do you think I should keep doing that?"

She looked at him for a long moment and then said, "There are things about you I don't know, but I understand the gist of what you're saying. Your will strengthens your abilities, and so you are able to strengthen yourself with the application of that attribute. I think, unless you feel you are suffering in a particular area, I'd continue that route. You'd do well to seek a mentor who understands your Core more thoroughly; I've little experience with spirit affinities."

"Well . . ." Victor thought about her words, found that he couldn't see an argument with them, and said simply, "Thanks."

He tried to ply her for more information as the dinner progressed, but Tes played him off, changing the topic frequently to more mundane subjects, like the meal, the music, various guests and their clothing, and even the weather. Victor was sure to keep an eye on Valla, watching to see if she was ready to leave, but his friend sat, rather at ease, eating her food and making what seemed to be polite conversation with the War Captain and the people seated nearby.

When the meal was over and people started to disburse, some going to dance, others walking off in pairs or small groups to drink elsewhere, Tes folded her napkin over her half-eaten dessert—an amazingly rich cake with a distinct coconut flavor—and stood up. "Excuse me, Victor. I have matters to attend in private. Please let your companion know that I'll seek her out tomorrow in the arena. Here." She handed Victor a shiny silver token with a pair of horns stamped into one side. "This will grant her access to my private spectator booth."

"Okay," Victor said, standing up. He cleared his throat and awkwardly said, "Thank you, Tes. Thanks for helping out Valla and for telling me so much about my world. I feel like a dumb kid more than ever, but I guess that's what happens when your eyes get opened up."

"The important thing is what you do now that your eyes are open. I look forward to witnessing your growth; the younger peoples of the universe, like those here in Coloss, are in for a treat." She chuckled and held out a hand, and Victor, ignorant as he was, knew he was supposed to kiss it. He blushed furiously, but he did it, taking her fingers lightly in his and just brushing the back of her hand with his lips.

"Well done, Victor," she laughed, and though he never took his eyes off her, she was gone by the time his brain registered that she'd pulled her fingers out of his grip.

"*Pinche* fucking crazy," he hissed, looking around the room for Valla. She was still standing near the head table, speaking to Blue and another man with enormous red-furred ears. Victor made his way over, standing a few feet to the side, waiting for her to make eye contact with him. After a moment, when the big-eared guy started speaking to Blue, Valla looked his way and nodded.

As he took the last few steps toward them, Valla said, "Thank you for dinner, War Captain. I must depart; my companion has a busy day tomorrow."

"Oh?" Blue said, feigning dismay by holding a hand to his chest. He looked at Victor and said, "Can you not manage to make your way home alone, lad?"

"I wouldn't be much of an escort if I left the lady here alone, would I?" Victor asked, struggling to keep a snarl out of his voice.

"I suppose not. What say you, Lady Valla?"

"I say I'm tired, sir. Thank you again, but I must be going." Valla sketched a half bow and then turned to leave. Victor nodded to Blue, noting the amusement in the man's eyes, and followed after her.

"You good, Valla?" he asked, lengthening his stride, so he walked beside her.

"Am I good?" she chuckled, shaking her head. "On the bright side, I had a wonderful meal and learned the names of many powerful people in Coloss. I suppose the gloomy news is that I must fight a woman far more powerful than I in a month's time."

"At least it's not in two days."

"Do I have you to thank for that?" Valla softly asked, glancing at him with arched eyebrows.

"Not exactly. That woman who made the, uh, prophecy wanted to help you out. I mean, I asked her to, but she said she likes an underdog. She's fucking strong, Valla, and she wants to help you prepare. I mean—" Victor glanced around the wide hallway they were walking through toward the front doors of the manor, noting the other people walking nearby, and said, "I'll tell you later, okay? Trust me, though; things aren't as grim as you think."

"I do trust you, Victor." Valla smiled and added, "A lot can happen in a month, right?"

"Damn right, *chica*."

8

❧❧

THE MADNESS OF CROWDS

Yeah," Victor said with a grunt as he pulled on his boots. "She said to show that token at the arena, and they'd let you sit in her box." He stood up from the little table in the central room of their suite and adjusted his belt, making sure he felt comfortable; it was time to get in some fights.

"And she's going to help me somehow, hmm?" Valla asked, flicking the silver token into the air and deftly catching it with her other hand.

"Trust me, Valla; she's the real deal. If anyone can help you prepare to beat that *bruja*, it's her. I'm pretty sure there's no one stronger than her in this whole city. Well, I might be wrong, but you'll see what I mean when you spend some time with her. Ready to go?" He moved over to the door, feeling a bit antsy about getting to the arena. He wanted to warm up a little and get a feel for the place before his first fight.

"Yes." Valla tucked the token into her belt and then led the way, opening the patio doors and stepping out into the courtyard. Victor followed, closing the door behind them. He had to hustle to catch up to her, and he sighed with irritation.

Valla had been less talkative than usual, even though she probably had a lot to say—what were the people like up at the high table? What did the Blue jerk talk about all night? How was she feeling? What could Victor do to help? He'd tried all those questions and more, but Valla wasn't talking. When they'd returned to the room, she'd said she was too tired, and that morning, she'd avoided him, staying in her room until right before it was time to leave.

"I wish you'd talk to me," he said as they walked through the inn and stepped out into the arena square.

"I know." She frowned but then surprised him by saying, "I'll bare my soul if you win all of your fights today."

"Oh, shit." Victor sighed, shaking his head.

"What?"

"Well, if you're promising something like that, you must think I'm going to lose. Damn, Valla, I thought you had more faith than that!"

She snorted and said, "Just don't die, all right?"

"That's the plan." With that, he grabbed her wrist and darted across the road to the steps leading up to the expansive plaza in front of the arena. They barely cleared the road before an enormous floating barge-like wagon loaded with soldiers in matching red armor whirred past. Its passage kicked up dust and sent a hot wave of steamy air chasing after them.

"They need crosswalks in this damn place," Victor growled as he hopped up the steps three at a time. He walked to the main gate and stopped near the mass of people loosely queued up to get inside. "I guess I have to go in through that other gate around the side. Meet you at the inn afterward?"

"Yes, I think it would be hard to find each other in the crowds; the inn would be best."

"Okay, well, get us a table in the common room; I'm sure I'll be thirsty. Also, while you're up there, see if any people are taking bets." He pulled out a sack of beads, handed it to her, then another—probably close to ten thousand beads—and she took them with a nod.

Victor turned and started to walk away, but Valla reached out and grabbed his arm. "Wait, Victor. I'm . . . well, I'm sorry I'm not good at things like this; communication isn't one of my talents." Her face was open, devoid of the makeup she'd worn the night before, but still full of color. Her green eyes were, for the first time he could remember, a bit bloodshot as she narrowed them and searched for words.

"Relax," Victor said with an easy smile. "I know you'll be rooting for me."

"I will. I'll share some words Shield Sergeant Grev said during my first deployment with the legion: The enemy can see your swords, they can see your armor, but they can't see your hearts. Show them what's in there. Never quit, never waver, and when you stand over them victorious, they'll know the iron in your blood." Valla spoke from her gut, her voice coming out husky, clipping each word in a kind of mantra, and Victor felt his back straightening and little goosebumps popping up at the nape of his neck.

"Damn," he said, lost for other words as his reticent, laconic friend spoke with such emotion. She offered him a brief smile, nodded, and then moved off to line up with the others waiting to gain entry. "No pressure," he muttered, turning to work his way around the arena to the fighters' gate.

The man at the gate acted as if he'd been expecting him and motioned him through. Victor walked down the stone-walled breezeway until he saw some other fighters he recognized from the previous day lingering near a side passage, and he walked over. "Yo," he said, "this where the fighters are supposed to go?"

The two were both Vesh: a big, rhinoceros-looking man, and a lanky, long-limbed woman who had black feathers for hair and long, talon-like nails at the tips of her elongated fingers. The big guy, his thick lips curling into a smile beneath the stout horn protruding where his nose should be, said, "Aye. The fight steward is down there. He'll show you to a ready room. Victor, wasn't it?"

"Yeah." Victor smiled and added, "I'm bad with names—don't think I caught yours."

"I'm Ronno, and this is Rekka; she's my sister."

"Hi," the woman said, waving at Victor almost shyly, leaning back against the wall and self-consciously adjusting her well-worn yellow-and-green lacquered chainmail vest.

"Cool to meet you guys," he said and started to step into the tunnel.

"Hold up, Victor," Ronno said, his deep voice rumbling. "You're new to Coloss, yes?"

"Yeah." Victor turned back toward him, starting to frown as he wondered what this was going to be about.

"We're trying to talk to all the participants in the tournament, trying to make a mercy pact."

"Mercy pact?"

"No one has to die today," Rekka said from behind Ronno's shoulder. "We're promising to grant mercy to anyone who yields in a fight. Will you do the same?"

Victor mulled it over for a moment, then said, "If I fight either of you, I'll show mercy if you yield, sure."

Ronno's smile spread even further, displaying enormous flat teeth. "Good! Luck to you then, brother." He reached out a stout, three-fingered hand, and Victor shook it, his grip awkward on the meaty appendage. Rekka smiled at him again, this time meeting his gaze with her dazzling yellow-flecked black eyes. Victor, ever at the mercy of his impulses, winked at her and then, grinning, turned to continue walking deeper into the bowels of the arena.

He felt good, happy that not everyone in Coloss, or more specifically, not all the fighters in Coloss, were jerks. He passed a few uniformed arena workers as he wound his way deeper into the facility, and soon he came to a large rectangular room with dozens of doors lining one side. Long benches filled the center of the room, sparsely populated by fighters and their friends, or perhaps teams was a better word. A man in an arena uniform, holding a softly glowing stone slate, stood near the entry hall, and Victor approached him.

"Ah, Victor, yes?"

"Right." Victor watched as the man scribbled on his slate with a matching stone stylus.

"Ready room one."

"One?" Victor wondered if the room assignment meant anything, but the man quickly dissuaded that notion.

"Yes, don't worry, lad; the first-round bouts and room assignments were randomly selected. That said, your first opponent will be in ready room two, and I have some rules to go over with you." He stared at Victor until it became apparent he was waiting for a response.

"Okay."

"Yes. Rule one: no fighting outside the arena. Rule two: all armor and magical items must be stowed in your ready room, save your primary weapon. A chest in your ready room will have a random set of armor for you to wear, though you can go without if you please."

"What? Wait, so I can't wear my own armor? What do you mean random?"

"A random selection will be available for you to wear, but you may wear your non-armored clothing if you'd prefer. None of the arena armors are enchanted other than for sizing."

Victor felt the man was being purposefully obtuse, and he had the urge to reach out and tweak one of his floppy, shaggy ears. "So, my helmet, my armor . . . what about my boots and my belt?"

"I'm happy you asked," the man said, pulling out a smooth black pointy wand and waving it over Victor, from his toes and up to his head. "Your boots, belt, armor, rings, amulet, and helmet will not be permitted into the arena."

"Fuck me," Victor sighed.

"You should be happy about this rule," the man tsked. "Some of the other participants have legendary artifacts that would make your trinkets pale in comparison."

"Right." Victor nodded, considering the words—he had no idea what kinds of things people might bring into the arena, and he supposed it was good there were limitations. "Right, but my axe is okay?"

"Yes, but, as I said, be aware that the combatants will employ many fine weapons today." The man was polite, but he had an officious air about him that was starting to rub Victor the wrong way.

"Any other rules?"

"Thank you for asking! In the next fifteen minutes, the passage from this room will be locked, and you'll need to spend your time between fights in your ready room or here. Remember rule number one, please. Should you win your first match, you'll be afforded limited first aid; the chest containing your belongings will remain locked until you finish the tournament. Should you lose but survive, you will be given back your belongings and escorted from this section of the arena."

"Are there any rules about that? I mean, letting people live during the fights?"

"It's frowned upon to slay a combatant who has asked for mercy, but it is not prohibited." The man's face remained impassive and his voice flat. Victor wouldn't have been able to tell his opinion on the matter. "If you'll excuse me, I see another fighter to whom I have yet to speak. Your ready room is there—the first door."

"Wait," Victor said, reaching toward the man but stopping short of grabbing him. When he turned back to Victor, he continued, "What about the other fights? I can't watch?"

"Apologies. I should have mentioned," the steward replied, pointing toward a large blank stone rectangle lining one wall of the room. "That view portal will display each contest."

"Oh, shit. Like an old-school TV . . ." Victor trailed off as the fight steward turned to speak to another fighter that had just walked into the room.

Victor walked over to the first iron-banded, wooden door, large enough for a Degh to walk through—enormous by human standards. Right away, he saw a figure he recognized leaning next to door number two—the giant Degh woman with curly blonde hair. He tried to remember her name, but the only thing Victor could think of was that it started with a K and had a distinctly feminine quality. Awkwardly, he tried to act as though he hadn't noticed her and made to open his door, reaching up to twist the handle that was at his shoulder level.

"Victor," she said, dashing his hopes of avoiding embarrassment and slipping inside his room.

"Hey . . ." he said, looking up at her and squinting, his shoulders lifting, unbidden, into a sheepish shrug.

"Kreecia," she laughed. "Darn! I think we'll have to fight first." She hooked her thumbs in her belt, and Victor noticed her bone-plated armor from before was gone, and she just wore some supple-looking leather pants and a sleeveless vest.

"Is that how this works? Rooms one and two fight, then three and four, etcetera?"

"I'm afraid so. Tell you what, cutie, I'll do my best not to kill you." She smiled, revealing a large gap between her top front teeth, then reached up to twirl one of her curls.

"I'll, uh, appreciate that. I'll try not to kill you, too. Please yield quickly, though—my axe is thirsty and not one to pull her punches."

"Oho! Spunky! I like it." She winked at him, and Victor couldn't help laughing.

"You know," he said, pulling his door open and stepping through, "I'm, like, half your size."

"Nothing that ever stopped me before. See you out there, cutie!" Her voice chased him through the door as it swung shut.

"That . . . would be a handful," he said, lifting Lifedrinker out of her loop. "Now I'm going to feel guilty if I chop off her leg or something, so let's try to take it a little easy on her, eh?" Lifedrinker hummed in his hand, her dark, living wood handle picking up the lights in the ready room, tiny stars blooming to life in the depths. "Damn, you're pretty, you know that?" He set her down on the bench that lined one of the walls, then looked around as he unbuckled his belt.

Like the rest of the arena, the room was walled with pale stone blocks. The bench he'd set Lifedrinker on lined one of the longer walls while two chests sat against the other. An iron portcullis blocked a passage leading up from the far wall, and Victor figured it led into the arena proper.

He walked over to the chests, both made of dark stone and both as big as his old varsity locker. He lifted the lid of the one on the left, and it swung open noiselessly on recessed hinges. The interior was empty, and he figured that was where he was supposed to deposit his armor and magical belongings.

The other chest opened just as effortlessly, and within was a leather-lined bronze breastplate and, to his horror, a skirt made of layered leather and bronze strips. "The fuck is this?" he asked the empty room, lifting it out to find, beneath it, knee-high boots and bronze-plated gauntlets. He took out the boots and gauntlets but tossed the skirt back into the chest. "I don't have any underwear that'll look good in that thing, sorry."

He dug around in one of his rings until he came up with a pair of sturdy leather pants, then he started changing. In the end, when he'd put on the boots, breastplate, gauntlets, and his own pants, he felt pretty good—they'd all resized to feel perfectly suited to his physique, and with his upper arms clear, he felt as he did in the old days when he'd first found his old badass vest in the dungeon near the mine.

He stowed all his valuables in the empty chest, then lifted Lifedrinker and began going through his axe forms, especially the combinations he'd learned with Polo Vosh and perfected while sparring with Valla.

He felt a little naked without the weight of his helmet, but he also felt light and fast, and a savage grin stretched his lips as Lifedrinker sang and snapped through the air. In the back of his mind, he'd been worried about who he might have to fight, but he began to hope his opponents, beyond the first match, would be assholes. He didn't want to spend the whole day pulling his punches.

Victor was deep into his routine when someone pounded on the door leading to the outer ready room. He finished up his combo, bringing Lifedrinker around in a snapping, upward hook meant to shear through an opponent's inner thigh; then, still holding her and sweating lightly, he turned to pull the door open. The fight steward stood there, rocking back and forth impatiently. He spoke almost immediately. "You're the first to fight today. When the portcullis opens, make your way up the ramp. You'll have one minute before a forfeit is declared."

"All right . . ." Victor started, but the man was already moving over to the next door. He was about to close the door when he saw a familiar face. Krista, the one name Victor could remember from the day before, stood smiling at him, her long canines glinting in the glow lamps.

"Hey, Deshi. I'm in room six—try to win your first two matches so we can dance, hmm?"

Victor eyed her up and down, noting that she wore armor much like his, though she hadn't turned her nose up at the skirt, and it looked kind of cool if he were being honest. More than that, though, he took in her spear—easily eight feet long, with a twenty-inch, razor-edged blade that winked with pale yellow crackling sparks. Not for the first time, Victor remembered his coach's words of wisdom and clamped his mouth tight, refusing to talk shit before a fight. He stepped back and closed his door with a thud.

If he'd had enough time, he might have begun to get into his head, begun to second-guess his enthusiasm to fight, and planted some doubts about whether he'd made the right decision. Fortunately, though, just a few minutes after he'd closed his door, the portcullis noisily ratcheted into the ceiling of the tunnel. "Right. Here we go, beautiful," he growled, hefting Lifedrinker and striding up the sloping stone passage toward the brightly lit opening fifty yards distant. He could already hear the noise of the crowd.

Victor's impulses warred with one another when he stepped out into the sunlight. One part of him wanted to turn around and forfeit. The other part wanted to hold up his arms and strut further into the sandy arena, basking in the attention of tens of thousands of people, something he'd never dreamed of in his old life. He settled for a compromise, walking calmly forward a half dozen paces, still holding Lifedrinker crossways in front of his waist.

The crowd was enormous, and so was the din. Cheering, howling, stomping, people shouting conversations at each other because other people were shouting, and behind it all, some kind of weird music that was mostly drums and pipes. Still, the beat was undeniable, and Victor found himself swaying to it as he waited for something to happen. He squinted up into the sunlight, the fiery orange-yellow orb just poking above the high, curved wall of the stadium.

He'd just turned toward the next passageway, the only other one with an open portcullis, when a loud, enthusiastic voice rang through the arena—an announcer. "Great people of Coloss! Great Warlord and War Captains! Our first fight of the low-tier tournament is about to begin. Before you stands the first challenger, a stranger to our world, an unknown quantity! Victor! What a name, don't you think? His very moniker proclaims his intention to win!"

The crowd erupted in louder cheers, and Victor couldn't help himself; he held Lifedrinker up and turned in a slow circle. He tried to make out faces, tried to see the box where Valla might be sitting, and tried to pick out the guy who was speaking, but it was impossible; thousands of people mingled together in a tremendous churning mass, becoming faceless in their multitudes.

The announcer continued, "Stepping into the arena to meet the challenger is our hometown beauty, the Damsel of Destruction, Kreecia!" Victor watched as Kreecia, wielding a two-handed, sledge-like hammer that had to weigh a thousand pounds, charged out of her tunnel, leaping a dozen feet into the air and landing with a tremendous crash, smashing her hammer into the sand. Victor felt the stone beneath the sand tremble at the concussion, and he took a step back to steady himself.

The crowd went absolutely insane, cheering and roaring so loudly that Victor almost lifted his hands to his ears. He stopped the impulse, though, hefting Lifedrinker and snarling. He cast Inspiring Presence, and though Kreecia was still intimidating with that gigantic hammer, he felt better about his odds. Watching her straighten up and ponderously swing the hammer, its head the size of a wheelbarrow, Victor used Sovereign Will to boost his agility and squared off with her.

"Are you ready?" the announcer shouted, and Victor realized the question wasn't directed at him or Kreecia when the crowd's roaring went up another octave. "Fight!"

The announcer had barely finished his shouted command when Kreecia squatted and launched herself into the air, lifting that ridiculous hammer high as though she meant to smash Victor, like a disobedient nail, into the ground. Victor channeled rage-attuned Energy into Lifedrinker, darted forward under the arc of her jump, and moving far faster than she, he leapt, hacking at her dangling left foot.

Kreecia's eyes widened, and she tried to pull her feet up, but so much of her brute strength was focused on managing her enormous maul, and Victor was moving so fast that despite her efforts, Lifedrinker cut a deep groove through her thick leather boot. Her edge, ever thirsty for flesh, tore into the top of Kreecia's foot, and even though it felt as if he'd struck an anvil, he felt confident he'd cracked some of those tiny bones.

Kreecia cried out and landed awkwardly, her hammer smashing into the sand with forward momentum rather than downward. The arena didn't shudder, but a spray of sand flew out as if a meteor had landed, leaving a trench six inches deep as Kreecia stumbled forward after her massive weapon. Inspired as he was, Victor knew better than to let up the pressure.

He charged after the giant woman. As she gained control of her hammer, clearly favoring her left foot, Victor was already on her, running past, hacking Lifedrinker sideways into the back of her knee with all his strength and momentum. It felt as though he'd taken an iron axe and smashed it into a massive knot in the trunk of a mesquite tree.

Lifedrinker bit, severing flesh, but when her gleaming Heart Silver edge struck the bones of Kreecia's leg, she was stopped short. The axe's handle vibrated with the impact, and Victor's eyes bulged at the concussive impact. Still, he didn't let go; it would take much more than that to pull Lifedrinker from his grasp. "*Mierda!*" he grunted, yanking Lifedrinker back and sideways, grinding through more of Kreecia's meaty leg but sliding along her adamant bone.

Kreecia howled in pain and fury, and if Victor hadn't been inspired or had his agility boosted, he might have died at that moment. She seemed to explode with bright orange Energy, and her hammer whistled through the air as she spun, sacrificing her balance to bring the hammer around sideways, directly at Victor. Still, he saw it coming just in time and dropped to roll through the sand. Howling like a freight train, the tremendous weapon destroyed nothing but air. Worse for Kreecia, she couldn't keep her grip as she fell to her back, and the hammer sailed toward the high stone wall of the arena.

Momentarily stunned by his close call, Victor watched the hammer smash into the arena wall with a resounding crash. Tiny fractures spread in the stone around the impact, and the hammer fell to the ground with a thud that he felt through his hands and knees as he clambered to his feet. He kept Kreecia in front of him as he stood, Lifedrinker ready, and approached the wounded woman, struggling to stand with a knee that wasn't working.

"I yield," she coughed, eyes bloodshot with tears of pain as she looked up from the sand. She'd given up trying to stand. Victor opened his mouth, but then he was cut off by the announcer's voice filling the air.

"Oh no! Our local heroine has fallen, and just like that, she's asking for mercy! Will the challenger grant it? Should the challenger grant it? Scream if you want to see more blood!"

The crowd's bloodthirsty howls rose to new heights, and Victor felt his blood stirring in response, felt his heart begin to thump with a different, heavy beat. The furious Energy at his Core started to seep into his pathways. His lips pulled back into a menacing, maniacal grin, and he lifted Lifedrinker high over his head.

9

VISUALIZING SUCCESS

Victor felt the roar of the crowd more than he heard it. He could feel their emotion and the Energy they were pouring out, flowing through the air toward him; it was palpable, thick, and hot, and his body and Core responded to it. He stretched his arm upward, Lifedrinker's edge glinting in the morning sunlight, and turned in a slow circle, displaying her gleaming silvery blade to each corner of the arena.

"I yield!" Kreecia said again, panting in pain.

Victor turned to her, his eyes dark with bloodlust, and she flinched back. He walked around her, circling, turned toward the high, crenellated stand where he assumed the nobility were seated, and roared. It wasn't anything spectacular, that roar—he was just his normal human size, not even berserk. Still, the savagery in his voice wasn't something that could be mistaken, and he drove it forth from his throat with a burst of potent, pure, rage-attuned Energy.

If the crowd responded to his scream, he couldn't tell—already, their thunderous noise was too much for his ears to filter. Still holding Lifedrinker high in his right hand, he stomped toward Kreecia and bared his teeth in a savage grin. He said, his voice heavy with subdued fury, held at bay by his iron will, "Don't worry." Then he casually lowered Lifedrinker and walked toward his tunnel, watching the portcullis, waiting for it to rise so he could get out of the focus of those mad people.

The crowd instantly turned on him. Roaring and cheering, screaming for blood one moment, then booing and hissing and stomping their feet the next.

Despite their intent to shame or infuriate him, Victor almost sighed with relief; something in his Core, in his heart, in the very center of his being had been responding to those mad cheers, and it was easier to breathe and think with the crowd losing its enthusiasm.

"Looks like the traveling warrior has decided to show mercy to our dear Kreecia! We all love a bloodbath, but let's rejoice! Kreecia lives to fight another day! Congratulations to Victor! He'll be back to fight in the next round."

Victor scanned the arena while waiting for his tunnel to open and saw that Kreecia was sitting up and that a steel door in the opposite wall had opened. A man dressed like an honest-to-God jester, complete with a funny hat and white face paint, had come through the opening and was cartwheeling toward her.

As his portcullis started to clank open, Victor saw the clownish figure produce a small vial and hand it to the wounded fighter. She drank it, and Victor nodded, turning to walk down the tunnel to his ready room. He felt almost instant relief as he descended into that cool stone tunnel, out of the glare of the sun and the crazy heat of the crowd's frenzy. Victor breathed more easily, the tension in his muscles relaxed, and his grip loosened on Lifedrinker's haft.

He didn't think there'd been any real risk of losing himself to that madness, that he'd execute Kreecia. No, he'd had complete control of himself the whole time, but what bothered him was how badly some part of himself had yearned for that release, yearned to be let loose from the cage where he held it, free to rampage, consequences be damned. "Is it the Quinametzin?" he asked Lifedrinker, lifting her to rest on his shoulder. "Is it just me? Some wild part of me that loves having a crowd go nuts for my actions?"

When he reentered his ready room, Victor was surprised to see a black lacquered box with a glimmering silver ribbon wrapped around it sitting on his bench. "Huh," he said, stepping over to it, laying Lifedrinker to the side, and pulling one end of the silvery bow. The ribbon unraveled effortlessly, and as it fell away from the box, it shimmered into motes of silvery light that faded away with a faint tinkling sound. "Cool." Victor picked up the box, about six inches square, and lifted the lid.

Inside, a gleaming platinum coin sat on a velvety black cushion. A note card was nestled within, and Victor lifted it to read: *Congratulations on your first-round victory! You've earned a Coloss Prize Token, redeemable at the City Stone.* Victor grinned, set the box and its contents atop the locked stone chest that held his other belongings, then picked up Lifedrinker and went out the door to the larger shared ready room. He wanted to watch the next fight.

When he pushed open his door, several people sitting on the central row of benches and watching the colorful "viewport" turned their heads his way, and a few nodded respectfully. He smiled and walked over to sit down, several feet between himself and the next gladiator. Victor wanted to be left alone, wanted just to watch his future competition, but he wasn't surprised when Krista's familiar voice said, "Lucky matchup on your first round, Deshi."

He ignored her, eyes trained on the screen, watching two Vesh fighting furiously in the center of the arena. One combatant was a man with dark, black fur and skin, spikes running down the middle of his skull and spine, and long, claw-tipped arms. The other was a woman that Victor would have sworn was half deer; she had antlers, soft, fuzzy fur on her cheeks, and a moist black nose.

"Not going to talk to us about your victory? Did you bribe the arena master to put you up against that slow oaf?"

"Quiet, Krista," a deep, menacing voice said, and Victor turned to see the speaker. Sitting on the floor in the corner, but still at eye level with most of the other combatants, was an enormous Degh giant. He had leathery, tanned skin, a shaven head, and glowering red eyes deeply set beneath a brooding brow. To Victor's astonishment, Krista didn't reply; she snarled and moved to sit on the bench a good dozen feet away. The huge Degh made eye contact with Victor, and though Victor nodded his appreciation, the giant looked away, almost dismissively.

Victor looked back to the viewport in time to see the deer-like woman, kneeling with a severed arm, being executed by the dark, spined Vesh. He'd cast some sort of spell, summoning ropy tendrils of shifting, razored sand that wrapped around her, and, as the crowd went wild, he held up a dark, taloned hand and made a fist. At the same time, his sandy bonds squeezed the woman, slicing her into several bloody segments.

"Damn him!" a familiar voice cursed, and Victor turned to see the rhino-nosed man, Ronno, standing to furiously smash a fist against the stone wall.

"Fair's fair," Krista said, though she didn't look happy. She stood and quickly walked to her ready room. Before anyone could reply, she stepped inside and shut the door.

"She's up now?" Victor asked, looking down the bench.

"Yeah," another Vesh woman said. Victor looked around to see who else was leaving, but then he realized only seven or eight people were watching—most of the combatants must have been in their ready rooms. He turned back to the viewport to watch, wishing he could hear what was going on out there, what the announcer was saying as Krista and a lanky, gold-scaled snake man squared off. "No, not snake man," he said softly to himself. "Yazzian."

The fight was brutal and fast. Krista's spear wasn't just for show; she knew how to use it. The Yazzian didn't wield a weapon, but he moved like liquid lightning, sliding around the arena in sparkling bursts, turning to throw balls of crackling Energy at Krista. The problem was, she wasn't any slower than he, and her spear seemed to have a will of its own, darting out to bridge the space between them, punching through crackling Energy shields, and relentlessly poking holes in the Yazzian, each one leaving him weaker and slower.

After her first strike, it was only a matter of time; the Yazzian left trails of dark blood in the sand, and after her third strike, he never had a chance to attempt to yield; Krista jerked the spear free, winked out of existence, and reappeared in a burst of red Energy behind the Yazzian, her spear firmly planted through his long serpentine neck. His spine must have been severed because he fell, limp and lifeless, to the sand.

"Damn. She can teleport?"

"Aye, but it tires her," said Ronno, still standing near the spot where his meaty rhino fist had cracked the stone wall.

"Fool to use it for no reason," another Yazzian said. "Now we all know."

"Most of us knew. Those of us that matter," the lurking giant in the corner rumbled.

"What's that supposed to mean?" the Yazzian asked, standing up, a gleaming, purple-limned rapier in its hand.

"Sit down, fool," Ronno said. "You'll be ejected for instigating violence out here. Not to mention, you don't want to fight Jast if you don't have to."

In response, the copper-scaled Yazzian walked to the seventh ready room door and disappeared within. Victor shrugged, looking to see that Jast hadn't reacted at all. He still sat in the corner, baleful red eyes trained on the viewport, completely ignoring everyone else. A few minutes later, Krista returned, flinging her ready room door open with a bang, laughing and bowing to the room. No one seemed impressed, and Victor studiously ignored her.

The next fight was between the rapier-wielding Yazzian and another giant Degh, and the Yazzian spent a good long while wearing him down with punctures and slashes, never suffering an injury from the giant's ponderous axe cleaves. Victor wasn't impressed with the Degh's axe work; if he had to guess, he'd say the man hadn't gotten past the improved stage—he definitely was strong, but his Energy usage was minuscule, and he wasn't fast. He wanted to ask if all Degh were slow, but he knew it would cause him some trouble, especially from the lurking giant, so he just resolved to keep watching.

After the Yazzian won, Jast, the giant in the corner, stood up and moved toward his ready room. Ronno called after him, "Jast, remember our agreement."

"If possible," the man rumbled, stepping through his door, making the enormous opening look almost small. Victor wondered what that had been about, but he soon learned. Watching the viewport, he saw Jast looming large, a great double-bladed, red-metal axe in his hands, staring at Ronno's sister, Rekka. Rekka looked like a child before him, her curved shortswords like toys.

"Shit," Victor breathed, glancing at Ronno. He saw how the big man sat—slumped on the bench, head in his hands, eyes down. He expected his sister to die. Victor felt for him and wondered how he'd handle such a situation. Would he stand by, or would he go fucking get her out? He figured he'd get her out—*ciertamente!* His earlier wondering about Deghs and whether they were all slow was answered while he watched Jast destroy Rekka. He moved with uncanny grace, easily staying on top of the much smaller, lithe, winged woman as she tried to circle and flank him.

Rekka managed to avoid his lashing axe cleaves for a few minutes. Inevitably, though, one of them struck home, and Rekka's legs fell away at the hips in a shower of blood that looked as if someone had tossed out a bucket of rubies, the way it glittered in the sunlight before splashing into the sand. Rekka's top half tumbled to a skidding stop, a copious pool of blood quickly formed around it, and Victor knew no potion would fix her.

Ronno didn't scream, didn't smash the wall, didn't wait to attack Jast. He stood, stomped to his ready room, and went inside without a word. "Damn, that's rough," Victor said as the door slammed shut.

"Rough indeed. I'd never enter a tournament with someone I loved." Victor looked to the speaker, a short, fox-eared Vesh woman. She wore tight leather armor, accentuating her feminine form, and, surprising to Victor, she had a quiver filled with silvery arrows on her back. She met his gaze, her golden irises twinkling as she smiled and said, "I'm Sanima."

"Cool to meet you. Yeah, I'm with you on that one. What if the arena master had put Ronno and Rekka against each other?"

"Indeed. What's your name, though?" she asked, standing from the bench to move closer. Victor found himself studying her, trying to see if anything other than her ears was fox-like, but she had normal, darkly tanned skin, and though her teeth were bright and sharp, they didn't look exactly like a canine's.

"Sorry; I'm Victor."

"You had some skill with that axe, and you move quickly. Should we battle together, I'll offer to spare your life if you'll do the same." She held out a slender hand, her nails sharp and painted green to match the makeup around her eyes.

"Yeah, for sure. I had the same thing going with Ronno and Rekka." Victor shook her hand, careful not to hold on to it longer than was polite.

"As did I. Ronno will fight Yarge now and may win. If so, he'll face Jast, his sister's killer, and that will be a bloody brawl."

Victor nodded, watching the screen as they cleared poor Rekka from the arena. He turned back to Sanima and said, "I guess, since we might fight, I shouldn't ask you about your secrets, but I couldn't help noticing you have a quiver on your back. They allow people to use bows in here?"

"Naturally. It's a legitimate weapon, recognized by the martial masters of all the great cities."

"Cool . . ." Victor said, trying to keep his expression neutral. He wasn't sure how he'd deal with a powerful Energy user that could pepper him with arrows from range. He could move fast, but he didn't have a teleport or anything like that. He supposed he'd call up his coyotes and use their speed and numbers to harry an archer. With that in mind, he nodded and looked back at the viewport.

Ronno was facing off with a Degh, who didn't seem so giant next to the rhino-like Vesh. He was still larger, but Ronno looked like a ball of thick skin and muscle with a horn, and Victor didn't envy the guy who had to fight him, enraged as he must be about his sister. His prediction proved correct—Ronno didn't use a weapon per se, but he had massive metal gauntlets that exploded with steam every time he punched his opponent.

The Degh wielded an enormous ball mace, but though he seemed to be striking hard enough to crack granite, Ronno shrugged off the blows, constantly pushing inside the Degh's guard to deliver bone-cracking, steam-exploding punches that sent the giant into a retreat. Victor didn't think the giant could continue to absorb those punishing blows, and he was right again—not five minutes into the match, the giant took a knee, and Ronno backed off, granting mercy.

Ronno didn't return to the shared ready room, and the subsequent fight went nearly as quickly as Victor's had. Another spear-wielding Vesh killed a giant Degh with a lightning thrust that put the spear through his massive chest, right into his heart. The arena-issued breastplate didn't seem to slow the spear, and Victor wasn't surprised because it had glowed with brilliant silver Energy as it streaked forward. Sanima tsked as she stood up from the bench.

"My turn. I suppose I'll face him in round two. He won't find me so easy to impale, though," she chuckled, sauntering through her ready room door. Victor looked around the nearly empty shared room and debated watching the next fight. If he'd counted correctly, it was the last one of the first round.

"One more, right?" he asked Krista, who'd been silently watching, completely ignoring him since her earlier victory.

"Right. Are you growing nervous, Deshi? Seen some displays of violence that give you pause?"

Victor contemplated ignoring her again, but he was slightly intrigued by her silence since her first match. "Looks like you have to fight that purple-rapier dude next. You nervous?"

"Garl is dangerous, and I'm going to have to concentrate, but he'll fall to my spear. You're the one who should be nervous—Harf is a vicious man. You saw how he cut Necla into pieces, and that was with an Energy attack. He's just as deadly with those claws."

"That so?" Victor couldn't help the smirk that turned his lips.

"Aye, Deshi. Run out now if you're smart. You've never faced such as us." She stood, leaning on her enormous spear, and Victor felt a chuckle fighting to escape his throat.

"Lady, I've seen shit that would make you piss yourself where you stand. I've been through worse than what that asshole did to that antlered lady. And I lived. Worry about your own shit."

"Antlered lady? Do you mean Necla? She was a friend, you scum." Krista bristled and bared her sharp canines, a low growl in her throat.

"Chill out. I'm not the guy who fucked her up." Victor stood up, hefting Lifedrinker, and turned his back to her, walking to his ready room. "I guess I'll see you in round three if you win again." Her growl chased him through the doorway and cut off abruptly as he let the door slam. "Fucking *pendeja*." He sighed and sat on his bench, trying to get his head back in the game—he was pretty sure his next fight would be more demanding than the first.

His mind kept returning to how his next opponent, apparently named Harf, had killed his opponent. He'd manipulated the sand into bladed, ropy tendrils, then sliced the woman he fought into pieces. How could Victor counter that? He could only hope he'd get a chance to employ his will attribute to shrug off the spell. Was it even real? Could sand have blades? Was it a mental attack? Victor began to realize he didn't know enough.

The problem Victor kept coming back to was that he was sure he could win if he went berserk or summoned his bear totem, but he was trying to save those cards for the third and fourth matches. "I'll use my coyotes to keep him off balance, I'll discourage him with fear, and I'll fucking cut him to shreds," Victor growled, repeatedly visualizing the combination.

He held Lifedrinker to his forehead, and he ran through it again and again in his mind. He imagined he was in the arena, preparing himself with a few spells, then he imagined the announcer starting the fight. In his visualization, he summoned his coyotes, dashed forward, projected his fear-attuned Energy, and, as the dark, spined Vesh faltered, he laid into him with Lifedrinker.

"Easy as one two three, right, beautiful?"

"Yes, Victor! We'll drive your enemy before us, water the soil with his blood, and bask in the adulation of the crowd!" Lifedrinker's voice was clearer than ever, ringing in his mind as the axe vibrated against his forehead, and Victor's heart thumped in response. His lips peeled back in a savage grin, and he gripped her haft with tremendous force, resulting in even more vibrations; the axe was eager.

"Goddamn right, we will." The portcullis clanked as it lifted into the ceiling, and Victor stood up, still baring his teeth. "Perfect fucking timing." He stalked up the hallway, his face a mask of determination and bloodlust. He wasn't worried about pulling his punches with this asshole, and for the first time in a while, he was looking forward to hurting someone.

He stalked into the arena, hardly noticing the crowd's noise this time, so intent was he on his visualizations for the upcoming battle. As soon as his feet touched the sand, he cast Sovereign Will to boost his agility; he had to strike fast. He cast Inspiring Presence, careful to consider everyone around him an enemy so they wouldn't benefit from the spell. As he stopped in the center of the arena and the announcer babbled about who he was, Victor stared at the other open tunnel, waiting for his opponent.

Harf loped out of the dark opening on his long, lean legs, his claws nearly dragging in the sand as he pulled his midnight flesh from his snout in a snarl, revealing enormous canines; the man looked as if he were half black-furred wolf and half man. If Victor saw him on Earth, before he'd ever met any of the peoples of Fanwath or this world, he'd think him a werewolf from a horror movie. The guy looked tough as hell, and for some reason, that only pissed Victor off more. He cast Channel Energy, flooding his pathways and Lifedrinker with rage-attuned Energy, and a growl rumbled in his chest as he began to glow with a dancing, baleful red aura.

The announcer's words were noise in his ears, his brain listening for one thing—the command to begin. Victor's muscles were flexed, ready to explode into action, and Lifedrinker hummed in his hands, lighter than air, eager to fly into battle. Victor could feel Harf gathering Energy of his own, getting prepared to attack him, but it felt like a trickle compared to the flood Victor had gathered.

Not only were his pathways humming with rage, his eyes bleeding the crimson fury of it, but Victor had gathered a thick band of fear-attuned Energy, and he'd primed his Project Spirit spell. When his brain registered the word "Fight!" he unleashed his attack, sending a cone of dark, twisted, writhing Energy right into Harf's face.

Victor could tell Harf had been releasing a spell as well; the sand around him had begun to shift, granules lifting into the air, but as soon as his wave of fear hit the Vesh caster, the man's will crumpled before his. Harf's eyes widened; he howled in dismay and fell to the sand, scrabbling backward in a panic. Victor didn't let up; he cast Manifest Spirit, summoning five dark, evil-looking companions that instantly began to howl and yip, charging at Harf.

Victor launched forward like a sprinter who'd heard the start tone, and just as he'd visualized, he went to work with Lifedrinker, employing her own brand of dark, bloody magic on his panicked, broken enemy. Harf never recovered his senses. He tried to hold out a hand to stop Victor, but Lifedrinker took it off at the elbow. On the backswing, Victor planted her firmly between two of Harf's ribs and left her there to siphon his Energy.

Victor's companions bit and pulled at Harf, yanking off hunks of bloody flesh and fur, shredding his leather armor. At the same time, Victor fell upon him, knees to his chest, and massive, furious, glowing-red fists smashing his toothy, snarling face into a dark, bloody pulp. All the while, Lifedrinker feasted, severing the flow of the Vesh's Energy, pulling it from his Core, and keeping him helpless and weak before the awful onslaught.

Victor never went berserk, never lost himself entirely to his rage, but he compartmentalized most of his mind, focusing only on delivering his plan of action, on destroying this enemy who had so callously done the same in his previous match. When Harf's body was still, Victor stood, and his coyotes stepped away to circle him, yipping and licking at their bloodstained muzzles and the thick, dripping strands hanging from his knuckles and fingers. He turned in a slow circle, chest heaving, eyes still mad with the thrill of battle as motes of Energy rose around him.

The motes were thick, more purple than gold, and when they flooded his body, Victor stood, grabbing Lifedrinker and holding her to the sky, absorbing the Energy and roaring back at the screaming, wildly cheering crowd.

*****Congratulations! You have achieved level 36 Spirit Carver, gained 10 will and 10 vitality, and have 8 attribute points to allocate.*****

*****Congratulations! You have earned a Class spell: Imbue Spirit, Basic.*****

*****Imbue Spirit, Basic: You are able to imbue an object or individual with a shard of your own spirit, granting some of your own power and will to the recipient. This effect will last until you recall your spirit shard. Energy Cost: Variable. Cooldown: Long.*****

10

THE MONARCH OF ATTRIBUTES

When Victor returned to his ready room, he saw another black, silver-ribboned box waiting for him atop the bench. Next to the box was a silver serving tray, and on the tray were several objects: a crystal pitcher filled with what looked like ice water, an empty crystal goblet, and a folded linen napkin on which rested a bisected sandwich that looked for all the world as if it was stuffed with pastrami and cheese.

"Cool," he said, setting Lifedrinker down and tugging at the bow on the box. As before, it fell away, dissolving into glittering, tinkling motes of dust. However, Victor's eyes weren't drawn to the little fireworks display; they'd settled on his bloody hand. His knuckles would have been one thing, but the backs of his hands, his nails, the space between his fingers—they were all coated in thick, dried blood.

He held his hands out in front of his face and squeezed them into fists. They weren't sore at all, which surprised him. In his old life, if he'd beaten a man's face until his skull began to crumble, his fists would have needed medical care. "I guess," he amended, having never done anything remotely like that when he lived on Earth.

The whole fight seemed kind of hazy to him; he'd so vividly pictured himself fighting, so carefully visualized his actions, that when he performed them in reality, it felt almost like just another repetition of his strategizing. Still, he remembered the feel of Harf's brow finally cracking under his onslaught and caving in with a wet crunch—that was what finally cooled

Victor's frenzied assault, brought him back to himself enough to stand up and absorb the Energy emanating out of the corpse he'd been pummeling.

He thought he should feel ashamed or guilty, but he didn't. Harf had demonstrated his viciousness. Victor knew there was a killer inside him, that he wasn't just the kid from Arizona anymore. He could spend his life hating himself, or he could accept the part of his spirit, the part that loved to fight, that enjoyed combat, and had no qualms about bashing in the skull of someone who had it coming.

"Did he have it coming?" Victor asked, flexing his blood-caked hands again. "Am I the judge?" He shook his head in resignation, picked up the pitcher, tilted it to his mouth, and drank half the water in several deep gulps. It was icy and clean and tasted better than anything he'd had in a long time. Stretching his neck until it popped, he sighed with pleasure. Then he tipped the pitcher over his cupped left palm, set it down, and briskly rubbed his hands together.

He yanked the linen napkin out from under the sandwich and scrubbed at his flesh, finally dropping the towel, now pink, on the bench. His hands weren't clean, but they weren't filthy anymore, and he felt that was a good representation of himself and his actions. He wasn't a shining knight of justice, but he wasn't a bad guy, either. Shrugging, he picked up the sandwich and devoured it in several enormous bites.

It didn't taste exactly like pastrami and cheese, but it definitely had a smoky, cured-meat flavor, and the bread was amazing. The crust had just the right amount of hardness to it, and the middle was chewy with a distinctly grainy flavor. Whatever the sauce was, Victor wished he had the recipe—creamy with a hint of tanginess, it complemented the meat nicely and added just the right level of moisture to make the bite palatable.

Feeling pretty damn good, with a pleasantly satisfied stomach, Victor lifted off the lid of the box. Just as before, a note card sat nestled in the black velvet interior next to a gleaming platinum coin like the one he'd received before. This time, however, the coin wasn't alone. A jar the size of a soda can stoppered with a huge cork lay next to it, and when Victor read the note card, he remembered the prize list he'd seen when he first signed up—it was the gall bladder of a crypt drake, whatever that was.

The note card reminded him that it was meant to be mixed by an Alchemist to "permanently enhance his strength and vitality." Victor was fairly sure the jar was made of crystal, and when he lifted it to look at the withered, dried hunk of dark gray flesh, he wrinkled his nose and said, "Not very appealing. I hope I can find an Alchemist that makes you into something tastier looking." He put the jar back in the box, closed it up, and set it atop the chest next to his round one prize.

When Victor stepped out into the common ready room, he was greeted by a much different scene than the one after his first round; only Sanima and Ronno were present. Ronno was sitting on the central bench, and Sanima was leaning against the blank stone where the viewport had been. She looked up at him, opened her eyes wider as though surprised, and nodded. "Congratulations."

Victor looked around the mostly empty room and then settled his gaze back on her, "What's the deal with the viewport?"

"They don't want us to know too much about each other before the final fights. We"—she gestured to Ronno—"didn't know you beat Harf until you came out of your ready room."

"You didn't see anyone bring me my prize or my snack?" Victor gestured with his thumb back into his room.

"No; the fight steward and his employees have other means to enter the ready rooms."

Victor nodded, then turned his gaze to Ronno. He wanted to tell him he was sorry about his sister, but he knew that would sound lame, and Victor couldn't imagine the big man would want any platitudes from a virtual stranger. Instead, he said, "Good luck with your fights." Then he turned and went back into his ready room, closing the door behind him.

He felt there was no point mingling with the other fighters if he couldn't watch them perform; Victor knew it was callous, but he didn't want to talk to them, didn't want to humanize them any further—they were his opponents, and he couldn't afford any more doubts. "Doubts lead to hesitation, and hesitation leads to getting myself fucking killed." He looked at the bench, saw the silver tray and dirty napkin were gone, and walked over to it, stretching out on his back, folding his arms under his head for a pillow.

He'd leaned Lifedrinker against the bench, and her beautiful dark wood haft jutted up next to his hip. As he looked at it, Victor saw the tiny motes of light, usually hidden in the depths of the wood, start to flicker and swirl, and he said, "Are you showing off, *preciosa?*" He picked up the axe and lifted it, constantly amazed at how the slightest twitch of his wrist or arm could move her, as though she waited for the indication from his flesh to show her what he wanted.

"You're looking good," he said, noting that the silvery veins of Heart Silver had thickened near her brilliant edge and that they stretched through the dark metal with more forks and branches than he remembered from the last time he'd looked at her. "What's gonna happen when there's more Heart Silver than . . . *cabron!*" he said, thumping a fist against his forehead. "I can't remember what that guy said your other metal was."

The axe hummed, light as a piece of balsa wood in his hands, and he knew she didn't care. Smiling, he rested Lifedrinker on his chest and closed his eyes. If Victor couldn't watch the fights, and he was stuck without any company other than his axe, he was determined to continue visualizing his victories. He knew one thing—if Krista won her fight that round, she'd be his next opponent, and he felt that she was the only fighter who definitely wanted to kill him. Knowing that, Victor decided he should start figuring out how to return the favor.

"So," he muttered to the ceiling, "she likes to use a spear, and she seems really fast. Coyotes? She might ignore them and stab me in the heart like that one guy . . ." He thought about it for a while, trying to think of the best skills and spells to use, and then he sat up with a start. "I leveled!" He pulled up his attribute points.

Strength:	135	Vitality:	150
Dexterity:	40	Agility:	63
Intelligence:	32	Will:	333

"So, with Sovereign Will, I can pump my physical stats by over a hundred now." He acted as though he was speaking to Lifedrinker, but he knew he was just talking aloud to help himself think. "My dexterity is getting too damn low. If I boost agility, all my physical stats are up way over a hundred, except for dex. Didn't Gorz or Lam—someone—explain that my ability to make adjustments with my weapon would suffer if my dexterity was outweighed too much by my strength or agility?"

"But, on the other hand—" He picked up Lifedrinker, gently rubbed his thumb along the cool, shiny metal of one of her veins, and continued, "Tes said to keep working on my will, and she's a *pinche* dragon." The truth was, Victor reasoned, he had eight points to spend, and with those eight points, he could raise his piddling dexterity to a slightly less piddling level, or he could bump up his epic will stat and make it even more epic. "Better to stand out for something awesome than try to be mediocre in everything," he said, applying his free points to will.

"Well, that's done. What's the deal with my new spell, though? I can 'grant some of my own power and will to the recipient.'" He thought about it a minute, looking at Lifedrinker and shaking his head. "Not going to experiment on you, beautiful. Let's see here." He looked down at his chest and the attractive but not very special bronze breastplate. It had spatters of blood on it, dry and rust colored.

"What about this piece of shit?" Victor held his hand to the cool metal and concentrated, activating his new spell pattern. As it formed in his pathways, he channeled inspiration-attuned Energy and the spell completed, flashing through his pathways, out through his hand, and into the metal of his armor. As the spell passed out of him, he felt a coldness in his Core and a general malaise that washed over him and then seemed to fade away.

The breastplate flashed with white-gold light, and Victor felt it grow heavier, more substantial, and it seemed to buzz with potential in such a way that he began to feel antsy, as though he wanted to leap into action. When he looked down at his armor, it seemed to gleam with an inner light.

"Huh," Victor said, wondering what the spell was doing for the breastplate. He tapped his knuckles against it, and they rebounded from the metal as if he'd hit electrified plastic, not bronze. "Weird . . ." Victor called up his attributes, looking for differences:

Energy Affinity:	3.1, Fear 9.4, Rage 9.1, Inspiration 7.4		Energy:	3062/3062 (3402)
Strength:	135	Vitality:	150	
Dexterity:	40	Agility:	63	
Intelligence:	32	Will:	307 (341)	

Looking at the numbers in parentheses, Victor realized that he'd lost ten percent of his will and ten percent of his maximum Energy. "So . . . so, like, part of my spirit is in this breastplate now?" He looked into his Core and pathways, saw the tether that connected him to the armor, and realized he could end the spell with a thought. "At least it's not permanent. Would it be worth it, though?"

Victor stood up abruptly, set Lifedrinker down, and began loosening the straps holding the breastplate onto his body. After pulling it off and setting it on the bench, he picked up Lifedrinker and said, "Okay, beautiful, please don't drain this breastplate; just try to hurt it." The axe vibrated in his hands, and with a grin, Victor lifted her high and brought her down on the breast-plate, aiming for the center and only using a fraction of his strength.

Victor's eyes almost bugged out of his head when a ghostly fist, flashing with brilliant white Energy, reached out of the breastplate and tried to bat Lifedrinker aside. She wasn't any old axe, though, and she struggled against the burst of spirit Energy. Still, the momentum of Victor's swing was ruined, and the axe glanced off the metal, leaving only a shiny, jagged scratch as she slid to the side. "Now that's pretty fuckin' badass!"

Victor quickly strapped the breastplate back in place, then he contemplated trying to cast the spell on more parts of his armor. He decided against it, though—at ten percent of his will and Energy per cast, he'd find himself running low pretty quickly if he did that.

He looked at Lifedrinker and again considered trying it out on her, but shook his head; something in his gut warned him off of it, at least until he could ask someone what might happen. She had a spirit of her own; what would happen if he put his in there with her, even just a part of it? "It might be fine; the spell says it works on people, too . . ." He vacillated for a long while, and eventually, his decision was made for him when the portcullis started to lift.

"Maybe next time," Victor said, hefting Lifedrinker and walking up the tunnel, his breastplate shimmering softly in the shadowy lightning. When he stepped out into the noise of the crowd and the glaring sun, now more than halfway toward its zenith, he was surprised to see Krista already waiting for him. The crowd's cheering intensified as she strode onto the sand, and the announcer howled his welcoming preamble with—what had to be—forced jubilation.

"It's Victor! The mad smasher of Harf the Terrible! Will Krista, the Spear Mistress, be able to put this savage down? What a battle awaits! I hope none of you are too squeamish, because these two have already displayed their willingness to part their foes from their most vital fluids!"

Victor continued to walk toward Krista. As he drew near the center of the arena, he cast Sovereign Will to boost his agility, and a System message flashed in his view, accompanied by a smattering of small golden Energy motes that quickly flooded into him.

"Oh! Bad luck for Krista! It looks like the otherworlder just improved one of his skills!"

*****Congratulations! You've learned the spell: Sovereign Will, Advanced.*****

*****Sovereign Will, Advanced: As an act of concentration, you can apply up to 33% of your total Will to any two of your physical attributes.*****

"Fucking A," Victor said, grinning as he wiped away the notification. Just like that, he'd gained more than a hundred points to one of his physical stats. As the announcer continued to babble, he recast the spell, focusing on enhancing his agility and vitality, and he felt his body respond. He was more nimble, more sturdy, and he felt like a million damn bucks. Lithely, he began to circle Krista, a slight bend in his knees, Lifedrinker held before him, and a madman's grin on his face.

Krista, for her part, didn't look happy. She held her spear, point forward, four or five feet of the shaft between her and Victor, the rest jutting out behind her. Her long, furry ears were pulled back, flat to her skull, and she frowned in concentration, eyes narrowed as she countered his movement, circling in the opposite direction.

"Look at these two!" the announcer roared. "So eager to get at each other! Who will win? Does anyone know? Even the Warlord is leaning forward on his throne! Has anyone seen such an exciting low-tier tournament? Could anyone believe so many great talents would participate? Just think! Neither of these two gladiators is even favored to win! Place your bets and get set for an epic bout! More excitement awaits as Jast and Sanima are set to battle after these two dogs! Make sure you stick around after the dust settles!"

"Ready yourselves, fighters!" the announcer roared, and Victor took the words to heart, finishing his preparatory spells. He boosted his acuity and readiness with Inspiring Presence, then cast Channel Spirit, causing himself and Lifedrinker to flare with red, rage-attuned Energy. Finally, he built his spell pattern for Manifest Spirit, readying his fear-based coyotes to spring forth.

All the while, Victor kept his eyes on Krista, and he knew she was also preparing herself. Dust began to swirl around her boots, and as she sidestepped, moving in a circle facing Victor, she seemed to move in jittery, phantom steps, trailing clouds of sand. Victor had to rotate faster and faster to match her. Then he felt a surge of hot Energy as her spear began to spark with electricity, and her eyes flashed like twin thunderstorms.

Victor began to feel the sun on the back of his neck, began to notice the smell of copper in the air, and the way the sand, though raked smooth, was darkly stained here and there. Was he really fighting in an arena? Was he really about to go toe to toe with that woman and her magical spear? What would his *abuela* think?

"Enough," he growled, shoving that part of himself down and letting his other half take the reins. His smile spread wider, his eyes narrowed, and Victor began to laugh, reveling in the things that had disturbed him before.

He breathed deeply through his nostrils, savoring the odor of blood and guts. He jerked his axe up to his chest, pumping it up and out to get a reaction from the crowd. When they howled and cheered, Victor howled back, and he saw Krista's face change—some of the confidence had bled away, and though her twisted snarl remained, Victor thought it looked hollow.

After an eon of babbling and haranguing, the announcer grew tired of ginning up the crowd or stalling—Victor had no idea which it was, but he'd certainly dragged out his intro longer than before. The shout to begin came at last as the announcer ramped up his voice, dragging out the words like a siren going off. "*Let's fight!*"

11

HOLLOW JUSTICE

If there was one thing Victor had always been good at, it was bursting into action at the signal to start. When he wrestled, there were times when he'd snap out of the down position at the ref's whistle before his opponent could even lock his hands tight. As the announcer shouted, "*Let's fight,*" Victor channeled that former self, exploding into motion, charging over the ground, summoning his coyotes, and hacking his axe at Krista all in the blink of an eye.

It would have been beautiful if Lifedrinker's edge had cleaved through the snarling woman, just as he'd planned, but it didn't go that way. Krista didn't stand still, and she proved just as fast as, or faster than, Victor. When his axe cleaved only the air, he jumped and rolled, feeling in his gut that the spear was coming in hot toward his side. He'd been right, and the crackling, lightning-charged spear just whispered over his back, sliding against his armor, but not enough to even scratch it.

Victor rolled to his feet, holding Lifedrinker ready, and he heard a yelp and high-pitched growls. He saw his coyotes leaping at Krista, tumbling back as her spear lashed out, and he only counted four. Already, she'd slain one. Victor growled and charged in again, hoping his hounds' distraction would serve to give him a clear shot with Lifedrinker. Krista impaled another coyote as he drew near, and when Lifedrinker whistled through the air at her, she seemed to shift and shimmer, and then again, he cut only the air.

Somehow she'd speared another of his coyotes as she fled Victor's assault, and Victor urged the last two to back off, to circle her and wait for the right moment. Krista made a mocking, pouty face, whistling to his pack and spitting into the sand. She jumped and slid toward one of his companions, and Victor leapt after her, but she shimmered, the sand shifted into the air, and suddenly she was behind him.

Rage began to pool in Victor's pathways, began to force its way into his heart and mind, and he desperately wanted to go berserk. As Krista's spear found his back, jamming toward his spine, his armor flared brilliantly, and a blazing, white-gold, ghostly fist reached out and smacked her spear aside. The crowd gasped in surprise, and Victor felt a surge of amusement that drowned out his rage as he whirled to face her.

"Enchanted your armor while you waited?" she snarled. "I'm fighting a gods-be-damned crafter?" She spat into the sand, and Victor ran toward her; he was here to fight, not banter. Once again, as he charged over the sand, she flickered and flashed, leaving nothing but a swirl of sand. Victor tried to anticipate the move, tried to adjust his momentum, priming his Project Spirit spell, hoping to catch her off guard with a blast of fear-attuned Energy.

Krista wasn't easily predicted, though; she attacked from directly behind him, and rather than go for a kill, stabbing at his torso—and its enchanted armor—to pierce his heart, she drove her long, wickedly sharp spear through the back of Victor's left thigh. He cried out as the razored blade slid through his thick, meaty leg, and jolts of powerful electricity coursed through his body. He convulsed and spasmed, but Victor did not let go of Lifedrinker. With his arms outstretched, his body jerking, and bloody saliva bubbling out of his clenched mouth, he clung to her haft while Krista twisted the spear.

When he realized he'd lost control of his body, fury filled Victor, and he was on the verge of berserking when he felt Lifedrinker buzzing in his hand. Suddenly his mind fixated on her, and he thought if she could resist the electrical charge, then by God, so could he. With a herculean surge of will, Victor brought his convulsing muscles into line and took two shaky, stumbling steps forward off Krista's spear.

With his vitality bolstered, Victor's thigh stopped bleeding almost immediately, and his spasming muscles settled as he turned to frown at Krista. She backed up a step, lifted her spear, and ran her long, pink tongue along the bloody flat of its blade, clearly putting a show on for the crowd; they roared in approval, and she smiled and said, "I'll feast on your loved ones when I'm done killing you here. I'll start with that blue bitch you brought along."

The crowd was screaming; the stands were booming with the stomps of their feet, and still, Victor heard Krista clearly—a benefit of evolved ears, he supposed. He saw the hateful, baleful glare she directed his way, and he remembered how she'd been instantly hostile to him. She beckoned him forward, flashing her long, bloody canines, spear alight with a fresh burst of lightning, and the sand dancing around her feet. He knew she'd make a fool of him time and time again if he kept charging like a bull.

"What's your problem anyway, *puta?*" Victor asked, starting to circle her again.

"I *devour* weaklings and interlopers, worm," she said, and rather than wait for Victor to charge, she flickered and faded from view, and he whirled, whipping Lifedrinker into a parrying downward, looping cut. He felt his axe make contact with the spear, knocking it aside, and Lifedrinker bucked and pulled, desperately trying to sink herself into the haft of that hated weapon. Victor pulled her back, though, and lunged forward, driving her gleaming edge toward Krista's throat.

Krista was no novice with the spear, and she whipped her dark weapon up and around, knocking Lifedrinker aside and drawing the needlelike point downward, just catching the top edge of Victor's forehead and raking it toward his eye. Victor jerked his head aside and danced backward, a curtain of blood flowing into his eye, stinging and obscuring his vision.

Victor knew she'd press the attack, so he willed his last two coyotes to leap at her, buying himself a moment to clear the blood from his eye; the cut had already stopped bleeding. He rubbed furiously at it, watching his poor, dark, smoky coyotes fight valiantly to the last, each succumbing to a lightning stab of Krista's spear. When none remained, Krista turned to Victor, the crowd roaring its enthusiasm.

"Ready to die, runt?" she snarled, stalking toward him, and Victor could feel her gathering Energy—far more than she had thus far.

He grimaced and growled. Something was wrong about this woman, so filled with hate. She was like a mad dog, and he began to see the need to defeat her more and more clearly. This fight wasn't a contest, a spectacle for people to enjoy. This was his duty—Krista needed to be put down.

He reached inward and pulled thick, surging ropes of Energy from each of the affinities at his Core. When he had them all in the iron grip of his will, he cast Harsh Light of Justice, fueled with enough Energy to cover every inch of the arena pit. Suddenly the pale yellow sun seemed to fade, and the sky washed out like an overexposed photo, more white than blue. The shadows along the arena wall disappeared, along with Victor's and Krista's, and as he looked around, Victor swore he could see every grain of sand, every drop of blood, every line of sweat running down Krista's face.

He saw her eyes narrow at first, then a pained look of panic filled them as she realized she was condemned; justice had come for her. On the other hand, Victor felt a fresh surge of vitality and a clear sense of purpose—it was time to bring this villain to heel. He stalked toward her, Lifedrinker light as a broomstick in his hands.

Even in her dismay, Krista rallied and completed her spell as he approached. A blazing, bright ball of Energy formed at the tip of her spear. She shifted oddly and streaked over the sand, moving to Victor's left and circling toward his back, and in the light of justice, it looked almost comical. She moved fast as an arrow, but obviously, and as he turned to track her with Lifedrinker, Victor realized she thought he couldn't see her.

She seemed surprised to see him staring at her as she leapt toward him with that blazing speartip. He stepped under it, a long, stretching lunge that lowered his center of gravity and allowed him to glide over the sand into her charge, his rear foot dragging like when he used to practice takedowns. Victor smiled as he watched her spear pass too high and too unwieldy to correct; he was inside her guard.

On the fly, Victor concentrated on his Sovereign Will spell and switched his boost to strength. He brought Lifedrinker across in a wide, sideways hack, using his forward momentum and prodigious might. The eager axe hit Krista full on, her gleaming Heart Silver edge ripping through the woman's abdomen. As Victor and Krista passed each other in that fraction of a second, she cried out; her spear flew through the air, and hot blood sprayed over Victor as her entrails fell, glistening like eels, onto the sand.

When Krista's spear impacted the arena's sand, the lightning gathered at its tip exploded in a ball of writhing, flashing lighting bolts that erupted with explosions in the air and against the sand, making little puddles of glass. The percussion of the thunder and lightning was accompanied by Krista's screams and gasps as she fruitlessly scrabbled at the sand, trying to pull her guts back into herself.

Something about the spell Victor had cast, about the justice hanging heavy in the air, wouldn't let him turn away as he watched her movements grow more and more feeble, her gasps more and more frail, and then, when stillness took her, he looked at the crowd and frowned. So many people in those stands deserved to have justice dealt to them. So many cheering, howling fools deserved a fate ten times worse than Krista had just been given. His hands clenched and twisted on Lifedrinker's haft, and he began looking for a way out of the pit.

Just as he took his first step, a surge of Energy flew into him, dark, heavy, purple-gold motes that lifted him from the sand, transfixing him and breaking his concentration on his spells. When he fell back to the sand, the world was once more lit normally by the sun, and he could hear the crowd's cries and the announcer's words, "Victor has stunned us again! What was that spell? That weird light? Will our local champion, Jast, be able to contend with this strange, otherworldly gladiator? Stick around, folks! The final battle will take place at noon!"

Victor glanced down at Krista's broken form, her life's blood and inside parts still glistening in the hot light, the scent of copper and shit heavy in the air, and he frowned. He couldn't find any joy in her death, only pity. She looked small and broken, and her face, smooth and relaxed in death's grip, looked pretty without the nasty snarl she'd always worn. Victor stood tall and slowly turned, facing into the stands, wishing he could find a friendly face among all those cheering, jeering people.

"Gladiator! Victorious Victor! Take a well-deserved rest; your greatest challenge lies ahead of you." The announcer's voice rang clear and loud over the noise of the crowd, and Victor turned to his tunnel, now open, and walked out of the arena, the crowd's hysteria fading behind him as he descended. He felt a little hollow, a little empty, and decided he didn't like being under the influence of justice-attuned Energy.

Even when Victor lost himself to rage, he at least felt alive; he felt that emotional release that washed over him as he came back to himself. Sometimes he felt guilt later, but it was better than this hollow, empty sensation, as if he'd made himself a tool for a force greater than himself. Was it all in his head? His justice Energy came from within him, just as his rage did; even the spell description said the light would "take on the morality of the caster." Still, he felt spent and used; he wondered if it was because the spell reflected a part of himself that was abstract and distant from his conscious mind.

"Maybe I'm just a lot closer to my rage, hmm?" he asked Lifedrinker, lifting her to rest on his shoulder as he made his way back into his ready room. Another prize box and tray of refreshments awaited him, and he ate his sandwich—identical to the one he'd already eaten—drank his water, and then pulled on the ribbon, opening the top of the box. Another Coloss prize token lay within, alongside a golden foil-wrapped package about the size of his thumb.

Victor picked up the note card and read about the prize. *Rock Wyrm Magma Horn: useful for making a breakthrough in Core development when properly prepared in an alchemical tincture.* Victor shrugged and closed up the box, setting it next to the other two atop his chest. He'd have plenty of time to think about prizes when the fighting was done. He stretched out on the bench, Lifedrinker beside him, and rested his eyes.

He tried not to dwell on his earlier fights, successful as they'd been. Victor wondered at that—the success he'd already had. The fights had been quick, for the most part, and he'd hardly been injured. His battle with Rellia had been a hell of a lot harder. Even the boss in the undead dungeon had been more of a struggle. He supposed much of it was that he'd improved; his Core was stronger, his axe skills were greater, and he'd gained experience and improved his attributes. "Still," he muttered, "everyone acted like I was a runt, a weakling in this world."

"Ahh, but you are only facing people still in the low tier," a man's voice said, and Victor nearly jumped out of his skin, flailing to catch Lifedrinker as he jerked up into a sitting position. "My apologies, sir; I merely came to collect your refreshment tray and to ask if you needed any first aid."

"Uh," Victor said, looking at the black-robed green insect guy. "Tong-pan," he corrected himself.

"Why, yes, sir. I'm a member of the Tong-pan people. May I?" the man asked, walking around Victor to pick up the silver tray from the far end of the bench. "Will you need any medical care? The fight steward noted you suffered injuries in your last match."

"Nah," Victor said, rubbing at the scabbed-over cut on his forehead and looking down at his bloodstained pant leg. "I heal fast." The puncture wound was still sore, but he knew it wouldn't start bleeding again, nor would it hinder his movement, especially if he kept his vitality boosted while waiting for his next match.

"I'm sorry I intruded upon your self-reflection, sir. I didn't mean to respond, but my mandibles are faster than my better judgment sometimes." He bowed several times quickly, his bright green carapace flashing as it reflected the glow lamp hanging above.

"No worries. It's a good reminder. I might be kicking ass so far, but I'm just fighting the weakest people in your city."

"No, no, sir! I beg to correct you; the people who fight in the arena are among our strongest; the vast majority of the populace is considered low tier, even if there are thousands in the mid and high tiers."

"Right. Makes sense, I guess. Seems that way in the world I came from, too. Ordinary people don't tend to have the freedom to build their strength; they're too worried about getting to work and feeding their families."

"Just so, sir. I'm afraid I must take my leave now before the fight steward thinks I'm giving you unfair attention." With that, the man turned and walked directly into the stone wall next to the chest containing Victor's belongings, disappearing through the blocks.

"The fuck?" Victor said, standing up and walking over to the wall. He pressed a hand against it and felt only cool, solid stone. Seeing how easily the man had come and gone from his room, Victor wondered who else could do such things. Was it an ability granted only to those who worked in the arena, or was it some magical ability that any person might learn? He knew if he cast the Inevitable Huntsman, he could move through solid barriers, but that was something a lot more complicated than whatever the Tong-pan had just done.

Frowning, he sat down, suddenly glad that he'd held back from displaying all his cards during his fight with Krista. He'd been tempted to go berserk, considering Jast couldn't watch his fight on the viewport. Now that he'd seen how easily some people could move in and out of the ready rooms, though, he felt vindicated in his decision to hold back. If Jast was the current arena champion, a hometown hero, there was a good chance he had a lot of powerful friends around. Someone might tell him about Victor's ace cards if they saw them in action.

"But they didn't," Victor said, lifting Lifedrinker and grinning. "Did they, beautiful?"

He lay back on the bench again and started to think about Jast. He'd only seen the guy in action once, and he'd been like a force of nature. Twelve feet tall, probably six hundred pounds, and fast as a damn striking cobra. "And he has a big fucking axe," Victor said, squeezing Lifedrinker's haft.

"I don't give a shit about that, though, lady. Polo had a big axe, and it didn't bother you. On the bright side, I don't need to hold back. We're going to go in there and show these fuckers what a real giant is—what someone with real Quinametzin blood can accomplish. We're going to show them how we fight when we let go, and when we're done, the crowd might be cheering, but they'll be fucking scared. They'll understand that being big doesn't make you a goddamn titan."

12

INTERVENTION

When the portcullis clanked open, Victor was ready. He had his game face on, Lifedrinker in his hands, and he felt nearly a hundred percent, physically. He strode into the passage leading up to the arena floor with purpose and vigor, and then a shadow separated itself from the wall and said, "Hold, gladiator."

"The fuck?" Victor growled, lifting his axe as though to strike the interloper.

"Hold!" the hooded figure urged, hands held up placatingly. It was a man—a Vesh, Victor was sure—some light revealing lean, muscular forearms and pointed black nails. "I will be brief; I know your time is limited."

"Speak." Victor continued to walk, though slowly.

"Your opponent, Jast, is the son of a powerful man—War Captain Black. Jast will grant mercy if you yield, and Black will reward you."

"Fuck that. I'm not throwing the fight." Victor increased his pace.

"Wait! The War Captain knows you wish to return to your world. He can make that happen." Those words gave Victor pause, and he slowly turned to face the hooded messenger.

"He can open a portal?"

"No, but one in his employ can."

"How can I believe you?"

"Jast always grants mercy if he doesn't strike a fatal blow before his opponent can yield. You have my word and the assurance of War Captain Black that his prize is real. We take honor seriously here in Coloss."

"Really? That's why you're trying to get me to throw the fight?"

"I . . ."

"I'm out of time. I'll think about it." Victor turned and stomped up the passage, his long legs moving him faster than most people would jog.

"See that you do!" the hooded man called after him, and Victor frowned.

"What an asshole," he growled, gripping Lifedrinker's haft. "Even if I don't take the deal, he's fucking thrown my game off." More than that, Victor was annoyed that he felt he had to consider the man's proposal. This was the only concrete offer he or Valla had been given to get home in a timely fashion. He'd won some prize tokens, which might be enough, but he wasn't sure. Additionally, he had to consider the idea that Jast might win, even if Victor didn't take a dive.

Victor looked around the arena, blinking his eyes in the blazing sun and doing his best to ignore the announcer's hysterical adulations. He was frustrated—pissed. He strode through the sand and lifted Lifedrinker, screaming his frustrations back at the crowd. They responded in kind, and the announcer had to stop speaking for a minute due to the clamor.

Victor smiled at the crowd's response to his frustration and threw his shoulders back, screaming, "*Fuck!*" It didn't seem to matter to them what he said; they roared back. Victor kicked some sand and looked around, waiting for his big opponent to show up.

While he waited, he frowned and muttered curses. Why did everything have to be complicated? Why couldn't he just have a good clean fight and beat the shit out of this guy? What would happen if he didn't take the asshole's deal? Would War Captain Black smite him down the moment he stepped out of the arena? He could only imagine the dude was high tier—more powerful than Victor could currently imagine.

"And here comes our champion!" the announcer said, finally getting Victor's attention. The crowd's hysteria rose to new heights as Jast, clad in armor similar to Victor's, strode out of his tunnel. He was enormous—something about his posture and how he held his massive, double-bladed great axe made him loom larger than when Victor had seen him in the common ready room. He stomped toward the center of the arena, stopping a half dozen paces from Victor and scowling down at him.

"Look at the fury on their faces, everyone! How will the mid-tier tournament match the excitement we've all experienced this morning? What a show! What a way to honor Horc! Your Warlord and Captains are on the edges of their seats, fighters! Don't disappoint!"

While the announcer continued to try to whip the crowd—and the fighters—into even more of a frenzy, Victor prepared himself. His armor was still enchanted with a shard of his spirit, and he knew he'd need to be strong and fast to face Jast, so he boosted his strength and agility with Sovereign Will. He cast Inspiring Presence, his grin widening as he started to notice how flimsy Jast's armor looked and how the giant seemed to favor his left side where he held the heavy end of his axe.

Jast's frown deepened, and Victor felt him gathering Energy of his own. Not for the first time, he wished he could tell more about what kind of spell an opponent was preparing, but he supposed it didn't matter; he had his strategy set. He built the pattern for Manifest Spirit, crafting it from pure, deep, rage-attuned Energy. On a whim, he channeled inspiration-attuned Energy into his axe and arms, hoping to outclass Jast before he had to play his aces.

"If I even play them," Victor grunted, still conflicted about the bullshit offer the hooded guy had made him.

"Say something, Deshi? Just yield quickly; my axe doesn't make small wounds." Jast grunted, squaring himself off and lowering his center of gravity.

As if on cue, the announcer howled, "*Fight!*"

Jast burst into motion, charging over the sand like an angry hippo, and Victor danced to the side, pushing the giant's enormous axe aside with Life-drinker. He'd cast Manifest Spirit as soon as he saw Jast take a step, and Victor danced back, trying to keep Jast facing him, while a great crimson shape began to coalesce out of a glowering red mist behind the giant fighter.

Jast grunted angrily as he recovered his axe's momentum and leapt at Victor, faster by ten times than the Degh Victor had earlier fought, but still slow enough for Victor to counter, carefully avoiding a direct test of his strength, using the giant's momentum to parry and block. As Jast's frustration mounted, Victor felt him gathering Energy to do something big, but then a titanic roar filled the arena, and Jast had his hands full.

Victor's gigantic, red-furred, fury-eyed cave bear leapt at the giant's back, and Jast barely whirled in time to get his axe between him and the great animal's claws and fangs. To his credit, Jast didn't fall or crumple under the onslaught; he screamed, and Victor felt his pent-up Energy release.

With a ringing clang, huge metallic blades materialized out of the air, like haftless axe-heads. They hung in the air around Jast, ten or more of them, and began to spin like a steel cyclone—a ring of razor-sharp blades that hacked and cut at the great bear as it furiously swiped and bit at Jast. Watching the bear's fur and shimmering spirit blood splash away, dissipating into red mist, Victor charged Jast's flank.

The ring of blades hung a foot or two away from the giant, and Victor slid in the sand, hacking Lifedrinker sideways toward the Degh's knee. He'd hoped to avoid the blades by going under them, but they seemed to have a mind of their own, and two corrected their trajectories to spin through the air in a collision course with Victor.

Victor doubled down, swinging Lifedrinker as hard as he could, her gleaming silvery edge limned with red fury, and as she made contact, he ducked his head low, trying to dodge one of the blades, trusting in his enchanted armor to save him from the other one. Lifedrinker bit deeply into Jast's flesh, sinking into the gap between his knee bones, and the giant screamed and stumbled.

Victor dodged the blade coming at his head. The other one he'd seen was knocked aside by his enchanted armor, but a third he hadn't noticed cleaved into his right side, parting his bronze plate as though it were paper and wedging between his ribs, cracking and separating them as it dug into his flesh. Victor moaned, his wind suddenly too feeble to scream, and rolled to the side, scrabbling away in agony.

As Victor pushed away through the sand, Lifedrinker still clutched grimly in one hand, he twisted to his uninjured side and watched as his great bear fought valiantly with the giant warrior. The bear had capitalized on Jast's stumble, ripping long, razored claws down the giant's chest, shredding his armor even worse than Victor's. Jast had almost fallen from the hack to the knee and the bear's swipe, and as he struggled to regain his balance, the bear charged.

Victor could see the bear had had enough—its eyes were red orbs of fury and frustration. It reared up on its hind legs, caution no longer a consideration, allowing the remaining blades to sink into its furry side as it brought its two enormous clawed paws down to rake the giant, clearly intent on shredding him to ribbons. Jast wasn't out of tricks, though, and he rolled back over one shoulder, leaving a great metal shield hanging in the air where, a second ago, he'd been standing.

Victor switched his Sovereign Will boost to strength and vitality and continued to inch backward in the sand, hoping his bear would distract Jast just a bit longer until the gaping wound in his side stitched itself together, at least partially—the magical blade had dissipated into metallic dust that, in turn, had shimmered away into mist. He'd only started to get his breath back when the bear came down on the shield Jast had created out of thin air, and with a tremendous clang, it stopped it short.

Victor's companion grunted, the Energy that animated it leaking in great gouts from the wounds left by the axe barrier and drizzling from its mouth. It looked toward Victor, pain and frustration in its eyes, and Victor knew it wanted to try again, wanted to keep fighting, but it was struggling to stand tall, and Victor couldn't take it. "Go on," he said. "You did your best; I got this." With that, the mighty crimson giant shimmered into fog that fell to the sand and faded away.

"Yield," a deep voice rumbled beside him, and Victor turned to regard Jast. The giant loomed over him, his enormous axe held high, ready to strike. Victor was still sitting in the sand, his left palm holding him up while his right hand clutched Lifedrinker. His side was still a mess, but he was already breathing better and could see the puddle of blood next to him had stopped growing.

At the giant's command, a million things ran through his mind—thoughts about Rellia and how she'd tried to get him to yield in a similar fight, thoughts about people he'd killed in arenas, thoughts about how he couldn't imagine living with himself if he caved now, even if it meant he was going to have a new, powerful enemy. More than anything, he wanted to kick this big bastard's ass and wipe that fucking superior, unsmiling glower off his face.

He opened his pathways and let rage flood them, and as he began to flicker with the power of it—a smoldering, red aura outlining his form, and deep, baleful red torches igniting in his eyes—he said, "I don't think I will."

"Fool," Jast said, his gigantic axe whistling through the air, aiming for the crook of Victor's neck and shoulder. Before the blade, falling like a guillotine, could sink into Victor's flesh, though, it stopped, frozen in place as if it had hit a block of granite. Jast looked confused for a moment, and then his eyes widened as it registered: Victor had grabbed hold of his axe, just below the blade, and he was standing, lifting the great axe in his left hand and holding Lifedrinker high in the air with the other.

Jast struggled, unable to comprehend what was happening; things weren't making sense. Victor was a tiny Deshi—how was he lifting his axe into an uncomfortable angle as he stood? How was he standing at all? As Jast let his eyes travel from the fist gripping his axe to Victor's face, he blanched; why was he looking up to see that glowering visage of fury? He opened his mouth, but no words would form on his tongue. What was happening?

Victor grunted, hacking Lifedrinker down into the iron-like haft of Jast's axe, and she ripped through the air like a crack of lightning, parting the wood with a concussion like thunder. Victor roared and flung the shortened great axe into the air, heedless of its trajectory; what cared he for the toys of a weakling? Jast stumbled back, released physically and mentally as he finally came to grips with his reality, but Victor wasn't ready to let him go.

Jast looked from the piece of wood in his hands to Victor, stomping toward him, and he dug deep into his Energy reserves to create his barrier of axe blades again. Victor roared—a sound that shook Jast to the bones, rattling his teeth and loosening something in his bowels—and charged through the spinning axe blades.

They slammed into him, biting his shoulder, side, leg, and arms, but the titan didn't seem to care; he kept coming and grabbed Jast by the throat, actually lifting him slightly into the air. Jast struggled against the enormous red-faced warrior's grip—tried with all his might to knock his hand away, but it only tightened, and things began to grow dark as he saw Victor lift his axe high, preparing a killing blow.

"*STOP*," a thunderous roar rang through the arena, but to Victor, it was a dim annoyance. Whoever thought they should intervene in his carnage would soon learn to think differently. This fool had dared to lift his hands against him; how could this weakling think to stand against the Quinametzin? He brought his axe down, aiming to split the giant's skull like a melon, but suddenly he was knocked, tumbling head over heels through the sand to crash into the wall of the arena.

Victor leapt to his feet, roaring in defiance and fury, looking around in his red-tinged vision to see what had happened. Jast lay crumpled in the sand, and standing above him was another giant, this one wearing heavy black armor and wielding a massive black metal shield, rectangular and thick. Had the fool dared to strike him with that? Victor roared again, and the crowd, hitherto ignored by him, shouted back. Victor lifted his arms, high over his head, wide, and Lifedrinker glinted, a brilliant, deadly hatchet in his mighty hand.

He basked in the adulation and screamed again, stalking toward the man in the black armor. Who was this challenger? The man hunkered down, standing over the fallen weakling, directing the flat, black metal of his shield toward Victor. "Stop!" he shouted again. "You are victorious!" Was that a note of pleading in his voice? Was this man here to give his respect? To beg for the weakling's life?

"You dare to strike me and then cower behind that metal?" Victor asked, though even in a question, his voice roared. He continued to stalk forward, his muscles bunched like enormous cables, the sand crunching under his steps and the crowd going wild. In some distant, removed part of his awareness, Victor knew the announcer was going into hysterics—the real kind, not the way he spoke to whip up the crowd.

Suddenly the ground shook, and another figure stood in the sand between Victor and the black armor-clad giant. He was a puny thing, wearing silvery armor and adorned with pretty white-feathered wings. Victor liked the looks of those feathers and began to imagine them adorning his armor and the haft of his mighty axe.

"Black, what are you doing?" the newcomer asked, and Victor paused his advance—there was power in that voice.

"My heir must live. I will pay reparations," the black-clad giant said, still crouching over his pathetic offspring.

"What say you, gladiator?" the powerful little man asked, turning to regard Victor's hulking form. "This sets a bad precedent; I'll make him pay you dearly for this transgression of the games."

Victor's rage had cooled significantly at the touch of the silvery little man's aura; he knew strength when he felt it, and something inside him was appeased by the potent being's attempts to be polite—at his show of respect. Victor began to assert himself in his own mind, pushing his Quinametzin alter ego to the side, and with an effort of will, he said, "I will respect your decision."

"Excellent." The silver-clad man snapped his beautiful wings wide and turned to face the area of the stands where box seats were set up. His voice carried over the noise, and as he spoke, people quieted. "Jast has yielded and, due to his father's intervention, is banned from the arena for one hundred years. The stranger is victorious!"

"Warlord!" the man in black said, straightening up.

"You've trespassed upon the sanctity of these games, Ardek. On Horc's Day, no less! We'll speak later, but for now, be grateful and show gratitude to this stranger to our city; he's within his rights to demand blood."

Victor felt his rage continuing to cool and knew he'd start to shift back to his usual self soon. He didn't want to appear small before these two men, not then. With that thought, he grunted and, Lifedrinker swinging loosely in his grip, started walking toward the portcullis that barred his tunnel.

"Gladiator . . . Deshi, I'm sorry, I forgot your name . . ." the silver-clad man called after him.

"Victor." He stopped and paused, turning to face the man fully, his voice rumbling out of his enormous chest, "I'm no Deshi. I'm a true titan, and should that man in black or his son seek another fight, I won't guarantee the safety of your city."

"Ho! Hear that, Black? This youngster has spirit! Victor, I'll see you at my Horc's Day feast tonight. There, Black will present you with his reparations." He didn't wait for Victor to answer; it was clear he considered it a settled matter. He snapped his wings with a *crack* and streaked into the air faster than mere feathers could have propelled him.

Victor entered his tunnel, leaving the howling crowd behind, his mind so busy he couldn't register the meaning of the announcer's words that chased after him. He felt his rage seeping away as he walked, felt Lifedrinker grow slightly heavier, bigger in his hand, and sighed. "It'll be good to get out of this cheap armor and get something to eat and maybe a couple beers. I wonder if Valla enjoyed the show."

13

※

BODYGUARD

You actually said that? You threatened the safety of the city?" Valla sat back and blew out a breath in amazement, shaking her head and lifting her mug of ale to sip at it while Victor laughed.

"When I'm berserk, it's like a different side of me comes out. Well, maybe a part of me becomes more pronounced." Victor shrugged and took a big pull of his own beer.

"At least the Warlord seemed to have a sense of humor. Tes told me he's nearly reached the twelfth tier."

"Fuck . . . seriously?"

"Yes, truly." Valla took another drink and said, "Well, you promised to tell me about the prizes you won, but I should tell you about our wagers first."

"You found a place to make bets?" Victor set his big mug of foamy, warm beer on the table and reached for the plate of sliced cured meats and cheese.

"I did, but the public bookmakers had limits on their bets for the first round, and after you crushed your first couple of opponents, your odds weren't as favorable as you might hope. Still, I turned your nine thousand beads into sixty-two. I . . . well, I did similarly well."

"Holy shit! Sixty-two thousand? I'd say we're sitting pretty with cash, huh? I mean, we should do some serious shopping before we head back to Fanwath, assuming we can get back with the tokens I won or with the help of someone powerful who happens to owe me." Victor grinned and winked, slightly buzzed from the beer. "You know, for interrupting my final match."

"Yes, everyone knows." Valla gestured to the crowded tavern, and Victor chuckled, remembering how people had crowded around when they'd first arrived, clapping him on the back, congratulating him, asking him questions about his fighting techniques, his giant form, and a million other things. Valla had finally grown tired of it and shouted them back, threatening to go elsewhere if they couldn't drink in peace, which caused the barkeep to take up her cause, chasing people away from their table.

"Anyway, the prizes." One by one, Victor pulled out his winnings to show Valla—the three prize tokens, the drake gall bladder, the magma horn, and finally, his grand prize, a glass jar containing a bloody heart about the size of one of Valla's fists. The glass was warm to the touch, and Victor knew it was enchanted to keep the heart as fresh as the moment it was pulled from the body of a spinefiend. He had no idea what a spinefiend was, but he was glad it sounded like a monster, not a person.

"If I remember correctly from the flyer you picked up at the arena, you need an Alchemist for the horn and gall bladder, but you're supposed to eat that heart raw?" The corner of Valla's mouth twisted down in an involuntary grimace, and Victor nodded sympathetically.

"Yeah. Sounds gross, huh?"

"Well, yes, but it's oddly fitting. It's meant to improve your bloodline, and didn't you have a bloodline vision involving the consumption of an enemy's heart?"

"Yeah. Holy shit . . . maybe I should go berserk before I eat it!"

"Is that safe?" Valla's eyes clouded, and her brows narrowed, and Victor knew she was remembering her encounter with his Aspect of Terror.

"I've got pretty good control of myself these days when I go berserk . . ." Victor drummed his fingers on the tabletop, thinking about it, and said, "When I first learned the spell, I had almost no self-control. I couldn't stop fighting until the rage left me. These days I can think, speak, I bet I could even cast other spells, though I've never tried . . ." He trailed off, noting that Valla didn't seem particularly put at ease.

He and Valla drank some more, and Victor ate more meat and cheese; then he shrugged and said, "I'll do it somewhere safe—outside the walls, even. You don't need to be anywhere near me, but I like the idea. I feel like I'll gain more from my bloodline if I'm in touch with it when I eat this thing."

"It makes sense," Valla finally said with a resigned sigh. "Perhaps we could ask the Warlord if he has a safe space for you to do it. What time are you supposed to go to his celebration?"

"Well, after the high-tier duels, I guess." Victor looked around and caught the barkeep's eye, waving him over. The big Vesh ambled through the crowd, his prodigious gut and hooved feet making his progress kind of comical, and by the time he arrived, Victor's inebriated grin had grown very wide.

"What can I do for you, Champion?"

"I'm supposed to go to the Warlord's feast tonight. Any idea what time I should head to his, uh . . . where does he live? A palace?"

"Ah, the Warlord lives in the citadel at the center of Coloss, atop King's Hill. Just keep following the roads with upward slopes, and you'll reach it. I bet the Warlord will start his party after the high-tier duels, which will be after the mid-tier tournament. A few hours after sunset, that's when I'd head up there." He looked at their table, the decimated meat and cheese platter, and their empty mugs and said, "Shall I send you some more food? Another round?"

Victor looked at Valla, and she nodded, so he said, "Yeah, that'd be good." After the barkeep grunted and walked away, Victor said, "So? What did you think of Tes?"

"She's amazing, as you said." Valla smiled, her pale blue cheeks a little flushed from the alcohol, and continued. "She wants to come with us on that monster hunt. We're still doing that, right? Even if your tokens allow us to travel back to Fanwath, I'd like to learn a few more things here. We have months until Rellia starts to panic."

"Really? That's a surprise," Victor chuckled. "I thought you'd be pushing me to go check out the City Stone right now . . ." Victor stopped speaking as Valla's eyes widened, and she leaned forward.

"Can we? We should see what these tokens will allow. It will give us a good idea about our next move, and we have hours before the Warlord's party starts."

"Well, we just ordered more food . . ."

"Put it in your ring; you can snack on the way." Valla laughed, tilting her mug to her face and downing the rest of her ale.

Victor laughed, too, and said, "Wow, you're in a very different mood than you were this morning."

"Tes made me feel a lot better about myself, about my chances in that duel, should we still be in this world when the time comes. Not to mention, I had a good time watching you beat up on the locals."

"All right, well, I'll go up to the bar, cancel our drinks, and grab my meat and cheese. Meet you outside." Victor stood up, his chair scraping noisily over the hard wooden planks of the floor, and pushed his way through the crowd up to the bar. People moved aside quickly, and a few clapped him on the shoulder. Victor smiled and burped, slapping people's backs in a comradely fashion as he edged around them, feeling quite good about his change in status with the locals.

He'd just stowed away his cheese tray and was edging his way through the crowd when he felt himself bump up against a man who might as well have been a pillar of iron, so little did he give. "'Scuse me," Victor grunted, pushing his way past some more easily shifted clientele, but the man reached out a hand and grasped his shoulder, giving it a squeeze and stopping him dead.

"Hold up, runt," a gravelly voice said, and though the volume was low, the words cut through Victor's foggy mind like a knife. He turned to regard the speaker more carefully and saw a Vesh with black scaled skin and folded leathery wings at his back. "You really caused some trouble for the War Captain today. Had to beat his son that way, did you?"

"It was an arena fight," Victor said, standing up straighter and turning to face the man. He could feel his aura pushing against him, like a palpable thickness in the air, and he knew this man was of a much higher tier than himself. He'd talked a big game when he was berserking in the arena, but Victor didn't think he should go around the city fighting people of unknown and likely prodigious power.

"You don't seem so tough now." The hand on his shoulder tightened, and Victor glanced at it, noting the black scales and thick, pointed, black nails.

"Are you part, uh, what are they called . . . Yazzian?"

"What the shit did you just say?" Suddenly the dark orbs beneath the man's scaled brow began to glow with furious golden Energy, and he leaned closer to Victor, his lips pulling back from long, sharp teeth.

"Oh, sorry. Was that insulting? I really didn't mean it that way . . ." Victor took a few steps back, slipping out of the man's grasp and making his way toward the doorway. The darkly scaled man scowled and stalked toward him. The crowd surged away from them, clearing some space, and Victor noticed the friendly banter and laughter that had filled the air was gone.

"Leave off him, Haz," a deep voice said from behind Victor, and he turned to see a Degh in a silvery helmet peering in through the too-small doorway.

"Gah, keep your nose out of this, Tronk," Haz growled, reaching for Victor's shoulder again.

"Don't think I will. Warlord 'imself sent me to look after the runt. Better get yourself back on a leash before you make more trouble for your master."

Suddenly Victor felt an enormous, powerful grip on his other shoulder, and he was pulled, stumbling back through the doorway and into the late afternoon sunlight. He almost stumbled, his arms cartwheeling to keep himself upright, but the hand stopped pulling and steadied him while he regained his balance.

"There we are," the same deep voice rumbled, and Victor realized it had been the Degh—Tronk, he supposed—that had pulled him out of the tavern. He jerked his head back toward the doorway and was relieved to see the scaly man hadn't followed; the crowd had reformed inside, obscuring his view. "I'll spend some time with you this evening, if you don't mind, lad."

"Uh, thanks. I wasn't looking for another fight right now."

"No, he wasn't," Valla said, and Victor realized she was standing behind the giant, frowning from just beneath his left elbow. "What did you say to that man, Victor? Couldn't you tell he was higher tier?"

"I didn't say anything . . ."

"Nar, there's nothin' he coulda done different. Haz is one of Black's lieutenants, and he holds a grudge for his master. Don't worry, though, folks. Our benevolent leader saw this comin' and sent me to keep ya company. I'm Tronk."

Victor regarded the huge man; he wore a silvery breastplate inlaid with golden sigils, an enormous sword strapped to his back, and a thick helmet that would give Victor's gift from Polo a run for its money when it came to angry-looking visages. More than that, like the Vesh inside the tavern, Tronk gave off a dense, dangerous aura—a kind of weight in the air that made it feel as if you were walking in water, each breath a bit of a struggle in his presence. Victor smiled and held out a hand, "Thanks, Tronk. I'm Victor, and my small blue friend is Valla."

"Right." Tronk nodded, squeezing Victor's hand between a few of his fingers. "The Warlord was a bit worried some o' Black's loyalists might try to earn some points by makin' you pay in the streets for what ya done in the arena. Nobody'll cross you with me around; I'm one of the Warlord's Fists."

"Fists?" Valla asked, moving next to Victor so she could look more directly at Tronk.

"Aye; there's ten o' us—we keep the peace and do some o' the Warlord's lighter work, get our hands dirty when he's busy with bigger messes."

"So, you're like our bodyguard tonight?"

"Tonight, tomorrow, maybe longer—depends 'ow long Black's feeling raw 'bout 'ow you embarrassed 'is son."

"Well, thanks. Uh, we were just going to try to get to the City Stone to see what I could do with the prize tokens I won. That all right?"

"Sure. Ya know the way?" Tronk hooked his thumbs in the oversized leather and metal-plated girdle he wore and looked up the street to his right.

"We figured it would be up in the Warlord's citadel," Valla said before Victor could respond.

"Aye, that's right. Follow me." Tronk started stomping up the sidewalk, and people scurried to clear the way for him. Victor and Valla hurried after, walking in his wake. Victor grinned and nudged Valla.

"Kinda cool not to have to worry about walking in the slow lane for a change." He nodded toward the Vesh and other human-sized people walking on the left side of the sidewalk.

"Aye," Valla nodded. "We're lucky he showed up. Maybe that man would have shown mercy on us because we're low tier, but he could have given us a very bad time."

"Us?" Victor frowned at Valla. "He was after me."

"How would I ever show my face to Rellia if I stood by and watched you slaughtered?" Valla scoffed and shook her head as though Victor had said something even dumber than usual.

"You don't need to get killed because of a vendetta some guy has against me. That wouldn't make life any easier for Rellia."

"No." Valla frowned and continued, "I suppose not. Still, I wouldn't be able to live with myself if I stood by and watched a comrade die."

"Maybe it wouldn't have been so bad, anyway. He might have just wanted to give me a good beating."

"Might be," Tronk rumbled over his shoulder. "Haz knows there'd be trouble wi' the Warlord if he killed ya." His boulder-like shoulders lifted, and Victor realized he was shrugging as he continued, "Though Haz mightn't care too much."

The walk to the citadel took a good half hour or more, even moving at the giant's pace as he cleared the way. The final street leading up to the citadel was steeply inclined, switching back east to west as it climbed the final stretch of King's Hill. At certain points, between gaps in the buildings, Victor and Valla paused to see the expanse of Coloss falling away below them. With the sky lit orange and crimson by the setting sun, Victor was reminded of just how far from home he really was.

The buildings were tightly packed together, and their rooftops, tiled in orange, green, copper, and bronze, created a magical tapestry of color that reflected the garish colors in the sky. All of this fell away toward a wall that seemed impossibly tall and wide—something that must have taken either enormous magic or a thousand years to build. When they finally rounded the last wide turn in the winding road and could see straight ahead to the Warlord's citadel, all the previous wonders fell away from Victor's mind.

Much like the great city wall, the citadel was constructed of gigantic rectangular stone blocks. It was square and rose in seven distinct tiers, each with crenellated ramparts built from the same great stones. Atop the ramparts, soldiers patrolled, tiny figures far from the ground, giving a sense of scale to the massive structure. Each side of the base had to be more than a mile long, and though it didn't seem so tall due to its tiered nature, Victor would have bet the central spire was higher than any of the skyscrapers in Tucson's downtown.

"Big," he said, words failing him.

"Aye. Luck is wi' us, though," Tronk grunted, still walking steadily toward the one and only monumental gate in the wall of the great building. "The City Stone's right in the middle on the ground floor." He trudged down the wide stone-paved roadway, and Victor followed, glancing at Valla and shrugging with a crooked grin.

"Pretty awesome building, if you ask me."

"Awful in its majesty," Valla nodded, suddenly quite sober.

"How many people live in there?" Victor asked, trying to hurry his steps to walk beside the giant.

"Dunno. Warlord has his troops, o' course—ten thousand strong. Then there's his children and their families and us Fists, and the servants, and . . . argh, it's too much to think about."

"Tronk, are all the Fists high tier? What about the Warlord's troops?" Valla, too, hurried her pace to walk beside Victor.

"The Fists, aye. His troops?" Tronk snorted, gesturing toward the gates and the dozen soldiers standing to either side with long, ornamental spears. "Most are like these—mid-tier."

"Do the War Captains have Fists or their equivalent?" Valla asked.

"Nar. Only the Warlord."

"So he maintains his power, his rule, through might." Valla nodded as though it was all making perfect sense.

"Yar. If a War Captain gets too uppity, we're sent to crack some 'eads."

"That how it is in the Empire?" Victor asked Valla as they began to pass in front of the soldiers. The troops neither moved nor spoke while they walked by, and Victor wondered if it would've been the same if Tronk weren't leading them.

"Certainly. The strongest families always work to maintain that strength, consolidating power through alliances and quelling any uprisings, even the hint of an uprising, before they can take root."

"Hope they don't know about Rellia's long-term plans." Victor winked at Valla, and her eyes widened in shock. He wondered if she was surprised that he knew Rellia was conspiring against the Old Powers in the Empire or if she simply didn't know what he was talking about. How much had Rellia shared with her?

"Rellia's not a fool," she said, pressing her lips together in a frown.

They passed under the gateway, wide enough to drive four buses through side by side and tall enough that Tronk could have stacked ten of his giant Degh friends on his shoulders before they touched the immense stone lintel. The gates, also made of carved or molded stone, hung on tremendous brass-colored hinges and had been pulled wide to allow clear passage. Beyond them, the entrance tunnel yawned like a man-made canyon leading to a brightly lit open area that looked for all the world like a park.

"City Stone's in the center o' the garden," Tronk rumbled, his pace unwavering as he continued trudging into the great structure. Even at the giant's pace, it took them a solid five or ten minutes to walk toward that brightly lit interior. Along the way, they passed many Vesh and a few Degh, but none of the other peoples of Coloss. They passed dozens of wide corridors leading off the main thoroughfare and half as many stairways leading up to tunnels and passages on different levels that led away from the great tunnel.

When they stepped into the manicured garden, the stone tunnel floor became more like a meandering cobbled path, and hanging above them was an artificial sun, or so it seemed to Victor. It blazed in yellow-gold splendor, giving off light and warmth. It was clearly not the real sun, though; Victor could shade his eyes and look at it, and he thought he saw crystalline tines poking out of a grand glass ball, swirling with Energy.

"That's awesome," he said, and Valla breathed deeply, looking around the park, nodding her agreement.

Grass grew on manicured lawns, trees rose up in cultivated groves, and hedgerows, fountains, and flower beds completed the picture. Though the trees made it difficult, Victor could shade his eyes and look beyond them to see that the citadel's walls encompassed the park, maybe a quarter mile long on each side.

"Is it always sunny?" Valla asked, following Tronk along the central cobbled pathway.

"Nar. When the real sun goes down, the caretakers will make it look like moonlight."

They walked in silence for a few minutes, Victor and Valla looking left and right, taking in the park's beauty, but soon they approached a dark stone monolith, thirty feet high and covered with silver and gold runes that seemed to shift and float just beneath the surface. An iron fence, fifteen feet tall and tipped with spikes, surrounded the stone, a single gateway opening onto the path on which Victor and the others approached.

Two soldiers, as big as Tronk and decked head to toe in gleaming plate mail, stood on either side of the gate. A woman wearing a rainbow-colored robe was between them atop a velvet-cushioned stool. She was petite, easily the smallest adult Victor had seen in Coloss; she had silver hair and brilliant blue eyes, and her skin looked for all the world like delicate, pale white porcelain. She even had seams at her neck, wrist, and finger joints, as though each part of her had been cast from a mold.

She looked at Tronk and his two charges and smiled, her thin, painted lips lifting in a strangely unnatural manner, and said, "Welcome. Please present your Coloss prize token in order to proceed."

14

CULTIVATION CHAMBER

Tronk stepped to the side, leaning against a nearby garden sculpture—a stone depiction of a bird with expansive plumage, sort of like a peacock. Valla also moved off the path, looking at Victor. He shrugged and approached the porcelain lady, fishing one of his prize tokens out of his storage ring.

"Ahh, yes. You may proceed, though please do not dally. People will be lining up to use the Stone soon." Her lips hardly moved on her smooth, painted face, and she spoke before Victor was within five feet of her, apparently able to confirm the token from a distance.

"Um, can my friend come with me?"

"You may bring a companion. Though, again, please do not linger long with the Stone." She gestured with one of her fragile-looking arms toward the open gateway, and Victor glanced from one silent armored guard to the other. They didn't move at all, and he began to wonder if people were inside those shiny metal carapaces or if they were some sort of automatons; the woman's strange nature added some weight to that theory in his estimation.

"Come on, Valla." Victor motioned her forward as he walked past the lady's stool, stepping under the wrought metal of the gate's archway. He could hear her behind him as he continued up the path toward the giant dark monolith. "This one's bigger than the one inside the Greatbone Mine."

"It's bigger than the ones in Persi Gables and Gelica, too," Valla said from behind him, her voice hushed.

"Do you think those guards were people? How would they stand so still?" Victor spoke over his shoulder as he continued up to the looming pillar, eyes struggling to follow the shifting, strange runes beneath its surface.

"I don't know, Victor, but nothing would surprise me in this place. Can you believe the scale of it?" Valla moved next to him as he stopped before the monolith.

"Yeah, this citadel is ridiculous. So, in the mine, I just had to put my hand on it. Guess this one's the same?"

"They all work that way." Valla nodded, reaching toward the stone. When her pale blue hand touched the dark surface, it crackled and popped, and she yelped, yanking her hand back. "It shocked me!"

"Well, you don't have one of these." Victor held up his token and winked at her, then he touched his palm to the stone. A System menu appeared in his vision, but this one was very different from the one he'd seen from the Stone in the Greatbone Mine.

Coloss Prize Token Exchange

Current Treasures Available for Exchange

Services

"Huh. It's a really limited menu. Can the ruler of a town or city change how the Stone works?"

"Oh yes. Whoever founds a settlement gains full control of the Stone and its services. As they grow the community, the System grants them more and more services, but they don't have to share any of them with the populace."

"Well, this one only lists two options—current treasures in exchange for tokens and 'services.' I'll see what kind of services there are first." Victor touched the second option, and another menu opened.

Coloss City Services

Acquire Coloss City Citizenship: 2 Prize Tokens, Revocation of Current Citizenship

City-to-City Transportation: Varied

Victor grunted and touched the second option.

City-to-City Transportation: Concentrate on your destination.

"Huh," Victor said again, his brow creasing as he tried to concentrate on Fanwath. His mind immediately pictured Persi Gables and the way it had looked from the hilltop out on the plains when he and Valla had first approached it.

Transport to Fanwath

Largest Hub: Tharcray, 3 Prize Tokens

Specified Hub: Persi Gables, 5 Prize Tokens

"How far is Tharcray from Persi Gables? Would it be hard to get back to Persi Gables from there?"

"It's far, but we could afford airship transport. We'd make it in less than a week. Why?"

"Sec," Victor replied, then he backed out of the menu and selected the option again, this time focusing on Tucson. He pictured the University of Arizona campus, at least the parts you could see from Speedway, where he'd driven by so many times with friends and family members. Before he could let his mind drift down memory lane, the screen changed, and a message appeared:

Invalid Selection: This location is not a System world.

"Figures," he muttered, moving back through the menu to the first page and selecting the "current treasures" option.

Available Treasure Exchange
Elixir of Regeneration: 1 Prize Token
Racial Boost, Basic: 1 Prize Token
Racial Boost, Improved: 2 Prize Tokens
Alchemical Ingredient, Advanced: 2 Prize Tokens
Racial Boost, Advanced: 3 Prize Tokens
Cultivation Breakthrough: 3 Prize Tokens
Alchemical Ingredient, Epic: 5 Prize Tokens
Racial Boost, Epic: 5 Prize Tokens (2 Available)
Stone of Sentience: 5 Prize Tokens
Alchemical Ingredient, Legendary: 10 Prize Tokens
Stone of Consciousness: 10 Prize Tokens (3 Available)
Epic Light Weapon: 10 Prize Tokens
Epic Heavy Weapon: 10 Prize Tokens
Epic Ranged Weapon: 12 Prize Tokens
Epic Energy Focus: 12 Prize Tokens
Random Legendary Treasure: 20 Prize Tokens

"*Chingado,*" Victor breathed.

"What? Tell me!" Valla nudged Victor's shoulder roughly, and he pulled his hand away from the Stone.

"Here," he said, holding out the prize token. "Check it out."

While Valla tentatively touched the Stone and then her eyes went glassy, Victor thought about the options. He could return to Fanwath immediately if he wanted, but that would leave Valla high and dry. He figured the two of them ought to be able to earn another couple of prize tokens fairly easily, so he felt some relief knowing there was a bright light at the end of the tunnel. Still, Victor was very curious about some of the more expensive items.

It seemed as though the stones of sentience and consciousness were meant to awaken a weapon, or maybe another item. What would happen if he used one on his helmet, for instance? He wondered why the Warlord didn't offer specific weapons rather than just categories of weapons as prizes. "Nah, it's obvious—he wants more people to spend more tokens trying to get the perfect prize."

"Hmm? Oh, the categories? I agree," Valla mumbled, still deeply engrossed in her study of the lists.

"I wonder what a legendary treasure is like, hmm?" Victor asked, nudging her.

"Oh, me too. I don't even know how to categorize treasures into tiers like that. What makes a weapon epic or legendary?"

"Good question."

"I'd sure like to get a stone of consciousness for Blue Razor. Even the sentience one; if she could feel, she might grow in power."

"Is that how that works?"

"I think . . ." Valla said, her words soft and trailing away as she continued to stare into space. "If you select the reward, it gives a brief description. Did you notice that?"

"What? No! I was afraid it would take my token if I touched the options."

"Well, I was right; it says that sentient weapons and other items can grow in power 'through their experiences.' Conscious items are the same, though they grow more quickly and can communicate. Lifedrinker must be conscious!"

"I coulda told you that," Victor scoffed. "She's real, Valla."

"I never questioned that . . ."

"Right, right. Sorry." Victor shook his head and added, "Thayla was always messing with me about Lifedrinker. You've never given me any shit."

"Correct." Valla smiled as she spoke, and a few seconds later, she said, "The racial advancement items all have the same description, though the higher-tier ones are supposedly more potent. I have a feeling there are myriad items in each category; the Warlord must have experts able to tell the strength of the treasures he puts in the exchange."

"Well, yeah, that would make sense."

"They seem quite reasonably priced, the racial boosts. How many ranks do you think an epic one would give?"

"No idea, but, yeah, I wish I had around fifty tokens so I could mess around with this stuff. Anyway, we better head out before that porcelain lady gets pissed."

"Right," Valla said, shaking her head slightly as she pulled away from the stone. She passed Victor's token back to him and added, "At the very least, we need to earn two more tokens. Unless we find another way home in the meantime."

"My thoughts exactly." Victor turned and walked down the path and through the gate in the fence. Tronk straightened up and lifted his thick lips into a smile at their approach.

"Done?" he rumbled, reaching up to rub at the stubble on his heavy chin.

"Yeah, we need to earn more tokens." Victor laughed and shook his head ruefully. "Some cool stuff available in there.'"

"Oh, aye. The Warlord knows 'is people; everyone works for 'is prize tokens, tradin' their greatest treasures away. Well, not everyone. You'll find plenty o' nice things for sale in Coloss." He shrugged and then added, "Where to?"

"How long until the Warlord's celebration? I'm supposed to show up for that."

"Hrmm. Sun's just set. Maybe three hours, maybe four."

"Do you know of a secure place where Victor can consume the heart he won? He'd like to use a rather dangerous spell when he does it." Valla stepped forward, glancing sidelong at the silent porcelain lady as she approached Tronk.

"Wait. Valla, I can't eat that now. Last time I advanced my race, I was out for days."

"What's yer racial rank?" Tronk asked, peering quizzically at Victor from beneath the heavy rim of his helmet.

"Uh—" Victor glanced at Valla, and she shrugged, so he said, "Improved Four."

Tronk frowned, noisily clearing his throat and then swallowing. "You could use the Warlord's cultivation chamber—nothin' you could muster would hurt that place, and the Energies in there would have ya up on yer feet in no time."

"He wouldn't mind?" Victor stared at the giant skeptically.

"Nar, he said ta give ya a tour an' ta keep ya busy." Tronk shrugged, and a slow smile spread on his face as he kept rubbing at his chin. "He lets Tronk use it."

"Well . . ." Victor began, but Valla nudged him and interrupted.

"That's a very kind offer, Tronk. Victor would love the opportunity."

Tronk nodded and grunted, straightening up, "Follow me." He turned and started stomping down the garden path, away from the City Stone and toward one of the side exits.

Victor glanced at the completely still porcelain lady and her two silver-plated guards, then waved awkwardly. The porcelain lady's painted eyes swiveled in their sockets and fell upon him, then her red-painted lips curled up into a smile. Victor returned the smile, though his looked more like a grimace, and hurried after Tronk.

"Kinda weird, don't you think?" he asked Valla as they followed after the giant.

"That a great master would let a near stranger use his cultivation room? Yes."

"No, I meant that the porcelain lady didn't say anything or even move when we came out."

"I'm fairly certain she's a construct, built to serve a purpose and not to have a personality."

"I don't know . . . she smiled at me. Did you mean that about the cultivation room? Is it weird that Tronk's taking us there? Do you think the Warlord will be pissed?"

"Nar," Tronk rumbled from up ahead, and Victor frowned, thumping his fist against his forehead. Of course a powerful Energy user would have good hearing. "He don't care. Warlord's been takin' a break from cultivatin'. His chamber's brim full; he even lets some o' the other Fists use it."

Victor looked at Valla and shrugged, and they continued to follow Tronk through the vaulted, highway-wide hallways and up massive stone stairwells where high steps were laid out next to ones half as tall. Victor and Valla climbed the shorter steps, and Tronk lumbered up the giant-sized flight. They continued this way, meandering through seemingly endless tunnels and climbing six more flights of stone steps before they came to their first doorway: a Degh-sized pair of bronze, rune-inscribed doors shimmering slightly with the Energy that held them secure.

"Are we at the top?" Valla asked.

"Near 'nuff." Tronk nodded.

"We didn't pass any rooms! Just massive corridors . . ." Valla's voice trailed off as Tronk rumbled a reply, interrupting her.

"Oh, there are plenty 'o rooms in this great building. We took the soldier path, though, where the Warlord's troops move when 'tis time to fight invaders."

"Does that happen often?" Valla pressed.

"Nar; every 'undred years or so."

"How old are you?" Victor asked before he could stop himself.

"Me? Three 'undred and some." Tronk shrugged, his metal pauldrons scrapping noisily against his breastplate with the movement.

"Damn." Victor nodded, figuring it made sense. If Rellia was sixty or so and Tier Five, the high-tier people in Coloss must be quite a lot older. Then he thought about his own rather meteoric rise and emended his estimation—it would take someone centuries unless they had high Energy affinity. Putting his thoughts together like that, he gave Valla an appraising look, really consciously appreciating her accomplishment for the first time; she had to be one of the youngest Tier Five people on all of Fanwath. Even Lam was near twice her age.

"Tronk, where are all the soldiers?" Valla asked, and Victor realized she'd made a good point; they'd hardly passed anyone as they traversed the citadel, only a scurrying servant here or there, usually laden with some sort of burden like heavy-looking baskets or laundry.

Tronk just shrugged and didn't offer any sort of reply; instead, he reached toward a smooth spot on the right-side door, resting his palm on the metal. With a shimmer and a click, the Energy barrier faded away, and the door popped ajar by a fraction of an inch. A wash of powerful Energy seemed to flow through that tiny crack in the doorway, and Victor's mouth filled with saliva as his body began to gravitate toward the door.

Valla made a small sound, like a gasp and a cry, and she rushed past him, reaching for the edge of the door, clearly intending to pull it wide, but Tronk reached down and grabbed hold of her wrist. "Nar, little blue one. Let the big man in first, and if there's time, I'll let ya cultivate for a while in there." His voice was calm and rumbled out of his big chest pleasantly, but Victor noticed that Valla had stopped short at his touch, and she nodded quickly, visibly battling with herself as she backed away from the door.

"In ya go, titan-blood," Tronk said, nodding to Victor.

"Titan-blood?" Victor had gained control of himself pretty easily while he watched Valla struggle, and now he stood before the door, basking in the rich Energy but wanting to know what Tronk knew of his bloodline.

"Yar, Warlord was excited to see ya in the arena when yer blood woke up. Reminded him o' the old Degh, the way we was afore our Ancestor Stone was busted an' Horc killed the wyrm at the center o' the Degh mountains." As he spoke, the big man's words were thick with emotion, and Victor felt a sadness—a loss—emanating from him that nearly made his eyes well up. Tronk's heavy lips curled down toward his prodigious chin, and Victor could see he was reliving some memory or another and that it was painful to him.

"Your people aren't what they once were?" Valla asked; apparently, she'd acclimated to the rich Energy in the air enough to speak—that, or Tronk's words had affected her, too.

"That's puttin' it light. Nar, we used to rule this world, we Degh. Long afore my time, though. 'Tis fine, though. I'm good and tough. Good enough." He shrugged and nodded as though he'd just talked himself into something.

"But the Warlord remembers how things were back then?" Victor glanced at Valla skeptically. "How old is he?"

"Dunno. Thousands o' years, though. Don't think any in Coloss are older." Tronk rapped his huge knuckles against the metal of the door and pulled it open a couple of feet. "In ya go now, titan-blood. Make us proud."

Victor nodded and gave Valla a quick glance.

"Go on," she urged. And Victor stepped into the thick Energy. As he looked about, taking in the chamber, he heard the massive door click shut behind him and felt the buzz of the Energy field coming back to life, sealing it tight. The room was shaped like the inside of a stone ball. The only part that wasn't curved was where the tall metal doors met the concave walls and ceiling. Steps rose from the base of the door up to a stone pedestal that sat in the middle of the spherical chamber.

As he slowly climbed the—human-sized—steps, Victor studied the walls, noting that thousands of little rune-inscribed bronze discs were mounted into the stone. To him, they looked like caps, as though they covered something. "Like maybe whatever all this Energy is coming from," Victor said, nodding to himself as he reached the pedestal. Standing there, inside the round room, he could feel the waves of Energy washing over him, coming from every direction.

The top of the spherical chamber was probably ten feet over his head, and the walls were just as far away; the pedestal put him dead in the middle of the space. "Huh. Maybe I'll sit down," Victor muttered, dropping down and putting himself into a lotus position on the stone platform. He took the jar containing the spinefiend heart out of his storage ring and set it on the floor before him, then he rested his hands on his knees and took several deep breaths, savoring the rich flow of Energy in the air.

"I wonder how fast I could level my Core if I sat in a place like this all the time? I wonder how hard it would be to make a space like this. I bet all those bronze discs have natural treasures under them." Suddenly Victor wondered if Tronk was wrong about the Warlord being okay with him using the cultivation chamber. What if he found out and flew there to yank Victor out and smash him like a bug? "Better get this going while I still can." Victor chuckled, then he built his pattern for Berserk, took a deep breath, and allowed his rage-attuned Energy to populate his pathways.

15

ANCESTORS

Victor felt the rage smoldering in his pathways, felt it surging through his veins with each *thump* of his mighty heart. He sat hunched over the little jar, his great fists clenching and unclenching as he heaved in and out each furious breath. Slowly, with a tremendous push of his will, he brought himself under control; he slowed his breathing and gradually relaxed his straining, bunched muscles.

"Hmm," his voice rumbled forth from his enormous chest, "let's see here." He picked up the jar, and his lips pulled back from his straight, white teeth as he felt its warmth. Victor grasped the top of the jar and twisted it loose, breaking the waxen seal. Suddenly the scent of copper, of bloody meat, wafted into his nostrils, and his grin widened.

Victor tilted the jar into his mouth, felt the warm hunk of tangy flesh fall into his mouth, and with zeal he began to chew the tough meat into pulp, savoring each squelching burst of hot, coppery liquid that drenched his tongue and rolled down the back of his throat. When he finally swallowed the last bit, Victor grunted, looking around the room in his red-haze-filtered vision, wondering what was supposed to happen.

For a moment, he forgot where he was, forgot why he'd gone berserk, and nearly let the rage slide out of his pathways and back into his Core, but then something happened. He felt a knot in his stomach, then a searing, white-hot pain, and he looked to the ceiling of the strange round room and screamed. Fire spread through his body like an eruption, and before his long ululating cry wound down, Victor fell back, his massive shoulders thumping against the stone of the pedestal—his vision went dark, and his consciousness slipped away.

Tenecoalt crouched among the rough-barked boles of the trees, peering down into a lush, verdant vale, the yellow orb of the Sun God hot and heavy in the air, provoking the moisture of the dense plant life and damp soil to rise in palpable, steamy waves. Tenecoalt loved it. He savored the heat, the humidity on his painted flesh, as he watched the green-scaled wyrm feasting. What a creature! What a worthy opponent! Tenecoalt felt his heart thump in anticipation; here was a beast deserving of his ancestors' attention.

He gripped his macuahuitl, newly crafted from the star metal he'd won from the clutches of a winged, lightning-riding stranger. So many strange men and creatures had been trespassing on his people's lands these last hundred years. So many men and creatures that had fallen to the might of the Quinametzin! He grinned savagely, eyes still tracking the mighty green monster below. How easily it had killed the powerful saber-clawed bear! "That was my heart to claim," Tenecoalt grumbled.

Moving through the trees, between the thick-leaved plants, he crept forward, a huge, white-clay-covered wraith. This fight would bring his ancestors to him; it would be a battle worthy of tales in the Ghost Lands. He glided down the slope, through the last of the trees, charging over the grassy slope toward his quarry. As his stride lengthened and he lifted his macuahuitl into the air, he threw off all pretense of stealth and howled a mighty war cry, flying toward the tremendous reptile's flank.

Tenecoalt was large for a Quinametzin, often towering head and shoulders over his brethren, but even his mighty frame seemed insignificant in the face of the enormous green wyrm as it whirled to confront his charge. The monstrosity was longer than a tall tree, thicker than five cave bears, with four legs, each big and heavy enough to smash a giant like Tenecoalt into the springy loam. It was dark green along its spine-covered back, but the scales faded to pale yellow where its prodigious belly dragged in the grass.

It was toward the low, hanging gut that Tenecoalt had meant to make his first strike, but he'd underestimated the speed of the mighty creature. It whirled, trampling the ground and whipping its long, deadly tail behind it as the monster brought its toothy maw to bear on him. Each of its hundred yellow-white fangs was as long as a spear, and they showered him with red-tinged saliva as they clamped shut, snapping the air with a thunderous crack.

The bite had been meant for Tenecoalt, aimed to part his top half from the bottom, but he was faster than that, more crafty, too. He slid under the monster's chin, burst up from the ground, exploding into the air like a springing, fangmaw fish, and dragged his impossibly sharp, unfathomably heavy macuahuitl along the scaly neck of the wyrm, pulling away scales, raking the flesh beneath them, and eliciting a furious roar from the monstrosity, so loud it shook the leaves from the nearby trees.

The wyrm bucked and thrashed, trying to twist into a position where it could bite at him again, but Tenecoalt was knocked aside by its surging shoulder, thrown briefly out of reach. He tumbled over the hot, damp grass and leapt to his feet, bellowing his own roar of challenge. He'd drawn first blood! "Come to me, Ancestors!" he screamed, charging toward the great serpent, rushing headlong at the jaws that would spell certain doom for him should they close over his mighty frame.

"Camaxtli hears your cry, warrior! Take my speed!" Suddenly, silver-white Energy bloomed around Tenecoalt, and he felt his arms and bones strain to contain the power. Where before he charged, now he flew over the grass, a comet, streaking too fast for the wyrm to track.

Tenecoalt hacked a terrible gash in its left foreleg as he flew by, leaving a trail of ripped, broken grass in his wake. Then, as he streaked along the length of the great beast, he smashed his dark, glinting macuahuitl into the wyrm's flank, dragging it for twenty lightning-laced steps before his surge of speed wore off and he had to roll away from the thrashing monster.

Tenecoalt tumbled through the grass, his last burst of Camaxtli's speed sending him flopping away from the wounded terror. He'd parted its scales and flesh, leaving a terrible wound that leaked gouts of gore with each of the monster's frenzied, writhing rolls; it was still trying to smash him, unaware that he'd rolled free.

Tenecoalt straightened up, and the wyrm caught sight of him. It ceased its flopping, rolling fury and stood, staring straight at him. Suddenly a deep, grating voice echoed through the vale. "Worm. Maggot! You dare to strike at the great Tu'vashele'kha'zat? Savor the bite you've taken—it will be your last!"

Tenecoalt held up his bloody macuahuitl and howled at the Sun, his deep, powerful voice ululating through the vale. Then he charged and again called on his ancestors, "Join me, Ancient Ones! Let us slay this boastful snake!"

He didn't let fear or panic enter his heart as he neared the monstrous creature—his ancestors didn't come to the aid of weaklings. As he drew close, his feet began to squelch in the hot-blood-covered grass, and he knew his ancestors would come or they wouldn't; either way, he was going to drive his macuahuitl into the wyrm's toothy snout.

The monster roared at him, hot breath billowing out over the meadow, ropy strings of bloody saliva accompanying the terrible sound. Still, Tenecoalt charged headlong into it, a grimace of determination on his face. The wyrm charged, Tenecoalt leapt, and then the sound he'd been hoping for came into his mind. "I am Guatamoc! Take my strength!"

An explosion of hot, red Energy erupted at Tenecoalt's Core, and he screamed in fury, pain, and exultation as his body stretched and his bones cracked. As he came down from his leap, he landed in front of the great wyrm with a thunderous crash, and the creature snapped its maw, aiming to remove his leg from his body. Tenecoalt pushed one mighty hand against its snout, holding it back just an inch from his flesh, and the wyrm's teeth clacked together with another powerful crack.

"I am not a snack for a slithering snake!" he roared, no longer having to look up at the monster but rather down. He hacked his macuahuitl, now tiny in his hand but still heavy, sharp, and more deadly than any weapon born of nature, into the wyrm's head and neck over and over. He drove its full length into the monster's flesh, ripping and shattering scales, pulling out hunks of meat and tendon with each stabbing, hacking blow.

"Ancestors! Savor the blood of our foe!" he screamed as he fought off the wyrm's thrashing, bucking attempts to get past his guard, to bite him, to claw at him, to whip its mighty tail into him. Tenecoalt stood firm, ducking, weaving, and fending off the beast with his free hand while he delivered wound after wound, drenching himself in wyrm blood.

As the monster grew tired and weak, he held it down with a gigantic knee on its snout and punched his star-metal-studded weapon through its eyes and then into its neck, twisting and yanking it out with great bloody strands of flesh.

When the wyrm lay still, and Tenecoalt stood exhausted next to its enormous head, he realized his ancestor's strength had left him long before he'd finished his bloody work. Still, it had been enough. He'd bested the monster with his skill; all he'd needed was Guatamoc's might to even the scales. He heaved an exhausted breath, lifted his bloody macuahuitl to the Sun, and screamed his victory into the sky, letting all know that the Quinametzin once again reigned supreme in this part of the jungle.

He stood, heaving for breath, clothed only in blood-caked clay, no longer white but pinkish red. It wasn't time to rest, though; he owed his ancestors tribute. Now it was time to find the beast's heart; he'd eat some, but the rest he would burn and send to the Ghost Lands to strengthen his ancestors so they might win more battles in those strange climes. "Thank you, Guatamoc and Camaxtli!" he breathed, moving to the wyrm's flank and looking for the best place to begin his bloody work.

* * *

Victor groaned and rolled to his side. He felt as though he'd been run over by a bus, a stark contrast to how he'd felt the last time he'd advanced his racial bloodline. Either the heart was a harsher catalyst or the chamber he was in, speeding his recovery, hadn't allowed him to convalesce as thoroughly. He sat up, rubbing at his eyes. In his dulled mental state, he felt as if he had something in them, but then he realized a System message was obscuring his view.

"Let's see here," he muttered, trying to focus on the weird floating text.

*****Congratulations! You have gained a new feat: Ancestral Bond.*****

*****Ancestral Bond: Your connection to your titanic bloodline has grown robust—like the Quinametzin primogenitors from which you trace your lineage, you have a deep connection to your ancestors. Should they be pleased with your efforts, and should your need be great, you may call on them, and they may come to your aid.*****

*****Congratulations! You've learned a new spell: Honor the Spirits, Improved.*****

*****Honor the Spirits, Improved: You understand, instinctually, what prizes from your conquered foes will please your Ancestral Spirits. With an effort of will, you can cause your Energy to devour your sacrifice, sending it to the Spirit Plane, where your Ancestors will consume it to grow in power. Energy Cost: 1000. Cooldown: Very Long.*****

"Uh," Victor grunted. "That's cool . . ." As he spoke, reading over the messages, Victor's mind wandered back to his vision, and his eyes bugged out. "Holy shit!" he breathed, remembering how it had felt to be Tenecoalt as his ancestors flooded him with power. "Fucking A!"

Victor wasn't sure they'd be so generous with him; he'd done nothing to earn their love so far, but somehow, he knew that if he worked at it, if he honored them, those spirits would come to him, too. They'd help him destroy his enemies. While he mulled it over and dismissed the System message, Victor's eyes fell on his hands, and he did a double take. "What the fuck?"

They were still his, for sure, but they looked different. The skin was darkly tanned, as always, but it had a more robust tint to it, a golden brownness that exuded vibrant strength. His fingers looked leaner, stronger, his nails like perfect, stone-hard pearls at the ends of them. He flexed his fists and felt as if he could smash stones in them.

He let his eyes run up his arms and noticed similar changes; his muscles and veins stood out beneath his robust, supple skin, and then he realized something: his scars were gone—every one of them. He stood up in a fluid, graceful motion and smiled at how pain-free he was. Whatever aches or exhaustion he'd felt upon waking up were gone. Looking around the little chamber, he noted his perspective had changed; he'd grown again.

Once leery of becoming "too big," Victor realized he didn't feel that way anymore. Either his experience with the Degh or his connection to his ancestors had altered that perspective—he felt good about it. "Let's see," he said, calling up his status sheet.

Status			
Name:	Victor Sandoval		
Race:	Human (Quinametzin Bloodline): Advanced 1		
Class:	Spirit Carver: Epic		
Level:	36		
Core:	Spirit Class: Improved 1		
Energy Affinity:	3.1, Fear 9.4, Rage 9.1, Inspiration 7.4	Energy:	3402/3402
Strength:	135	Vitality:	150
Dexterity:	40	Agility:	63
Intelligence:	32	Will:	341
Points Available:	0		
Titles & Feats:	Titanic Rage, Ancestral Bond, Flame-Touched		

"Whoa, advanced," he said, resting his hand on Lifedrinker, unconsciously covering his chatting with himself by directing his words toward her. "That means I gained . . ." He counted on his fingers. "Six ranks? Hell yeah!"

He rested his hand on his chest. "Gorz," he asked, "how tall am I now?" No response was forthcoming, so Victor fished the amulet from his shirt and held it in his hand. It was warm where it had been resting against his chest, but he couldn't feel anything else coming from it. "Gorz?" he tried again, and suddenly a spike of unreasonable panic jolted his heart. Unreasonable because he'd hardly spoken to the spirit fragment over the last few months. As he realized this, his panic turned to hot shame, and he put the amulet back around his neck.

"I don't know what's happening with you, Gorz, buddy. If you're gone, I hope you went to a better place, back to your whole self, even. If not, I'm going to ask an Artificer how I can help you." Victor noted a new resonance to his voice, a deeper register, and he shook his head, wondering just how much he'd changed.

He walked over to the big metal doors, reaching a hand toward them, feeling the hum of Energy still holding them sealed shut. He pushed against the left one, the one Tronk had opened for him, but it didn't budge. Not knowing what else to do, Victor rapped his knuckles against the metal, smiling at how it echoed and reverberated through the charged metal.

Almost immediately, he felt the Energy field fall away, and then the door clicked, and Tronk pulled it wide, looking into the room with his eyes squinted against the brightness. For the first time, Victor realized he'd never seen any source for the illumination. It seemed to be coming from the stone itself, and he wondered if it was a by-product of all the Energy sources stored in the cultivation chamber.

"Titan-blood. I feel greater strength within ya; yer aura stands out, even as we bask in the flow from the chamber." Tronk stepped aside, and Victor stepped out, finally laying eyes on Valla; she'd hung back in the shadow of the giant.

"Ancestors, Victor. You're up to Tronk's shoulder now."

"Aye, big fer someone who ain't a Degh."

Victor looked at Tronk, then Valla, and his heart began to thump as he realized she was right. She'd always been smaller than he, but now her head barely came to his stomach, and Tronk, well, Tronk was gigantic, and Victor a lot smaller—Valla had been exaggerating. Still, his perspective had shifted quite a lot. "Shit, man. I already had a hard time fitting through doorways back on Fanwath," he groused.

"Good luck getting comfortable in a normal bed," Valla snorted.

"All right, all right. How long was I in there?"

"Maybe an hour or two? Great Mother, Victor! You look like a . . . like you've been cut from marble—no, bronze. Well, I mean, you don't look like metal, but Old Bones, you look supernatural!"

"Valla! Did you just cuss at me twice in one sentence? I'll report you to Rellia; she'll need to wash that mouth out with soap."

Valla's mouth fell open, and her eyes widened, but then they narrowed, and she smiled. "Actually, that was two sentences, and if you think that was bad, you should hear how Rellia speaks!"

Tronk yawned hugely and grunted, rubbing at the top of his head, and Victor turned to him. "What should we do now, Tronk? We still have some time before we have to see the Warlord?"

"Nar, not too much. Better stick 'round the citadel. Your wee blue friend want to try the chamber?" Tronk turned to Valla and pointed toward the still open door.

"I . . . sure, I would. When will I get another chance like that?" She started toward the open door.

"If ya stay 'round Coloss fer a while, ya might get his permission to use it more often. If'n titan-blood here agrees to the Warlord's terms . . ."

"Terms?" Victor asked, his voice rising in surprise.

"Yar, he said sommat 'bout you acceptin' the champion prize—to fight in the Gazra's Day Tournament. Said I might hafta watch over ya fer a month or more." Tronk spoke flatly and shrugged as though he weren't dropping something of a bombshell. Valla paused at the doorway then looked back at Victor, and she, too, shrugged.

"We wanted more prize tokens, Victor, and I wanted to be here long enough to put that she-wolf in her place."

"Oh man," he said, reaching up to run his hand through his hair, and maddeningly, the only thought that came to his mind and out of his mouth was, "I need a haircut."

16

A SLEEPING GIANT

Ah! Victor! The champion of the lower-tier tourney, everyone!" The War-lord's words held a tint of amusement that bordered on scorn, at least in Victor's mind, and he had a hard time finding a friendly expression as he strode toward the dais. Only the people mingling nearby bothered to turn at the Warlord's words, halting their conversations long enough to observe the minor spectacle.

"He's a big one for a Deshi," one of the scantily-clad Vesh women hanging about near the Warlord's thronelike chair said, her lips curling into a seductive smile, exposing fangs that complemented her lupine eyes and long black claws.

"Not a Deshi, Tawnla, not a Deshi," the Warlord said, holding up a hand as though to push the words back into the woman's mouth. "No, Victor is a man from another world entirely, and his bloodline is quite potent, as you'd know if you'd managed to look away from your cup of wine during his match!"

Victor stood before the dais, dozens of eyes on him, but hundreds of others seemed utterly unaware or uncaring of his arrival, which was fine by him. Valla and Tronk stood back near one of the refreshment tables, watching, he was sure, to see how this would play out. "Warlord," he said, sketching a half bow that would have been sloppy if his body were capable of ungraceful movements.

It seemed the more he advanced his racial traits, the more palpable were the effects of his superhuman attributes. He'd noticed it before as he pro-gressed, feeling stronger, healthier, his fingers more nimble, but this latest advancement was the most tangible. He wondered if there were certain "hard caps" on attributes governed by a person's racial advancement.

Though Victor's strength and agility were the same after his ordeal in the cultivation chamber, he felt significantly more potent and agile. More than that, he felt sharper—nuances of expression and the repercussions of his words were more obvious. He still felt like himself, but it was more like his average, his baseline, was what his most inspired moments used to be.

"I welcome you, Victor . . . Tell me, from whence do you hail? Have you a surname or a title you'd like me to use?"

"I . . . I have a few, Warlord, but I'd be happy to simply be known as Victor of Tucson, the place of my birth." Victor wasn't sure why he said those words, but he imagined it had something to do with nostalgia; he knew he'd likely never go back to Tucson, but it felt good to remind himself and the universe that it existed and that he had roots none of them would or could ever understand.

"You heard it! Victor of Tucson! What a show you put on for us today! I must say, you appear different to me. Have you already partaken of your grand prize?"

Victor breathed deeply, contemplating his words as he looked around the crowded hall. Musicians played loudly from a stage off to his left, and people mingled and danced in every direction—the Warlord's dais stood at the center of the room, though it was hardly the center of attention. To his right, where Valla and Tronk stood, were rows and rows of tables laden with meats, fruits, steaming platters, magically heated pots and trays, and piles of pastries. His stomach rumbled as he cleared his throat to reply.

"I did, thank you. I used your cultivation chamber at Tronk's insistence."

He smiled, baring his perfect straight white teeth, devoid of cavities or fillings and strong enough to bite through a plank of oak. "Oho? Tronk's been known to take liberties with my chamber, but this is a new level! Ha! Well, Victor, how would you like to have access to that chamber for another month? I'd let you use it whenever you found it convenient."

"For a month, Warlord?" Victor asked, stepping a bit closer. He noticed the Warlord didn't have any guards, didn't seem to mind people crowding around his chair, and didn't shy away but rather leaned forward as Victor approached.

"That's right. You won the tournament, so you've gained a wild card entry into the Gazra's Day Tournament next month. Naturally, you'd be competing under my flag, and I can't have you wanting for training opportunities."

"I'm not familiar with the tournaments or, well, any of the customs in this world, sir," Victor said, rubbing his chin. "Is it different from today's tournament?"

"Yes! It's grander, Victor, and champions from the twelve great cities will compete. You'll represent Coloss alongside Yabbo, our current champion. Because we're hosting, Coloss gets two spots on the ladder."

"Yabbo? I didn't see him today."

"You must not have watched the mid-tier tournament, hmm? Oh, I didn't mention that the Gazra's Day tournament is mid-tier only. You'll need to work on your level a bit, but I think you'll do well, Victor." The Warlord spoke offhandedly as though it wasn't a big deal at all, but Victor's throat caught mid-swallow.

"Ahem." Victor glanced at the people watching the conversation—a dozen or so Vesh of varying sizes and animalistic natures. He saw how their eyes gleamed hungrily though their lips smiled pleasantly. "I'm yet to reach Tier Four, Warlord."

"True, but you're so strong for your level, Victor! Think of the glory you'll achieve for Coloss should you win a match or two! I'm sure you can make your way to Tier Five before the tournament, don't you think? I'll give you access to my chamber, and you can train with Yabbo. Why, I heard you're signed up for a monster hunt leaving in two days! Surely you'll gain a level or two fighting desert wyrms!"

"I . . ." Victor shrugged—it wouldn't hurt to act as if he was willing to go along with things for now; if he found a way off this world before the tournament and wanted to bail, at least he'd have some time to use the Warlord's facilities. "I'll give it a try. If I don't make it to Tier Five, I'll be disqualified?"

"No, no, no," the Warlord chuckled, "I'll sign an exception. Trust me, Victor, you're going to bring glory to Coloss, even if you're a bit under level. That reminds me! Doesn't Black owe you a prize?" He spoke to the gathered nobility, his voice suddenly cutting through the noise of the hall. "Black!" The word, spoken like a summons, echoed through the great room, and Victor suddenly felt an inkling of the aura the Warlord was holding in check—a power so dense, so concentrated, he felt as if he were standing next to a bomb primed to explode.

The Warlord looked like a handsome human, though a strange one with white feathers for hair, even his eyebrows. His wings were folded and hung behind him, giving the illusion of a chair back, but as the Warlord shifted, Victor saw that his "throne" was a fancy stool. His white feathery eyebrows narrowed as his summons went unanswered for a few seconds, but then the smile returned to his lips as he heard something Victor could not. "He comes." The Warlord nodded and motioned for Victor to step to the side.

Victor turned toward the wide-open double doors, past the throng of servants lingering about with trays of refreshments to offer guests as they arrived. A few heartbeats passed, and then heavy clanking steps echoed over the hubbub of the crowd, and a familiar figure loomed into view, stomping through the open doors—the giant Degh, still clad in black plate armor, though his head was now uncovered.

Black was a big Degh, though not any larger than his son, and he didn't seem so intimidating to Victor—not after he'd cowered behind his great shield in the face of Victor's rage in the arena. A part of Victor's mind, the more rational, intelligent part, knew the War Captain likely hadn't wanted to fight him, not because he was afraid, but because he didn't want to anger the Warlord any further. Still, Victor stood tall and watched him approach impassively.

"Warlord," Black rumbled, coming to a stop in front of the dais next to Victor and bowing his head.

"War Captain. Thank you for being so prompt. My new charge, Victor of Tucson, is weary and would like to retire soon. Have you some words for him?" The Warlord wore a sardonic smile and shifted on his chair to lean sideways, crossing one long, silk-clad leg over the other.

"Aye," Black said, pivoting to face Victor, looking down from atop his boulder-like armored chest. "Congratulations on your victory today. I'm sorry I intervened, but I have only one son and am willing to pay the consequences for keeping him alive."

"Thank you," Victor said, then he glanced around, noting that the hall had grown far quieter than when he'd been speaking to the Warlord alone. He raised his voice, speaking so that more people could easily hear, and said, "I can't blame you. I'd do just about anything for the people I love, too."

"Well said!" the Warlord crowed, clapping his hands together. Victor was startled as the sound that emerged from their contact was more a *boom* than a clap, and the spell of silence that seemed to have hung over the hall was dispersed—people again began to talk and laugh, and the music took on new life, increasing in intensity. "And Victor's prize?" the Warlord asked, more quietly, his words directed at Black.

"Yes." Black produced a polished wooden box engraved with silvery runes. It was about the size of a shoebox, and he held it out on one giant palm toward Victor. War Captain Black was not a young man; he had gray and black hair, grizzled stubble, and wrinkled extra skin sagging around his pale brown eyes, but he managed a smile that looked genuine as Victor reached toward his offered prize. "I learned, during the tournament, that you have a Spirit Core. This is a prize that sat in my family's vaults for generations, waiting for a scion who could make use of it."

As Victor took the box, heavier than it looked, into his hands, the Warlord said, "Tell us more, Black. What's this ancient treasure, and what's it got to do with a Spirit Core? Surely not some dusty heirloom you found convenient to foist off on this newcomer?"

"Nay, Warlord, not a foisting, but an exceptional prize. Can ya nay feel the Energy coming from that shielded box?" As the War Captain spoke, Victor knew his words were true; he felt a tingling sensation in the palms of his hands where they touched the wood. They itched with it, and he felt a deep urge to rip the box open, exposing the contents. He knew that if his will weren't so strong, he'd struggle to resist the temptation. As it was, though, Victor held the box close and looked to the Warlord, listening to his conversation with Black.

"I feel it, aye. Okay, enough mysteries. Tell us!"

"'Tis a fragment of one of my ancestors. A piece of a mighty ancestor's soul—a shard of the Ancestor Stone itself. Silent these many generations, waiting for one of our kind to be able to commune with it. We've not had a Spirit Core among us since the fracture, and the Degh wise ones fear we never will. Now, here comes a man with titan blood in his veins, with a mighty connection to the spirit realm, and here I am, beholden to him. Some in my clan are angry, but the wise ones are in agreement: it's not chance that Victor came here; our ancestor awaits him."

The hall had grown quiet again, and Victor got the impression that Black rarely spoke at such length. He felt emotions warring within him at the giant's words—honor, pride, sympathy, sorrow, even shame. Why shame, he wondered, but he knew the answer: was he really deserving? "I . . . Thank you, War Captain," he said as the eyes in the hall fell on him.

"Well said! A prize well given and well received! Let us rejoice! Victor," the Warlord said, his words breaking the spell in the hall once again, signaling a return to revelry, "I trust you'll allow me to provide accommodations for you and your companion? Stay as long as you like, but when you're ready to retire, Tronk will show you to your quarters. Think long and hard about my offer; I'd love to help you improve over the next few weeks and do Coloss proud on Gazra's Day."

"Thank you, Warlord," Victor said, bending at the waist ever so slightly, still clutching the rune-covered box to his chest. The Warlord smiled and then turned to speak to one of the women standing nearby, and though he was only a few feet away, Victor couldn't make out his words—he'd been dismissed.

"Victor, might I have another word?" Black asked, turning toward him.

"Of course . . ."

"Follow me to the refreshments? My throat is parched."

"Sure." Victor followed the War Captain through the crowd to one of the tables where pitchers of icy juice and bottles of strangely labeled alcohol were gathered. He saw Valla and Tronk move toward them, but they hung back, perhaps intuiting that he and War Captain Black had more words to exchange.

"Do you understand what I've given you?" Black asked as he picked up a large crystal goblet and poured the shimmering green contents of a bottle into it.

"Sort of—I've had some experience with spirit shards in the past."

"This is likely different," the giant rumbled. "This shard is taken from a massive crystal where once our people's great ancestors continued their existence after living in this world. The shard in that box isn't a tiny fragment of my ancestor's soul, but rather most of it—a nearly complete being that lies dormant, waiting for the touch of a Spirit Caster. But not just any Spirit Caster—one with the right bloodline. I believe he'll speak to you."

"What happened to your, um, Ancestor Stone?"

"It's a long story and not one I'll enjoy reliving in this crowded hall. Come to me in my estate, sit with me and drink, tell me about what my ancestor says to you, and I'll share what I know. To be honest, Victor, if you are able to speak to my ancestor in that shard, then you'll probably know more about the fracture than I do."

"Are Spirit Casters really so rare here?"

"Among the Degh, aye—unheard of for a hundred generations. There are some among the Vesh, but our ancestors won't speak to them, won't even stir."

"If I come to you," Victor said, reaching for a goblet and a pitcher of something that looked like fruit punch, "to share what I've learned, can you please ask your more . . . enthusiastic supporters to not attack me?"

"Aye. I'll put the word out. You'll have my protection going forward. I wish I could tell you more about the shard. I'm not sure how you're supposed to reach my ancestor, but I hope it will be clear to you as a Spirit Caster. I hope my ancestor will have much to teach you." The giant lifted his goblet, drained the contents, set it on the table, and reached out to clap Victor on the shoulder. "I'm off—not in the mood to celebrate tonight, but perhaps I will be down the road. Perhaps with my ancestor's aid, you'll have something good to share with me."

He didn't wait for Victor to respond; War Captain Black stomped out of the hall, walking directly through groups of Vesh and Degh, interrupting conversations and ignoring greetings and curses alike. Victor felt a presence at his elbow and looked down to see Valla. "Hey," he said, smiling.

"That went well. What an interesting encounter!"

"Yeah, did you hear about the tournament? About the Warlord's invitation to stay here?"

"Yes. Tronk said the invitation extends to us both, me being your 'companion' and all." Valla wore a smirk, and Victor smiled along with her.

"At least you won't need to worry about Blue messing with you if you're staying in the Warlord's citadel."

"What makes you think I don't want him 'messing' with me?" Valla asked with a wink, and Victor's mouth fell open.

"I . . ."

"When d'ya want Tronk to show yer rooms to ya?" a voice rumbled behind him, and Victor whirled to see the giant, armor-clad man taking a bite from a huge slab of meat, still attached to a bone.

"Can we go now?" Valla asked, and Victor couldn't blame her; it had been a long day, and he was dog-tired.

"Yeah. That good with you, Tronk?"

"Yar." Tronk turned and started ambling toward the big doorway, and Victor and Valla followed in his wake. They traversed hallways that were a good deal more narrow than the ones they'd used to get to the cultivation chamber but still plenty large for Tronk's easy passage. The hall where the celebration was being held was near the ground floor, so their journey included several flights of stone stairs.

These more narrow hallways were often carpeted down the center, and Victor caught himself trying to estimate the size of the carpet rolls needed to furnish a place like the Warlord's citadel. "They've got to be enchanted," he said, imagining the need to replace them every few years and the enormous undertaking it would be.

"What?" Valla asked.

"The carpets—I mean, they've got to be enchanted to self-repair, don't you think? Can you imagine replacing miles and miles of carpeting?"

"Yar, they are," Tronk rumbled from up ahead. Valla chuckled, shaking her head.

"You think of strange things, Victor. Are you going to tell me about that box you're clutching to your chest? I heard Black's words when he presented it, but you act like you know more."

"I don't know more, but I feel more," Victor said with a shrug. "It's definitely something powerful, and I know I don't want to put it in a storage container; let's put it that way."

"What will you do with it?"

"Um, well, when we get to our rooms, I'm going to take it out of this box, for starters." He paused, thinking about it, gauging his excitement and measuring it against his exhaustion, and then said, "Yeah. I'm going to take it out of its box and go from there. I have a feeling I'll know what to do." Victor smiled and tucked the box under one arm so he could lower his other hand to give Valla's shoulder a nudge. "You don't expect me to wait around when I've got something this cool to check out, do you?"

17

A BARGAIN FOR ANSWERS

Tronk had shown him and Valla to their suite and then grumbled about being hungry as he walked off down the hallway. He hadn't said whether he'd come back or when, and Victor decided not to worry about it. Their rooms were simple but elegant, with high ceilings, large furniture, and plenty of space.

A central sitting area separated two bedrooms, each with a built-in bathing chamber. The floors and walls were appointed with polished marble, oil paintings, and thick carpets woven from fine materials. The balcony let in the light of the nearly full moon, exposing a view of an entire quarter of the city. The view alone ensured that no inn in the city could compete with the Warlord's guest accommodations. Victor opened the balcony doors and stepped outside.

He breathed deeply of the fresh, crisp air, then went back inside to sit on one of the long couches in the central room, staring at the box he'd set on the table when they'd first arrived—the box Black had given him. While not large enough for a Degh, the furniture was comfortable for Victor, and he wondered at that; was it too large for a person Valla's size or for Vesh? He couldn't ask her because she'd gone into her room and closed the door when they'd arrived, saying something about practicing a cultivation technique Tes had shown her.

He thought about what he was doing; should he get some sleep before he tackled the mystery of Black's gift? Victor laughed, thinking about himself hitting the pillow and how his mind would wander to the idea of an ancient giant ancestor waiting to speak to him through a magical soul shard. There was no way he'd be able to sleep. The next day wasn't going to be taxing, anyway; he and Valla were planning to go shopping and to speak with an Alchemist and an Artificer—maybe do some training if there was time.

Shrugging to himself, Victor pulled the box containing the spirit shard closer. There wasn't a lock on the box, but the sides of the lid had two brass circles, slightly indented on the edge, and when Victor pressed them both with his forefingers, it clicked and popped open. A wash of Energy, warm and vibrant, rolled out of the box, and Victor inhaled deeply, enjoying its feel as images of warm kitchens and family gatherings rushed through his mind.

As the feeling faded and the Energy pulse subsided, he studied the long jagged crystal resting on the box's padded black-velvet interior. It was about eight inches long, thick as his wrist at the base, tapering to a jagged point on the other end. The center of the crystal pulsed with dim pink light, and the left edge of the shard looked sharp enough to cut flesh. Victor tentatively reached into the box and grasped the shard with his left hand, careful to grip it around the smooth, rounded side and not to squeeze against that sharp edge.

The crystal wasn't warm, as Victor had expected. It felt cool in his palm and slightly rough where he'd thought it would be smooth. He held it closer to his eye, examining the faintly pink surface, and saw it was filled with tiny pores. He gently rubbed his thumb against it, feeling the bumps of the nearly microscopic holes and wondering what the whole crystal had looked like before it had been fractured. Was what he held a significant piece or just a tiny sliver of a massive stone?

"Well . . ." he said, wondering how to proceed but knowing in his gut that he needed to connect to it, to touch the crystal's Energy with his own. "Do I pull your Energy to me, or do I send my Energy into you? Does it matter?" Tentatively, Victor reached out with his will, trying to tug at the pink, pulsing heart of the crystal. The Energy was there, dense and powerful, and it slipped from his grasp like sand through a person's fingers. "All right, then. You want to see who you're dealing with first, hmm?"

Victor reached into his Core and pulled out a thread of inspiration-attuned Energy, ready to send it into the crystal, but then he had a second thought. Should he only use a part of his Core, or should he give this ancestor dwelling in the shard a fuller picture of himself? Victor tugged threads of rage and fear-attuned Energy into his pathways, winding them around his inspiration thread. Then, with the woven ribbon firmly held together with his will, he pushed it out through his pathways into the crystal.

Suddenly he felt a tug on his Energy, felt his Core abruptly surge, pushing more and more of it into his pathways as the threads became ribbons, became ropes, became flowing rivers of Energy. The crystal was no longer cool in his hand; it had grown warm and then uncomfortably hot as the pink Energy softly pulsing at the center grew brilliant, the radiant aura expanding like a halo at first, but then like an enormous bloom, filling Victor's vision and obscuring everything else.

Victor gripped the crystal with one hand and shielded his eyes with the other, trying to focus inwardly on his Core. He saw his Energy drawing low and readied his will, prepared to cut off the flow before he was drained dry. As if anticipating his intentions, though, the surge suddenly stopped, and the flood became a trickle, and he was left with nearly a quarter of his Energy intact. He was just about to look away from his Core when a deep voice rumbled nearby.

"Is it true? A scion at long last? You have a different feel about you, titan-blood. Your Energy is thick and rich with so many flavors—has so much changed?"

Victor opened his eyes to see that he sat in a strange featureless plane. Angles of light and shadow were the only hints of any structure, but sitting cross-legged in front of him was a being that didn't lack for substance; a giant, with a demeanor and hulking presence that put Black to shame, glowered down at him. He had dark skin covered with runic tattoos etched with bright turquoise, ochre, and emerald inks. His face was stern, with a prominent brow, an aquiline nose, and cheek and jawbones like etched granite.

The giant's eyes blazed with power, a bright pink that matched the Energy Victor had seen in the crystal. Again, the titan cleared his throat and rumbled, "Well? Will you speak, or are you dumbstruck?"

"Well, yeah, I guess I am a little bit—dumbstruck, I mean." Victor cleared his throat and then said, "I'm Victor."

"Victor. Not a name one in my clan would take. You're from one of the others, then, not a Stone Heart? The Black Sun? The Lake Lords?"

"Uh, none of the above. I'm not from your world. Are you aware of how long you've been without a visitor?"

"Time is different here, and I can feel . . . a separation." The giant scowled, his heavy black brows drawing together. "Where are my kin? My ancestors and brothers? My father and uncles? It's strange. Tell me, then, stranger, how come you to the Ancestor Stone? Why have my sons not removed your head?"

"Well, I guess you know less than Black thought you would. I have some . . . hard news for you."

"Go on, speak plainly." The giant leaned forward, his muscles rippling along his bare chest and midriff. It dawned on Victor that the giant was nearly naked, wearing a simple leather loincloth.

"Well, first of all, I'm new to this world. I'm from Fanwath and Earth before that. One of your descendants awarded me a shard with a powerful spirit. You see, a long time ago, thousands of years, your Ancestor Stone was shattered . . ."

"*Lies!*" the giant erupted, leaping to his feet, fury on his face. Victor scrambled up also, backing away and holding his hands out.

"I'm not lying! Can't you tell? Can't you feel that I'm not being deceptive? What good would it do me to lie about this?"

The giant paced back and forth, scowling, and Victor swore he could see tendrils of steam rising off his tattooed shoulders. "Continue your tale."

"Well, the Degh who gave me the shard said it was part of the Ancestor Stone, said that he and his people had lost the ability to connect to you through it, that since the shattering, none of them had been born with a Spirit Core."

The giant looked up from where he'd been pacing, brooding, his eyes on the strange, shapeless ground. When those pink, luminescent orbs focused on Victor's eyes, Victor gazed back, unblinking, unflinching. He had nothing but true words for the giant and wanted him to see that. "No Spirit Cores? For thousands of years?"

"A hundred generations, I think, is how he put it."

"Gods be good," the giant rumbled softly. "Could it be? Have I languished so long? How did the Stone fracture? I remember . . . I remember Bavarak . . . yes, it was Bavarak I last spoke to. Something about a war with the upstarts, the mutants from Ghol. Vesh, I believe they called themselves. Is that how it happened? Did the Vesh crack our Ancestor Stone?"

"I don't know." Victor held his hands out, palms up, as though to display his lack of an answer. "I can try to learn more—try to find answers for you."

"And what of you, Victor? Why come to me? Your blood feels strong; I sense a kinship. You're no giant, but you're no weakling, either. Do you seek knowledge?" The brooding giant sat again, a fluid motion in which he almost seemed to collapse as he sat on the floor, his long, powerful legs folding beneath him. Victor followed suit, sitting in front of him.

"Yes. I was pulled from my home, forced to fight, forced to learn what I could from enemies and friends, though few have had any clue about my talents—my bloodline. I need help. More and more, I'm faced with enemies whose power eclipses my own, whose intentions are less than kind. I need guidance if I'm going to survive the challenges before me." Victor sat back, staring at the giant, his mind torn between pride at his eloquent speech and shock . . . at his eloquent speech. Had he truly changed so much?

"Hmm," the giant rumbled, lifting a hand to his chin. "Do you speak true? You will help me to learn of my people's fate?"

"Yes." Victor nodded once, with conviction.

"If there is aught you can do to help, will you? I must know what happened to my people, why they're so cursed, and if they can be helped—if the damage can be repaired."

"I . . . I want to help you, but my time in this world is limited. I have people depending on me back on Fanwath." Victor faced the giant as he spoke, worried there might be another outburst, but the giant's only reaction was a deepening of his already prodigious frown.

"And me? You planned to take me with you from my homeworld?" His voice didn't betray any anger, but Victor could feel a hidden edge, like violence on the verge of erupting.

"I hadn't thought about that. I didn't know what to expect when I won the crystal. Now that I've met you, I wouldn't take you from your world if you don't want me to."

"Am I the last?" the giant asked, though the question didn't seem directed at Victor. He glanced up into the weird, shapeless space around them, and it looked as though his eyes were focused on something. Victor tried to follow his gaze but saw only the weird void.

"Victor, did you hear of any other shards? Are there others of us lingering in fragments of the Ancestor Stone?"

"I don't know. I can ask . . ."

"Very well, Victor. As a show of good faith, I'll answer any two questions you have about your growth, your nature, or your Core. If you return with more answers to my questions, I'll help you further. Agreed?"

"Agreed!" Victor's mouth blurted before his mind could think about it.

"Good. Speak your questions, then."

Victor didn't have to think about his first question—he'd been wondering it for a while now. "My bloodline leads back to my distant ancestors, a race of giants—titans—called Quinametzin. As I further my racial advancement, I seem to grow larger, but not truly giant like the Degh or the Quinametzin . . ." The giant opened his mouth to say something, but Victor hurriedly kept speaking.

"One aspect of my Core is rage. When I cast Berserk, using my rage-attuned Energy, I take on the aspect of my ancestors—I'm a true titan for a while. Is there any way for me to assume that aspect without my rage? Perhaps with a different Energy attunement, or none at all? Will I keep growing as I improve my racial bloodline?"

The giant stared at him for a moment after he'd stopped speaking, and finally, he rumbled, "Finished?"

"Yes."

"You tried to sneak more than one question into that one. I'll indulge you, but only because you seem an honest soul. There are spells that might ignite your bloodline, spells other than your Berserk. I might know one. As to your second question, the one you tried to sneak in, I'll indulge it because I don't have a good answer—I don't know. I've not heard of the Quinametzin, but I know titan blood is strong, and I feel it pulsing in your veins. You may eventually take the full form of your ancestors if you continue to evolve your race. You may not."

"Any chance you could . . ."

"Careful! One more I'll allow, Victor. When you return to me with answers, we can arrange a new bargain."

"Right. Um, before I ask my next question, I feel like I need to describe myself to you, what I've been doing with my levels and attributes, my spells and skills, and my Core. Would that be all right?"

"Go on," the giant rumbled, seeming to settle further into the ground, affecting a more comfortable, contemplative pose.

"Well, I've had a few different classes. I'm Level Thirty-Six, by the way. You see, it all started when I formed my Core out of rage-attuned Energy . . ." Victor spent the better part of an hour—well, what seemed like an hour—in that timeless place, describing his classes, his Core, his spells and skills, and how he'd spent most of his attribute points on will. The giant grunted every so often, listening and frowning, occasionally asking for clarification, especially when Victor described the effects of his spells.

When Victor finally finished, and the echoes of his words had faded away, the giant lifted his head and said, "An intriguing tale, Victor. You've done well for a man with little guidance. I would have been proud to have you in my clan. Tell me, then, what is a question I can answer for you?"

"Well," Victor sighed and shook his head, smiling ruefully, "this feels like a stupid question, but I'm banking on finding you some answers, hopefully, so we can speak and cooperate more fluidly."

"Go on!" the giant barked, clearly growing tired of the buildup.

"All right, all right. I want to know, what the hell should I do with my attribute points? The ones I get that I can allocate. I've been dumping them in will as several other people have advised—is that wise?"

"Truly? Do you ask such a simple question? Victor, you've learned the art of dominating your physical nature with the power of your will. Do you desire strength? You have it. Do you demand speed from your body? You have it! Such power was so very rare in my time; very few Spirit Casters had such control of their physical nature. Already, you've explained that your ability has doubled in potency—you are able to improve not one but two aspects of your physical nature with an effort of your will. Why would you not continue to refine that ability?

"Yes, Victor, should your class continue to grant you unallocated attribute points, you should put them into your will. Build it up so it towers like a monument of stubbornness, a fulcrum on which you can bend the nature of reality. Flesh and bone will rend and break before the might of your insubordinate desire."

"Thank you . . . Can I know your name, Ancestor?" Victor asked, deciding it was appropriate to honor the ancient spirit with the title.

"I am Khul Bach, founder of the Stone Heart Clan."

"Khul Bach? I've noticed the Degh I've met in Coloss don't use surnames . . ."

"*Coloss?*" Khul roared, erupting to his feet again. "That den of Vesh villainy?"

"Yeah, um, it's the only city I've visited so far." Victor stood up, taking a step back from the enraged giant.

"There are Degh in Coloss? Did we conquer them, then?"

"No. There's a Vesh in charge of Coloss, though he seems at peace with the Degh. His name is . . . " Victor struggled to remember the Warlord's name. Everyone referred to him as 'Warlord,' but he knew he'd heard his name a time or three. "Let's see, it's . . . Thor? Thorg? Thoa . . ."

"Thoargh!" Khul roared, spitting the word like a curse. "So the bastard has broken the clans? The upstart about whom Bavarak sought our counsel, our guidance to destroy . . ." Suddenly, Khul's face fell, and he seemed to slump. "Did we fail so miserably? Was it we who wrote our own doom?"

"I don't know, Khul, um, Mr. Bach . . ." Victor trailed off, his earlier brilliance with words dashed by his awkward tongue.

"Khul Bach, Victor. Use my whole name for respect—are your people so different?"

"No, not so different, just a little mix-up with the System's Language Integration. Listen, I'll get you more answers. I'll come back as soon as I can, all right?"

"Good. Yes. I must think on what you've told me. Pull your Energy back to yourself, Victor. You'll find very little time has passed on the material plane."

"Oh? All right, let me see here." Victor concentrated and reached out into the thick Energy hanging in the air and began to pull, tugging it toward himself, toward his pathways, and then, like water down a drain, it rushed into him, and when he opened his eyes, he was sitting alone. He'd sunk back into the couch cushions but didn't feel cramped; he almost felt rested.

The night was quiet, save a single dark blue bird that sat on the balcony railing, trilling a haunting song, something like, "*Ta-twee-ta-twee-ta-ta-ta-twee.*" When Victor stood up and walked toward the open doors, the bird spread its azure wings and whistled shrilly as it glided down toward the city, spiraling away from him on an invisible updraft. Victor watched it go, wondering what it was called.

He thought back to Khul Bach and their conversation. He thought about all the different threads that were starting to pull him in different directions in this new world, and he wondered what he would do. How could he possibly deal with so many things in a month or two?

18

A STROLL THROUGH COLOSS

Y ou will wait fer me?" Tronk asked, reluctant to leave Victor at the Alchemist's shop. It was near noon, the sun brilliant in the pale, faintly green-tinged sky, and Victor had suggested they kill two birds with one stone—he'd talk to the Alchemist about mixing up the rewards he'd won in the arena, and Tronk would take Valla to see Tes; she'd promised to show Valla a new spell that would utilize both of her affinities.

"Yeah, I'll wait here, Tronk. When you get back, we'll hit up an Artificer. Is that all right? No one's going to mess with me at some random Alchemist's shop. I'll stay inside."

"Yar. Sounds fine. I'll be back in less than an hour."

"You don't need to guide me, Tronk," Valla said, her fists on her hips, a look of annoyance on her face.

"Warlord said to keep both safe. Said Victor's foes might use you." Tronk shrugged and gestured with his hand for Valla to follow as he began to lumber up the street with his odd but fast rolling gait.

"Can't argue with that," Victor said, smiling at Valla. She huffed and turned to follow the giant, and Victor opened the door, stepping into the aromatic shop. The front end of the store was narrow, only a few feet separating the door from the counter. Behind the counter, though, rows of shelves lined with colorful bottles, wooden boxes, jars, tins, and little sacks filled a much bigger space.

"Welcome," said a Vesh woman with coppery skin, white hair, and a pleasant facial expression. Victor thought she was rather beautiful and would have thought she was human if not for the fact that her left arm was a sucker-covered tentacle, gently swishing a rag over the top of the counter.

"Thanks," he said, approaching her and digging through his ring for the two prizes from the arena. Victor took a deep breath and smiled; he hadn't expected such a heavy scent of cinnamon, and he wondered if it was from a potion or if the shopkeeper was cooking something in the back room. He set the jar and the gold foil package on the counter, and she leaned close, brows narrowing and her upturned little nose wiggling as she examined them.

"May I?" she asked, the tip of her tentacle arm hovering near the jar containing the crypt drake gall bladder.

"Sure." He watched as her tentacle gripped the jar and tilted it so the bottom faced her, and then she smiled.

"Ah! An arena prize? Are you that off-worlder everyone's talking about?"

"Oh, maybe. I'm Victor."

"Good to meet you! I'm Shouza. So, a crypt drake gall bladder, hmm? I can make the tincture you're looking for. It'll take me a few days. What's this other?" She set the jar down and picked up the foil-wrapped package. "Dense Energy! Should I leave the foil on?"

"I don't know if it matters—it's a rock wyrm magma horn. Whatever that is. It's supposed to . . ."

"Help with Core breakthroughs, aye. I can make the tincture from this at the same time—different equipment is required. Since you're providing the ingredients—well, the most expensive ones—I'll charge a nominal fee: a hundred beads each. Fair?"

"Well, it seems steep to me . . ."

"You can shop around if you want," Shouza said, setting the package down and shrugging, her earlier smile disappearing as she pressed her lips into a line. "Anything else I can do for you?"

"Well, hang on," Victor said, pushing the two prizes toward her, "I didn't say I wouldn't pay—it just feels like a lot to me. I'm not from around here, remember?"

"Oh, sure." Shouza's frown softened, and she scooped up the two packages in her tentacle, deftly gripping them both despite her lack of digits. "So, three days at the earliest. Okay?"

"Yeah, that's fine. I guess I'm going on a monster hunt tomorrow, so I'll probably be gone a little while." Victor sniffed deeply, savoring the aroma in the air, then let his eyes travel over the shelves, wondering what was in all those bottles, jars, vials, bags, canisters, and boxes. "Got anything you'd recommend I bring along on a monster hunt?"

"What are you hunting?" Shouza deftly deposited his prizes under the counter and then turned toward the shelves behind her.

"I'm not really sure; maybe some kind of wyrm? I think the Warlord mentioned that, though how he even knows about the hunt I'm signed up for, I have no idea."

"Wyrms are not to be trifled with. I hope you're with a strong company."

"Uh, Spears of the Sun or something like that . . ."

"I'm not familiar." Shouza wrinkled her nose again, but this time she didn't look annoyed, more perplexed. "I'd recommend something to help with poisonous fumes. Some of the wyrm species have glands that excrete clouds of gas." She turned and ran her tentacle along the shelves and added, "You can never go wrong with healing, especially proactive healing. Do you have a stock of regeneration potions?"

"Proactive healing? I have some healing potions I bought back in Gelica, er, a city in my homeworld." It felt strange calling Fanwath his homeworld, but Victor didn't want to overcomplicate the conversation.

"But not regeneration? It's hard to drink a healing potion if you've been disabled or if you're unconscious. Drink a regeneration potion before a fight, and if you're hurt within a few minutes, the effect will heal you."

"Really? How long will it last?"

"Depends on how much you're willing to pay." She walked farther back to the next row of shelves, scooped up several different potions, and brought them back to the counter. She set them down in a neat row, and once again, Victor was impressed by the dexterity of her long, flesh-toned, sucker-covered appendage. He tore his eyes away from it to look at the bottles—all smaller than a soft drink bottle but each shaped slightly differently, with variously colored glass and wildly different contents.

Shouza pointed to the furthest one to Victor's left, a dark blue corked vial, and said, "This one will heal terrible wounds but will only last in your system for around a minute. Should you be wounded after that, it will have no beneficial effect."

"So . . . when you say 'terrible wounds,' what are we talking about? Like, will it regrow limbs? Fix a smashed skull?"

"No, it will knit flesh and bone, but it will not resurrect you or regrow lost limbs. It's possible if you were just mostly dead . . . I mean, if your heart were pierced, but your spirit still clung to your body, the repair might save you—a ruined brain, though? Not likely."

"Do any of them regrow lost limbs?" Victor had wondered about that for a long while—he'd learned from conversations with Rellia, Thayla, and others that advancing one's race could mend a missing appendage, but he'd never seen anyone selling potions that could do it.

"Sure." Shouza's tentacle skipped over the next two potions and settled on a heavy crystal jar with a red, wax-sealed lid. The contents within looked like shimmering purple jam to Victor. "This one, if consumed, will remain potent for nearly an hour and will mend anything shy of a severed head. Caution, though, warrior: when I say 'remain potent,' I mean it will lay dormant, ready to heal you—it will only do so for a short while, as the Energy is drained away from each wound mended."

"How much?"

"Twelve thousand beads. I would also consider trading it for Coloss prize tokens."

"That's impressive, but I'll need to think about it. Do you have anything in between?" Victor eyed the potions she'd skipped over.

"Yes, of course. These two are both quite powerful and capable of healing many dire injuries. The white-waxed jar contains a potion that will remain potent for nearly an hour, and the blue-waxed jar has similar healing properties but will only last in your system for around ten minutes—it's a great deal less expensive."

"What are their prices?" Victor frowned, thinking about how much he wanted to spend on consumables.

"Two thousand for the white, five hundred for the blue."

"I'll buy . . . four of the blue ones." Victor shrugged. He'd rarely been in a fight that lasted longer than ten minutes; he supposed it would be nice to be able to chug a potion and not worry about injuries for an hour, but Coloss had a lot of interesting things for sale, and he didn't want to blow all his money in one place.

"And would you like some poison-immunity tinctures in case you face such a wyrm?" Shouza scooped up the potions Victor had rejected and returned them to the shelves, picking up three more of the blue-waxed jars in the process.

"How much are they?"

"They're each one thousand beads but will protect you for more than an hour."

Victor thought about it—he wasn't sure, not even fifty percent, if he had to put a number on it, what he'd be hunting, but he figured it wouldn't hurt to have one on hand. Frowning, he thought about Valla and said, "I'll buy two."

"So . . . four thousand beads? Sound right?"

"No . . . oh, for the regeneration potions, too. Yeah. Hey, you know how you're making a tincture that will supposedly improve my strength and vitality? Do you sell more things like that? Permanent boosts?"

"I do, though you have to be careful—there are diminishing returns based on an individual's tolerance. Have you used such things before?"

"Never . . ." Victor shrugged; he hadn't even known they existed prior to seeing the award listed on the arena flyer.

"Then you'll likely gain a large boost from the tincture you're paying me to create." She paused, and Victor could see she was battling with some inner dilemma. She opened her mouth two or three times to start speaking and finally said, "I'll tell you this—I don't have anything that potent in stock, and should you use one of my lesser tinctures, it may dull the effect. I'd wait until you've consumed your prize before going down that road."

"Well, thanks for your honesty, Shouza. You've earned some loyalty from me as a customer." Victor smiled, and Shouza returned the gesture, her rosy lips pulling back from surprisingly crooked but white teeth.

"Good! Here, let me get your poison resistance drops." She turned and walked further back through her stock, and Victor pulled out a sack of beads. "Hey, do you have one of those counting things? I mean, for beads?"

"Yes," Shouza said, returning with two tiny dark green vials. "Just tilt these into your mouth and hold the liquid under your tongue as long as possible, and you'll have the best results."

"Right, thanks," Victor said, putting them and the regeneration potions into his storage ring. Shouza used a magical rod to count out his payment.

"Hey, I have a few old potions and things that have been gathering dust in my storage ring. Mind looking at them for me?"

"Sure! I love seeing treasures and mysterious mixtures!" She leaned forward with a new gleam in her eyes.

"Okay, um," Victor dug around in his ring and produced a leather bandolier holding five green flasks—he honestly couldn't remember where he'd gotten it. "Here," he said, laying it before her. Shouza plucked out one of the vials and popped the cork, lifting it to her nose and nodding.

"As I suspected—poison. Not a particularly strong one, either. Still, if one were to consume this or coat a blade with it, it would make someone with a rather low vitality quite ill."

"Oh." Victor nodded, then took the bandolier back and slipped it into his ring. "One more," he said, then he took out the large wax-sealed jar of what he'd always assumed was blood, which he had looted from the ghoul champion so many months ago in the dungeon by Greatbone Mine.

"This is more special!" Shouza said, leaning close and sniffing at the seal. "I can read its Energy density from here. This . . . I'd need to run some tests on this, but I think it's meant to be consumed and will be quite beneficial; this may be an item like we were just speaking about, something that will boost an attribute or two."

"If I leave it with you, will you identify it?"

"I will. Depending on what I find out, there will be a fee." She grinned, unashamed.

Victor laughed, then turned to look out the window, wondering how long he had to wait for Tronk. He was surprised to see the giant already there, sitting on the stoop, too large to come through the door easily. "Sounds fair enough. I guess I'm off—I'll see you in a few days."

"Glad to have met you, Victor. Your ingredients are in good hands; I'll ensure you have great results. Just remember to recommend me to your friends."

"Oh, I will. Thanks again." Victor moved to the door; a tiny voice in the back of his head wondered if he was being stupid, leaving his prizes with a complete stranger. Still, the rational part of his brain reminded him that Tronk had recommended the shop and that he knew where to find Shouza should she betray his trust. He stepped into the warm, slightly humid air and clapped Tronk on his massive shoulder—the giant had eschewed his plate armor and wore a thick, well-worn, and scarred leather jerkin instead. "Ready, boss?"

"Yar," the giant rumbled, clambering to his feet. "Got what ya needed?"

"Yep, she seemed pretty cool." He saw Tronk's blank expression and added, "She was nice and seemed to know what she was doing."

"Mmhmm." Tronk nodded, then posed a question. "What kinds of magic items you want? Gotta think of the best place to take ya."

"Well, I need help with a magical item that stopped working—an amulet with a spirit inside it. Other than that, I'm kinda just wanting to shop around. I'd say take me to the best Artificer you know to start with."

"Right." Tronk nodded and started walking, taking the opposite direction from where he'd led Valla. "Back to the citadel—Fough works for the Warlord, knows the most."

"Shit, really? Should've started there."

"Yar. Next time I talk to you more before we leave." With those simple words, Tronk picked up his pace and began overtaking other pedestrians. Victor followed in his wake, easily keeping up, though his legs were still a good deal shorter than the giant's. While they made their way through the city, Victor's mind wandered to his experience the night before, to his conversation with Khul Bach.

He wanted to get some answer for the ancient spirit right away, but he'd been putting off these basic necessities and wanted to honor his promise to Valla; they'd agreed on how this day would go. He figured if he finished early enough, he could ask Tronk to take him to see Black that evening. Maybe he could get a few answers before he left on his monster hunt.

"Tronk!" a high-pitched voice shouted from above, disrupting Victor's musings. He looked up, as did the giant, to see a female Degh leaning out of a window, two stories up, in the tall, narrow building they were passing by. "Tronk! Where are you going? I haven't seen you down at the Red Harpy for days!"

"Ugh," Tronk grunted, stopping and holding a hand out to indicate Victor should pause, too. He looked around, a slight frown on his face, as though he was trying to see who might be watching this exchange, but then he cupped a hand to his mouth and hollered, "Hi, Bell! Been busy. Not much time fer drinks. Maybe later tonight." He shrugged and turned to leave, but Bell—Victor couldn't believe he'd finally met someone with a name that wouldn't be weird on Earth—wasn't having it.

"Wait, Tronk! I'll walk with you."

"Nar!" Tronk said, turning back to the window, but it was too late; the giantess had already slipped away. "Balls . . ." the giant grumbled.

"What's the story?" Victor asked, amused at the giant's discomfort.

"No story. Bell's a friend, but she talks too . . ."

"Tronk! I'm here," Bell announced, slamming the door to the building open and bounding down the steps. She was a giant, no doubt about it, taller than Victor by a head, but she was a good deal shorter than Tronk and significantly more lean. She wore tight leather pants, high boots, and a velvety green vest that showed off her bracelet-covered, swarthy arms. As she strode past Victor to squeeze Tronk into a hug, Victor saw that she had curly, coppery hair pulled into a ponytail and bright green eyes that twinkled with mischief.

"Ugh, Bell! Not in the street! I'm a Fist!" Tronk's cheeks had reddened, and he looked for all the world like a little kid embarrassed by his mother's affections. He finally extricated himself and started walking, clearly flustered, and only looked back for Victor after several steps. "I gotta take Victor somewhere. Come with me if ya want," he grunted.

"Victor?" Bell asked, turning, for the first time, toward Tronk's charge.

"Yar, he's important to the Warlord, and some folks wanna smash 'im."

"Victor! From the arena!" Bell held out a hand, and Victor smiled, reaching out to shake it. "I knew Tronk must be busy with something important—no way he'd avoid me for days and days without a good reason!"

"I was wi' ya two nights ago, Bell!" Tronk groused, resuming his stomping progress toward the keep. Victor followed along, and Bell walked beside them, a little in front of Victor and a little behind Tronk.

"Did Tronk tell you about me? I bet he couldn't stop mentioning me!"

"Uh, well, I haven't had a lot of time to speak with Tronk . . ."

"Oh, really? Well, I'm sure he'll tell you all about me next time you have a bit of a break. Where are we going, fellas?"

"Ta see Fough," Tronk muttered.

"Fough? Fough the Artificer?"

"Yar."

"Oh, well, I'll wait outside. He's a bit much for me."

"Yar. Just Victor will go in. You and me can talk while we wait."

"I knew you missed me!" Bell quickened her next two steps to catch up to Tronk and reached to take his hand. The giant groaned and shook his hand a few times, but there was no helping it—Bell's grip must have been secure. Victor smiled, amused, then a weird feeling hit him, and he suddenly experienced an almost violent wave of nostalgia, a feeling he'd not experienced much in his young life. He thought about Marcy and about Chandri; he thought about Teil and even Thayla, and he suddenly felt very alone.

He looked down at himself and sighed, shaking his head. Even if he wanted to go back to Chandri, how could he? She'd joked about his size when he was a full foot shorter and a lot smaller. He knew it was a dumb thought—people of all sorts of different sizes got together, but he couldn't help how his mind jumped to irrational conclusions, couldn't help his feelings. "You're being stupid, Victor," he muttered, reaching up to furiously scrub at his short hair, trying to shake the feeling off.

He looked around, taking in the wild variations in the peoples of Coloss—
the giant Degh, the Vesh, the Yazzians, the Tong-pan. He'd seen a dragon
lady, and he'd seen people on Fanwath of all sorts of sizes and shapes—Lam
was huge for a Ghelli! As far as he knew, there were thousands of worlds he
could visit with ten thousand different types of people. Who was he to worry
about being a little bigger than the people he cared about? Victor nodded,
happy to see the citadel coming into view, and decided to quit worrying about
things he couldn't control.

19

A MATTER OF DENSITY

In here?" Victor asked, gesturing toward the stone archway opening onto a dim, downward-sloping tunnel.

"Yar. Fough's place is down there. Not comfortable for me." Tronk eyed Victor up and down and said, "Not comfortable for you, either, but better than me."

"Okay," Victor sighed, scratching at his stiff, short hair. "Where will I find you when I'm done?"

"Central gardens with Bell."

"What about Valla? Are you going to get her? Escort her back here?"

"Nar, the lady, Tes, said she would get her back. Her aura was heavy—Tronk thinks she's safe."

"Yeah." Victor slapped a hand on the stone lintel of the archway, bending slightly to look down the length of the tunnel; he'd have to stoop the whole way. "Makes sense. Well, I'll see you in a while, then." He started in, Tronk's rumbled farewell echoing strangely down the long, sloping path. They were two levels beneath the ground floor of the citadel already, and the tunnel's incline was taking him deeper still. It seemed Fough liked his seclusion.

As he meandered down the tunnel, walking past small, closed doors, he began to appreciate his evolved body and high vitality—despite his stooped posture, his neck and back felt fine. He knew he'd get sore eventually, but with his long-legged pace, Victor hoped he'd reach Fough's lair before that happened.

"Let's see," he muttered as he came to a junction. "What did he say? Pass the doors, left, then left, and I'd come to some steps." Victor turned left, and in another ten minutes, he'd found the cramped stone stairwell and, growing impatient, he hopped down them three at a time. A short walk up an even narrower tunnel brought him to a solid wooden door, beneath which steady yellow light leaked.

Victor's eyes had grown accustomed to the murk, only having the occasional glow lamp to navigate by, and the bright light was a welcome sight. He strode up to the door and knocked on it three times with his knuckles.

"Come," a raspy voice said immediately. Victor twisted the door handle and pushed it open. When he stepped through, he was pleased to find himself in a vaulted chamber. He straightened up and looked around. A man wearing black silky robes, complete with a deeply cowled hood, was hunched over a table, carefully etching something into a sheet of shimmering silvery metal. Around him were what looked like the cluttered contents of several warehouses' worth of esoteric goods.

Books, boxes, wooden tubes, metal rods, crates, bolts of material, and tools of every sort Victor could imagine were piled on tabletops, precariously stuffed onto shelves, and stacked into piles that teetered and leaned against each other and the high walls. Everything was illuminated by a high chandelier from which spilled brilliant yellow-white light, shed by numerous crystals that radiated more brightly than any glow lamps Victor had yet seen.

"The Warlord sent you?" Fough asked, not looking up from his work.

"Not exactly." Victor reached behind himself and pushed the door closed with a click. The walls of the chamber were crafted from the same square gray blocks of the tunnels he'd been traversing, but here, on the inside of Fough's workshop, Victor could see they were coated with a thin layer of soot—he wondered if it was the residue of experiments gone awry.

"Well? Who are you, then?" Fough's voice had a sibilance to it that seemed familiar, and Victor began to suspect the Artificer was a member of the Yazzian people, like Boaegh. He supposed it made sense, considering the slight similarity in their names.

"I'm a guest of the Warlord. I have some questions and work for an Artificer, and my escort, Tronk, said you were the right person to speak to." Victor stepped toward the table on which Fough worked, noticing the rich pile of the carpet he stepped onto—despite the stone underneath it, he felt as though he sank a good inch into the soft fabric.

"Hmm. Pose your questions while I finish this up." Fough had yet to look up, and the only parts of him Victor could see were his slender, delicately scaled green fingers.

"All right," Victor said, lifting Gorz's chain over his head and setting the amulet on the table. "I'll start with this. There's a spirit in this amulet—well, a spirit shard. He used to be very talkative, but lately, he's been quieter, and as of yesterday, I can't get him to respond to me. He complained about losing time and feeling . . . Shit, I don't remember his exact words, but he said something about wondering if he was being pulled back to his 'larger soul.'"

"Mmhmm," Fough said, carefully etching another rune into his metallic sheet. "Has the amulet been subject to powerful Energies?"

"Uh . . ." Victor thought about the question. He thought about his own spells, how he transformed with huge surges of rage-attuned Energy to become a berserking giant. He thought about his powerful justice and fear-based transformations, then he thought about the spells that had been used against him, particularly the fire cast by Boaegh. "Yeah, it has. I guess there's also the portal we went through to come here. Does that matter?"

"A world portal? Was it stable?"

"I don't know . . ."

"All right, just a moment, just a moment; I take it back, don't tell me any more—I need to concentrate." Fough continued etching, and Victor stood as patiently as he could, straightening his back and flexing his neck, watching the tiny, delicate etchings the Artificer was making; they were complicated and beautiful, and they reminded him of the patterns he'd created in his pathways to build his Energy weaves. A minute turned into five, turned into fifteen, and then Fough sighed and set his slightly humming, green-metal etching tool onto the tabletop. It buzzed against the wood until he released it, and then it lay still.

"Done?" Victor asked, looking into the man's bright yellow serpent eyes as he straightened, giving Victor his attention.

"For now, yes." To Victor's surprise, the Yazzian affected a very human-like smile, and it softened his weird, alien appearance a great deal. "This amulet, hmm?" He picked up Gorz's amulet in his nimble fingers and turned it over, giving it a good look. Victor felt a surge of Energy, and Fough's eyes pulsed with golden light for a brief second or two.

"See anything?"

"Oh yes. Quite an old artifact, isn't it? I can see the Energy lines, the entrapment runes, and the persona-regulating ciphers—those I'm not familiar with and would need a key to understand fully. I don't need the key to see that many of the binding materials, woven through the metal of the amulet, have weakened. There are gaps in the rings, and some runes are completely worn away. I'd say your entrapped spirit has fled this plane of existence, friend." He set the amulet on the table and shrugged.

"Seriously? He wasn't trying to flee, though . . . He seemed confused by what was happening to him."

"A simple fragment, regulated by this amulet to behave a certain way. No, it's likely there was truth to its assumptions—the greater whole of the spirit, from which the fragment was taken, was exerting a pull. It might not have been a conscious effort; as fragments of rock might gather around a planet, forming into a ring and then into a moon, pieces of a spirit gravitate toward each other. With holes in the bindings, this one slipped free and no longer lingers on this plane with us."

"Damn. I was starting to wonder if I'd done something to cause his problems, like, I've been a bit neglectful . . ." Victor trailed off, not really wanting to bare his soul to this stranger.

"Well, your amulet needed some maintenance, but with you not being an Artificer, I'm not surprised you didn't realize it. I could repair it, help you to trap a new spirit within. It won't be the same, but the amulet has the enchantments to force a similar behavior—it will perform the same functions it used to."

"Wait . . . so Gorz wasn't obsessed with memorizing things and mapping? The amulet made him do that shit?"

"Gorz was the spirit's name? Yes, it's likely the amulet enforced those traits."

"I'll fucking melt it down, then. I wouldn't enslave a spirit." Victor struggled with the emotions fighting for dominance within him—guilt, anger, regret, and even disgust. While his outburst vented some of his anger, a real sense of loss suddenly hit him so hard that he had to take a step back.

Gorz was gone. Gorz, the friendly voice that had guided him out of despair in the mines, helped him to master his inspiration attunement. Gorz, who had given him advice and shown him the path to take in the darkest depths of the world. He was gone, and Victor hadn't even properly said goodbye.

"Are you all right?" Fough asked. It wasn't easy to see the emotion on his hairless, scaly face, but his eyes seemed slightly widened, and Victor wondered what his own face looked like to elicit such a question.

"Not really, no. I figured Gorz's issue was solvable. I didn't think the last time I spoke to him was . . . the last time I would speak to him. Goddamn it." Victor stepped forward to pick up the amulet, but as he reached for it, Fough spoke.

"I'd buy it from you just to study the cipher—I've not seen that quality of work in some time. I'll swear to properly destroy it when I'm done."

Victor picked up the amulet, ignoring the man's words. He concentrated, closed his eyes, and reached out, "speaking" to Gorz in his head, as he used to. *Are you there, buddy? Are you really gone?*" No reply was forthcoming, though he stood there for several seconds repeating the question, his eyes closed. To his credit, Fough didn't speak or attempt to interrupt him. When Victor finally opened his eyes, the Artificer shrugged his narrow shoulders.

"I wouldn't lie about a thing like this; there is no presence in that amulet."

Victor sighed heavily and hung the amulet over his head again, tucking it down beneath his shimmering scale armor. "Sorry, but I'm going to hang onto it for a while—sentimental reasons."

"I understand. Let me know if you change your mind about letting me study it."

"Yeah." Victor didn't think he would—why would he want to help this guy learn to enslave spirits better? He supposed there might be legitimate reasons for knowing how to do whatever the maker of Gorz's amulet had done. Maybe some spirits went willingly into objects, but he didn't like the idea that they could be forced to behave a certain way. His mind raced down various lines of thought—what if the spirit was evil? What if a person willingly separated a shard of their soul for such a purpose?

There might be cases where the creation of such an object wasn't inherently wrong, but Victor wasn't interested in exploring them at the moment. He just hoped Gorz had found a better existence than he'd been forced into for the last several thousand years.

"Is there aught else I can help you with?" Fough asked, gesturing to his table, indicating the work he'd been doing.

"Yeah. A few things, I'd bet, but first, a question that's been tickling the back of my mind: Are there limits to the magical resizing effects on items? Take my armor, for instance—I sometimes grow in size, like, as big as a Degh . . . bigger. So far, it's held up." Victor grabbed the material of his shimmersteel armor at the sleeve, tugging on it as if to illustrate its sturdiness. "What if I grew even more? How is it possible? I mean, magical materials are expensive. Couldn't someone just make a small piece of armor, enchant it to grow to the size of the wearer, and then have a giant put it on? Then they could melt it down, making more and more of their material."

Fough held up a hand, interrupting Victor's monologue. "No, no, no. That's not how the magic works. Do you know about the tiny building blocks of the universe? The atomic level?"

"Yeah . . ."

"When an Artificer creates an object that can shift its size, he or she puts a spell on the material, charging it with ambient Energy used to shrink or expand the space between those atoms. It works up to a certain limit, but eventually, the object's material will degrade. High-quality materials with high Energy density can withstand this more than others, using their deep stores of Energy to bridge the gaps, especially if the resizing is temporary." Fough paused for a minute and really looked at Victor, his eyes running up and down his figure from his boots to his bare head glowing faintly yellow as he channeled some sort of spell.

"Your boots are in dire straits. Your pants don't seem bad; are they new?"

"Yeah, I have quite a few pairs."

"Your armor is made from very high-quality material. Whatever resizing you're forcing it to go through is taking a bit of a toll, but I think it could withstand the punishment for quite some time before it started to bleed its Energy and begin to unravel."

"Fuck, seriously?"

"Oh yes. I'll let you in on a little secret—if you want your gear to last longer, many, many times longer, you should have it crafted for your largest size and then bond with it while you're small. It's much easier on materials to shrink than to stretch."

"Ah, no shit? So I should get some Degh-sized gear while I'm here, hmm?"

"Here? As in Coloss?"

"Right. Not here." Victor gestured around the cluttered room.

"Well, I do have quite a stock of objects I've worked on over the years. Anything you're particularly interested in?" As though mimicking Victor, Fough gestured around his workspace, his eyes lingering on some steel-strapped trunks tucked against one wall.

"Maybe. Just a sec; can you check something else out?" Victor reached into his storage ring and pulled out Polo's gift, the enormously heavy Kethian Juggernaut helmet. His muscles straining, he carefully set it on the table so that he didn't shatter any of the boards.

"Ah! Wondrous," Fough said, nodding. His eyes flared with the familiar golden glow, and then he smiled. "You've no worries about this item; that's some of the densest metal I've ever seen, and its natural size is a great deal larger than this. Yes . . . some sort of deep metal." He reached out to touch the helmet, gently scraping one of his pointy black nails against its surface. "Very dense Energy. Look! The noseguard is slowly sinking into the wood."

"Yeah, sorry 'bout that," Victor said, reaching out to touch the helmet and sending it back into his storage ring. Sure enough, several indentations remained on the wooden top of Fough's worktable.

"Not to worry; you can see the scrapes and stains I've left behind—it's meant for working on, not admiring." Fough rubbed his hand over the wood, pausing to smear a black stain into the grain with his thumb. "I was dying some fabric earlier."

"Well, do you have any armor similarly dense? Preferably something made for a big Degh."

"I'm the Warlord's Artificer; what do you think?" Again, the Yazzian smiled, and though it didn't show any teeth, it was a pleasant expression. "I have a wyrm-scale vest that would suit you well. I can also help with your footwear."

"Wyrm scale?"

"Oh yes. Fabulous material, the scales of an adult wyrm. Difficult to work with, difficult to enchant, but in the right hands . . ." Fough held up his long, slender, green fingers, allowing Victor's imagination to finish the statement.

"Are wyrms related to dragons?"

"Yes! Wyrms are dragons' brutish, flightless cousins. Well, according to the texts I've studied. They're not nearly as intelligent, but still quite dangerous and powerful."

"Have you ever seen a dragon?" Victor wondered how Tes felt about the people of Coloss hunting her "brutish cousins."

"No, not in the flesh. There's a skull in Maposh—they built their great cathedral around it."

"Maposh? That another city around here?"

"Well, not exactly 'around here.' Maposh is beyond the Serpent Sea and then some thousand leagues inland." Fough turned and walked over to the banded trunks Victor had spotted earlier and began to clear a space on the rug in front of them. "Come, let me make some room here, and then I'll show you the vest. You won't be disappointed."

Victor nodded and stepped around a pile of leather sacks and a rack of long wooden staves so that he could watch while Fough dragged boxes, books, and various other items to other parts of his cluttered space, clearing a large section of rug in front of the centermost trunk. "You could use some help organizing this place, I'd say."

"Oh, it's not a matter of help . . . well, yes, it is. I do need the help; whenever I get started doing it on my own, I get interrupted. The Warlord keeps me busy. It's just that I need an assistant I can trust, and I haven't found one yet. Not for a long while."

"Really?"

"Yes. I had an apprentice, but he went into business on his own. I'm sorely tempted to create a construct that will serve my needs, but it's terribly costly and difficult to make one that can learn, and such functionality would be essential to the job." He grunted as he shifted the last object—a foot-long cylinder that rattled as though it was filled with marbles.

"There's no one in this whole city you can trust?"

"Ah, I didn't say that; I said I couldn't find an assistant I could trust. The people I trust in this city do not want to work for me, categorically!" He chuckled as he flipped open the trunk, revealing what looked like a deep, black void to Victor. "Bear with me—thousands of objects in here."

"Oh, right. A dimensional container."

"Just so, just so," Fough said in his raspy voice, and then he snapped his fingers and said, "Aha!" He gestured with his left hand and suddenly, with a heavy rattling *clunk*, a hauberk, easily twice the size of Victor's current armored shirt, flopped down on the thick carpet. It gleamed in the bright light, hundreds—thousands—of pearlescent black scales glinting as Victor moved closer, sucking a breath through his teeth.

"*Chingado*," he said, leaning close, admiring the craftsmanship.

"I was going to sell it to Black, but the bastard contracted his own armorsmith and refused to even look at it."

"The scales are amazing, but what about that leather they're stitched into?" Victor couldn't take his eyes off the vest. The scales were brilliant, and he could feel the Energy within them, but the black, supple material they were stitched to looked like something special as well. It gleamed as though it was freshly oiled; he wanted to put it on, to feel that rich texture for himself.

"That's not leather; it's hell queen silk."

"Excuse me?" Victor straightened up and jerked his eyes away from the armor. "What's a hell queen?"

Fough chuckled and said, "A type of spider. Sounds worse than it is . . . well, no, it doesn't. They're called that because their venom has been described as synonymous with a visit to hell. Metaphorically, of course; I've never visited one of the abyssal planes, but I can't imagine just being there would be torturous. There are those who would argue the point, however. Oh, and they're called queens because males of the species don't live long—the females consume them after mating."

"So, uh, it looks awesome, but I imagine it's expensive, huh?"

"I'd part with it for five prize tokens. I'm happy to entertain other offers."

"I'm not really looking to trade any prize tokens. How about beads?"

"Well, the scales and silk were quite expensive, then you have my enchantment and crafting fees. I couldn't let it go for less than two hundred thousand."

"Fuck me."

Fough grinned at Victor's outburst and said, "Too rich for your blood? I'll take other trades; have you been on any monster hunts lately? Have any interesting trophies?"

"No, but I'm going on one tomorrow. I'll come to see you if I get anything I don't want. What's the benefit of the armor besides being dense in Energy and able to resize a lot?"

"Oh, you'll never need to fear these materials unraveling; they'll hold up, especially considering I made it so large to begin with. More than that, it will provide excellent protection—I'd invite you to strike it with your axe, but it looks like a hungry weapon. I can see the Heart Silver veins; it's ready to evolve soon, if I'm not mistaken, and I'm afraid it would feast upon the hauberk's Energy."

"Really?"

"Oh yes. I was quite taken with it as I examined your equipment. You wouldn't be looking to trade it, would you?"

Victor frowned and put his hand atop Lifedrinker's metallic head. "Her. And not for a million beads, *pendejo*."

"I didn't mean any offense," Fough held up his hands, smiling again, his yellow eyes slightly squinting as though apologetic or embarrassed—Victor couldn't quite read the emotion. "I'll hold the hauberk for you, hmm? If you're going on a hunt, I bet you'll come away with some real prizes you might trade. As a show of good faith, how about I give you a pair of boots? Hmm? I have quite a few gathering dust in here."

"I can't argue with free boots." Victor shrugged and smiled, removing his hand from Lifedrinker.

Twenty minutes later, Victor was striding up a long, wide corridor on his way back to the ground floor of the citadel. His new boots were black—it had been that or a pair of pale yellow ones, and Victor wasn't ready to make that kind of fashion statement in Coloss. They had thick, grippy soles made from a material much like rubber but entirely synthesized by Fough from various rare ingredients. He claimed they'd never burn or melt and that he'd really have to try to lose his footing.

The uppers were polished to a near mirror sheen, and when Victor had frowned at the flashiness of them, Fough had reassured him, saying that the shine wasn't permanent; he'd have to buff them now and then to keep them looking so sharp. Victor had no intention of doing so. Still, they were comfortable and had been sized for a Degh before he bonded with them. They were dense with Energy and would last him a very long time if Fough were to be believed.

Victor was annoyed at how long he'd been in there and how expensive everything seemed in Coloss. On the other hand, he had to remind himself that he'd only been there a few days and was already significantly richer than when he'd arrived. He was beginning to look forward to the monster hunt and hoped he'd have a chance to score some big points with the hunt master; it sounded as if there were great rewards to be had.

More than anything, he had a vague hollow feeling in the pit of his stomach, and he knew it was from what he'd learned about Gorz. He felt as if a friend had died. He wanted to go sit in a tavern and get drunk. He wanted to tell people about Gorz, but he didn't think anyone would get it, not even Valla, which only added to the hollowness. Was he really that alone? He felt a slight vibration at his hip, and he looked down to see Lifedrinker, and a smile turned the corners of his lips upward. Had she felt his thoughts, or maybe, at least, his emotions?

"Well, beautiful," he said, holding his hand against Lifedrinker's cool metal, "at least that guy confirmed what I thought; you're pretty damn special. What do you say we go find out what Black knows about the Ancestor Stone? Maybe I can get the old giant in the crystal to give me a few more secrets before we leave on the hunt tomorrow."

20

A KIND VOICE IN A DARK PLACE

"That's right," Victor growled, growing irritated by the black-plated guard's questioning. "War Captain Black wanted me to check in, to tell him about my experience with the ancestor shard."

"Yar," Tronk said, from behind him, looming over his left shoulder. The giant hadn't been exactly excited to lead Victor to the War Captain's estate, but he'd shrugged and said something about there still being hours of light left and then said goodbye to Bell. She'd been a little more difficult to shake than that, though, following them for several minutes through the upper districts of the city until Tronk had finally promised to meet her at their favorite spot after Victor and Valla left on their monster hunt.

"Yes, and I've told you the War Captain isn't seeing visitors this evening . . ."

"Move," Tronk said, striding forward, shoving the Vesh-sized guard out of the way and dragging the long sliding gate open several feet. "Fist comin' through. Official business," he rumbled as several other guards rushed out of the gatehouse. None of them spoke, though, nor lifted a hand toward Tronk. The giant nodded at them, then motioned for Victor to follow, trundling up the long cobbled drive toward the gloomy black-marble villa.

"They didn't want to mess with you, did they?" Victor asked, quickening his steps so he came up beside Tronk.

"Nar, they know better. Only one in this place tha' might give me a workout is Black hisself."

"He's the strongest?" Victor asked, a little surprised.

"'Course. Aren't the leaders the strongest in yer world?"

"Earth? Definitely not—most wealthy, most influential, I suppose. Fanwath? I don't think so; there seems to be a degree of contrast between political power and raw power. It's certainly a little different than here."

Tronk shrugged and stomped up the steps, ignoring the black-clad footmen and approaching the enormous doors at the front of the big, imposing edifice. The left door opened before he crashed into it, and a liveried servant stood panting, holding it open to the side. "Lord Fist, will you need to see the War Captain on this visit?"

"Yar."

"Please go to the Midnight Parlor, and I'll bring him the news of your arrival."

"Uh-huh." Tronk strode off, and Victor followed, amused at how the giant had made himself at home. Most of the guards and servants at Black's villa were Vesh, though he thought he counted a higher percentage of Degh than he'd seen elsewhere. It made sense to him—Black was Degh, and his home was built to accommodate him and his family. Surely there were friends and relations from wherever the Degh hailed that he'd wanted to hire.

In Victor's opinion, the villa was a depressing place—the lights were dim, the wall panels stained dark grays and blacks, and black marble was ubiquitous, used for floors, pillars, and trim. Gloomy artwork abounded—black marble busts and statues, paintings of nighttime scenes, and rugs and carpeting that were all predominantly, no surprise here, black.

Tronk led him, purposefully and without pause, to a small parlor with a servant's station in the corner and comfortable, darkly upholstered couches and chairs arrayed on dark carpeting. Victor figured out rather quickly why it was called the Midnight Parlor; the Energy lamp that supplied the light in the room was a faded yellow-green and hung near the apex of the high domed ceiling, almost like a replica of the moon that was just now rising outside.

While the place was gloomy, it was interesting, and Victor and Tronk had no trouble getting comfortable in oversized, overstuffed chairs. While they waited for Black, a servant wearing a black velvety uniform brought refreshments—some sort of chilled wine and a bowl of cut, nearly-frozen fruit. Victor availed himself of the snacks, pleased by the mixture of tart and sweet samples and enjoying the pale, cold wine—the first time he could remember having wine that wasn't dark red.

"Victor, and my old friend, Tronk. Thank you for visiting; can I assume you have some news of the shard?" Black strode into the room, still enormous, still intimidating, but no longer wearing heavy plate armor. He wore comfortable-looking black pants that were baggy at the top and tapered at the ankles. A loose button-front shirt, also black, hung from his shoulders, only partially fastened by the bottom few buttons.

Black was a handsome, if borderline elderly, man with dark, peppered gray and black hair and a full, well-maintained beard. His eyes, buried in the folds of decades—or centuries—of crow's-feet, were bright, pale brown, and full of depth. Victor could tell the man was holding back his aura, much the way Tronk and the Warlord did, and he wondered just how many people were of such power that they needed to restrain themselves on a constant basis. Valla had said Victor's aura was heavy, but he didn't feel he did anything to contain it.

"Hullo, Black," Tronk rumbled, reaching for a scoop of chilled fruit, heedless of the sticky mess he was making of his hand.

"Hello," Victor said, standing up and holding out his hand. "I do have some news and some questions. Can we talk here?"

"Aye." Black nodded, stomping forward and grasping Victor firmly by the wrist. Victor squeezed the giant's wrist in return and was pleased that his grip felt firm on the thick, powerful appendage. "This is a good place; we won't be bothered." He released Victor's arm and sat in a chair across from him and Tronk, and Victor sat back down.

"I made contact with your ancestor," Victor said, not interested in beating around the bush.

"Truly?" Black's eyes opened widely, and he leaned forward, his mouth partially open, as though he wanted to speak but clearly held himself back, waiting for Victor to expound.

"Yes, no lie." Victor nodded. "He's well, with all of his faculties, but he's lost time and has no idea what's happened outside the Stone since its shattering. The last person he remembers speaking to is someone named Bavarak. Does that ring a bell?"

"Ring a bell? Ah, I get your meaning, Victor. Yes, I know who Bavarak is . . . was. He died during the Breaking. Aye, Tronk?"

"Yar."

"The Breaking?" Victor pressed.

"The war between the Degh and the Vesh. Well, and the Yazzians—they aided the Vesh. When the snakes besieged our cities to the south, distracting us, the Vesh did the unthinkable: raided our homelands, calling up the seas to drown Ulhavat—the island from which our ancestors hailed."

"And broke your Ancestor Stone?"

"Aye. The Warlord himself led the attack long before my time. What's this to do with the ancestor, though, Victor? Am I just serving to assuage his curiosity, or is there a larger purpose for your visit? I'd hoped you'd be giving me answers—a way to restore my people's lost glory."

"I want to give you answers. I want to help you, but the ancestor wasn't ready to tell me everything he knows; I'm not one of your people, if you hadn't noticed." Victor leaned closer to Tronk as if to demonstrate his differences and snorted at himself, pleased with his attempt at levity.

"So he sent you for more information before he would help us?" Black didn't seem amused.

"He doesn't know enough to help you yet. He wanted to know another thing: is he the last one? Are there other shards of the Ancestor Stone?"

"Aye, there are others. Most of the clans have one, and the Warlord has three. Some were left where they lay too long, and dungeons grew around them. I know of seventeen shards altogether."

"Did you . . ." Victor paused, trying to think of how he should phrase the question without sounding insulting. "Did your people not try to put them together? The ones the clans hold, I mean?"

"Of course. Those of us who could agree, at least." Black frowned and rubbed at his chin. "This was back when the fracture was new, and my people were freshly conquered. The accounts I've read seemed to indicate that great Energies repulsed the shards, pushing them away from each other. It didn't help that none of my people with a Spirit Core escaped the fracturing alive."

"I think that information will be interesting to your ancestor. He seemed . . ." Again, Victor broke off his speech, trying to choose his words delicately. "Dismayed. Yeah, he seemed dismayed that your people were in Coloss, that you were working and living with the Vesh. He called them 'upstart mutants.' He knew the Warlord, by the way—said he was the one who stirred the Vesh up to wage war."

"Aye, Warlord Thoargh is ancient and powerful." Black frowned, and Victor thought he could hear the giant's molars grinding. "We don't serve him, not exactly, but we don't have the numbers or the strength to be our own people again. Some of us"—he gestured to Tronk—"think it wiser to work with the Vesh, grateful that we still exist as a people, though our numbers dwindle year to year."

"He broke us," Tronk said, stretching back. "Broke us, then let us live, part o' his empire."

"Empire? I thought Coloss was a city-state."

"A city-state with ten million square miles of countryside under its direct control. A city-state with a dozen other city-states subservient to it. An empire in everything but name," Black said.

"Enough," Tronk rumbled, sitting up and making a vague gesture at the air around them. "This topic ain't somethin' the Warlord wants to 'ear about."

"Aye, brother," Black said, scooting forward and looking directly into Victor's eyes. "Victor, please tell the ancestor about our situation. Tell him about the loss of Ulhavat. Tell him our people diminish each year, each generation weaker and fewer than the one before. Keep his counsel to yourself and only speak of it among Degh you can trust—Tronk and I should be the extent of this circle, for now."

"Yar," Tronk grunted, scooting forward to stand up. "Time we 'eaded back, Victor."

"All right," Victor said, standing. He felt he had enough information to please the ancestor and wanted to get back to the citadel to check on Valla, anyway. Black walked them to the door, and as he and Tronk stepped through, he offered some parting words.

"Victor, no one from my household will cause you trouble, and it's known the Warlord is sponsoring you, at least until Gazra's Day. You shouldn't run into any trouble from the citizens of Coloss, but watch yourself should you leave the city—I'd hate to lose your connection to my ancestor before aught could be gained from it."

"I'll be careful, War Captain. Thanks for the heads-up."

"I'll hope to hear from you again soon," Black called after them as Victor and Tronk made their way down the steps and up the lane. Victor raised his hand up and waved in answer. Then he turned to regard Tronk.

"So, you're friends with Black?"

"Friends. Cousins." Tronk shrugged. He didn't offer any other explanation, and Victor decided to let the matter rest for now. He had a lot to mull over while they walked. The more Victor learned about the Degh and their situation, the more tragic it seemed. He had a hard time reconciling his experiences with the Warlord with the image he had of a conqueror who drove an entire race of people into submission, destroying their home—an entire island—and diminishing their potency in so many ways.

Something about their Ancestor Stone seemed to make the Degh different from the other peoples Victor had encountered in this world and on Fanwath. Why were they weaker individually because of this stone's breaking? Why would there be fewer of them each generation? Why would they keep growing weaker? He hoped the ancestor in the shard would be able to shed some light on the matter, but if not, he hoped he'd be happy with the information enough to give Victor some more guidance as a mentor.

When they returned to the citadel and Tronk led Victor to his suite, he found Valla within, sitting on the rich, thick rug at the center of their seating area, deep in meditation. He could feel the Energy swirling in the air around her and wondered why she was cultivating there instead of in the Warlord's cultivation chamber. Despite his attempt to be quiet, she heard him moving around and opened her eyes. "You're back."

"Hey, Valla." Victor sat in one of the chairs positioned so he could speak to her while looking out the windows toward the city. Valla shifted to face him directly. "Your time with Tes go well?"

"Very well! She . . . I still have a hard time saying this, it seems unbelievable to me, but she thinks I can improve my Energy affinity by perfecting my cultivation method; she thinks I'll be able to gradually increase it to a level half again as high as it is. Victor, no one on Fanwath knows how to do that! Well, no one who's ever spoken of it."

"Seriously? Can I ask . . ."

"Right now, I have equal affinities for iron and air—both are four point one."

"And she thinks she can help you get those into the . . . sixes?"

"Yes!"

"That's fucking great, Valla!" Victor clapped his hands together enthusiastically. "I told you she knew a lot!"

"It helps that she has elemental affinities herself, I think."

"No doubt." Victor, of course, couldn't stop his mind from running away with the obvious question: if Valla could improve her affinities, could he? Did it work differently for spirit affinities? Regardless of anything else, he was excited to see that there were rules about Energy and Cores that the people on Fanwath didn't yet know; there might be a lot more to discover on Zaafor than he'd first considered. "Anything else? She teach you any cool spells or anything?"

"No, but she hinted at being excited to speak to you during the hunt. She went on and on during the tournament about your potential. It was . . . tedious."

"Oh? You didn't mention that yesterday!"

"Well, it was your big day, and I didn't want to sound sour. I'm in a much better mood after the progress I made today. Tes thinks I'm going to master this cultivation drill in no time. She's such a good teacher! Victor, I think she's a lot more powerful than she seems . . ." Valla spoke the last in a hushed voice, as though she worried about eavesdroppers.

"Yeah. You've noticed she looks human, like me, right? I think the people here assume she's a Vesh with no obvious . . . mutations—is that the right word?"

"I've noticed. I asked Tes about it, and she said she and you might share some ancestry but that she's not human."

"Mmhmm," Victor said, rubbing at his chin. He supposed Tes would have told Valla she was a dragon if she wanted her to know. "Sounds about right. I knew she wasn't from Zaafor, anyway."

"I asked her if she could help us open a gateway to Fanwath, and she wouldn't answer me directly, but she said, 'I don't think you'll need to worry about that.'"

"Really? Well, for what it's worth, I think she's right. Speaking of which, did you find out where we're supposed to meet our hunting company? I completely forgot to ask Tronk about it."

"Yes, Tes told me we should meet her at the gate to the wastes at dawn." Valla's eyes suddenly widened as though she'd just remembered something, and she said, "Oh, Victor! How did things go with the Artificer? Did you get help with your amulet?"

Victor's face fell, and he sighed, falling back in his chair, tilting his eyes so he looked up at the white plastered ceiling. "Not exactly help, no. The Artificer thinks the enchantments on the amulet got weakened from time and exposure to Energy. He thinks Gorz slipped away, well his fragment did, and he thinks it's gone to join the greater part of his spirit."

"Oh?" Valla asked, lithely springing to her feet and coming closer to Victor. There wasn't a chair nearby, but she put a hand on his wrist and leaned toward him, concern in her eyes. "Are you upset about it?"

"I . . ." Victor wanted to vent; he wanted to talk about how he really felt, but something choked the words in his throat, and he said, "I guess it's good that he's not trapped anymore. Who knows what his spirit will get up to now that it's free."

"That's true," Valla said, giving his wrist another squeeze, but her eyes narrowed as she stared at him, as he avoided making eye contact. "Something's bothering you, though."

Victor sat up, looked at her, saw the sincerity on her face, and sighed. "I'm upset, yeah. I'm upset with myself. This shit has happened to me before, and it fucking guts me that I let it happen again. I didn't even know it was happening."

Valla's eyes narrowed in confusion, and she said, "I'm not following . . ."

"I've done this with friends before. When I was fifteen, I had a friend. His name was Chris, and we were pretty good friends—hung out a lot around the neighborhood, you know?" Valla nodded, and he continued, "Well, one summer, he stopped coming around and started hanging around with these other dudes. I just shrugged it off. 'Guess he's too cool for me,' I said—never even fucking texted him about it or anything." He could see Valla was confused by his words, but he kept pushing through the memory.

"Well, the months went by, and I knew less and less about what he was up to, and then one day, I got to school, and they called me to the counselor's office. They were calling all the people they thought were close to Chris. He was dead. The rumor I heard was that he was running from the cops on his dirt bike, wiped out on some gravel, and slid his head into the curb. My fucking friend was dead! He'd gotten wrapped up with some dudes that had him running product from some asshole on the south side up to our neighborhood."

"Product?"

"Drugs. It doesn't matter. The point is, I fucking just let him go, never bothered him, never tried to get him to tell me what was up, never told him to get away from those assholes. And then he was dead."

"And you feel like Gorz is the same?"

"Well, I sure as hell neglected the shit out of him. I could have taken him to an Artificer sooner. Maybe if I'd spent more time chatting with him in Persi Gables, I'd have seen he had a problem. Now he's gone."

"It's not the same, though, Victor. Gorz was a trapped spirit; you could say he's better off, and it wouldn't be a euphemism."

"I know logically that it's different, but it doesn't feel different, you know?" Victor put his hand on his stomach, right beneath his heart. "It feels like I've got a hole here, as though I fucked up somehow and lost something—some-one—important." He shook his head and rubbed at his eyes, embarrassed that he was getting so emotional over the amulet, over the spirit shard. "It's just—in the back of my mind, I always knew Gorz was there, but like in my past, I was too wrapped up with my own shit to give him the attention he needed. Meanwhile, I could talk to him anytime I needed to. He . . . he helped me get through some pretty grim shit, Valla."

Valla stared at him for a few seconds, but rather than speak right away, she gave him a smile and took his hand, tugging him to his feet. "Come on, Victor. Let's go out on the balcony. I have some very special whiskey I've been saving for a special occasion. Let's send your friend off with a toast."

"Valla, you don't have . . ."

"No. Don't protest; come on. I've been wanting an excuse to drink this, and it sounds like Gorz deserves our well wishes to send him off. He's got a great journey ahead of him!"

"Yeah." Victor nodded, walking with her to the door, comforted to know she was here with him, and before he could say it, she spoke.

"I'm glad you're here with me, Victor. How alone and scared I'd be in this strange world without you! I won't diminish your feelings, but I'll tell you that, from what I've seen, you're an excellent friend. You're dependable, you care about how people feel, and I know you didn't mean to neglect Gorz. You missed a chance to say goodbye, but here's another. Tell your friend how you feel."

Valla had been placing objects on the balcony railing while she spoke—a black crystal bottle with a red waxed cork top and two square, short crystal glasses. She broke the seal on the cork, twisted it out of the bottle, and poured the glasses full of a rich, vaporous, amber liquid. She handed one glass to Victor, picked up the other one, then looked at him expectantly.

"All right," Victor said, licking his lips. The heady scent of the liquor's vapors filled the air, wafting into his nose, and the smoky odor was making his mouth water. "Gorz." Victor cleared his throat, shaking his head ruefully, then tried again, "Gorz, you were a dependable, kind voice in a dark, terrible place. You saved me from despair on more than one occasion, and just knowing you were there was a comfort that got me through a lot of bad shit. You were a great friend, and you deserved better from me. I'll honor your memory, and I hope there's some way we might meet again—maybe in your next life."

Valla lifted her glass, and Victor clinked his against it, then they both drank. The liquor burned his throat, but it warmed his body instantly, and a tingle of numbness touched his nose and cheeks. "Whew," he said, blowing out a vaporous breath and waving a hand in front of his face. "Strong stuff!"

"Yes! Another?" Valla asked, already pouring her glass full. Victor nodded, and that night they stood out under the stars, looking down at the immense sea of lights that was Coloss, and Gorz received many toasts in his honor.

21

GUIDANCE

Sometime around midnight, Valla went to bed, and Victor sat by himself on the balcony, endlessly entertained by the sea of lights that stretched away from the citadel. Beyond the city wall was a sea of darkness, not a single light to be seen as far as the horizon. "Coloss is like a . . ." Victor paused and thought, trying to come up with something clever, poetic even. "Coloss is like a pile of glittering jewels, poured out by a colossus in the middle of the desert."

Victor laughed and patted Lifedrinker's living wood haft, where she rested across his knees. "That was fucking terrible. Remind me not to try to make a living as a poet." He was a little drunk, mostly just buzzed and relaxed, but behind the easy laughter lurked darker emotions—loss, anger, self-loathing, and embarrassment.

"Why'd I have to go and tell Valla all that shit?" he growled, standing up abruptly. He carried Lifedrinker through the sitting room of their suite and then into his bedroom. He placed the axe on the dresser top where the box containing the ancestor's shard sat waiting for him. He wished he could put it in a storage container but knew better than that; the spirit within would suffer in such an environment.

Victor was tired but not sleepy, and he decided to spend some time with the ancestor; with the hunt starting in the morning, he wasn't sure when he'd get another good chance. He took the faintly pink crystal from the box, cradled it in his hands, and sat down on the rug at the foot of his bed. The last time he'd spoken with the ancient spirit within, scant seconds had passed in the world, so he wasn't worried about the safety of his person while he communed with the ancestor.

Clearing his mind, Victor gathered his Energies and pushed them out into the shard, and as before, he felt his Core surge, flooding the fragment with his three affinities, until the world faded away and in a bloom of brilliant light, he once again sat before Khul Bach in the strange white and gray, sharp-angled plane.

"You return," the giant said, his stern gaze softening slightly, perhaps pleased that Victor had kept his promise.

"Yes," Victor said, clearing his throat. "I had a chance to speak with Black, um, the Degh who gave me this shard—I think his real name is Ardek." Victor shrugged.

"And? You have information for me? Answers about the fate of my people?"

"Yeah . . ." Victor gathered his thoughts, then tried to share what he'd learned as succinctly as possible. "The Warlord who rules Coloss rules a lot of the world, I guess; other city-states and their leaders pay him fealty. He's the one who destroyed your people, well, with a Vesh army and the help of the Yazzians. According to Black, they caused the seas to rise up and flood your homeland, and in the process, they managed to shatter your Ancestor Stone."

"Impossible!" Khul Bach said, slamming a fist into his palm, but Victor felt it was more surprise than disbelief that caused the outburst.

"I have more," Victor said, waiting to see if the giant would continue fuming, but the giant didn't object further, so he continued. "Black knows about seventeen different shards from the Ancestor Stone. He says most of the clans have at least one and that the Warlord has several. He says some were left too long, and dungeons grew around them, whatever that means. Um, I'm supposed to tell you he's begging you for help—he says the Degh have grown weaker and fewer in number with every generation."

"Why will they not speak to me themselves?"

"Didn't I explain that last time? Black said that when the Ancestor Stone was destroyed, Degh with Spirit Cores died, and none have been born since."

"I . . ." Khul Bach opened his mouth to speak, but then his eyes narrowed, and he shook his head. His face fell, and he said, "It's our fault. Our hubris, our ambition, did this."

"What?" Victor had been expecting Khul Bach to rage about the Warlord, insisting that Victor kill him or something.

"We created the Ancestor Stone as a way to take control of our destiny; our bloodlines, our knowledge, our . . . ancestors, all there, tangible, ready to augment and enhance the younger generations. I can see how the Spirit Casters of my people would have been shattered with the stone; their connections were deep and permanent. With them gone, with the stone destroyed, our people languish, the great magics we created to bind us to the stone serving to harm rather than aid."

"Is there anything that can be done?"

"Aye, a powerful Spirit Caster must mend the stone." Khul Bach frowned and glowered at Victor rubbing at his chin. "You won't do. Not yet. What level did you say you'd attained? Forty?"

"Thirty-Six."

"Ancestors!" Khul Bach growled, squeezing his fists so tightly that Victor could hear the strain of the flesh on his knuckles. "One runt. One child to face the man who conquered a race of titans. This won't do."

"Uh, yeah. I've felt the Warlord's aura, and I think he could whip my ass pretty easily."

"Yes. You'll need to be much stronger. I'll need to make you stronger."

"Hold on a minute, Khul Bach." Victor held up his hands, and when the giant glowered at him, he continued, "I have a lot on my plate. I need to go back to my world, at least for a while; there's an entire army and huge households depending on me. We're supposed to conquer some new lands, and I think that will probably take a while . . ."

"Conquering is good, Victor. You'll gain strength, which you need."

"So, you're cool with me not challenging the Warlord right away?"

"Ha! I'm not a fool; you'll gain strength, you'll become a powerful force with my instruction, you'll gather my people and what shards you can under your banner, and then, only then, will you challenge the Warlord." Khul Bach's voice grew louder as he spoke, and his fists gradually lifted until they were over his head, and his final words came out as a shout.

"Hold up! Fucking hell, man! I'm not looking for another war! Besides, why would your people win now, when they're weaker and fewer than when the Warlord last beat them? What if I could get my hands on the Warlord's shards without fighting him? Maybe he doesn't care about them all that much . . ."

"Don't be naive; the man holds them for a reason!" Khul Bach growled, leaning closer to Victor, fury in his eyes. Victor knew the anger wasn't really directed toward him, but he felt as if he needed to take a step back to settle the giant down, so he held up his hands and cleared his throat.

"Hold on! We need to get some things straight." Khul Bach glowered but held his tongue, and Victor continued, "Of course I want your guidance! I know you have a lot to teach me, and I've wanted a real mentor for a long time. That doesn't mean I'm going to throw away my life and my freedom for it. I can find what I need elsewhere; it might be hard and take me decades or even centuries, but I'll be doing what I want, of my own free will. Do you get me?"

"So you would leave my people to languish? You'd have them whither away to nothing?"

"I'm not saying that. I'm not saying I won't help them, but I need you to know that I'll do it when I think I'm ready and when I don't have other people already depending on me." Victor held the giant's gaze, difficult as it was. He felt as if he were lifting weights with his eyeballs, struggling to hold up under the mountain-sized aura bleeding out of the giant's oddly pink-hued eyes.

"A bargain well struck," the giant said at last, his posture softening and his deep frown relaxing. "When you're ready, then. I, too, think you need work. Much of it."

"Right . . ."

"Your Core is pathetic. Do you never cultivate?"

"I cultivate . . ." Victor's voice lost its stern conviction, raising an octave on the word, and he frowned, annoyed with himself.

"Not enough. Your Core should be in the advanced stages. What's your highest ranked spell?"

"Um, Berserk and Sovereign Will are both advanced."

"Passable," the giant sniffed, then added, "but barely. You should use them at every opportunity. Berserk frees your titan blood, no? And Sovereign Will, your ability to force your body to rise to greatness? What attributes are you currently enhancing?"

"Well, none; I'm not fighting or anything . . ."

"Bash's Blood, boy! You should be using it always! Because you aren't planning a fight doesn't mean your enemies feel the same!"

"It takes concentration . . ."

"How much? How hard is it?"

"It's like . . . it's like trying to hold your eyes open without blinking; I can do it, and I can do it for a long time, but it starts to wear on me."

"Then you must keep using it, practice it until it feels more like breath-ing. Eventually, you'll feel worse without it than with it. Do you understand?"

"Yes." Victor nodded.

"Good! We want that spell to grow into the epic range as soon as possible. I believe you'll experience a great breakthrough when that happens. Now, tell me about your Core. I know you have three affinities. I know you're in the improved ranks, but why? Do you hate to cultivate?"

"I'm just . . . I'm just always busy, and yeah, cultivating is a pain in the ass, especially my rage and fear affinities; I have to live through those emotions. I have to grind through them like a fucking miner trying to get a nugget of gold out of a mountain of stone."

"Show me," the giant said, and Victor knew what he meant; he expected him to do some cultivating at that moment.

"In here?"

"You'll struggle to gain any strength cultivating here because of the nature of this place; it's outside the flow of time, but you can still show me your method."

"All right," Victor sighed, and then he closed his eyes and turned his gaze inward, pulling up one of the constructs he'd built from his memories, a construct of rage. He studied it, wrapped his mind around it, felt the raw heat of his fury, his animosity—it was a construct built from a memory concerning his cousins, one of the many times they'd bullied him, speaking Spanish about him, teasing him about his "*gringa*" mother.

He remembered them laughing at how he only understood a few of their words and mimicking the way his mom walked and spoke; he'd only been a little boy then, and his mom had been everything to him—his dad, Hernan Sandoval, did shift work for the military in Nevada, flew out of Phoenix, and was sometimes gone for weeks. Victor remembered feeling like an outcast, an outsider in his own family, only happy when his mom took him home. He and his mom had been a team, and she'd done everything for him. Then she'd died.

Victor felt the fury building in his pathways and worked it, pushing, driving, gathering, and pulling it into his Core. He wallowed in his construct, soaking it in, becoming the rage that simmered there in his past. He didn't know how long he sat like that, running through his drill, but he knew it was a good long while before the giant cleared his throat and gave him a nudge.

"Enough, Victor." When Victor looked up at him, he saw the giant's face was troubled and that much of his earlier hostility had faded. "Rage is a difficult affinity, lad. I see the pain on your face while you struggle with it. Who taught you that drill?"

"Well, I mostly learned it myself through experimentation. When I first had to cultivate, I wasn't much more than a slave, and I didn't have any real help."

"Then you should be proud. Your drill is potent, and if the Energy were richer around you, I believe you'd be pulling great swaths of it into your pathways, converting it to rage, strengthening your Core with each repetition. Still, there's room for improvement. The method you use to gather the Energy, condense it, and siphon it into your Core needs work.

"Did you know that Energy calls to Energy? The more you leave in your pathways, the faster you'll pull more in, and the faster it will convert to rage or whatever affinity you're cultivating. You must learn to fill your pathways to bursting, then to siphon off only half of that Energy, leaving the rest to build up another rotation more quickly."

"I get it." Victor nodded. "I can do that, Khul Bach."

"Good. When you return, I'll expect your Core to be stronger. So, tell me about your spirit totems. You mentioned the spell last time we spoke."

"They're fragments of my own soul, as far as I understand . . ." Victor spent what felt like hours going over his spells with Khul Bach—how he learned them, what they did, what rank they'd gotten to, and what his plans were as far as improving each one. The answer to that last question always tended to be some variation of "Well, I hadn't really thought about it; I just planned to keep using them and hope they improve."

Khul told Victor that the best way for him to improve his abilities was to pick one or two and focus on them, then go on to the next. Sure, it helped to use them all whenever he needed them, but he wanted Victor to get some skills and spells into the epic level as quickly as possible. That said, he insisted that Victor go berserk at every possibility and keep himself boosted by Sovereign Will at all times.

"Really? You want me berserking when I'm not even in a fight?" Victor said when Khul delivered that last instruction.

"Yes. You have the will to manage it. If you push that spell beyond epic into legendary, it's likely to morph; I have high hopes for it. Should you fully master yourself under its influence, it won't exactly be a 'berserking' spell, will it?"

"Spells can change . . ." Victor stopped himself before he finished the question. Of course spells could change; he'd seen it himself as he'd used different Energy to cast them, or when they'd increased in level from basic to improved or beyond—they gained new effects or became more potent.

"I see the light blooming behind your dim eyes, apprentice. You may yet learn. So, here are my orders: Never go a waking moment without Sovereign Will active. If you must rest your mind from time to time, that's permitted, but only so long as you absolutely have to. Secondly, you must use your Berserk ability whenever possible, and you must practice casting other spells while under its influence."

"Fuck, man. My traveling companions aren't really going to love this . . ."

"Good! People should fear and respect you. You're the descendent of titans, and by the Ancestors, all the gods, and their children, I'm going to make you into a worthy scion. Now, tell me about your axe."

"Lifedrinker? How do you know about her?"

Khul pointed to Victor's waist and said, "Its echo is here with you."

"What . . ." Victor looked down, but he didn't see what Khul was pointing at. He'd left Lifedrinker on his dresser. "I don't see her."

"Because your mind knows where it is. The echo of its spirit is heavy, though, and closely tied to your own."

"Her," Victor said, frowning. "She's alive and not an 'it.'"

"Ah, yes. Of course. So, *she* speaks to you?"

"Yeah," Victor said, then he spent another long while telling Khul all about Lifedrinker.

"A worthy weapon for my scion! And you think she's coming close to an evolution?"

"Yeah, I'm sure of it!" Victor said, grinning proudly, as though Lifedrinker were his child and he was telling another parent about her accomplishments at school.

"Let's hope she grows. A strong spirit is good, but you'll need a mighty weapon to take on the Vesh."

"I'm not taking on the Vesh . . ."

"Not yet!" Khul said, holding up a hand to forestall argument. "When next you slay an enemy, be sure to let your axe feast! More than that, don't forget to honor your ancestors. Have I given you enough to work on? You should bring my shard with you, of course; we can speak while you're on your hunt."

"About that," Victor said, frowning. "Your shard is pretty large, and it's in a box. It's not exactly convenient to carry around."

"Do *not* put me in a dimensional container!" Khul roared.

"I know, I know! Is there anything else I can do?"

"Yes, a simple solution exists: have the shard built into an amulet or some such, and have the Artificer reduce the size of it. Just be sure that when the shard is removed from the jewelry, it will retain its original form. Easily done, and the size of the shard will not affect me at all. Just don't damage it!"

"Oh? All right, that doesn't sound bad, then. Okay, Khul Bach, I think I should get going—you've given me plenty to work on."

"Yes. Speak to me as soon as you're able. I'll want a thorough update on your progress."

Victor nodded, and then he gathered up his Energy. When he opened his eyes, he was sitting in his room, and the moon still hung high in the sky outside his window. Victor hopped to his feet, one fist tight around the ancestor shard, then he walked over and scooped up Lifedrinker, slipping her into his belt. He strode with purpose through the suite and out the door, then broke into a jog.

He'd made it to the first stairwell when he frowned and concentrated, casting Sovereign Will to boost his vitality and strength; then as he hurried down the steps, Victor cast Berserk. Red-tinged fury filled his vision, and a growl slipped past his lips, but he kept moving, realizing he was now striding easily down the Degh side of the steps. Occasional growls escaped him, and his fists were clenched and ready to strike out, one holding tightly to the ancestor shard.

He was glad it was the dead of night and nobody was out and about in the hallways; Victor kept looking for something to fight and kept catching himself doing so, but he growled, and with an effort of will, he pushed the rage out of his mind, let it fester in his pathways, let it simmer in his heart, ready to explode, but kept his mind cool. It was a struggle to do so without ending the Berserk spell altogether, and he found the exercise both taxing and rewarding; he could do this.

When he'd descended several levels and came to the cramped, narrow tunnels that led deeper still, he finally allowed the spell to fade and breathed a deep sigh of relief; he felt as if he'd just done several circuits around a weight room, using every machine along the way. Still, he felt good and knew his advanced body wouldn't let him down, so he crouched low and hurried through the tunnels, making his way to Fough's workshop.

The door was slightly ajar, and when Victor peered through, he saw Fough sitting at the same table where he'd last seen him, only this time, he was poring over a densely inscribed stone tablet. "Come in," the Artificer said without looking up.

"Hey," Victor said, stepping into the room and straightening his back with a sigh.

"Thought of something you need at the last minute?" Fough asked, a wry smile on his face as he looked up from his tablet.

"Yeah, actually." Victor stepped forward with the ancestor shard and then said, "I need a convenient way to carry this, and maybe some more like it, but I can't put it in a dimensional container because . . ."

"Because a powerful spirit lies within," Fough said, standing up from his stool and stepping back from the shard.

"Yeah, exactly."

"Well, I can help you—the spirit, it's not hostile, is it?"

"No. Shouldn't be anyway." Victor kept his grip on the shard, pleased by its gentle pink glow.

"How many others do you anticipate needing to accommodate?"

"Well, at least eighteen." Victor didn't know why he said that, why he was trying to prepare for all the other shards when he knew damn well it would be a long time—maybe many years—before he'd need to worry about them, but something about it felt right.

Fough's eyes narrowed, and he held his chin between his thumb and fore-finger, the scales glittering ever so slightly in the glow of the lamps. "What about a bracer? I could make a bracer and enchant it to hold the shard and others like it; When you touch the shard to the socket, it will decrease in size and sink into it."

"Would I be able to remove it, and would the shard return to its normal size and shape?"

"Naturally." Fough moved off to rummage in one of his trunks as if he'd finished with Victor.

"Can you do it now? I mean, I can pay extra for the short timing, but I gotta leave town at dawn . . ."

"Yes, yes. I'm intrigued. I have a bracer I can modify if I can just find it." Fough continued to rummage in the trunk, nothing but a black void visible to Victor within its four sides.

A thought occurred to Victor as he looked around himself. He was in one of the only open areas in the room, standing on a large rug before Fough's primary workbench. "Well, I don't want to alarm you, but I'm supposed to be practicing a spell; I'm going to increase in size a bit while you're working . . ."

22

INTO THE WASTES

Victor stood outside the city gates, watching the other members of the hunting company gather beneath the dawn-lit sky; stars were still visible, but a hint of orange and yellow painted the eastern horizon. Valla shifted beside him, also watching the procession of animals, wagons, and people. So far, Victor had counted nearly fifty people and half that many beasts and vehicles.

He flexed his left fist, looking down at the thick band of dark metal covering his forearm's lower half. Fough's bracer had been designed for a Degh and made from a very dense, "Energy rich" metal—some kind of ore that Victor had already forgotten the name of. Still, it was sturdy, and Fough had fitted the inner surface with gold-colored rings—another metal Victor couldn't name—in three columns of six; the center topmost was occupied by a pink gem that winked at him in the dim light.

Victor still didn't understand the magic that took the long, jagged ancestor shard and condensed it into a gemstone. He'd been worried that the crystal shard had been altered somehow when he'd first touched it to the ring. The magic had snatched it from his fingers and snapped it into the mounting, making it much smaller and rounder than when he'd been holding it. Fough had reassured him, though, touching the gem and twisting it, pulling it away, suddenly long and jagged once again.

"Pretty cool," he muttered, rubbing a thumb over the pink gem. He'd already confirmed that he could still commune with the giant's spirit even when the shard was mounted on the bracer.

"Your new bracer?" Valla asked, shifting to look up at him.

"Yeah—the way the magic changes the size and shape of the shard."

"Mmhmm. Just remember, you have a lot to do before you traipse off around this world looking for more shards. We need to get back to Fanwath . . ."

"I know, I know." Victor sighed heavily and then changed the subject. "I feel like we should have bought some mounts. Most of the hunters are mounted." He gestured to a nearby Degh riding on the back of a lumbering lizard-like creature with black and orange scales.

"Many aren't, though. Besides, I need to practice my movement spells, and you, well, you're supposed to be berserk; do you think a mount would tolerate that?"

Victor opened his mouth to reply but realized he didn't have any argument. He shrugged and said, "Yeah, I guess you have a point. Damn!" he sighed, blowing out a deep breath, "It's going to be a pain in the ass running around all these people while I'm berserk."

Valla chuckled, eyes still on the other hunters gathering into a loose line. Victor followed her gaze and saw Cayle, the woman who'd recruited them, yelling at some Vesh in a wagon, hollering about how every person and vehicle would need to keep up; she wasn't slowing down for anyone. Valla cleared her throat and said, "Have you tried spirit walking here? I wonder if you can reach your friends among the hunters . . ."

"Oh, I tried. The spirit plane was strange here. I only stood around for a few minutes, looking at the weird way the desert was reflected there. I couldn't feel any hint of Old Mother or Thayla, but there were plenty of other presences—heavy, old powers, and I felt like they'd noticed me, too. I ended the spell before I found out who they were."

"It sounds frightening. It's strange to think about; I can't wrap my head around it, really—the idea of multiple 'planes' of reality. If you were on the spirit plane here and on Fanwath, why couldn't you travel to where your friends were?"

"I don't know. Maybe I can, or maybe someone with the right skills and power can. Maybe the spirit plane is just as big as this one, and it would be like walking millions of lightyears or whatever separates this world from Fanwath."

They stood in silence after that, Valla deep in thought and Victor watching the procession, trying to build up the strength of will to make himself cast Berserk again. He'd switched his Sovereign Will bonus to vitality and agility, figuring it would make travel easier. Even with his vitality boosted, though, he felt a little tired; he hadn't slept at all the night before. Dawn had nearly come by when Fough finished with his bracer, and he hadn't wanted to try to sleep for the scant hour or two before the sun appeared.

"Victor and Valla!" Cayle called, striding toward them with her magical tablet clutched in one hand. "Happy to see you showed up."

"Glad to be here," Victor said, grinning and reaching out a hand to grasp her wrist.

"Should we travel with any particular part of the procession?" Valla asked as Cayle clasped his wrist.

"Suit yourselves. It's probably safest with the wagons, but you'll see more action if you're near the vanguard. No mounts? Well, we move at a decent pace, but nothing a strong Energy user should struggle to match." She grinned and pointed toward the front of the gathered hunters and said, "My mount is up there; see her? The sky ferraga?"

"Sky ferraga?" Victor squinted, trying to see where she pointed.

"The winged serpent off to the side, there; the one with the yellow and black scales. She's not big enough to fly with me yet, but I'll be terrorizing the skies on her back in another fifty years!" She laughed and stomped off to check in another group of hunters—three Yazzians in their plain, earth-toned robes.

"That would be cool," Victor said to Valla as they watched her walk away. "A flying mount, I mean."

"It sounds amazing but dangerous. I supposed you'd have to have an elaborate saddle. Speaking of which, I miss Uvu."

"Yeah, your cat would love it around here."

"No, he wouldn't. He'd hate all these other predatory mounts. I'd have to ride him a good distance from the train."

"Hello, Victor. Valla." Victor jerked his head toward the voice and saw Tes standing between the two of them and the gate; she'd approached noiselessly. He smiled when he saw her attire: high blue-stained leather boots that came to her knees, white stockings that rose higher, and then a simple pale yellow dress that fell to about mid-thigh, cinched at the waist by a delicate-looking, laced blue ribbon. Her hair picked up the yellow and orange highlights in the morning sun, and the delicate blonde curls framed her face as though she were waiting for a professional modeling shoot.

"Uh," Victor said, struggling to decide if he should comment on her appearance or if it was one of those situations where his mouth was going to get him in trouble.

"You look like you're going for a picnic, Tes!" Valla said, chuckling and stepping forward to take Tes's delicate-looking hand in her own.

"Well, I have all I need in storage, and I see no reason to be uncomfortable while traveling. I don't plan to fight any of the creatures we encounter anyway. I've no need for prize tokens." She smiled, scrunching her hazel eyes. For some reason, Victor had remembered them being blue, but he couldn't be sure if his memory was playing tricks on him or if they'd changed color one of the times he'd encountered her.

"So, you're really coming along to help Valla train? That's pretty cool of you, Tes."

"Not just Valla. I've a thing or two to show you, my burly friend. Am I mistaken, or have you grown in stature since Blue's rather memorable party?" She stepped toward him, and suddenly she was looking him almost in the eye, towering over Valla. The growth had been instant and so thoroughly unexpected that Victor had to shake his head and blink his eyes to force some order back into his perception.

"Gah!" Valla said, also shocked by the shift in Tes's size. "What sort of spell is that? Did you really grow, or is that an illusion?"

"Bit of both, dear," Tes said, grinning at Victor. "Well? I believe I heard your companion mention that you're supposed to be working on your Berserk ability. Let's see!"

"You heard that . . ." Valla started to ask, but Victor knew better than to try to understand the woman—dragon. He had a feeling she could do a great deal more than she let on; if she wanted to listen to their conversation from a distance, that seemed like a tiny fraction of her capabilities. As Valla spoke, he sighed and released the spell he'd been building up, already intent on following Khul Bach's instructions.

As the rage flooded his pathways and his vision tinted red, his perspective shifted, and he was looking down at Tes again, Valla more like a child than a grown woman beside her. He'd already begun to find it easier to hold most of his rage from his mind, letting it simmer and fume in his pathways, thumping with red-hot waves through his body with each of his heartbeats. He grunted and tried to smile at Tes, but a smile was a bit more to ask for than he could manage while berserk—it came out like a savage, bloodthirsty grin.

"Goodness," Tes said, glancing at Valla. "Even better up close! Can you feel the heat of his aura? That's the smoldering potential of an elder being—a true titan. Victor, you've done well to connect so deeply to your ancestor. Your bloodline is strong! I can feel it thrumming, and my heart sings with it. I feel a kinship; our ancestors used to hunt under the same moon."

"Where are you from, Tes?" Valla asked, a puzzled look on her face.

Before Tes could reply, though, Victor rumbled, "I need to move. I feel the urge to fight." It was true. His blood boiled and seethed, his muscles twitched, and his eyes kept darting around, looking for the reason he was there; where was his enemy? Surely there must be one nearby. Why were all these weaklings loitering around? He knew the ones near him, they were friends, but those others . . . no, they weren't enemies. He had work to do; he needed to travel, needed to find a monster to slay.

"Come!" Tes said, and suddenly she was larger yet again, standing just a bit shorter than Victor's towering, hulking form. "I know the route the hunt will take; let us get a head start, and perhaps you can tussle with a beast or two!" She laughed and started jogging, her long legs carrying her away from the gates, dust stirring beneath her feet, and her short, frilly yellow dress trailing behind her.

Victor didn't have to think twice; he saw the pretty lady in yellow running away, knew she wanted him to chase, and knew no reason why he shouldn't. He jerked Lifedrinker from his belt, holding her in one hand, and ignoring the procession of weaklings and a few truly overbearing auras, he charged after her. His furious rage, held tightly in check by his will, found a new outlet; rather than killing, he was hunting, and he lifted his head and roared with delight, savoring the thrill of the chase.

If he'd had eyes for anything other than his quarry, always so close but just a bit too far away to leap upon, Victor would have seen a much smaller figure trailing close behind him. Valla ran, blue sword in hand, her legs a blur of dusty wind and occasional bright flickers of lightning. Further back, a woman mounted atop a long, colorful serpent rode up and down the line of hunters, excoriating them, shouting that the hunt was afoot and they'd be left out.

They ate up the miles, long, powerful legs that never tired carrying them up and down dusty hillsides and past the scattered scrubs and cacti; they didn't follow a road or trail, but Victor didn't have the presence of mind to wonder if Tes truly knew the way; he had one thing in mind—catch the woman in yellow. Every time he started to get close, she'd pull away, and the constant frustration kept his fury bright in his eyes.

Victor remembered Khul Bach's words, though: he was supposed to practice casting other spells while berserk, so he tried. He reached into his Core and saw that his pathways were thick with rage and that his Core was slowly growing dimmer, but he ignored that. He clumsily yanked at a strand of inspiration and tried to cast Inspiring Presence. Could he do it? Could he be beserk and also an inspirational force on the field of battle? He'd often wondered.

He felt the inspiration-attuned Energy fight for space in his pathways, felt it gather into the pattern for his spell, and then, with a rush of clarity, it flooded outward, and his rage receded. Victor stumbled as he rapidly decreased in size, and the urgency of the chase left him. Still, he was a big, fast man, and now he was inspired, and he laughed, pushing his legs to pump harder as he ran after the slender giantess in the yellow dress, her blue ribbon of a belt trailing behind her.

Tes stopped, though, and when he caught up to her, laughing, Valla close on his heels, she smiled and said. "You're not quite ready for that, Victor. Your rage dominates your pathways, and the inspiration fights with it for space; they're both potent spells. You'll need to level your Core and expand your pathways to manage both at once."

She paused and glanced at Valla with a smile, then back toward a narrow gully between some scrub-covered hills, "I sense a pack of sand spiders ahead; you should go berserk again—you're trying to improve that spell, right?"

"Right . . ."

"Hurry then, before Valla kills them all," she said, running toward the gully. Valla howled and charged after her.

"Shit!" Victor said, jogging after them and looking to his Core—his rage was nearly half depleted, but he figured he could manage another Berserk. "How long can I hold it, though," he grunted, canceling his Inspiring Presence and quickly casting Berserk. It failed to take hold, and he realized it was still on cooldown. "No fucking fair!" he wailed into the sky, watching Valla and Tes shrinking with distance as they ran into the hills.

He started running, really running, not jogging. Part of him wanted to cast the Inevitable Huntsman, but he knew better—he didn't know exactly how to choose his quarry when that spell took shape, and he didn't want to lose control of himself. "Come on," he grunted, pushing himself as hard as he could, straining his leg muscles, pumping his lungs like a bellows as he tore over the rocky, barren soil, leaping shrubs and cacti, never wavering from his beeline toward the splash of yellow in the distance.

When he finally entered the gully, the low scrub-covered hills rising around him, he looked at his Core again, saw his rage nearly recovered, and tried to cast his Berserk. As the rage flooded into him, as his perspective changed with his renewed height, and as his muscles surged with power, he roared in furious excitement, leaping a dozen yards up the side of a hill.

He tore through the dirt and smashed a brittle tree apart, the only obstacle in his path that he couldn't leap. He saw the yellow-clad woman stop, standing before a brush-covered depression, and then the more diminutive whirlwind of a woman—Valla, he reminded his dulled, angry mind—kept running. He was half a mile away when the sand and shrubs burst upward into the air, and dozens of pony-sized, furry, brown and orange arachnids exploded out of the ground, charging toward his friend.

Victor renewed his frenzied pace, roaring out a challenge as he leapt and ran over the desert landscape. He allowed his berserking Energy to flare through him, pulling back his will. As his body heated up with the volatile power of his rage-attuned Energy, he seemed to find a new gear, exploding over the ground, leaving smashed and ruined obstacles in his dust-clouded wake.

His thoughts had grown blissfully simple; all the background noise that lived in the corners of his mind faded away, and only one single objective filled the totality of his consciousness—kill the creatures that threatened his friend. With the joy of simplicity of purpose, Victor leapt into battle, Lifedrinker singing like a whistling executioner as he whipped her left and right, wading through the frantic, clicking, hissing, thrashing arachnids.

Lifedrinker severed limbs, smashed carapaces, tore through fangs, and cleaved apart clusters of black, bulbous eyes. Gore flew in her wake, and Victor's other hand didn't idly rest while she worked. He grabbed legs, yanking spiders left and right, smashing them together and flinging them apart. All the while, he suffered countless bites and stabs from the creatures' claw-hooked legs.

He was in full, glorious rage, though, and Victor's body was far sturdier than the last time enemies had swarmed him. The bites left shallow punctures in his flesh that mended almost instantly, and the claws scraped along his thick, sturdy skin, leaving a wake of pink healed flesh; he hardly lost a drop of blood before the shallow injuries on his arms, neck, and legs closed up.

When he finally cleared a path to Valla, he found her surrounded by charged, metallic dust, jolts of stabbing electricity flashing out to strike the spiders that leapt at her, stunning and scorching them. Her blue sword was like a long specter's finger, leaving dead and broken spiders with each liquid flick of its metallic touch.

Victor was so lost in his rage that he couldn't register Valla's effortless grace, couldn't see that she was holding her own just fine. He simply saw her and knew she was a friend in need, so he continued to rampage, leaping upon a particularly large spider and burying Lifedrinker into its fuzzy, many-eyed head. She sank in, and he heard her Valkyrie war cry and laughed with gore-soaked madness. He let Lifedrinker go and leapt away into the legs and snapping fangs of another group of spiders.

Victor grabbed spiders' limbs and punched spiders' abdomens; he grabbed fangs and pulled, breaking the chelicerae and pulling them free, trailing gray flesh and blue blood. Victor sank into the mad, gore-filled horror of battle, and when the rage finally stopped flowing from his depleted Core, he fell back into himself, a smaller, less titanic warrior. Then, he channeled his inspiration-attuned Energy and began to battle with wits and adroitness rather than brute, mad force.

He'd come out of his rage empty-handed, and knowing finding Lifedrinker amid the carnage would take too long, he pulled out his old baton. At first, it bounced from his foes, harming them not at all, but he cast Channel Spirit, flooding it with fear-attuned Energy, and it began to have an effect, warping and smashing spider flesh with weird purple-black clouds born from each concussive strike.

He ducked, rolled, slid, and leapt, avoiding the remaining spiders' bites and claws. Several times he found himself face to face with a rearing, hissing spider, and he lunged forward, feinting low and then driving up with his heavy, dense juggernaut helm into the fangs and hard carapaces, cracking them like eggs.

When he finally stood, some fifty yards away from Valla, both of them surrounded with mounds of gory, twitching dead spiders, it felt as though he'd been fighting for hours. Tes, still as tall as a Degh, stood to the side, spotless and fresh in her yellow dress, and clapped. "Well fought! Brace yourselves!"

"Huh?" Victor looked around; was there another threat? But then he saw it—thick globes of purple Energy were forming around the site of their battle, coalescing out of the air around the dead arachnids.

In moments they began to flow together, creating two streams. One surged toward Valla, and the other, thicker stream exploded toward Victor, poleaxing him with its flow, lifting him high in the air. He imagined something similar was happening to Valla, but he couldn't spare her a glance; his vision was filled with explosions of light, and his mind was drowned in the powerful euphoric effect.

When he finally came back to himself, Victor saw a System message waiting for him.

*****Congratulations! You have achieved level 38 Spirit Carver, gained 20 will and 20 vitality, and have 16 attribute points to allocate.*****

"Two levels?" he said, laughing.

"Congratulations, Victor and Valla!" Tes called, stepping closer, and Victor realized she'd matched his height again.

"I leveled!" Valla called. "And my Steel Tempest spell is already improved! You were right, Tes." She started to jog through the mess toward Tes and Victor.

"I can feel the hunt master and her troupe approaching. She'll take stock of the slain monsters and award you your prizes. Don't frown, Victor! You're working as part of a monster-hunting company—all kills must be shared. If I sense more packs like this, I'll try to lead you away so you can get the majority of the kills, but you'll want the others around if we meet something much stronger."

"Huh," Victor managed to say, his mind still reeling from the Energy rush and the battle before it.

"Thank you, Tes!" Valla said. "Before I learned the spell you showed me, there's no way I would have survived that. I think I killed nearly ten of the monsters, and I'm hardly scratched!"

"Of course! I said I'd help, didn't I?" Tes laughed, and then a horn sounded, and she glanced over her shoulder, then back at Victor. "They're almost here. Better pick up your axe—she's going to draw some greedy stares now that she's evolved."

Victor's eyes bugged out, and he quickly started scanning the battlefield. "She's . . . evolved?"

23

❊

REAPING THE REWARDS

Victor followed Tes's gaze to the giant arachnid corpse near the center of the gully and started kicking his way through the corpses toward it. Sure enough, as he walked around the lifeless body, its legs hanging in the air, curled inward, he saw a long, dark haft sticking out of the creature's head. He recognized it as Lifedrinker's living wood handle. Still, it was different—longer, broader, and the tiny twinkling motes of light that usually lay deep within the grain, only visible in the right light, were decidedly more pronounced.

"*Que bonita!*" he whispered through teeth clenched in nervous anticipation. He shoved the bloody, broken legs aside and reached out to grasp her haft, and a jolt of Energy hit him when his fingers wrapped around the wood. It felt familiar and different at the same time, and his grin widened as the axe seemed to sink into his grip eagerly, humming and vibrating ever so slightly.

"I can hear them growing close; come with me to stand near Victor, Valla. I'll need to calm Cayle's anger." Victor heard Tes speaking, but he couldn't concentrate on her; he had eyes only for Lifedrinker as he pulled her thick, long handle sideways, cracking the spider's carapace and freeing her head. He lifted her clear of the fuzzy, monstrous arachnid and held her up in the bright sunlight.

"Holy shit," he said, and he heard Valla's intake of breath, echoing the sentiment. Lifedrinker's Heart Silver core had spread through the black metal, nearly obscuring it to the point where only thin streaks of black lingered in the brilliant, much larger, silvery axe-head. Her blade had grown significantly, and the heavy, thick spike at the back looked ready to punch through four inches of solid steel without a problem, so wickedly did it glint in the light.

If he gripped her past the halfway point on her handle, he could still swing the axe one-handed, but she was definitely bigger and meant to be used with both hands now—at least while he wasn't the size of a Quinametzin. "I'm going to need a better way to carry her . . ." he started to say, but then a crystal-clear, feminine voice, high, sharp, and fierce, entered his mind.

"Victor, my love, do I please you?"

"Fuck yes, you do, Lifedrinker!"

"All I ever wanted, all I ever want, is to help you crush your foes. Didn't we have such fun with these many-legged weaklings? Victor, when will you make yourself large again? When can we lay waste to more of your enemies?"

"Ha!" Victor couldn't help the laugh and the huge smile that had spread on his face. "Soon, beautiful, soon. We're on a hunt now; there should be more for us to fight."

"She speaks to you?" Tes asked, walking closer, Valla close beside her.

"Yes, more than ever. She's hungry for more battle."

"Talk to your flesh-mates. I'll be close when you need me."

"Thank you, Lifedrinker," Victor said, resting her haft on his shoulder, the massive, silvery axe gleaming in the sunlight next to his head. He turned to speak to Tes and Valla, but then a commotion between the hills caught his attention, and he turned to see several enormous beasts—mounts—carrying their riders into the gully and the scene of spider carnage.

In the lead was Cayle on her thirty-foot, black-and-yellow serpent mount. This close to the creature, Victor could see its wings, folded back and rather anemic; he figured they must grow as the creature aged. Cayle didn't look happy as she pulled her snake to a stop and leapt down, crunching her boot through the exoskeleton of a dead spider's leg.

Several others also dismounted, but only one came forward with Cayle— a hulking, black-furred Vesh with four arms. He held a coppery spear that had to be twelve feet long from its tasseled haft to its needle-sharp tip, and his thick-nosed, heavy-browed face was twisted with rage. Before Cayle could speak, he growled, "I should crack your legs, runt!" With his words, a wave of anger and strength poured out, and Victor had to take a step back—this was no low-level Colossian.

"Quiet, Forx," Cayle said, holding up a hand, but she didn't look happy either. She'd kept her wings folded behind her, but her brow was furrowed under her thick, white horn, and her chocolate eyes held storm clouds within their murky depths. "When you sign on with my company, you don't race off to kill hordes on your own. I'd planned to pass this way purposefully—we often find trophies in this gully."

"It's my fault, Cayle," Tes said, stepping in front of Victor and Valla. "I led them off, thought this would be a good initiation for them. Of course, they'll share the prizes, but you have to admit, they need the experience."

"So do plenty others!" Forx roared, veins standing out on his ruddy forehead and saliva feathering out with his breath.

"Calm yourself," Tes said, and suddenly Forx blanched and stepped back. Victor had a good idea why; Tes probably gave him a taste of her aura.

Cayle seemed not to have noticed anything, though, and said, "Tes, I appreciate you're used to doing things your way around the city; I know you have the War Captains' ears, that they and the Warlord respect you. I won't hold a grudge, but I'd appreciate it if you let me run my hunt without such interference—it makes me look bad and makes it hard to keep everyone in line. Are we agreed?"

"Yes, Cayle. I'll speak to you before I do anything so impulsive again." Tes held out a hand, and Cayle took it; the two women stared at each other for a moment, and then Cayle nodded.

"Well, we've got some harvesting to do!" She turned and started hollering to the others who'd arrived at the gully but had hung back to watch how things played out. "Right! No venom glands from sand spiders, but I want hearts, fangs, claws, spinnerets, silk glands, and any piece of carapace bigger than a square foot!"

Some people started moving toward the battle scene, but others hung back, and Cayle shouted, "I'm a fair hunt master, people! If you help harvest, you will be rewarded. If you laze about, your share will be docked!"

"You'll want the book lungs and ovaries from the females, too, Cayle," Tes said quietly, a hand before her lips.

"That's right. Thank you," Cayle nodded and then shouted the orders.

"Come, Victor, Valla," Tes said. "I'll teach you how to harvest a sand spider."

It took the hunting party the better part of two hours to comb through the bloody corpses, carving off carapaces, slicing out organs, and piling them all on large tarps that Cayle watched over, making some sort of tally on her magical clipboard. Tes kept her promise, showing Valla and Victor how to slice away the salvageable large pieces of carapace and how to make sense of the mess within the spiders' abdomens. Victor enjoyed the removal of the fangs the most, as it didn't require as much carving and wasn't nearly as odiferous a pursuit.

In the end, when Cayle awarded the treasures, he and Valla each received a sizeable pile of parts—several large hunks of carapace, a dozen fangs each, and six of each organ, including the hearts. Victor stared at his blue-spattered prizes for a long while, and then he started putting them into his ring, saving the longest pair of fangs and the biggest heart.

"What are you doing?" Valla asked, watching how Victor stared at the long, weirdly tubular spider heart.

"Are you going to eat it?" Tes asked, grinning over Valla's head.

"Not this one. I might eat some of the others, but I'll wait 'til I'm berserk. No, this one is for my ancestors, along with these fangs."

"They're valuable, Victor!" Valla said. "I heard some of the others talking—we already have enough monster parts to trade for a prize token if we're crafty with our dealing."

"I need to start earning my ancestors' favor, Valla. I know it's hard to understand, but it'll be worth it."

"I believe him," Tes said. After watching Victor stare at the trophies for another minute, she prompted, "Well? The hunting party is getting ready to move again soon . . ."

"What Energy attunement should I use? Does it matter?"

"Oh? You haven't done this before?"

"No."

"I don't know the right answer, but if I were you, I'd cast the spell with my inspiration-attuned Energy; it seems fitting for a man seeking his ancestors' help and guidance."

"Yeah. I was thinking the same—I was afraid they might take offense at rage- or fear-tainted offerings." Victor nodded and concentrated on the bloody heart and the two fangs he'd rested atop it, and then he cast Honor the Spirits for the first time. He clamped down on his rage and fear Energy pools and allowed his inspiration to feed the spell.

As the pattern completed and the Energy rushed out of him, brilliant white flames engulfed the spider trophies, but not a bit of smoke rose from them; they flared like a chemical reaction and then faded away, nothing left of the fangs or heart, not even ash or charred soil where they'd been resting.

"An expensive offering," Tes said, nodding. "I hope your ancestors appreciate it."

"Yeah." Victor shrugged, then looked at the column of hunters, their mounts, wagons, and retainers starting to wend their way out of the gully through a different gap in the hills. "So, we gotta stay with the rest of 'em from now on?"

"No," Tes chuckled. "I already spoke to Cayle about another potential target on the way—I've caught the scent of a juvenile rock wyrm a league or so to the north; she doesn't want to pursue it but has given us permission to have a look."

"Why doesn't she . . ." Valla started, but Tes had anticipated the question.

"It could take hours to track it down, and she doesn't want to move the whole hunt that far off course for a single juvenile—she's hoping to take on an adult blood wyrm at Vagrant's Oasis, quite a different sort of challenge."

"You're cool with us hunting wyrms?" Victor asked, then clamped his mouth shut; he'd forgotten Valla didn't know Tes's true nature.

"Why wouldn't I be 'cool' with it?" Tes laughed and started hiking up the side of a hill to the north, moving directly perpendicular to the rest of the hunting party.

"Come on," Valla said, hurrying after her. Victor shrugged and started jogging to catch up. When he was halfway up the hill, well away from the other mounts and people in the hunting party, he cast Berserk and fought with himself for a while until he'd gotten under control. By then, Tes was a distant yellow figure near the top of the hill, and he grinned as he laid eyes on his quarry.

With a barbaric roar, he began to leap in long bounds up the slope, quickly catching Valla. She was startled by his outburst but cast her movement spell, keeping pace with him. In his haze of diminished cognition and feeling the urge to fight, Victor was moderately pleased to find he didn't have to struggle with any hostility aimed at Valla; it seemed his berserk Quinametzin self had grown used to her presence and didn't consider her a threat.

He chased the woman in yellow for a long while, up and down hills, and as before, she managed to keep herself just out of his reach no matter how he thought to surprise her with a well-timed leap down a steep slope or a sudden sprint as he drew near. The frustration made it easy to maintain his rage. However, when she finally stopped and he drew near, Victor asserted his will and calmed himself, reminding his furious alter ego that she was his ally and helping him train.

"Hold your rage, Victor; keep it simmering. Look to your Core. Have you much left to draw upon?" Tes asked as he and Valla came up beside her, Victor looming to her right and Valla crouched low, a small figure to her left.

Victor did as she asked, finding it harder than usual to turn his gaze inward, well aware that it was his fury that made it difficult—he wanted to scan the horizon for a foe, wanted to lash out and strike something. Still, he forced himself, and there, quickly pulsating with hot fervor next to his other pools of Energy, stood his rage, more than half depleted. "Half," he grumbled.

"Perhaps a snack is in order. Do you not have more hearts within your storage?"

"Those are valuable . . ." Valla started to say but gave up, shaking her head as Victor produced one of the long, strangely shaped spider hearts.

His mouth began to salivate the moment he saw it, the moment he *smelled* it. He didn't wait for an invitation or for second thoughts; he tore into the thick, rubbery meat with his powerful incisors, ripping off a gory hunk, blue blood spattering down his chin. Valla looked away, but Tes watched him with eager eyes.

Victor swallowed his first bite and chomped into the heart for a second as he felt the lump of meat sink into his gut—it was satisfying on a level he could hardly describe, but rather than be calmed by the pleasure, his rage surged, and his fury and bloodlust rose to new peaks. He hungrily gobbled the heart, one huge, ripping bite after another. All the while, he felt something occurring within him—the meat was flooding his channels with Energy, so much that it surged into his Core, pushing it past full until, with a satisfying pulse, it expanded.

*****Congratulations! You have improved your Core to rank: Improved 2.*****

Victor wiped the message away, too eager to fight to bother reading it. "Full," he grunted, noting how Tes anxiously watched him.

"Brilliant," she laughed, then pointed down the hillside to a long expanse of rocky, sandy land. "See how the ground tremors ever so slightly?"

"Ugh," Victor grunted, nodding.

"Valla, now's your chance to try the spell Elementalist Troft showed you. Target that spot of ground with your Lightning Strike."

"From here?"

"Yes—we have the height, and you can clearly see your target. I think it will work." She didn't wait for Valla to acknowledge her instructions; she turned to Victor and, reaching a hand between his shoulder blades, gave him a shove, shouting, "Titan! Charge that spot! There's a beast there that dares to challenge you!"

Victor didn't need further urging—his tall, beautiful friend said a beast wanted to fight. How could he not charge into battle? As he ran down the hill, he released his hold on his rage, letting it flow heavy and rich into his pathways—all of them. His vision turned blood red, and Victor screamed a horrible challenge, holding Lifedrinker's gleaming blade high over his head as he bounded down the rocky slope.

Just as he reached the base of the hill, a yellow-white fork of lightning flashed out of the blue sky, cracking into the sandy ground, nearly blinding him with its brilliance. When it faded, he had a dark spot in his vision—the afterimage of the bolt. He didn't slow, though; instead, he roared into the sky, hectoring the source of the lightning, his enraged mind already having forgotten that Valla was the caster. It didn't matter, though; something was there to answer his challenge.

A horn the size of Victor's thick, muscular arm burst out of the sand, followed by a stone-plated head from which two baleful red eyes glared. The monster saw Victor leaping over the sand, axe high, and continued to surge forth, a six-foot section of neck coming clear of the ground before two brown-and-gray scaled forelimbs pulled free of the rocky soil, stomping down and clawing as it scrabbled to deliver itself from the grasping dirt.

The wyrm was half emerged, some twenty feet of rock-scaled monstrosity, when Victor made the final leap that brought him sailing toward its horn-plated head. The monster roared at him, lifting its spike-bearded chin and opening its maw, revealing dozens of foot-long teeth, well-designed for the ripping of flesh and bone.

However, Victor was no docile plate of meat, ready to be consumed. He was a leaping, screaming titan. His muscles bunched like enormous steel cables, and Lifedrinker screamed along with him, tearing through the air like a falling comet. Though he wasn't as massive as the young wyrm, Victor probably weighed close to a thousand pounds with the added mass of his Kethian juggernaut helm, and his strength was prodigious. When he crashed into the wyrm's head, he gripped its snout horn with his left hand and delivered Lifedrinker's edge into the side of its skull just behind its left eye with the other.

Lifedrinker screamed in excitement and frenzied battle lust, and the sound her edge made as it smashed and cut through scales, flesh, and bone was like a small automobile colliding with a telephone pole. The wyrm, still half in the ground, didn't stand a chance; that blow alone nearly killed it, and Lifedrinker was so deeply set in the side of its skull that when Victor released her handle, the beast had no hope of dislodging her—Lifedrinker pulled herself further in, and thick rivulets of Energy began to stream into the axe.

Victor lifted his hands and blood-spattered face to the sun and screamed his triumph, watching the wyrm thrash and flop in its death throes. Standing there, arms upraised, face hot with the brilliance of the solar light, he felt a joy in his soul that he'd rarely felt before—this was what he was made for. He was a fighter, a gladiator, a titan, and a killer of beasts, monsters, and men. Nothing felt so good as fulfilling his purpose. Once more, as the rage began to fade and his enemy's thrashing ceased, he lifted his head to the sky and screamed his titanic bloodlust.

"Well done, Victor," Tes said, walking up behind him, Valla trailing a bit further behind, her wide eyes tracing the length of the mighty wyrm. "Let your rage cool now, titan. It's time to rest and reap your rewards."

24

NIGHT CAMP

Victor strode forward to retrieve Lifedrinker from the dead wyrm, but before he could grab hold of her haft, he saw great motes of purple-gold Energy forming up around the gigantic corpse. He paused and stood back, bracing himself; it looked like a lot of Energy. Sure enough, the motes coalesced into a wide, shimmering pool, and then most of it surged toward him while a thin stream streaked toward Valla. Once again, Victor was lifted into the air, held helpless by the massive influx of Energy and the euphoric well-being that came with it.

It was such a surge that Victor felt he might gain another level, but it didn't happen; when he fell back to the ground, he had no System messages waiting for him. "I must be close, though," he said, voice thick with emotion and endorphins. "God, that's some feeling!"

"I can only imagine; I've never pulled a stream so robust," Valla said, though she looked quite pleased.

"Just wait," Tes said to Valla, resting her hand on her shoulder. "When you've improved that lightning strike and built up your well of Energy, you'll be able to smite large groups of enemies; throw a few dozen of those out into a battlefield, and when all's said and done, you'll collect quite the reward.

"A few dozen? I was nearly exhausted from just the one!"

"Naturally, we have a lot of work to do, but you're on the right road now. Victor, get your axe, and then I'll show you how to harvest a rock wyrm!"

"Right," Victor said, but before he grabbed Lifedrinker, he pulled up his status sheet and allocated his free points into his will attribute—he should have done it after fighting the arachnids, but at least he'd remembered now. "Three seventy-seven will," he said, grinning at Tes and Valla.

"Oh, Ancestors!" Valla hissed, stepping forward to give him a punch in the shoulder.

"Hey!" Victor laughed, then reached up to grab Lifedrinker's haft and pull her free, with a squelching crunch, from the wyrm's skull.

"Settle down, dears," Tes said, chuckling. "Shall I start listing off my attributes?"

"Yes!" Victor and Valla both said, eager to hear just how strong the woman was, but Tes laughed and shook her head. She held out her right hand, and suddenly an ivory-hilted, bone-colored knife was resting in her palm; its eight-inch blade was long, tapered to a needle point, and curved ever so slightly. It was the knife's blade that had Victor's eyes bugging out, though; it shimmered with red light, and wisps of smoke or steam drifted off it, curling away into the pale blue sky.

"I'll train you to clean this corpse with my hell blade, but you'll eventually have to get your own carving knife. Fair warning: this knife is going to spoil you."

"Hell blade?" Valla softly asked, leaning close to look at the wicked edge.

"Oh yes. It's crafted from the fang of a greater pit fiend and charged with hell-attuned Energy. We'll make short work of our job with this beauty." As if to illustrate, Tes stepped closer to the wyrm's head, and with two quick swipes of the knife, she removed one of its long white teeth, leaving a smoking hole in the creature's gums.

"There's a 'hell' Energy?" Victor asked, still stuck on the implications.

"Yes, but don't get too worked up about it; there are many planes—as you should know, being able to Spirit Walk—and some of them are categorized as 'hells.' It's nothing to do with some of the other meanings and connotations the word might have for you."

"All right," Victor said, shrugging. "So, how much of this bad boy is worth saving?"

"A lot of it!" Tes laughed, then she said, "Now, watch more closely. I'll cut out one more tooth, then you two can take over. We'll go bit by bit, but we should hurry because once we start to spill the offal from our prize"—she patted a hand against the horns jutting from the wyrm's chin—"some larger predators might be drawn to the smell."

By the time they'd finished carving out valuable parts of the wyrm's carcass, the sun was sinking toward the western horizon, and Victor and Valla were soaked in wyrm blood up to their shoulders. They'd learned to carve out horns, teeth, glands, organs, claws, and some plate-like, rocky scales. Tes taught them how to tell which scales were worth saving and which weren't—the more mature plates had a coppery sheen if you rubbed them with oil, and she said they'd be valuable to crafters.

Victor and Valla shared the spoils, though it didn't really matter—they'd probably pool their resources when they got back to town anyway. Still, Valla insisted Victor take the heart, and he nodded his agreement; he was curious what his Quinametzin alter ego would think of it. Of the other parts, Tes said the wyrm's venom sacs—Victor hadn't even realized it was venomous—were the most valuable.

Valla took one, and he did as well, but he cast Honor the Spirits on it, and Tes watched with gleaming, eager eyes while his spell consumed the valuable prize. Valla's look was more one of horror, as though she were watching a child pour priceless liquor into the sink. While he watched the brilliant flames consume the big, greenish-yellow organ, Victor said, as if by instinct, "Take this offering, Ancestors! Grow stronger in your realm!"

"Do they linger there?" Valla asked when it was over. "Your ancestors, I mean? I always thought most ancestors move on to . . . other things. My elders taught me to honor my ancestors, but it's more an homage; we believe that most spirits move on and that only those that want to meddle tend to stick around."

"I think Quinametzin are different. I don't know how, exactly, but when I had my bloodline vision, my ancestor believed that when he sent his offering into the spirit realm, it found its way to his ancestors and made them stronger. In turn, they'd sometimes grant him some of their strength."

"Quinametzin? The name for your titan bloodline?" Valla asked, clarifying.
"Yeah."

"Your ancestor, the one walking through your blood, was wise. The spirit plane is a gateway to many realms. A powerful being could easily send messages or Energy through it from one realm or plane to another. I wonder where your ancestors live and fight!" Tes looked into the sky for a moment, eyes narrowed in contemplation, then said, "Likely many different worlds and realms and planes—your spell and your spirit must have a way of finding them."

"Pretty cool," Victor said, nodding. He tried to imagine it—dying and then finding his way, as a spirit, to a new place, some kind of new existence, and he wondered what sorts of challenges he'd face; surely the ideas of heaven and hell had to come from somewhere. He wondered if spirits went wherever they wanted or if something from their past might pull them in a particular direction. He wondered if they always forgot their old lives when they left the spirit plane or if some of them remembered something somehow.

Victor was pleased to know that this existence, though it might end, wouldn't necessarily mean the end of him. As he contemplated an afterlife, and as they walked, their prizes safely stored in their dimensional containers, another thought occurred to him, and he asked, "Tes, you told me that many strong bloodlines existed in my homeworld, that lots of elder races mingled with humans. Does that mean I might have more than one bloodline?"

"I would think so, given how many generations have passed since the elder peoples walked your Earth. If you dream of waking more of them, though, I have some bad news. Your Quinametzin bloodline must have been the strongest, closest to the surface when you went digging around in your blood. As you've pulled it further out of the past, into your pumping blood and cells, it surely has pushed any other bloodlines further down. I've never seen a person wake more than one bloodline from an elder heritage."

"Ah." Victor nodded, slightly crestfallen; he'd had some unvoiced dreams of gaining wings or something cool like that one day.

"Don't be glum, titan-blood. Few bloodlines can compare to that of a titan—I don't mean giant, mind you. You know the difference, yes?"

"I don't . . ." Valla said from Tes's other side.

"Ah." Tes turned to smile at Valla and said, "It's a matter of Energy density and potential. A titan, while a giant, is not the same as a giant who is not a titan. Titans"—she paused as if considering her words—"are known for destruction and dominance. They're clever and powerful and sometimes rise to such levels of power that other peoples view them as gods. Giants are different; they might resemble a titan, but their potential isn't on the same scale—their Energy affinity and innate abilities are simply on different levels. It's like comparing a newborn member of your race, Valla, an Ardeni, with one who's advanced their race into legendary status."

"Are they related, though? Khul Bach"—Victor touched his bracer—"thinks I'm somehow related to him."

"Related, indeed, but the Degh are not simple giants; they're fallen titans. Surely he's explained that to you?"

"Their Ancestor Stone . . ."

"Exactly. They made a pact, a blood rite, and fueled it with spirit Energy. Their Ancestor Stone granted them great potency, but its destruction ruined them. I've been studying the histories of this world a bit while I've been in Coloss."

"Khul wants me to help the Degh here. When I'm stronger."

"Much stronger, I'd hope." Tes laughed. "You have powerful abilities, a potent combination of affinities, and, obviously, your bloodline, but you're no match for Warlord Thoargh, and sadly, I cannot help you with him or those loyal to him; I've made a pact."

"Yeah, no, I don't plan to try to rebuild the Ancestor Stone anytime soon. Maybe someday, though." Victor felt a little guilty saying "maybe," considering the agreement he'd made with Khul Bach, but he knew he was just playing things down; he really did intend to help the giant and his people someday.

"It'll be dark soon," Valla said. "Should we hurry?"

"We'll come upon the hunters' train in a dozen miles; already, they move to make camp."

"How do you know that stuff, Tes? Like, how did you know where to find the spiders and the wyrm?" Victor looked from Tes to Valla, who shrugged.

"My senses are . . . robust." Tes laughed and reached over to tousle Victor's hair. "Come, shall we hurry as Valla suggests?" She started running, and Victor sighed, then looked at Valla.

"She'll only tell us what she wants us to know. Have you figured that out?"

"Yes . . ." Valla looked ready to say more, but Tes interrupted her.

"I can hear you two! Come!" She laughed, pulling away from them, dust rising in her wake. Valla cast her movement spell, a cloud of swirling, electrically charged wind surrounding her feet as she bolted after Tes's yellow, streaming skirts.

"Oh hell," Victor sighed, shifting Lifedrinker where she rested against his shoulder and breaking into a jog. "Guess I might as well keep practicing," he grunted as he cast Berserk, and then, red fury clouding his vision, he dashed and leapt after the two women, a maniac's grin on his face.

When they came within sight of the hunters' camp, Tes stopped and let Victor "catch" her, encouraging him to let his rage fade away. When he'd cooled down and they walked past the perimeter guards, Victor was tired and hoped there wouldn't be anything more to do before he got some sleep; he'd gotten precisely none the night before. Unfortunately, the hunters' camp wasn't a place to quickly find sleep.

The strange beasts the people of Coloss used for mounts were staked around the tents, bedrolls, and campfires of the hunters, but they made quite a racket as the moons rose—howls, grunts, yowls, and hisses. The noises were exceptional not because of their variety but because of their volume; many of the mounts were sized for Degh, and their voices had a way of rolling through the night and echoing over the desert landscape that Victor found jarring. Valla was no different, and when she voiced a complaint, a nearby hunter walked over.

He was an old, grizzled fellow with two chipped bull horns and a prodigious underbite from which four long tusks sprouted. "Don't ye worry 'bout it, lass. Them beasties will get quiet after a bit—they're just letting each other know who they are. You'll get used to 'em soon, anyhow. Why, I couldn't sleep without them lovely sounds—means there ain't any adult wyrms or drakes attacking."

"Well put, old-timer," Tes said, looking up from where she was laying out a bedroll.

"Old-timer? Why, I ought . . . nah, I'm jus' joking. I'm old, all right." He laughed and then moved back to his campfire.

"Funny fellow," Tes said, and Victor noticed she'd made herself an average human's size again while he hadn't been looking.

"Tes, I have a tent if you want to share," Valla said, pulling out her fancy camping equipment and beginning to set it up in the spot Tes had commandeered for them.

"What the hell?" Victor laughed. "I never got an invite like that . . ."

"I imagine you're too large and smelly," Tes laughed.

"I see how this trip is going to be," Victor sighed, then dug around in his ring for his own bedroll and small, one-man tent, glancing over his shoulder every so often to watch the two women put together Valla's sizable tent and populate it with all the furniture she kept in her storage containers—armchairs, tables, carpets, a canopied bed, and several glow lamps. "I swear to God, when we get back to town, I'm buying a shitload of camping gear, and by camping gear, I mean a huge tent and a bunch of furniture."

"You can put your bedroll on the rug here," Valla said.

"Well, thanks." Victor laughed, getting up and moving it over. "I don't remember your tent being quite this big before . . ."

"It's got a few different appearances. Rellia bought it for me when I left for the Legion."

"Tes," a new voice called from just outside. Victor recognized Cayle and straightened up from where he'd been laying out his bedroll.

"Yes, Cayle?" Tes asked, lithely springing up from one of Valla's armchairs.

"How was your wyrm hunt?"

"One juvenile . . . Do you want the spoils?"

"No, no. You offered, and I declined to bring the hunt, so you should keep them. I have another request."

"You want me to bring your brother the next time we break off?" Tes asked, and Cayle laughed.

"I'm that transparent?"

"No, but it's logical; he's low tier, and you want him to learn, just as Victor and Valla are learning. Of course, we'll let him come along if we break off again."

"Thank you, Tes! I appreciate it; he hates when I'm hanging over him, feels like I'm trying to fill in for our mother."

"Not to worry. What time do you think you'll break camp in the morning? There's a cave on the way, well, a couple of leagues south of Boil's Crossing—that's your next stop, yes? I can take these two and your brother to check it out; I've heard rumors of night brutes. If you don't mind, we'll get going at dawn."

"Night brutes, huh? Are you sure that's wise? Barn's only Level Thirty-Two."

"I'll watch over him, and Victor and Valla are more capable than you think. We should be able to reach the crossing by late afternoon—sooner if the rumors aren't true and we've nothing to fight in the caves."

Cayle gave Tes a long look, then let her eyes drift to Valla and Victor, and he saw her stare at Lifedrinker for a long couple of heartbeats. "Okay, Tes. I'll have Barn up and ready at dawn."

"Perfect!" Tes smiled as she watched Cayle walk away, then she flicked her fingers, and Victor's ears popped. Valla reached up to her ears with a puzzled expression, so Victor figured she'd been included in the spell. "I'm quite sure there are night brutes there. This will be wonderful experience; they're usually around Tier Seven, but they're simple beasts—all muscle and fear-attuned Energy; something you should be able to counter, if I'm right, eh, Victor?"

"I, uh, yeah, I should be able to . . ."

"Yes. This will be excellent—I predict a minimum of two levels for you each. Barn shouldn't be a problem; I'll have him turtle up behind his big shield, and you two can do most of the killing."

"Two more levels, Tes?" Valla said, shaking her head. "Ancestors! I'm glad we met you."

"Oh, I am too, Valla. It might seem like I'm doing you a big favor, and I am, but I fully anticipate a return on my investment." She laughed, plopped back down in one of Valla's chairs, and added, "Besides, I'm having a lot of fun!"

"Where are you from, Tes?" Valla asked, sitting in a chair opposite her, leaving the one with its back to the tent opening for Victor. He sighed, stood up from where he'd put out his bedroll, and walked over to sit while he listened. "I mean, you told me your people had common ancestry with Victor's, but you're not from his world. Can I know about your home?"

"Sure you can, Valla, but you heard that popping in your ears, right? That means our conversation is private, and I expect it to stay that way."

"Understood," Valla said, leaning forward to deposit an Energy-powered teakettle on the little table between the chairs.

"Tea?" Victor groaned and produced a bottle of cheb-cheb he'd gotten from Tellen's clan.

"Drinking, Victor?" Tes tsked. "You've still got cultivating to do!"

Victor groaned; he'd wanted to sleep soon, but he knew she was right—he'd promised Khul Bach to work on his Core. "It's from Fanwath; it won't be enough to get me drunk, especially with my vitality boosted."

"Ah, well, does it have a good flavor? Pour me a glass."

"Well, me too, then!" Valla said, putting away her kettle.

"That's the spirit," Victor laughed, finding three matching crystal tumblers in his second ring. "I bought these in Gelica; please don't break 'em 'cause they're my favorites. See how the bottom is nice and heavy?"

"Tut!" Tes said. "If I break one, I'll give you one better; you should know that by now!"

"Fair." Victor smiled, breaking the seal on his bottle of booze and pouring a couple of fingers for each of them. "I have thick fingers." He laughed.

"Tes, my question?" Valla pressed.

"I'm from Aradnue—a beautiful, ancient world. My people were masters of Energy before the System was an inkling of an idea near the center of the universes."

"An elder race?" Valla breathed, leaning forward.

"That's right, but I'm not so old myself—young, in fact, if you ask my closest kin."

"Can you tell me about your world?" Valla asked. "What are the cities like? Are your people numerous? What sorts of wonders you must have!"

Tes answered some of Valla's questions and several more from Victor, but while she spoke, he kept thinking about Earth, about the cities humans had created and the things they'd accomplished, like building ships to try to explore the universe.

He was proud of his people in that moment because, despite the fantastic things Tes described, the dragons had accomplished them all with magic—in Victor's opinion, humans had it pretty damn hard, coming from a dead world with no magic and short life spans, and they'd done some awesome things. He tempered his pride with the sobering thought that they'd also done some terrible things.

Tes was telling Valla about a tower atop a mighty mountain that stretched so high into the skies of Aradnue that one could see halfway around the planet's circumference from its top level. It sounded like hyperbole to Victor, but he supposed with magic, anything was possible. He wanted to see something like that, wanted to experience wonders so far beyond what was on Fanwath or this world—Zaafor—that people like the Warlord could only dream of them. Abruptly he stood up and said, "I'm going to cultivate."

25

IMBUE SPIRIT

The next day, true to her word, Tes led Victor, Valla, and Barn—a large, gray-plate-armored man with long, thick quills for hair and a very ruddy complexion that didn't do a lot to complement his bulging black eyes—out of camp before most of the other hunters had begun to wake. Barn wasn't a talkative fellow, and he seemed grumpy, despite the opportunity Tes was providing for the three of them. They traveled on foot, as usual, and fifteen minutes into their jogging progress, Tes started to urge Victor to cast Berserk.

"It's too early, Tes!" he moaned, not looking forward to battling his alter-ego for control.

"Did you level your Core last night?"

"No, but I just did yesterday! It'll likely take a while, don't you think?"

"Maybe, but maybe your brutish self will have a hunger for another heart. You still have some, yes?"

"Yeah . . ."

"Including the wyrm heart." She grinned and added, "What a meal that'll make!"

Valla snorted in amusement, shaking her head, and Victor turned to her. "This funny for you? Must be nice to eat what and when you want with no one badgering you about it!" He was mostly joking; he was glad Valla was starting to feel comfortable enough with him to laugh a bit at his expense.

He glanced at Barn, saw his glowering face and how he kept his eyes straight ahead, inhaling and blowing out his air in a steady cadence as they jogged, and said, "What's up, Barn? You have a bossy woman in your life, too, huh? Irritated that your sister sent you along with us?"

"Huh," he replied, then spat to the side into the dusty soil. "Sorry you got stuck babysitting me—Cayle saw me drinking with some of the other hunters last night and probably decided to send me off on runt duty."

"Runt duty?" Tes laughed, shaking her head. "Your sister did you a big favor, young man." Victor almost laughed at Tes's tone and choice of words, but he could see Barn's red cheeks getting redder with irritation. Tes continued, "You're going to see a lot more action today than the rest of the hunters, especially without a bunch of high-tier experts stealing all the glory."

"Really?" Barn gave Tes a second look and raised his weird, prickly eyebrows.

"Really. We're off to clear out a night brute nest." Tes winked at him as his mouth fell open, and he struggled for words, but then she turned back to Victor. "Nice attempt to change the subject, but don't you think it's about time you brought out your oversized friend?"

"Wait, last night I had a thought, and I wanted to ask you something . . ."

"Just the one?" Valla asked, interrupting him, and it took a minute for him to see the joke.

"What the hell, *chica*?" he asked, a laugh bubbling up, unbidden. "You've got jokes today! Okay, fair game. No more mister nice guy." He gave her shoulder a shove as she grinned, then he turned back to Tes. "Anyway, I was wondering, if someone summoned me, do you think it's possible to summon my *abuela*?"

"Your grandmother . . . It may be possible. I'm not an expert on that sort of magic, but with your blood, I'm fairly sure a summoning ritual could be made to target a person related to you. I'm not sure if it can be more specifically targeted. I feel like you were a bit of an unexpected result when summoned; the people who pulled you from your homeworld didn't seem pleased with you, if I recall your tale correctly. Didn't you say they dumped you into some fighting pits or sold you off . . ."

"That's right. But still, they must have had something that tied the spell to me, right?" He glanced at Valla and said, "Isn't that what Rellia's investigator found?"

"Yes, 'biological material.'"

"Likely blood. You didn't get any answers from the mage responsible?" Tes deftly leapt over a thorny bush as they continued running.

"No . . . he wasn't in a talking mood. There's the guy who hired him, though. What was his name, Valla?"

"Ap'Gravin. Boaegh hadn't been working with him for a long while, though . . ."

"Still, that ap'Gravin dude might have been the one who gave him the blood for summoning me."

"Yes, it may be worth pursuing." Valla nodded. "Provided we ever get back to Fanwath."

"I would investigate." Tes nodded. "If you find out what material was used and more about the summoning ritual, you may well be able to do the same for your grandmother. Do you think she'd appreciate it?"

"I . . ." Victor was about to say that, of course, she'd want to come to a world of magic and be with her grandson, but then he thought about her devotion to the Catholic Church. He thought about all the killing he'd done, and he tried to imagine his grandmother doing anything violent and couldn't. Would she thrive in a world like this? Did it matter? He could give her treasures to advance her race. He could teach her to cultivate, and, sure, she may never gain a lot of levels, but she'd be alive. "I need to think about it some more, but maybe."

"All right. It's time, Victor; no more stalling. Barn, do you have a movement spell?" Tes held up a hand, and they all slowed to a walk as she spoke.

"No, but I have a clockwork mount."

"Take it out, please. We're about to pick up the pace."

"Right," Barn stopped and stared into the sky for a moment, wiggling around the fingers of his gauntleted left hand, and then a brass-colored cube appeared in front of him in the dirt. It was about a foot to each side, and when Barn leaned forward and touched it, it began to vibrate and click noisily. It bounced once, then long, thin rods shot out of the four top corners. They writhed in the air for a second, and then the box underwent transformations too fast for Victor's eyes to follow.

More shorter rods shot out, and they stretched and bounced, and in less than a minute, a four-limbed mechanical skeleton shaped vaguely like a horse crouched before Barn, steam erupting from ports along its ridged spine, accompanied by clicks and whirring sounds.

"Shit," Victor said, taking a step back and admiring the weird mount. "Do you have a saddle?"

"Sure," Barn said, producing a cushioned leather seat that he strapped onto the top of the ridged metallic spine. Several pegs jutted out from the sides of the mount's "ribs" that he fastened it to.

"That's a marvel," Valla said, stepping around the faintly shuddering mechanical horse.

"Yeah, it's cool as hell." Victor reached a hand toward the rune-covered head of the mount and then said, "Safe to touch?"

"Yep." Barn nodded, then sprang into his saddle. Victor rested his palm against the metal, wondering if it was hot, but it felt just slightly warm.

"Is it fast?"

"Fast enough," Tes answered for Barn. She turned to Victor and stared pointedly, and he sighed.

"Fine, here goes." He cast Berserk, and there ended his relaxing morning. Tes, as usual, watched him transform with eager eyes, grinning at his involuntary growl as the red rage filled his vision and his Quinametzin self took in his surroundings. He had a terrible urge to smash the mechanical creature nearby, but Victor held himself in check, and then, as Tes sprang away, suddenly nearly as tall as Victor, he roared and charged after her.

At some point, Tes had changed her yellow dress for a pale blue one, and her ribboned belt trailed behind her, a shade of lavender that beckoned and taunted Victor over the miles. Valla and Barn seemed content to follow several dozen yards behind his brutish, leaping, growling figure as he futilely tried to catch the lithely running woman. Somewhere, in a corner of his mind, Victor's rational self wondered just how fast Tes could run if she wanted to.

He tried to remember her dragon form when she'd given him a glimpse. Had she had wings? Yes, he chuckled, and the emotion translated to a wild, crazed laugh coming from his titanic form—of course she'd had wings! He almost lost his rage as he imagined flying, soaring through the blue expanse, feeling the wind as it whistled over him . . . Victor shook his head and roared, urging more rage to pump out of his Core and furiously breaking into a sprint up a long, hard-packed hillside.

They seemed to be following a southwesterly heading, and their journey stretched into the afternoon. Tes didn't have to stop and urge Victor to release his rage when they arrived; his red-hot Energy had begun to fail several minutes before, and he was running as his usual self, trailing far behind Tes, Barn, and Valla. A part of him was irritated; why wasn't she pausing to let him recover? Then he figured they must be getting close, and she just wanted to get there and wait for him.

The desert still stretched endlessly around them, but they'd progressed into some low rocky hills for the last dozen miles, and it was at the base of one such hill where Victor finally caught up to the others; they were all sitting on a large red blanket. Tes was reclining, back in her more diminutive form, drinking from a crystal flask, and Barn was stuffing his face with a huge, dripping sandwich filled with meat. Valla waved to him, then returned to what she'd been doing—writing in her Far Scribe book.

"Don't mind me," he huffed, leaning over, hands on his knees, purposefully breathing much harder than he needed.

"Oh, do sit down, Victor." Tes chuckled. "Why didn't you eat a heart?" She pressed her lips into a pout as she asked the question, and Victor was struck by how beautiful she was. She had such big, clear eyes, and their greenish-brown irises glittered in the sunlight, and then there were those rosy lips and . . . He shook his head. He knew better; was her appearance even real? She was a dragon under all that beauty, right?

He grunted and sat down, forcing a frown, and he thought he saw something like approval in Tes's eyes as she looked away and took another drink from her flask. "Well," he said, "I'm not going to lie—I forgot about the hearts until I'd already lost my rage, and I'm, well, I'm just not up to eating a raw monster heart when I'm not mad with fury."

"I'll help you remember next time," she said. "Eat something. Drink. The cave is up yonder among those tumbled boulders."

"Okay." Victor sat across from Tes, next to Valla, and dug around in his storage ring until he found some bread, butter, and a bowl of still steaming noodle soup he'd bought months ago in Gelica.

"That smells good," Valla said, leaning close to sniff his bowl.

"You want some?"

"No, thank you. I don't like to be full before a battle."

"Yeah, I used to be the same when I wrestled. I think that's mostly because I was worried about making weight, though."

"You're a grappler?" Barn asked around his mouthful of sandwich.

"Yeah. Well, not as much as I used to be. I've become quite fond of fighting with an axe." He patted Lifedrinker, where he'd laid her next to him.

Tes eyed him and the axe and then said, "I'll make you a proper sling for that axe when we camp tonight."

"Really? Thanks, Tes. Yeah, she outgrew the loop I had on my belt . . ."

"Yes, I'll make you a shoulder sling so the head rests further up under your arm."

"You craft?" Valla asked, looking up from her book.

"Oh, I have a hobby or ten. Speaking of which . . ." She produced two small vials and tossed one to Barn and one to Valla. "Should you find yourselves in dire straits, quaff those."

Barn held it up, peering with one bulging, solid black eye into the milky contents. "What's it do? Heal?"

"No, you'll discorporate for a time and be drawn toward this rod." Tes held up a rune-covered dull-gray rod about a foot long and, reaching back over the edge of the blanket, firmly drove it into the hard-packed dirt.

"Truly?" Valla said, her eyes widening. "I don't think I can afford such a gift, Tes." She held it toward the woman, and Tes chuckled.

"Not to worry—I crafted it myself, and I'm hoping you won't need it. Still, I did promise to help you and Barn; I wouldn't be much of a mentor if I didn't give you an escape plan before walking into a night brute nest."

Victor watched the exchange with an arched eyebrow, waiting for the explanation for why he'd not been offered one of the escape potions, but when none was forthcoming, he just chuckled to himself and took another big spoonful of soup. "I wish it wasn't so hot out; I was in the mood for soup, but it would be so much better if the weather were chilly."

"What about Victor?" Valla asked for him, ignoring the small talk about soup.

"He's going to be completely berserk, and the night brute's magic will have little effect on him. Speaking of which, Victor, tell me about that Imbue Spirit spell again."

Victor let go of his spoon and straightened up, looking over the blanket at Tes. "I've cast it on my armor before. Basically, it takes a little piece of my spirit and puts it into an object. Well, also an individual, according to the description."

"And?"

"Oh, when I cast it on my armor, I used inspiration-attuned Energy, and it seemed to gain a bit of a will of its own. When I was about to be struck, it was like a ghostly hand reached out and parried."

"Truly?" Valla seemed impressed, leaning back from her book with wide eyes.

"But you haven't cast it upon a person yet?"

"Nope."

"I believe you mentioned you're able to make Energy attunements other than the three in your Core, yes?"

"Right. Courage and justice."

"Courage?" Barn said, an eager note in his voice. "That'll come in handy against night brutes!"

Tes clapped her hands and nodded at Barn. "Exactly! Victor, can you try to imbue Valla with a bit of your spirit using courage-attuned Energy?"

"Imbue me with his spirit? Will he be in control of me?"

"It says I'll grant some of my 'power and will' to the recipient, not that I'll gain control of them."

"You trust Victor, yes?" Tes asked, locking eyes with Valla.

"Of course . . ." She licked her lips, and Victor felt a little sorry for her being put on the spot like that. "Okay, Victor."

"Right. Give me your hand." He turned his hand so it rested on his knee, palm up, and waited for Valla to place her much smaller blue fingers in his. She hesitated at first, but then her brows drew together, and with a determined, perhaps involuntary growl, she reached forward and snatched three of Victor's fingers in her grip.

"Careful, Victor; be sure to channel the correct Energy," Tes said, leaning forward, that familiar, eager gleam in her eyes. Barn brushed the crumbs from his hands and audibly gulped his last bite, also shifting to watch what happened.

Victor still held his bowl of soup in his other hand and sighed as he sent it into his storage ring, only half eaten. He closed his eyes, focusing on his Core. His rage-attuned Energy was already nearly full, pulsing balefully, and he smiled at its familiar heat, gently tugging some of the Energy out of it to combine with inspiration, building the weave for courage in his pathways. When it was ready, he clamped down hard on his fear attunement, then cast Imbue Spirit.

The spell took shape and pulled forth more of his two Energies, filling the pattern to bursting with courage, and then he sent it forth into Valla. While the Energy flowed out of him into her, he watched, locking his gaze with her seafoam green eyes. He felt her grip tighten on his fingers, saw her shoulders curl forward with tension, and then she pulsed, briefly limned in a golden glow, and her eyes blazed with it, the green giving way to brilliant red-gold. Her lips peeled back in a smile, and she laughed.

Victor knew the spell was complete, so he let go of her, but Valla held on, squeezing his fingers, her eyes still shining with brilliant golden light. "Is this what it feels like to be you?" she asked brightly. "Ancestors! I feel ready to fight anything!" She gave his fingers another squeeze, then let go and hopped to her feet. "I still have control of myself, so that's good . . ."

"I believe the spell has imbued you with some of Victor's will and clearly with courage. You should fare well against the night brutes' magical attacks. I think because your armor was inert, Victor, your will played a more . . . active role in its imbuement." Tes stood and continued, "Can you spare the Energy for a similar boon to Barn?"

Victor had suffered a brief moment of weakness and nausea just as he had when he'd cast the spell in the arena, but he felt fine already. "Each casting costs me ten percent of my will and ten percent of my maximum Energy. I should be good . . ."

"Yes; your will is prodigious, and you'll be berserk. I think you'll be fine." Tes nodded, then gestured for Barn to move closer to Victor.

"I feel incredible! This is amazing, Victor; nothing will stop us!" Valla had produced her blue sword and moved off to the side, performing the forms of her fighting style against imaginary enemies.

"Glad you like it," Victor said. Then Barn reached out a thick, pinkish-red hand, and Victor grasped it, noting how dense the calluses were on the man's palm. "Courage again?" he asked Tes.

"Yes, for this battle. I do wonder, though, what would happen should you use your fear affinity . . ." Tes smiled mischievously as she spoke, and Victor saw a change in the way her eyes glinted as she looked at Barn; it reminded him of a cat playing with a mouse.

"Uh, please don't," Barn said, tugging his hand. Victor held on, though, and shook his head.

"*Tranquilo, hombre.*" He gripped tighter, then just as before, he built the pattern for courage and cast his Imbue Spirit spell. Barn's body, just like Valla's, briefly pulsed with golden Energy, and then his eyes took on the red-gold glow of courage. In Victor's opinion, it was a massive upgrade from his usual bulging, bug-like eyes. Barn immediately released Victor's hand and jumped to his feet with a whoop.

"Outstanding! Let's crush some enemies!"

"Get your shield out, Barn," Tes said, chuckling as she, too, stood. Victor groaned and clambered up, barely making it to his feet before Tes summoned her blanket back into storage.

Victor shook his head, trying to clear it; the malaise after casting the second imbue had hit him a lot harder. "Hey! What if I wasn't ready to . . ."

"Oh, hush." Tes laughed. "You know you were."

"Yeah"—Victor chuckled—"good call." He stretched, popping his back between his shoulders, trying to play off his sudden fatigue. He knew he'd adjust and didn't want Tes to think he needed to cancel one of the imbue spells.

"Okay," Tes said, looking at her three charges—Valla dancing about with her long, blue blade flicking through the air, Barn shrugging his arm into the straps of a shield nearly as big as he was, and Victor. "Pick up your lady axe, Victor, and call forth your titan self; it's time we plumb the dark depths for glorious battle."

26

NIGHT BRUTES

When Victor—hulking, furious, eager for battle—stepped into the gravel and scree-strewn cave entrance, his nostrils were assailed by a pungent scent, something like a cross between shit and ammonia. He scanned the long, craggy walls and ceiling, trying to find a source for the smell, but he didn't see it. Growling, he strode forward, brushing past the little man covered in metal and his even smaller blue friend.

Before he stooped down to delve deeper, Victor glanced over his shoulder to see the approving nod of the tall, fair-haired woman, the one who led him on chase after chase. He grinned at the gleam in her eyes, eager to show her what he could do, eager to water this filthy hole with the blood of his foes. He kicked his way through the loose rocks, and as they gave way to his boots, the smell intensified, and Victor saw smears of black and white on the stones.

"Shit," he grunted, then hunched low to pass through the jagged tunnel entrance, his helmet crunching through the rock, sending a trickle of dust and gravel down his neck and back. When he descended a few feet and the cave's entrance became obscured by the cavern walls, his eyes began to adjust. He saw rough walls, more gravel, and the tendrils and ropes of ancient roots jutting out of the walls and ceiling.

Victor surged down the slope, kicking and smashing his way past more rocks and yanking or hacking away long roots. He had no patience for obstacles. "Careful, Victor," the small voice of his blue friend said, and he wondered what she meant. Had he hurt her with a tossed, broken root?

"Back up," he grunted, considering the matter solved. He felt the urgency of battle lust and didn't want to pause for the small ones. They said something, speaking to one another, but their words didn't register with him; why should he listen to the mewling of children? Something in this pit thought to challenge him, sought to spill his blood and stop his heart, and that was all he could focus upon. It was enough.

He surged down, eyes blazing with rage, shoulders low, head forward, smashing through the ofttimes too narrow tunnel, the thought of a collapse never crossing his mind. Every time he felt his rage begin to wane, Victor reached into his Core and urged more of it into his pathways; he knew there were limits to the hot Energy, but he wasn't near them yet. Ten minutes or more went by as he slid and stomped through the tunnels, ever downward, following the stench as it grew stronger and stronger, bringing water to his eyes and fueling his fury.

He began to hear coughs and more chatter from his smaller companions as they struggled to keep up, clambering over piles of loose rocks that Victor leapt or stepped across. Again, he tuned the sounds out. Let the tall woman aid the less fit; he was too close to slacken his pace now. His instincts proved right—one more twist in the tunnel, one more slide down a loosely packed slope of stones, and he found himself in an enormous cavern.

Victor looked around, and as he took in a breath, ready to bellow a challenge, hundreds of baleful red eyes opened in the black depths of the cavernous ceiling. The slow susurration of leathery wings unfolding and the weird barking chirps that echoed out of the darkness did nothing to cool Victor's bloodlust. Rather, the sounds further enraged him; why were his enemies hanging up in the blackness where he couldn't reach them?

He strode forward over the suddenly damp cavern floor, squelching his boots through thick pads of moss and lichen and . . . other things. He lifted Lifedrinker in the air, and he bellowed his fury. Suddenly the red lantern-like eyes moved. They dropped through the blackness, dozens of them, and then the owners of those eyes came into sight, falling on twelve-foot wings through the damp, dark air, clicking and barking as they descended toward the screaming, red-limned madman.

"He went down this slope," Valla said, nimbly leaping from one large rock to the next, trying not to slide on the smaller, loose stones.

"Aye," Barn grunted, trying to balance with his immense shield on one arm and a heavy-looking gray ball mace in his other hand. He had similar gray plate armor on almost every part of his body, and Valla knew it must be hard to keep from falling on these loose rocks with all that weight and lack of mobility. She looked up the dark tunnel behind him, wondering where Tes had gotten to, and that's when she heard Victor's furious roar.

"He's found them!" she said, trying to increase her pace. Weird sounds echoed up the tunnel, clicking, hissing, and coughing barks. So many at once that, whatever night brutes might be, there must have been dozens of them.

"Gods, be good! That sounds like a lot of them!" Barn groaned with a note of panic tinging his words.

"Come on!" Valla said, finally giving into gravity and leaping more recklessly down the slope. She slipped about halfway down and slid a dozen feet through the gravel on her backside, but when she used her momentum to hop to her feet, she'd made it to the bottom. She glanced back to see Barn sliding after her, and she smiled; he might be nervous, but Victor's spell still had his eyes gleaming with golden Energy—he wouldn't turn and run, not yet.

She hurried down the stretch of tunnel toward a wide, moss-covered opening and noted how the yellow and green fuzz seemed to grow out of the cave like a carpet. Blackness filled the space beyond, but she could hear Victor screaming and howling amid the cacophony of the night brutes. "I *think* that's the night brutes," she amended, still hurrying forward. When she came to the opening, and the darkness seemed to wrap around her palpably, she felt an icy grip take hold of her heart, and she almost fled.

Something flared within her, though, bright, powerful, and full of hope and encouragement, and she knew it was Victor's will, his fragment of courage-attuned Energy. The black tendrils fell back, and Valla whipped her long, blue sword forward, wishing she could part the hazy, tangible shadows with its edge. The clamor was almost too much for her, the screams, the clicks, and the weird, underlying rasping sound—something like scales rubbing on scales.

"It's black as a wyrm's asshole in there," Barn said, coming up behind her. Valla nodded and tried to summon an Energy orb, the first spell she'd ever learned, a light for when she was in the dark. The Energy poured out of her into her hand, and the ball of yellow light flared brightly. She winced in its glare and frowned when she saw it didn't illuminate more than a foot of the space beyond the cavern opening.

"That's no help," Valla said.

"Victor! Summon your courageous light for your companions!" Tes called out from somewhere ahead, her voice clear as a crystal bell despite the din of battle. Before her words registered, Valla's mind boggled at the idea—how had Tes gotten ahead of them? Before she could ponder her words, though, she heard Victor yell again—one of his strange curses from his homeworld—and then, high in the air, a new sun was born.

"No, not a sun," she hissed, gripping Barn's shoulder as she watched the rip in the darkness from which a dazzling, broad fan of reddish-golden light poured down to the cavern's floor, creating a vast pool of light that chased the clinging darkness away. Valla and Barn both gasped at what they saw in that brilliant radiance.

Dozens, no, hundreds of hulking, black-scaled forms, something like a cross between a human and a bat, writhed on the ground, all surging toward a singular gigantic combatant—Victor, in the full glory of his titanic form. He stood head and shoulders above the brutes; he was larger, glowing redder, and more muscle-bound than ever. Valla guessed him to be nearing fourteen feet in height, and Lifedrinker, though she'd grown much recently, was still a one-handed weapon in his hands.

The axe screamed, glinting like a falling star in the reflected light of Victor's courage spell as she hacked limbs, heads, wings, and scales. Victor bellowed in counterpoint to the axe's cries, grabbing the thick, muscle-bound night brutes by their wrists or necks and flinging them away, smashing them into one another to give himself room to maneuver.

"Blood of the Gods!" Barn hissed. "Look at the mess he's making." He looked at Valla, and his red-gold eyes seemed eager; she knew hers were a match.

"Let's get in there!"

Tes watched from her perch on the cavern wall as her two less enthusiastic charges finally joined the fray. Barn held his tower shield before himself as he waded into the back of the thrashing, jockeying brutes. Valla held back and threw out her lightning strike, targeting the center rear of the mass, blasting at least two of the creatures solidly enough to stun them. "Well done!" Tes called, laughing.

This was an enormous nest, bigger than she'd hoped. She'd wondered, briefly, if it was too much—the creatures were rated a solid three tiers higher than Victor, but they were stupid, slow, and unimaginative, and relied on their powerful darkness and fear auras to claim their victims, neither of which worked very well around her charges, not with Victor's courage boon. And Victor, well, Victor was a monster.

Somehow he'd flooded his channels with more rage than Tes had ever seen, sprouting another foot in height and gaining a significant amount of mass. "Did the ancestor lurking in your blood see the brutes and grow furious at their size?" She chuckled. As if in response, Victor bellowed another mighty yawp and split a brute from crown to crotch with that wonderful axe of his.

"What a treat to watch this old bloodline come to life again!" Tes laughed. She'd have so much to tell Yek'nakkara'ma'shohon. Hadn't he told her it would be a waste of her time to come to this part of the universe? "Wait until you see this memory, old uncle!"

One of the brutes slipped up behind Victor and raked its claws, both sets, down his back, ripping his lovely, shimmering armor and shredding the skin beneath. Victor roared, whirled, cleaved both of the night brute's taloned hands off, and kicked it in the chest, sending it flying into a cluster of the creatures, knocking several of them sprawling.

Tes narrowed her eyes, willing her vision to zoom in on Victor's back, and watched as the deep grooves in his flesh filled in with scar tissue before her eyes. "Elder Gods, but you heal fast!" Something about the attack seemed to have driven Victor's rage to new heights, and he went into a veritable frenzy as he charged among the monsters, hacking, throwing, tripping, and headbutting them. He was like a mad bull among swine, utterly brutalizing the brutes, never giving them a chance to press him with their sheer numbers.

When she'd watched him in the arena, Tes had known there was something special about Victor, and it wasn't just his ability to berserk—his spirit Core was so rich with potential, so overflowing with raw emotion, she'd had to shield herself from it when she first spoke to him. His aura was profound and pulled like the undertow of an ocean.

She'd marveled that the lesser folk in Coloss seemed oblivious to it, but then she'd considered how sensitive her people were, especially to the weight of feelings, and had realized that they simply didn't have the capacity to comprehend everything pouring out of the barbaric young man.

"I'll need to teach him some more control of that aura if he's going to visit some of the older sectors of this universe."

A different sort of scream interrupted her musing, and Tes jerked her eyes away from Victor to see that fifty or more of the night brutes had turned on Valla and Barn. Valla fought like a dervish, using the Steel Tempest spell Tes had taught her. It kept the brutes at bay just long enough for her to dance out of their reach, though it couldn't harm them overmuch. Still, that sword of hers did plenty of hurting—she could surely dance a beautiful dance with that blade.

It became clear that it was in response to Barn's rather dire straits that Valla had screamed—the big armored oaf was nearly buried under the onslaught of night brutes. One of them had peeled back the top of the Vesh's shield and was working to drive its long, fanged snout over the obstacle, gnashing its teeth inches from Barn's throat. Tes glanced at Victor, wondering if his enraged mind would try to aid his companion or not. He was still madly brutalizing the horde near the cavern's center, oblivious.

"Do I intervene? Should I give Victor a hint and see if he can save the Vesh? Oh, bother! I did make a promise to Cayle. Drink your escape potion, you dolt!" When it was clear Barn wouldn't be able to manage even that much, Tes sighed and centered a lightning blast on the group of night brutes pressing the man. An arc of blue electricity flared out of her hand, shredding the darkness hanging nearby to tatters and then exploding into the pack of monsters, reducing them—every single one—to charred corpses.

Valla had fallen back, shielding her eyes, and Barn was sent flopping head over heels from the explosion, but the brutes who'd been pressing them were no more. Tes smirked. "Sorry about stealing those kills, my darlings." She glanced over the cavern floor, trying to get a count on the still-living brutes—Victor had maimed or killed more than half, but it looked to her as if his furious red aura was waning. She licked her lips, smiling with anticipation, and sent a whisper into his ear, "Aren't you hungry from your efforts, titan? Why not send the brutes running? Give them a taste of true fear and then have a feast while they regroup?"

In the midst of his frenzy, Victor heard a familiar, lilting voice in his ear, *"Aren't you hungry from your efforts, titan? Why not send the brutes running? Give them a taste of true fear and then have a feast while they regroup?"* Even in his rage, he knew what she meant, and when he thought of the hearts in his storage ring, his mouth filled with saliva.

He looked around at the scattered night brutes—a few pursued him as he rampaged, a dozen or two, while others milled about, bewildered by the furious beating he'd been dishing out or stunned by the mighty bolt of thunder that had erupted out of the darkness. "Yes," he grumbled, hacking his beautiful axe through another scaly, flat, shelf-like brute skull. "Why shouldn't I?"

Purposefully, Victor reined in some of his fury, forcing himself to act with his mind instead of his instinct, and then he moved out of his circle of radiance into the dark, clinging shadows generated by the night brutes. The blackness wasn't nearly as thick as when he'd first arrived, a mere echo of what it had been now that so many of the brutes had been slain or wounded. One of the largest of the creatures tried to follow him, leapt at him, and he met it in the throat with Lifedrinker's shimmering edge.

Blood and viscera spattered, and Victor reached into his Core and grasped his fear-attuned Energy, using his will to gather up a massive river of it. It moved sluggishly, the rage in his pathways pushing against it, fighting for space, but Victor forced it through. Then he cast Project Spirit, driving it out in a cone of writhing, purple-black, miasmic Energy that slithered through the darkness to seep into the minds of the dozens of brutes that tried to press their advantage now that Victor was out of the light.

Victor saw them slow, saw the red gleam of their wide eyes dim and darken, saw how they shook their heads and struggled, unable to comprehend what was happening. They were the makers of fear; how could fear be taking hold in their dull minds? Victor finished off their resistance with an enormous roar, digging it out of the center of his gut, sending out the frustration and rage of countless torments in a palpable wave.

The night brutes broke, leaping away, flapping their wings, howling in madness as they flung themselves to the heights of the cavern or its far, shadowy edges. Victor laughed in his maniacal fury, and, the memory of the seductive voice fresh in his mind, he dug out the heavy, red, still-warm heart of the rock wyrm. Saliva gathered in his mouth at the scent of hot copper, and he bit a huge, grisly chunk out of it, ripping through the tough meat with his powerful jaw.

It was good, far better than the arachnid heart. Victor chuckled and grunted, heaving for breath through his nose as he worked to devour it. By the third bite, he could feel the heat spreading through his stomach, out into his pathways. He saw the red fury of his vision darken and deepen, and he knew his Energy was being replenished.

He noisily grunted as he swallowed another bite. Then the Energy began to grow heavier, hotter, seeping out through his pathways into his flesh and bones, saturating his every cell, enriching and strengthening them. Victor ate with such a frenzy, speeding his wild wolfing of the meat as he felt its effects begin to infuse him, that he made short work of the heart. Panting, blood coating his mouth and chin, his chest and his hands, he lifted his head to the cavern ceiling and howled his glory, rewarded by a System message, even in the heat of battle.

*****Congratulations! You have advanced your race: Advanced 2.*****
*****Congratulations! You have gained 10 vitality.*****

Victor laughed madly, a giant, blood-covered visage of terror, his armor hanging in shreds, a gleaming, red-soaked axe hanging loosely from one mighty fist. He roared and roared, stomping and fuming, hectoring his enemies, daring them to return. He walked well away from his circle of light, shouting, raging, and brandishing Lifedrinker, furious that his enemies had yet to answer his challenges.

He thought he saw movement in the shadows near the far edge of the cavern wall. He turned toward it, stomping farther from his small friends and the bright rays of courage-attuned Energy, and then, with a grating rumble of shifting earth and stone, something roared back at him, something with a voice so loud and furious that it shook the walls of the enormous cavern.

Some might have fled from such a sound; some might have cowered. Victor laughed. He lifted Lifedrinker over his head and stalked into the darkness, leaning into the noise, unable to feel fear, unable to consider caution in his absolute and utter, furious madness.

27

A LOT TO CHEW

The roar sounded again, and Victor ducked his head slightly, so the crown of his weighty helm led the way forward. He was furious, ready to fight, eyes blazing with the deep red Energy of his rage, but still aware of the rocks and dust falling from the high cavernous ceiling. They crashed on his mighty shoulders and shattered and bounced away from his immovable helmet, and Victor shouted, blood-drenched, ragged and savage in his anticipation.

He'd stalked some thirty paces deeper into the enormous cavern when he finally saw his new challenger. More accurately, he saw its eyes. Where the night brutes stood ten or a dozen feet in height, and their eyes were the size of small, red-glowing saucers, these new ones were angular, baleful, and hung some thirty feet in the air, surrounded by clinging, shifting shadows.

Victor lifted Lifedrinker and charged forward, too enraged from his battle, from his meal, and from his surging Energy to consider consequences. Perhaps a tiny voice of reason existed in his violence-oriented mind; maybe he simply had good instincts for battle. Whatever the cause, he ducked and rolled as a shifting wave of shadow swooped toward him, and claws like scimitars, dripping with inky darkness, cut the air above him.

He surged to his feet and continued his charge, frustrated that his foe was still wreathed in shadows, infuriated that it wouldn't show him its face. An echo of himself, a tiny voice railing at the barrier of his rage, seemed to shout, "Put some light on it, fool!" Before he could evaluate the advice from his rational self, he saw a curtain of thicker darkness shift before him and tried to roll again, but a scaly, spear-taloned foot crashed into him, sending him flying a dozen yards until he smashed into a rocky, moss-covered cavern wall.

Victor, especially enraged and full of Quinametzin vigor and pride, wasn't one to lie around. He rebounded from the wall, drove his feet against it, and performed a somersault, racing, mad-faced and still eager, back toward his foe. Before he closed the distance, though, he growled, in a voice few would recognize as his, "How about some light?" Then again he cast Dauntless Radiance, and the darkness split high above, and a great ray of golden-red illumination fell on his foe.

As the light bathed the immense monstrosity, blasting the shadows away, its dark scales began to smolder, black steam and smoke rising, and it howled in furious agony. Victor, despite his madness, paused, stunned by the visage of the horror before him. It was three times the size of the other night brutes but lankier, with a more humanoid face. Its lack of an elongated snout didn't seem to diminish the size or number of fangs that filled its great maw, made visible as it roared, shaking its head side to side in Victor's light.

Victor leapt straight for the long, muscular, black-scaled left leg of the monster, hacking with everything he had, aiming Lifedrinker's wicked edge for the creature's knee. She screamed her eager bloodlust, the air rippling behind her, such was her velocity. The atrocity was still distracted by the light, reaching up to claw at the high rip in the air where Victor's courage-attuned Energy poured forth, and it didn't even try to move, didn't lift its leg to step, didn't swipe at Victor to block his blow.

Lifedrinker impacted the midnight scales of that knee hard enough to create a small concussive shockwave that would have felled an ordinary person, flattening them with the grinding *crash*. Victor, to his horror and suddenly sober mind, felt Lifedrinker's haft crack as she rebounded. The impact had shaken even his mighty Quinametzin bones, reverberating up through his arm and into his neck, stunning him as the force of his tremendous blow was absorbed and reflected into him.

He stumbled away from the monstrous leg, Lifedrinker hanging slightly crookedly from his hand, and shook his head, trying to clear the ringing and regain his clarity of thought. That's when the creature, still smoking from the light, still screaming its outrage, reached down and swatted Victor with its great, razored, inky claws, dragging enormous furrows through the flesh of his chest, shoulders, and stomach. The blow sent him head over heels, a dozen, two dozen, three dozen yards, to tumble and flop over the stone, where he bounced to rest among a pile of dead night brutes.

* * *

Tes heard the roar, and her head jerked away from where she'd been watching Valla and Barn. She willed her eyes to see further into the dark, peering through the magical shadows to the far wall of the cavern where a small tunnel led away. The stone above the tunnel had cracked, and it looked to be widening, great hunks of moss-covered stone falling to tumble and bounce on the cavern floor.

She reached out with her senses, willing whatever was roaring, whatever was coming, to reveal itself to her. What had she missed? That didn't sound like a night brute. When her senses couldn't pierce the stone and the thick veil of darkness-attuned Energy hanging behind it, she glanced back at Victor and saw his rage was surging beyond anything she'd yet seen—his aura dancing along his frame like baleful red flames. He screamed into the blackness, stalking toward the sound. "Oh dear," she muttered.

Tes gathered her Energy and, with a surge of will, teleported to the bottom of the cavern, appearing in a crackling flash of blue lightning behind Barn and Valla. "Time to go," she said. They both whirled to see the source of the noise her lightning had made, and when they saw her and heard her words, Barn immediately started making his way toward the rough, narrow tunnel that led up to the surface. Not Valla, though; she watched Barn walking away, then turned back to the darkness where screams and roars echoed and reverberated.

"What about Victor?"

"I'll stay with him, help him flee if necessary." She knew it would be; anything that could obscure itself from her would be too much for the titan-blood.

"Promise?" Valla asked, finally starting to follow Barn.

"Of course. Come now, no time to waste." Another titanic roar shook the cavern, and Tes watched as loose rocks and dust tumbled from the high ceiling. "I mean it—go!" That got Valla moving, and soon she was behind Barn, urging him onward as they slipped into the tunnel. "At least I don't have to worry about those two . . ." she started to muse aloud when red-gold light split the thick darkness, and she laid her eyes on the source of the commotion.

"Old Gods," she hissed, rushing forward. "What are you?" The creature was at least three times Victor's size, smoking and steaming from Victor's light. Its eyes and scales reminded her of the night brutes, but that's where the similarity ended. It was lanky where they were hulking, more humanoid and less monstrous in its design. More than that, malevolence reeked from the creature, and Tes could finally begin to get its measure, and she didn't like what she was feeling.

Again she hissed, "What are you," as she streaked through the shadows, noting that the night brutes themselves were nowhere to be seen. "So they don't count you a friend, hmm? Or maybe they're worried you'll mistake them as part of your meal?" She saw Victor gather himself and, as the monstrosity was distracted by his blazing light, charge forward to smash his axe into its knee. "Poor fool doesn't know how to flee."

There was no mistaking the cracking boom that echoed out from the source of impact; that lovely axe of his wasn't a match for those scales. Tes was contemplating the best way to extricate Victor and herself when the terror stopped fussing with the courage-attuned light and swiped at the young titan-blood. "Oh . . ." Tes said, her heart doing a flip in her chest as she saw those gigantic, darkness-tainted talons slash him and send him flying through the air, back to where the bulk of the night brute battle had taken place.

The creature strode forward, baleful red eyes focused on the fallen man, and Tes stood up straight, calling out with a voice that cut through the distance like a needle through parchment, "That's enough of that."

The monstrosity froze in its tracks and turned toward her, and, if she wasn't mistaken, she saw a look of puzzlement on its shadowy, brutish face. "I think I should let you look me in the eyes instead of down upon me," Tes hissed, then began to unravel her carefully woven disguise, releasing the bonds of Energy on her flesh, allowing it to stretch and change. In just a few heartbeats, she crouched in the no longer expansive cavern, easily thrice the mass of the shadowy giant.

"What are you," she growled, her enormous voice rumbling out, shaking dust loose from the ceiling and causing the mysterious monster to flinch back. There, fully back to her natural self, Tes allowed her prodigious senses to stretch forth, and she read the truth of things, saw through the creature's scales and flesh to its Core and spirit, and a laugh like cracking thunder escaped her mighty jaws. "A prince of night brutes, hmm? My, but I wonder what you ate to advance your monstrous race so. I suppose it doesn't matter now. Still, your heart will make a lovely gift for my young friend. Should he earn it, that is."

Tes breathed deeply, expanding her gigantic lungs, sucking the air out of the cavern, devouring the lingering shadows, and causing Victor's light to flicker and fade. The night brute prince, a monster, but not a suicidal one, turned to flee, springing toward the wide crevice from which it had crawled. It managed three long strides before Tes exhaled, and a torrent of jagged blue arcs of lightning blasted into its back.

The burst of Energy lit up the cavern as if a new sun had been birthed, and any lingering magical shadows were utterly evaporated. Victor's light of courage winked out in the face of the surge, and the prince was stopped in its tracks, transfixed by the jolts, so much electrical Energy tearing through it that its head, hands, and feet exploded to allow faster egress. "I hope I didn't ruin your organs with that," Tes grumbled, striding forward on her enormous taloned feet. "I thought you'd resist me a bit more, honestly."

With her greater senses awake, Tes was aware of Valla and Barn and knew they'd reached the surface. She also knew Victor lived, that his prodigious regeneration had saved him, mended the worst of his gashes before his rage had fled his unconscious body. "Hmm," she rumbled, sniffing at the night prince's corpse. "Something good is still within. Old Gods, I'm hungry, though. Should I save this snack for him?"

Tes dragged a long, blue-black talon over the smoldering flesh of the prince's back, peeling back the meat and clipping through its adamant ribs, each one *pinging* loudly, echoing around the cavern. A little more digging revealed a smoldering heart, and Tes neatly plucked it out with two of her talons. "Hmm, I smell . . . I smell change. I smell Energy. I smell a mystery. Not enough for me, though. A drop in an ocean. For him, though; for my young friend . . ." The heart disappeared, slipped into one of Tes's many dimensional containers.

Tes turned and sidled through the cavern to where Victor lay, his hand, even in his dashed and broken state, still firmly wrapped around the hilt of his lady axe. "Endearing," she said, her enormous predator's maw turning up at the corners into a smile. "Hmm, can't have you waking with me looking like this, can I? Oh, bother, time to squeeze into something a bit more petite."

Tes willed her form to contract and to change; she had to pour out a prodigious amount of Energy to bind her molecules into a more diminutive form, had to expend even more to make herself lighter so that her bipedal feet didn't crack or shatter the floors she strode upon. When she stood before Victor, a woman much closer to his size, she was exhausted. "A lot of trouble you've put me through today. Still, you're amusing, at least. More than amusing."

Tes sat on a tumbled stone, watching him sleep while she gathered some Energy. What a handsome human! "Well, I don't have many to compare you against, but still . . ." She liked how his dark brows shielded his—when he was wakeful—piercing eyes, how his straight, powerful nose almost curved downward at the tip. She liked the laugh lines at the corners of his eyes and the dimple in his strong chin. He had such straight white teeth, and he loved to show them when he smiled and laughed.

"How are you so full of joy? I think I'd be quite bitter had I suffered what you've been through." At her words, he shifted and groaned, and Tes stood up. She moved closer and reached down to pick up Victor's free hand, and then she cast Steps of the Tempest, encasing him and herself in its Energy, and with a flicker of her will, she flashed out of the cavern and up the long, crumbling slope of the tunnel, out into the brilliant sunlight.

When she stopped, Victor lay in the sand, just as he'd lain in the cavern. Tes crouched beside him and softly said, "I can feel it gathering below. Some Energy is coming your way."

"Is he okay?" Valla asked from beside her, and Tes straightened to look at the blue-skinned, lovely woman.

"Oh, aye. He'll be right as rain in a moment—well, scarred, but fine. You and Barn should brace yourselves. Some Energy flows this way."

"Some . . ." Valla said, then realization dawned on her. "From the night brutes."

"Yes, dear Valla."

"What was that thing, Tes?" Barn asked, but before Tes could answer, several winding, flashing, coiling ropes of Energy surged out of the gravel-strewn cave and poured into the four of them. The thickest, by far, silver-tinted and wild, flowed into Tes. She frowned as she absorbed it, pulling it into her Core and replenishing more of her spent power. She frowned because she'd rather it went to one of her charges. Still, they were reaping their own rewards.

Victor had been lifted off the ground by his flood of silver-tinged purple Energy. Valla and Barn had much smaller shares, but still, they looked ecstatic, and she figured they'd gained a level. When Victor settled back to the dusty ground, his eyes were open, but they weren't happy; he'd lifted his axe and stared at the jagged crack in its elegant handle.

*****Congratulations! You have achieved level 40 Spirit Carver, gained 20 will and 20 vitality, and have 16 attribute points to allocate.*****

*****Level 40 Class refinement is available. Class refinement is permanent. Human Energy cultivators will next be offered a Class refinement selection at level 50. To view your options and make your selection, access the menu through your status page.*****

*****Congratulations! You have achieved level 42. Attribute advancement is being banked until you have completed your level 40 refinement selection. Any progress beyond level 40 will be lost if you lose consciousness before making the selection.*****

Victor brushed aside the System messages and lifted Lifedrinker so he could look at her more easily. When the Energy surge had woken him, he'd quickly realized where he was—Tes must have dragged him out of the cave. He wondered what that thing had been, how it had so easily brushed off his attack, but he didn't really care, not while Lifedrinker lay wounded in his grip. "¿*Qué pasó, hermosa?*"

"Is she hurt?" Valla asked, stepping over the rocky ground to kneel close to him.

"I fucking split her haft . . ."

"It will heal, Victor," Tes said. "Bind it up with some strips of cloth; give the wood time to mend. It's alive and full of Energy; she'll be none the worse for the wear, though she may bear a scar for a while—until you help her to evolve again, I'd say."

Victor sighed with relief at the words. He knew Lifedrinker would live if her haft broke, or he used to know that—when she'd evolved and grown with her haft, it seemed to have become more a part of her than the old handles she'd had in the past. He sat up and summoned one of his shirts from his storage ring, ripping it into long lengths of cloth.

"I have bandages . . ." Valla started to say, but he'd already begun to tear the shirt, so he just shrugged.

"Small price to pay. I'm sorry, beautiful," he said as he tightly bound her split handle together, tying the strips of cloth into knots.

"I leveled!" Barn said, apparently done dwelling on Victor and his damaged axe. "Hey, what was that thing, Tes?"

"A night brute prince." Tes smiled and laughed. "Beyond Level One Hundred and quite evolved, if I'm not mistaken. You're lucky to escape with just a few new scars, Victor."

"I think I bit off more than I could chew. Did you pull me out? Thanks, Tes."

"My pleasure; it's a joy to watch such verve for combat!"

"Are you sure it won't follow?" Barn asked, backing away from the cave entrance.

"No need to worry, Barn." Tes laughed, moving over to slap the big Vesh's back, making his armor rattle as dust and bits of gravel fell out of it. "I killed it."

"Seriously?" Victor asked, his voice raising slightly with excitement.

"Oh yes. I'm sorry, but I hit him with a bit too much lightning—ruined most of his organs. Still, his bones are worth much. We should harvest everything we can—from the night brutes, too. I think you'll earn more from this nest than most of the hunters on this expedition."

"Sounds like a plan, Tes. Thank you again for the rescue." Victor gently squeezed Lifedrinker's haft, ensuring the bindings he'd put on were holding her damaged wood tightly together. "What about you?" he asked Valla, changing the subject before he forgot to ask.

"What about me?" She looked confused.

"Did you level, too?"

"Oh! Yes!" Valla smiled and hooked her thumbs in her belt, pulling her shoulders back proudly. "What about you?

"Yep! How about it, Tes? Wanna give me some advice on my next refinement?"

28

WEIGHTY DECISIONS

Y ou're Level Forty already?" Valla asked, her face twisted in something between admiration and disgust.

"Actually, I'm Level Forty-Two, but the System says it's holding two levels until I go through my class refinement . . ."

"Ancient Fathers! Weren't you Thirty-Six back in Coloss?" Valla shook her head and then sat on a rock to more easily scrub the ichorous black blood from her sword. Barn sat in the shade of a boulder nearby and worked with a small sledgehammer, trying to straighten his shield. Victor turned to Tes and shrugged.

"It's a product of your high Energy affinity and, well, the fact that you did a lot of killing—the killing of things far more Energy dense than yourself."

"Is that how you describe levels? More dense with Energy?"

"Creatures like giant spiders and night brutes don't necessarily have levels, but they gather Energy, yes, and they evolve and grow in strength. These night brutes were once a colony of cave scavengers. Over a century or two, they gathered Energy and natural treasures to become what you fought down there. The prince was on another scale; it's likely he stumbled upon a potent bloodline treasure deep below the surface."

Victor frowned, contemplating her words. Tes looked from Victor to the others, then said more loudly, "We'll rest for a while; clean up your gear and contemplate your improvements. I'll help Victor with his class, and then we'll harvest the night brutes."

"My armor's wrecked," Victor said, looking at the tattered shreds of his scale shirt. It had completely lost its integrity and luster when the night brute prince raked its talons through it.

"Well, it's a pity, but you need something more sturdy anyway. I'm sure one of the Degh back with the caravan will have an old breastplate or something you can barter for. You can look for something better when you get back to town."

"Yeah, I guess." Victor shrugged out of the ruined armor, sending it into his storage ring, and then he took off his shredded, bloodstained shirt. Tes stepped forward and traced one of the new, pinkish-white scars traversing his torso from the left shoulder to the right side of his stomach.

"You're lucky you have such rapid healing while enraged." Her light, cool touch had brought goosebumps to his flesh, and Victor shifted uncomfortably, forcing himself to look within his ring for a clean shirt. He pulled it out and stuffed his head through the neck hole.

"Yeah, I know. I'd be dead two dozen times if it weren't for my ability to heal when I cast Berserk." He shrugged his arms into the shirt and pulled it down.

"Well? Tell me about your class choices."

"I haven't looked yet. Should I allocate my free attribute points first? I always wonder if the choices are determined the moment I hit the refinement level, or if I can still influence them . . ."

"No, the System isn't so flexible. It has made its decision on what to offer you, and nothing you do will change that, short of a System-granted boon designed to enhance those choices."

"Are those hard to come by?"

"Exceedingly. When individuals win them from dungeons or challenges, they rarely put them up for public sale." Tes stepped a few yards away to pick up a large, flat boulder that had to have weighed three hundred pounds and carried it over so she could more comfortably sit near Victor. Victor shook his head and smirked, and Tes said, "What's so amusing?"

"I mean, don't you have chairs in your storage rings?"

"Ha! Indeed I do. Still, I'm comfortable enough. Come, let's see what the System has thought of your progress these last ten levels." She leaned forward, eyes eager.

Victor nodded, opened his status menu, and then selected the class refinement option. He read through the first option:

*****Class refinement option 1: Titanic Warrior, Epic. Prerequisite: The strong presence of a titanic bloodline originating from an elder race. You've**

begun to unlock the secrets of your ancestry. By leveraging your bloodline to form Class abilities, you will continue to build on the synergy between your Class and your heritage. Class attributes: Strength, Vitality, Will.***

"The first option I've seen before. It's called Titanic Warrior."

"Read it to me," Tes said, resting her chin atop a fist as she leaned her elbow onto her knee. Victor complied, and she nodded, grinning. "Your current class is epic tier, correct?" When Victor nodded, she continued, "I like this option; it's good to lean into your bloodline, considering its strength. Still, let's see what else the System has in store for you."

Victor swiped the option aside, and a new one appeared in his vision:

*****Class refinement option 2: Spirit Warden, Epic. Prerequisites: Spirit Core, ability to manifest spirit aspects and traverse the Spirit Plane. Your forays into the realm of spirits have given you deep connections to those lands that border the veil. Harness that understanding to further your abilities and enhance your potency. Class attributes: Will, Intelligence, Unbound.*****

"That's a new one," Victor said, eyes narrowing as he read it aloud.

"Interesting! Your spirit companions—totems—are already quite powerful. I imagine great versatility lies down this path. Well . . . let's not overly contemplate this yet. What's the third option? The System isn't very creative—if it's going to offer you a legendary refinement, it will likely be the final option."

"All right." Victor waved the option away, and the third came into view:

*****Class refinement option 3: Titanic Rager, Legendary. Prerequisites: Spirit Core, Rage Affinity, Titanic Bloodline. Your deep connections to your titanic bloodline and powerful rage affinity have converged to bring forth your legendary potential. Class attributes: Strength, Vitality. System Note: Selecting this refinement will alter several of your abilities and have an extreme impact on your Energy affinities.*****

"Shit," Victor said, reading the description.

"Do tell!"

"You were right; it's a legendary class, but . . . Well, here, I'll read it to you." As Victor read the wording of the selection to Tes, her eyes widened, and her grin broadened, but she surprised him by ultimately shaking her head.

"I don't like it."

"Huh?"

"The System 'note' at the end; I've only seen that a few times in my travels and studies, and it generally accompanies truly profound changes in the individual. Some people don't care; they want power at any cost and embrace the change, but with this class, with rage as its focus, I worry that you might be changed very much indeed—to the point where you wouldn't recognize yourself, and I don't mean physically."

"Damn," Victor said, rubbing his chin with his long, powerful fingers. He held his hand out in front of his face, made a fist, and then said, "I've changed a lot, Tes. I'm not much like the kid who got summoned to Fanwath, but, well, inside, I know I'm still me. Do you think this class would change that?"

"That's exactly what I worry about. That was your final option, yes? Usually, the System only offers three options as people progre—"

"Hang on," Victor said, having just swiped the option aside to see if there were more. "There's another!"

*****Class refinement option 4: Titanic Herald, Legendary. Prerequisites: Sufficiently advanced titanic bloodline. You have embraced your ancient bloodline, giving air and light to a people who have faded from this universe. Continue down this path; give this world and others a reason to know the name of your great, ancient progenitors. Class attributes: Strength, Vitality, Agility, Dexterity, Intelligence, Will.*****

"Uh," Victor quickly swiped the "window" to the side to see if there were more options but was met with a final message:

*****Class refinement option 5: No Refinement - You are pleased with the path on which you find yourself and choose to continue until your next refinement option.*****

"Yes?" Tes prompted.

"Uh," he repeated, licking his lips. "It's another legendary option—Titanic Herald. It sounds . . . interesting."

"Are you going to make me ask?" Tes reached forward and gripped Victor's wrist, her fingers like warm, steel bands clad in velvety smooth skin.

"No, sorry; my mind's just whirling." Victor read her the class description, and Tes's eyes widened, and, though Victor couldn't imagine how, they seemed to shine more than ever with eagerness.

"This is very interesting, Victor! How many total attribute points did you get with each of your current class levels?"

"Um, twenty-eight."

Tes nodded and said, "Not dissimilar to most System-bound peoples. You're likely to get thirty-six with a legendary class. That difference alone should narrow your decision down to your final two options. The only reason I would ever counsel against taking a legendary option would be because you're trying to reach a specific class and a lesser rarity was a stepping stone or because your legendary options had drawbacks that outweighed the benefit."

"Like you think the, um, Titanic Rager would have?"

"The System rarely provides warnings; when it does, it's wise to consider them deeply."

"The final option, the Herald, doesn't have any unbound attributes, but it lists every attribute. I haven't seen that before."

"Usually, in a description like that, the first listed attribute is awarded the most points. That's not always true, though. Sometimes the attributes are increased equally, and the listing order is arbitrary. I would theorize that the Titanic Herald Class is not specialized; it's meant to help you gain further mastery of your bloodline. Future refinements will likely lead to specializations, perhaps into classes that the System designs to mimic your progenitors' ancient professions."

"Designed to mimic?"

Tes glanced from Victor to Barn and Valla, then did her little trick that caused his ears to pop, and said, "Dragons and other elder peoples did not have the System around to make our classes for us. We learned to master Energy on our own, and the skills and spells we spent our time specializing in became our 'classes,' though each of us was rather unique.

"The System tries to make Energy more accessible for people newer to Energy. It creates classes and helps to guide you through the process. Some might call it altruistic, but others know it's selfish—as you gather Energy and grow in power, so too does the System's tax from your efforts grow. It leeches but a tiny fraction of the Energy you gather, but combine the 'tax' of a trillion people, and you see why the System has grown so ubiquitous and difficult to circumvent."

"So, as I uncover my bloodline, the System is learning about the Quinametzin, and it might offer me refinements that it finds . . . through me?"

"That's right."

Victor sat there, contemplating Tes's words and also the decision he had to make. He, of course, saw the value in the legendary class, but he also felt a little strange about it. Victor was a human; if he kept pushing his bloodline, would he lose that? Would he become more Quinametzin than human? Before he could stop himself, he gave voice to his concern, "Tes, will I start to lose my humanity if I keep pulling out my bloodline?"

She smiled at him and gave his wrist another squeeze. "You're so different from dragons and titans I've met, and I mean real titans, Victor. Even when you're enraged, well, maybe not at your most mad, like when you charged the night brute prince, you usually display some part of your nature—you, not the Quinametzin.

"How many times have I let you catch me as you chase behind as a berserk lunatic? You never offered me harm; you never even spoke a cross word. There's too much of your human heritage in here"—she touched his chest with her other hand—"for the Quinametzin to drive it out. You might become a titan, of sorts, someday, but you'll never be solely Quinametzin."

"Well, give me a minute to think, would you? Thanks for the advice, Tes." She nodded and stood up, glanced at him one last time, a sly smile on her lips, then walked over to Valla. Victor sighed, stretched, and then put his finger on the pink gem of his bracer, sending forth a trickle of Energy. The world shifted, the colors bled away, and once again, he was inside the strange, angular world of the ancestor shard, standing before Khul Bach.

"My student returns and stronger than before, I see."

"Hello, Khul Bach." Victor offered a half-hearted wave. "I thought I should give you a chance to weigh in on my class refinement options."

"Wise." Khul Bach nodded solemnly. "Read them each to me, lad."

"Right. Option one . . ." Victor read through each option, and, to his credit, Khul Bach never interrupted him, listening and nodding as he progressed. When Victor finished, he grunted and rubbed at his chin, mulling things over for several moments before he spoke.

"What do you think, Victor?"

"Well, I think it would be smart to take a legendary class. I'm worried, though, about losing myself, my nature, to the Quinametzin in my blood."

"You would like my opinion?"

"Yes! That's why I'm here."

"Mmhmm. I'll tell you what I want you to choose, and then I'll tell you what you should select. Perhaps they're the same."

"You don't know?"

"I'm still thinking it through. Let's go through my thoughts: I want a scion who will one day be able to bring my people back to glory, someone who can save us from withering into obscurity. A 'Titanic Rager' might well win many battles, but will he be crafty and versatile enough for the great challenges to come? Perhaps. Perhaps he could slaughter his way to each of the shards and unite the Ancestor Stone. Perhaps he'd cause so much strife and misery and become so focused on slaughter that he'd lose sight of the greater goals, though.

"No, I'd rather you chose one of the epic options over that one, Victor. The choice, to me, is obvious; you should select the final class and herald in your titanic bloodline. Are you not intent on saving the Degh? Do we not want to restore my people's titanic nature? It seems a perfect match."

"So, I should pick that one." Victor nodded.

"Wait, Victor. I wouldn't be a good mentor if we didn't discuss why it would be a good choice for you." Khul Bach leaned forward and thumped a thick round finger into Victor's chest as he spoke.

"Right . . ."

"Do you enjoy your rage affinity? So much that you'd like to give up the others?"

"I . . . feel close to my rage, and if I'm being honest, I like the release I feel when I give in to it. I'd gladly give up my fear affinity, but . . . no—I can't see myself willingly parting with my inspiration attunement."

"The System is warning you about this for a reason; I believe if you accept the Titanic Rager Class, your rage will grow lopsided in your Core to the point that it may drive out the other affinities. The Herald Class, though, offers you a balance of attributes. It offers you a chance to gain power and knowledge and learn from your bloodline to find a specialization you can happily embrace. I'm certain it's the right choice for you. What causes you to hesitate?"

"You'll scoff at me, but I'm worried about becoming too much like the Quinametzin ancestor I see in my bloodline visions; already, I act differently when I'm berserk through my Titanic Rage feat. I not only act differently, I think differently—sometimes I catch myself thinking and speaking like I'm a Quinametzin, and . . . it's weird. I get so fucking full of myself and, like, reckless. I act as if it's my right to smash anyone who dares to stand up to me."

"Ah. So these Quinametzin from which you gain your titan blood were a haughty people? Likely they dominated their place in the universe for millennia, long enough to grow certain that they were the strongest of peoples. We Degh suffered from similar delusions for a while, but we had our challenges. Still, it's possible we never reached the heights of your progenitors; I don't believe we ever felt it our right to conquer all whom we met—a difference in culture, perhaps.

"Still, no matter the strength of your bloodline and how sincerely you embrace it, you are still Victor, and if you assert your will against your instincts, if you keep in mind your desire to keep those traits that you value in your heart and spirit, your bloodline will not overpower that nature. It's possible the ancestor you've witnessed through your visions does not holistically represent the Quinametzin; could it not be possible that you had other ancestors who weren't so brutally domineering? Perhaps you'll meet others as you explore more deeply."

"Uh, I guess it's possible, yeah." Victor liked the way Khul Bach spoke, the rhythm of his words, and his logical, positive way of exploring the topic. "I feel better about things, Khul Bach. Thank you for your advice."

"I've had a long time to think and have vicariously experienced many lives, Victor. I'm happy to share my wisdom with you because I want to see you succeed, and I'll always be honest in reminding you that I have selfish reasons for that. Still, I have begun to grow fond of your spirit, and I'd like to help you prosper and flourish. Trust my advice."

"I'll give it the weight it deserves. Thanks again. I'll be back soon," Victor said, then he severed his connection to the shard. The world snapped into being around him: the bright blue sky, Valla speaking softly to Tes, Barn banging away at his shield, and the hard rock under his butt. Victor sighed and opened his status sheet, pushing his sixteen free points into will; for all he knew, they were the last free points he'd ever get, and he wanted to give his will a final boost. He looked at his status:

Status				
Name:	**Victor Sandoval**			
Race:	**Human (Quinametzin Bloodline): Advanced 2**			
Class:	**Spirit Carver: Epic**			
Level:	**40 (42)**			
Core:	**Spirit Class : Improved 2**			
Energy Affinity:	**3.1, Fear 9.4, Rage 9.1, Inspiration 7.4**		**Energy:**	**3963/3963**
Strength:	**135**	**Vitality:**	**200**	
Dexterity:	**40**	**Agility:**	**63**	
Intelligence:	**32**	**Will:**	**413**	
Points Available:	**0**			
Titles & Feats:	**Titanic Rage, Ancestral Bond, Flame-Touched**			

"Well, here goes," he said, then opened the refinement menu and selected the fourth option, Titanic Herald.

29

A HERALD'S FIRST DAY

When Victor selected his class option, he was imbued with a sense of well-being, power, and confidence; he immediately felt that he'd done the right thing—this was his path. Energy surged through him, infusing every nook and cranny of his body, and he lifted his head back and howled at the pale blue sky, unable to contain his exuberance. System messages queued up for him to read, and he flipped through them, one by one, his grin widening with each.

Congratulations! You have refined your Class: Titanic Herald. Class feat gained, Titanic Constitution: Your titanic bloodline has enriched and fortified the microscopic structures of your body, from your blood to your bones, to the hairs on your head. Henceforth, you will automatically receive 5 bonus points in vitality each time you gain a level.

Congratulations! You have achieved level 41 Titanic Herald and gained 6 strength, 11 vitality, 6 dexterity, 6 agility, 6 intelligence, and 6 will.

Congratulations! You have earned a Class spell: Titanic Aspect, Basic.

Titanic Aspect, Basic: For a brief time, present yourself as the herald of your bloodline. Gain the aspect of a true Quinametzin Titan while maintaining cognizance and the utility of your full array of spells and skills. Energy Cost: 1000. Cooldown: Long.

Congratulations! You have achieved level 42 Titanic Herald and gained 6 strength, 11 vitality, 6 dexterity, 6 agility, 6 intelligence, and 6 will.

*****Congratulations! You have earned a Class skill: Titanic Leap, Basic.*****

*****Titanic Leap, Basic: Whenever your form reflects the aspect of your titanic bloodline, you will find that you are able to leap quickly and powerfully, covering distances seemingly implausible, even considering your tremendous size and power.*****

"I see you made a decision," Tes called from where she sat next to Valla. Victor grinned at her then stood up, stretching his back and lifting Lifedrinker to his shoulder. She hummed and vibrated against his thick muscles, and Victor squeezed her haft.

"Soon, *chica*. Soon, we'll fight again." He raised his voice and said, "I gained a shitload of stats with this new class." He walked toward Tes and Valla, then continued, "I feel fantastic; do I look different?"

"More hale. Your aura bleeds out, pushing more heavily than ever. Tes, can't you teach him to rein that in?" Valla shifted back, her hands behind her on the flat rock where she rested, looking up at Victor with squinting eyes and a friendly smile. He realized the sun was behind him, so he squatted down to make it easier for the two women to look him in the eyes.

"I can and will, but that's a lesson for camp. It's about time we harvested those night brutes and got on our way. Here." She produced her hell blade and handed it, hilt first, to Victor. "Go start carving the bones out of that prince; you shouldn't have much trouble, using that knife. We'll catch up. You can tell me about your new class features when I get there."

"Oh, all right . . ." Victor stood up and then looked down at the two women with a raised eyebrow. "Did I interrupt something?"

"Tes was helping me understand how to better shape one of my spells when you started howling." Valla chuckled.

"Oh, damn. Yeah." Victor rubbed at his head ruefully. "I was just excited." He glanced over at Barn, who was still frowning as he worked to smooth out his shield, then he said, curiosity getting the better of him, "Doesn't his shield self-repair?"

"You can see how thick it is." Tes tsked. "He needs to hammer it into a semblance of the correct shape, or the self-repair will take ages."

"Aha, yeah. Got it." Victor turned toward the cave entrance, then, on a whim, he cast his new spell, Titanic Aspect. He felt Energy surge out of his Core, all three of his affinities. It flooded his body, filling his pathways and then pouring into his veins, skin, and bones. He arched his back, looked up at the sky, and involuntarily roared as he expanded with the power of his spell.

For the first time he could remember, he stood, huge and menacing but fully himself. No red rage filled his vision, no urge to fight or kill—he was just Victor but . . . more.

Victor shifted and turned over one of his boulder-like shoulders, a broad grin on his face, and said, "See you down there." His voice rumbled out, and he laughed as he heard it bouncing off the rocky sides of the cave opening.

Tes's eyes were alight with glee as she studied him, and she nudged Valla's shoulder and said, "Our young titan is showing off. Should we be impressed?"

"Oh, I suppose it would do more damage to his ego than it's worth dealing with if we didn't 'ooh' and 'ahh' a little bit." She giggled, and Victor snorted, happy to see their good mood, even if it was at his expense.

"I don't think you guys get it! I'm not berserk right now!" He laughed again as if to prove his good mood, then waved and started into the cave.

By the time his Titanic Aspect wore off, he'd pulled most of the night brute prince's ribs from its charred remains, and he was working to carve out the bones in its legs when Tes and the others arrived. Between the four of them and Tes's uncanny talent for butchery, they managed to gather the valuable remains from the battle in just under four hours. After sharing out monster trophies, Tes's three charges each had a stack of precious bones from the prince and dozens of organs from the lesser brutes.

It was nearly dusk when they started north toward a place called Boil's Crossing. Victor resumed his practice with Berserk, running madly after Tes through the desert wasteland while Valla and Barn, on his mechanical mount, kept pace just a few dozen yards behind him. The sun slipped away behind the western horizon, but the sky remained pink and purple for a long while before fading into night. A couple of hours into their run, Tes paused, and when Victor caught her, she smiled at him.

"Aren't you hungry, titan-blood?"

Victor tried to take stock of himself, grunting with suppressed anger, his fists clenched as his eyes kept darting past Tes, looking for something hostile to fight. With an effort, he turned his attention inward, saw his rage nearly depleted, and growled, "Yes."

"Perhaps one of those brutes' hearts might be a worthy meal?" She grinned, somehow just as tall as he was, though still graceful, still beautiful, and as Victor looked into her gleaming eyes, he felt his rage begin to fade away. She punched him in the chest, not hard, but enough to jostle him and provoke a snarl, and she said, "Hurry now, angry one! Eat before your fury fades!"

"Ungh," Victor said, reaching into his storage ring for one of the dozen or so night brute hearts he'd salvaged. It fit in his mighty palm, dark maroon and glistening with undried blood. Victor's mouth began to gather saliva as he looked at it, and he didn't need further encouragement to devour the hunk of raw, tough muscle. Each swallowed lump of Energy-filled flesh flooded his pathways with red Energy, filled him to bursting, then pushed his Core to the point where it swelled and flared, pulsing like a miniature sun.

Part of Victor knew it was about to advance again, but his enraged mind didn't care. The pretty lady in the colorful dress was running away again, and he needed to catch her. He howled and yelled, aware that his companions were behind him; his pack was on the hunt, and a fight surely awaited them if he could only catch the lady.

The procession they made, their forms silhouetted against the darkening horizon, must have been a spectacle for any casual observer—a tall woman sprinting, endlessly energetic, with her ribbon of a belt and those in her hair flowing behind her, a great, hulking brute, leaping and charging, ever gaining on the woman, only to have her dart ahead out of his reach, and then a much smaller figure, bathed in jolts of electricity and wind, keeping pace with the brute. And, bringing up the rear, a squat, powerful figure encased in metal and riding upon a steaming, clanking metallic horse.

Not long before they came into sight of the crossing, Victor's rage-attuned Energy faded, and Tes didn't stop to encourage him to recharge it. She did slow, though, and when Victor, panting and sweating, crested the last hill atop which she stood, she gestured down to a brightly lit cluster of stone buildings gathered around the near side of a mighty stone bridge. Looking at the bridge, Victor let his eyes drift to the left and right and saw a dark ribbon in the starlit desert, and he said, "A river?"

"The river." Tes nodded. "The only one in the wastes. Even with its life-blood so rich, nothing much grows around it, though."

"The buildings are Boil's Crossing?" Valla asked.

"Yes, and you can see the hunters have already arrived." She pointed to a staked-out circle of monstrous mounts near the most prominent structure. Bright lights flared from its windows, and Victor could see people gathered outside on a cobbled patio, glow lamps hanging from posts, and small fires burning against the encroaching darkness.

"An inn?" Barn grunted from atop his clicking, hissing mount.

"Aye." Tes nodded. "Who's hungry?"

"I am!" Victor grunted.

"How could you be? I saw that meal you had an hour ago!" Valla didn't hide the note of disgust in her voice.

"Don't judge your comrade," Tes said, resting a hand on Valla's shoulder. "He has a mighty furnace to fuel."

Victor reached up to his chin, noticed it was still tacky with dried blood, and shook his head. "I don't blame you, Valla."

His response made her frown a little, and she glanced from Tes to Victor, then back again, and she opened her mouth as if to say something, but then she closed it again. The moment passed, and Barn said, "Well, I'm starved. Let's get down there." Without waiting for a reply, the big Vesh steered his weird mount down the slight incline, urging it into a canter, kicking up some dust.

Tes put an arm over Victor's shoulders, and he realized she'd matched his height again. She urged him forward, walking with him, and Valla hurried to keep pace, walking on Tes's other side. "You've both made much progress in the last couple of days. I'm proud of you," Tes said, reaching down with her other hand to squeeze Valla's shoulder. "We'll get a good night's rest, and then in a day's hard travel, the hunting party will hopefully find its quarry. I think the two of you have a good chance to claim a piece of the prize!"

"I notice you never take a split of the trophies from the kills, Tes. Is it all too beneath you?" Valla asked, smiling up at the taller woman.

"Beneath me? No, not necessarily, but I have plenty of treasures and trophies. The things I seek are a bit more rare." As she spoke, she glanced at Victor, and that sly smile and gleam in her eyes returned; he began to wonder what exactly she sought from him. He knew she wanted some of his blood. Was that all? He knew she found his bloodline and his antics while berserk entertaining; did dragons get bored of life to the point where following around someone like Victor spiced things up?

As they approached the inn, Victor watched Barn's horse explode into steam as it shifted and shrank, its many moving parts pulling in on themselves until only a quivering, metallic, clockwork cube remained. He picked it up, stowed it away, and then turned toward the trio as they strolled up. "Thanks for everything, Tes." He moved his gaze from left to right and added, "Nice to meet you, Valla and Victor."

"It was a pleasure, Barn," Valla said, reaching up to thump her fist against his armored shoulder.

"Yeah, take it easy." Victor waved, hanging back by Tes's side.

"You can join us anytime," Tes said. "Tell your sister I was good to you, will you?"

"Of course! I had a lot of fun, and that was a fast level for me." He eyed Victor again, sighed heavily, turned toward the inn's cobbled courtyard, and walked away, his heavy armor and bulky body giving him an awkward, rolling gait.

"He envies you, Victor." Tes hadn't entirely removed her arm from him; she'd loosened her hold, letting her arm slip off but still clung to his shoulder with her hand, and she squeezed it.

"Who wouldn't?" Valla asked. "He levels quickly and has such a potent mix of bloodline abilities and class skills . . . I'm glad I'm not his enemy."

"Sheesh. Is that all I am to people? An enemy or an ally? We're friends, Valla." Tes's grip on his shoulder tightened, and Victor rather liked the feeling; it was friendly and reassuring, and he could feel the Energy in her hand. If *he* were glad anyone wasn't his enemy, it was Tes.

"No. No, I know, Victor. I'm sorry; I was just thinking in terms of what we have waiting for us when we get back to Fanwath. I'm pleased you're Rellia's . . . *my* ally."

"Splendid!" Tes said, letting go of Victor and clapping her hands. "I was wondering what we'd talk about over dinner, and that sounds like an entertaining topic. Tell me about Fanwath and what you have waiting for you!" She strode ahead of them, not waiting for a reply, and Victor shrugged at Valla. She nodded, and they followed after, through the smoky courtyard with its braziers and glow lamps, past several hunters Victor recognized. Some of them called out, and Tes waved and bowed.

They claimed a table inside, next to a big stone hearth, and Tes ordered them several dishes she claimed were local delicacies. They reminded Victor of Indian food, with similar spices and textures, much like curry. The food was served with warm, grainy bread with a thick crust that tasted wonderful when smothered with the herbed butter that came along with it.

Victor ate a lot, more than he had in a long while, and Tes and Valla laughed about it several times, interrupting Valla's tale about the Untamed Marches and Rellia and her conflict with the other nobles in her household. Victor was a little surprised by how free Valla was with Rellia's secrets, but he figured it didn't matter—they were in a completely different world, and Tes had proven herself powerful enough to dig any secrets she wanted out of them if she really wanted to.

They drank a lot and laughed even more. At one point, Cayle joined their table and shared a toast with them, thanking Tes for getting her brother some fighting experience. She didn't stay long, though, and the trio were left to their own devices, telling tales, rolling dice, and joking about one another—with a preponderance of the quips made at Victor's expense.

Several different musical artists entertained the patrons of the tavern throughout the night, the last of whom was a woman who played the lute alone on stage and sang in a haunting voice about war and loss, love and death, and generally put a damper on things. Tes proclaimed it an excellent time to get some sleep, so they retired to a proper common room—a big space behind the tavern where cots were lined up for weary travelers to sleep in.

Victor claimed a cot big enough for a Degh, and Tes and Valla found empty beds nearby, and the three of them fell into sleep rather quickly. At least, Victor thought they did; he only really knew for sure that he did. The next thing he knew, bright light was streaming through windows, and the smells of bacon and fresh bread filled the air.

After a hearty breakfast, the hunters gathered outside, and Victor gravitated toward the rear of the column, where he could see Valla and Tes standing near a large wagon filled with barrels. Valla hadn't been at breakfast, and when Victor first approached the pair, he waved and called out, "Hey! How'd you sleep?"

"Not at all, to be honest. Too many people in one room. Too much snoring and grunting and, excuse me, farting. I spent the evening near the mounts, cultivating and enjoying the fresh air." Valla folded her arms in front of her chest as she spoke, a frown touching her lips at the memory.

"Oh? Well, I didn't hear a thing. Closed my eyes, and the next thing I knew, the sun was shining through the windows." Victor shrugged.

"You see, Tes? He even has to boast about being a better sleeper than I am!"

Tes chuckled and said, "With what his body went through yesterday, I'm surprised he was able to wake up. You'll be fine and are probably better off for the cultivation you got in. Well," she said, looking around at the hunters getting mounted and lining up, "I don't have a field trip for us today. We'll travel with the column and camp tonight, and I have a strong feeling we'll find Cayle's quarry on the morrow."

"Should I berserk again?" Victor asked, a note of dread in his voice. He didn't want to have to battle with himself all day around the column of hunters, cargo handlers, and beasts.

"I have another idea." Tes backed away from the wagon, walked a dozen steps, toes to heel, as if she was measuring something, then nodded and said,

"Stand behind me." Victor and Valla hurried over to stand behind her, and she nodded, then gestured with her hand, moving it as though she were pulling something large from a sack in front of her. Suddenly a bronze platform the size of an SUV appeared. It floated above the ground, kicking up a bit of dust on an invisible air current that seemed to be holding it aloft.

"What's this?" Valla asked, walking forward and leaning over to look under the platform. Victor copied her, and sure enough, nothing but air separated it from the ground. The platform was about four inches thick, twelve feet long, and six feet wide. The surface was carved with myriad runic symbols, many of which were inlaid with precious-looking metals like silver and gold.

"A travel platform I won from a rather combative wizard on a different world. I rarely use it, but I think today you both would benefit from some study and cultivation. Victor, your Core is ready to burst, so you may as well push it through to the next level. While you do that, I'll craft you a new sling for that axe, and then I'll give you some lessons on aura control. Valla, I have two more spells to teach you before we meet the wyrm tomorrow. Go ahead! Hop aboard." Tes laughed as she saw Valla eagerly pushing against the platform, not moving it at all.

"Seriously?" Victor laughed. "I get to ride in comfort and style? Tes, you're the best!" He laughed again and leapt aboard the floating platform, and when his full bulk made contact with the rear quarter, it dipped, though only a few inches, and then it resettled, completely stable. "This thing is awesome! How fast is it?"

"Depending on how much energy the driver puts into it, very fast. I have plenty of Energy, so we'll keep up with the caravan rather easily." She climbed aboard and sat near the front, and Victor held out a hand to pull Valla up. She found a seat near the middle and immediately began to pull notebooks and writing utensils from her storage ring. Victor sighed, watching her, imagining she'd definitely be the type of student with straight A's in school. He sat at the back as Cayle blew a horn near the front of the column, and the hunters got moving.

Victor hung his legs over the platform's edge and watched the countryside go by. When they got to the bridge, he stood up to look over the edge, watching the slow, dark green water lazily ripple by beneath the stone structure. Something with enormous, rough scales surged up momentarily, splashing loudly as it dove back under, and he reminded himself not to swim in that water.

30

OLD TREASURES AND AURAS

Sometime around midday, Victor broke through and leveled his Core. As each of his orbs of attuned Energy surged and pulsed, then contracted on themselves, slightly denser than before, Victor looked up and smiled with satisfaction. He'd made a lot of progress since coming to Zaafor, and he had a feeling he'd make a lot more before he and Valla left. He looked at his Energy status.

Energy Affinity:	3.1, Fear 9.4, Rage 9.1, Inspiration 7.4	Energy:	5280/5280

He waved it away and looked at Tes, who sat near the front of the floating platform working with some leather straps, and said, "Hey, why'd my Energy go up so much when I gained those levels back at the night brute cave? I only got six points in will and intelligence each level . . ."

"Maximum Energy is influenced much more by intelligence than will. Will improves your recovery rate to a greater degree, though." She didn't look up as she answered, and her quick reply made it clear that she'd anticipated what he was thinking. As if to prove that point, she answered his next question before he could ask it. "Each rank you gain in your Core should give you a boost of around one hundred Energy. Is that right?"

"Yeah!"

She nodded and said, "Most advanced races receive a similar boon."

"Advanced races?"

"Those with a decent connection to Energy—a measurable affinity and the ability to work it into spells or abilities. Some creatures have Cores and Energy, but their affinity is so low that it simply works through them as an extension of their natural instincts."

"Huh." Victor nodded. He looked away from Tes to his left, where Valla sat studying spell patterns, and then over her head to the vast, endless wastes. "We're going to have a chance to camp and rest before we hunt the wyrm, right?"

Tes closed her eyes and seemed to concentrate momentarily, then she nodded and said, "Yes, I'd say so."

"I need to honor my ancestors before the hunt."

That got Tes to look up from her work, and she narrowed her eyes and grinned at Victor. "Wonderful idea!"

Victor smiled, and then, while waiting for Tes to finish her work, he sorted through his storage containers, going over some of his long neglected treasures. He had two items he'd gained back in the dungeon attached to Greatbone Mine that had sat, lurking as grim reminders of that foul place, in his dimensional pouch. He'd always intended to have someone with knowledge look at them but never seemed to get around to it.

The first, he could easily explain why he'd left alone—the twisted, silvery-green crown of the cultist who'd been guarding the portal to the dungeon. Victor loathed the idea of touching it, but he couldn't find the fear that used to keep his fingers away; if the thing tried to poison or curse him, he'd smash it down with his will. That determination firm in his mind, he snatched it out of his bag and held it in front of himself.

It was cold, and something definitely writhed beneath the metal, touching his flesh with its sickly Energy but quickly retreating as it felt his aura. Victor grinned at it and then looked at Tes. She'd lifted her head from her leatherworking and wrinkled her nose at him. "What's this, then?"

"A crown I found a long time ago. I used to be afraid to touch it, but it now seems more afraid of me. Do you know what it is?"

Tes stared at the crown for a moment, and Victor could feel the Energy build up behind her eyes as they glowed briefly. She shrugged and said, "It's a vile thing, possessed by a mad spirit bent on twisting the minds of those who wear the crown into worshipping a long-dead being—some sort of demon, if my feeling is right."

"Oh, shit. I probably shouldn't have had it in my dimensional container . . ."

"It was mad long before you acquired it. I get the impression it was dormant, hidden for millennia before it was found rather recently."

"You could tell all that by looking at it?" Valla asked, looking up from her studies.

"Oh yes. I have very robust senses for that sort of thing." Tes winked at Valla, then looked down at her project, but she continued speaking, "I would think your ancestors could make use of the Energy within that crown quite handily."

"Oh?" Victor grinned at the idea. "Not a bad thought—I can let them deal with the nasty spirit." He put the crown back into his container and pulled out his other item—the choker he'd won from the dungeon boss. Frost began to form on his fingers where they touched it, and he gingerly set it down on the platform before him so he could better look at it. The choker was pale blue with seven different crystals, all shaped like runes that held no meaning to Victor.

"Ah," Tes said, leaning closer and peering at the choker. "This is another matter. What a lovely item!"

"I can feel it from here!" Valla said. "It's heavy with elemental Energy."

"Yes, currently charged with a water attunement, but I think it can hold other elements. Where did you get this one, Victor?"

"From a dungeon boss. I was only Tier Two, so I didn't think it could be that great . . ."

"You were only Tier Two, but what was the boss?" Valla asked, eyes still locked on the choker.

"Uh, good question." Victor shrugged.

"Regardless, that item is quite valuable. May I?" Tes asked, leaning further forward, arm outstretched but stopping short of touching the choker.

"Yeah, sure."

Tes picked up the necklace, and Victor noted with interest that frost didn't seem to form on her fingers. She smiled as she turned it around in her hands and then said, "This is a focus for the primary elements. A focus and an elaborate power cell." She glanced around at the wagons and mounts traveling nearby, then held the choker out to the side. A moment later, Victor sucked in his breath as he watched an honest-to-goodness miniature winter squall stir up out of the hot, sandy wasteland and blow rapidly away into the distance leaving six inches of snow in its wake.

"Holy shit!"

"Ha! Well, I purged it of water Energy. It's ready to receive a different element. If only you had a friend who could channel some sort of elemental

Energy, Victor." She gave him an obnoxious wink and nodded toward Valla, who was still staring out into the wasteland, watching the black, swirling cloud as it faded into the distance.

"Do you want it, Valla?" Victor asked, quick to take the hint.

"Hmm?" She jerked her head back to Victor and then glanced over at Tes, still holding the choker delicately in one hand. "I couldn't, Victor! It's a precious artifact!"

"True." Tes nodded. "Though you are working together, and surely Victor would want his partner to have every advantage. Besides, you could owe him one. Perhaps you'll win a prize that he could benefit from someday. Would you rather he kept it stowed away, gathering dust, or sold it for some beads?"

"Yeah." Victor nodded. "What Tes said."

"Here." Tes tossed the necklace to Valla. "I've removed my bond. It will always work as a focus, but you'll need to spend some hours charging it to use the power cell function."

"Power cell?" Valla asked, gently holding the pale blue choker, running the runes between her thumb and forefinger.

"A generic term for items that can hold a store of Energy. Once you've charged it, you'll be able to amplify spells you cast with the stored Energy. Until it's depleted, then you'll need to spend time charging it again."

"Oh, right. Back home, they're usually called power stones because, well, because we tend to use gems for the purpose."

"Yes." Tes nodded, then turned back to her leatherwork.

"Thank you, Victor," Valla said, gesturing with the delicate, beautiful choker.

"You're welcome. I hope it works well for you."

"It's the loveliest thing anyone's ever given me. I'll be sure to flaunt it to Rellia when we return." Valla grinned as she put it around her neck, hooking the clasp at the rear. A moment later, Victor saw little charges of electricity flicker over the runes.

"It looks really nice on you." Feeling some heat in his cheeks, he glanced away and almost laughed at himself. "You're charging it?" he asked to change the subject.

"Yes, it's quite easy! I just focus a strand of Energy from my Core through my pathways into it, and it slowly absorbs it. I'll need to rest before it's full, unless . . . I think I can keep up with the draw if I cultivate at the same time."

"Yes, you should, and as you grow in power, it will become more and more easy." Tes held up the leather strap she was working with and eyeballed Victor briefly before nodding and picking up her stitching tool.

Victor continued to organize his rings, moving mundane items into one and his more valued items into another. For a while, he spaced out sorting through the ring he'd won from Jikrak, the one filled with building supplies for a "hermitage." He wondered how valuable those materials were; it seemed like a lot of exotically named woods and stone, glass and fixtures, tiles and . . .

"What do you think?" Tes interrupted his thoughts. He jerked his attention away from his dimensional container and looked at the leather harness she'd made for him. It was a work of beautiful craftsmanship, and Victor knew some Energy must have gone into it. Runes lined the leather, silver rivets held the axe-loop part to the shoulder harness, and soft white fur lined the inside of the strap that would rest on his shoulder. The ring meant to go around Lifedrinker was also silver, and Victor wondered what he'd do if she outgrew it.

"It's wonderful, Tes. Thank you!"

"Try it on," Tes said, and Victor nodded, reaching out to take it and then hanging it over his neck so it rested crossways over his chest. The loop for Lifedrinker rested against his ribs about at the height of his elbow. "Stand up and put her in there."

"Right." Victor stood, lifting Lifedrinker from the floor of the floating platform, and then slipped her haft through the ring. She hung there, comfortably snug against his body, her handle hanging down alongside his leg.

"If she evolves to become larger, the ring will resize itself. I also enchanted the whole thing to grow and self-repair. I used Boilercrock leather—very dense and capable of holding a lot of Energy, so you can get quite large without harming it.

"Sheesh, Tes!" Victor said, rubbing the dark, supple hide between his fingers. "I didn't expect something this nice. Can I pay you or something?"

"Foolish man!" Tes scoffed, "Don't offer to pay for gifts, especially when given by one of"—she glanced around—"my type of people!"

"Right. I *am* foolish, Tes. I didn't mean any offense." Victor spoke earnestly, and his words brought a smile to Tes's face.

"Good! Now, I sensed your Core expanding. Are you ready to learn to rein in that aura a bit?"

"Please!" Valla said, smirking.

"Hey! Didn't I just give you a fancy necklace?"

"I'm sorry!" She chuckled, holding up her hands in surrender, then turning back to her spell pattern.

"Mmhmm." Victor grinned, then he took Lifedrinker out of her loop and sat back down, resting her on the platform next to him.

"You could tilt her handle back so you can sit with her still in the harness," Tes said, watching him.

"Yeah, but I don't know; I like to give her room to breathe when I'm not walking around."

"Does she speak to you often?" Tes leaned forward, and Victor saw her hand twitch as though she was about to reach for the axe but held herself back.

"Do you want to hold her?" he asked rather than answer her question.

"May I?" Tes reached forward, taking the invitation as answer enough, and very carefully picked Lifedrinker up by the haft, her fingers wrapping around the dark, star-speckled wood just beneath her metallic head. "Oh, she's wonderful!" Tes's eyes lit up as she turned Lifedrinker this way and that, staring into the depths of her living wood haft. She traced some dark streaks of metal in the shiny Heart Silver with a finger, one of her blonde eyebrows raising with interest.

"Her edge used to be the only shiny part; the Heart Silver spread as she woke up and evolved. She speaks to me, but not all the time, to answer your earlier question, by the way. When it first started, I felt like I could feel her emotions before I could hear her words."

"I've seen many conscious weapons, but this one has such a strong spirit, Victor. She must love you." Tes smiled and handed the axe back to him, and Victor rested her on his knees.

"Well, it's mutual. We've seen a lot together."

"A brave man to open his heart so. I like that about you, Victor; I think you'd proclaim your love for your axe no matter who listened."

"He would." Valla didn't look up; her words were quick and spoken from experience. Tes laughed, and Victor shrugged.

"All right, let's get down to business. Victor, you have a powerful will for one so young and newly into the fourth tier. I think you'll find this lesson very easy." She looked into his eyes and waited for Victor to nod before she continued. "You can feel others' auras, yes?"

"Yes, especially from powerful people like the Warlord or Tronk or . . . well, or you."

"Mmhmm, but you don't feel the pressure of my aura right now, do you?"

"No." Victor frowned, trying to remember the last time Tes's aura had pressed down on him.

"That's because I'm holding it back. It takes some conscious effort, but less and less the more practiced you become. In some worlds, were you to walk around with an overbearing aura, it would be taken as a signal that you sought violence or that your will was so weak that you couldn't contain yourself. We don't want that to happen to you, do we? When you unleash your aura, you want it to be intentional."

"Makes sense."

"So, just as you manipulate Energy with your will, you must learn to pull your aura back and hold it down. The first step to that process is being able to see it. Close your eyes and turn your attention to your Core." Victor did so, finding it easy to look "inward" at his Core and the three orbs of Energy therein. "Now, expand your view, keep the Core at the center of your awareness, but allow your perception to see your pathways. Simply widen the perspective.

Victor tried to do as she asked, but he felt his view of his Core slipping away as he looked at his pathways, and he grunted in frustration. Somehow able to see his problem, Tes spoke again. "Slowly; relax and broaden your view, but keep that Core at the center, don't look away. Let your pathways fill your peripheral vision."

Victor nodded and tried again, carefully focusing on his inspiration-attuned Energy and letting his inward-seeing eye expand its field of view. He almost whooped with glee when it began to work, and he saw his pathways stretching away from the Core at the center of his perception.

Victor continued trying to expand his view, and soon he saw the extent of those pathways, all the way to his fingertips, toes, and the center of his forehead. When he smiled with satisfaction, he noticed something. At the edges of his perception, outside his pathways, hung a flickering, pulsing curtain of reddish-purple light, glowing as it surged and retracted, seemingly at random.

"Holy shit," he breathed, "I think I see my aura."

"I knew you'd be a quick study!" Tes sounded almost smug. "Reach out with your will and pull that aura in. Hold it tight to the edges of your pathways."

"All right," Victor said, gritting his teeth, squeezing his eyes tight, and twisting his lips in concentration. He pulled at that pulsing field outside his pathways and managed to restrain part of it while other parts flared out. "It's hard to get ahold of it all!"

"Come, Victor. I've seen people with half your will do this. Keep your focus on your Core! Don't look at one part of the aura and grab at it. Reach out like you're casting a net and pull it all in." Victor decided to take her words literally, and he envisioned his will forming into a net. He urged it to expand, wrapping around that pulsing, flaring aura and pulling it to himself, binding it tightly to the edges of his pathways.

"Whoa!" Valla said.

"You did it!" Tes cried, clapping her hands.

"Ancestors! I can't remember the last time I wasn't under that pressure . . ."

Victor opened his eyes, his mouth wide in a smile of pride, and then Valla reached up and cradled her head, groaning. "Ugh! You let go!"

"Doh! Shit." Victor closed his eyes and began to repeat the process.

"Victor, you'll need to maintain some concentration on holding your aura back. With practice, it will get easier and easier, and, eventually, you won't even realize you're doing it."

"Let me see here," Victor said, biting his tongue in concentration as he finally reasserted his web of willpower, pulling back his surging aura. For the next several hours, he worked on the process, slowly allowing more and more of his attention to leave the view of his Core and trying to interact with the world while a part of his mind kept concentrating on holding back his aura. He got better at it, but by the time the wagons were grinding to a halt at the base of some low, rocky hills, he had a blinding headache, and with an apologetic shrug to Valla, he let it go.

"Well, I had quite a long break from it, and I'll get used to it again. Promise me you'll keep working at it, though!" she said, standing up and stretching.

"I will, Valla. Promise." He looked over at Tes, who'd hopped off the platform and was looking around the campsite, presumably choosing a spot for the three of them to set up their tent. "Hey," he said, turning away from Tes and back to Valla, "I'm going to sacrifice some stuff to my ancestors. Wanna watch?"

31

GLORY FOR THE GHOSTS

Victor looked through his piles of monster trophies, allowing his instinct to guide his hand as he pulled specimen after specimen out of his dimensional container and stacked them together on the sandy ground of the waste. At the bottom of the pile was the cultist crown, and he knew in his gut that his ancestors in the spirit plane—or Ghost Lands, as Tenecoalt called that otherworldly realm—would appreciate it as an offering. He wondered about that; would they like it for its Energy, or would they consume the spirit lurking within? At this point, nothing would surprise him.

Dawn was just brightening the eastern horizon, and most of the hunters were still sleeping off their excessive drinking from the night before. There had been no partying for Victor and Valla; they'd spent most of the evening in the tent working on assignments from Tes. Victor shook his head and grinned as he recalled the conversation that had spurred those hours of study.

"Tes," he'd asked, watching the woman, now small enough to comfortably sit in one of Valla's plush chairs, "how do you keep changing your size so easily?"

"Oh? You've noticed?" She laughed.

"Yes! When I'm . . . bigger and running through the waste, you're my height. When we stop to talk, and I'm my usual size, you're my height. When you need to sit in a comfortable chair built for a much smaller person, you seem to fit just fine. What gives?"

Tes wrinkled her nose and shifted so she could pull her legs up under her, leaning against one heavily cushioned arm of the chair. She gave Victor a long, penetrating look and asked, "Are you wanting to sit in small chairs, or are you worried about dwarfing the people you've known, afraid you'll grow more distant in their hearts because of your size disparity?"

Victor glanced at Valla, still peering intently at a spell pattern she was trying to duplicate, and then his ears popped, and he turned back to Tes—she'd cast her privacy spell, perhaps to spare his feelings. "I guess so. Everyone I knew before I came to this world was pretty much human-sized. I think it would be cool to fit in anywhere I went . . ."

"Well, I can't help you with that—fitting in anywhere, I mean. The spell I have requires very Energy-dense flesh and is able, with the expenditure of enormous amounts of Energy, to make me nearly any size smaller than originally but not larger. I suppose I could modify it to do so, but the expense . . ." she trailed off, clearly trying to envision the idea.

"Would it work on me?" Victor felt hope in his chest and was surprised by it—he'd thought he'd come to terms with his largeness.

"I think so; your titan ancestry, your bloodline, has begun to manifest quite significantly in your physical form. I'm not sure you have the Energy to alter yourself by much, but if you study the spell, you should be able to accomplish much as you grow in power. I believe your inspiration-attuned Energy would be a good fit for the magic."

"Would you teach me?" Victor leaned forward, going so far as to scoot over the rug, so he sat closer to Tes's chair.

"This is ancient magic, Victor. Many of my kin would be quite cross with me for sharing it, assuming you could master the pattern—it's quite complex." Something about the crooked grin on Tes's face and the way she leaned forward to match his posture told Victor she wasn't worried about what her kin might think.

"So, will you?" he pressed.

"I will. Tonight, I'll give you a tenth of the pattern. Prove to me that you can master that much, and I'll give you more."

Victor chuckled as he stacked a long rib bone from the night brute prince onto the pile. He'd been up all night studying the wild, twisting, shifting pattern that Tes had drawn out for him on a piece of magical parchment. She'd said the most challenging part of the pattern would be forcing his Energy into it, but Victor knew he could master his Energy—his will was strong enough. No, for him the hard part was comprehending the insane complexity of it and then trying to force his clumsy fingers to recreate parts of it.

Still, Victor knew he'd get it eventually, especially if he could manage to make a few more levels and boost his intelligence and dexterity a bit more.

When he thought of Tes and remembered the glimpse she'd given him of her dragon form, he could only imagine the kind of Energy that went into shrinking that massive body into a petite woman; he didn't need anything so severe, just the ability to shave off a foot or two when he wanted to exist among his smaller friends more comfortably.

He heard footsteps crunching in the sand behind him and turned to see Valla approaching. She looked past him to the pile of monster organs and bones and said, "Quite an expensive offering."

"My ancestors battle in the Ghost Lands, and these are the least of the scraps I can offer," Victor said before he even realized he was speaking. Were those his words? Were they the words of Tenecoalt? Was he human or Quinametzin? "I'm starting to think like one of them," he said, deciding it had been him, but with ideas that were new to his conscious mind.

"Well, you've advanced your bloodline a lot. It makes sense. There's nothing wrong with learning and gaining new ideas and ideals, though. I think it's wonderful that you can connect yourself so viscerally to your ancestors."

"Well, let's say I have a lot more respect for you—I mean the Ardeni and Shadeni—and your reverence for your ancestors."

Valla smiled and stepped forward, reaching up to rest one of her small blue hands on his arm above his elbow. "Are you ready?"

"Yeah." Victor glanced back toward the tent, hoping to see Tes approaching, but she'd not returned from wherever she'd gone. After giving Victor the pattern to study, she'd said something about finding a dice game and a "strong enough drink." He shrugged, turned to the pile of offerings, gathered his Energy, and cast Honor the Spirits.

White, heatless flames burst into existence at the base of the pile and rapidly spread through it, sending ghostly smoke into the air that faded into nothing. No smell accompanied the burn, and though the light was brilliant while it lasted, there was no afterimage in Victor's eyes after it faded. It was as though the whole thing hadn't been real. Still, the offerings were gone, and Victor felt a deep satisfaction in his heart; his ancestors would be pleased.

"That's such a pretty spell," Valla said, squeezing his arm.

"Yeah." Victor inhaled deeply and smiled, turning to look down at Valla.

"So, I noticed you were still sitting there poring over that spell pattern Tes gave you when I finally went to sleep. What are you trying to learn?" she asked, meeting his gaze.

"What are *you* trying to learn?" Victor countered. "You studied all day on the platform and then all night in the tent!"

"I finally got it!" Valla laughed, apparently fine with his redirection. "Watch!" she said, backing up, and then Blue Razor was in her hands. She concentrated momentarily, and the sword crackled with white coruscating electrical Energy, surging and pulsing. She turned toward the desert and swung the sword in a downward, angled slash, and the white, pulsing electricity leapt off the blade, rippling and crackling into the night in a vast arc. "Cut of the Storm's Fury!" Valla laughed.

"Pretty dramatic spell name, but shit, that was cool!" Victor held out his hand, meaning for Valla to slap it, but she sort of gripped his fingers awkwardly, clearly not used to the custom. Victor chuckled, squeezed her hand back, and said, "That's awesome, Valla. You're going to mess that *pendeja* up when that duel comes around."

"I know it's childish, petty even, but I'm looking forward to it."

"You're not the one who started that shit!" Victor said. "That chick was downright nasty, and she's the one who wants to make your skin into a cloak! If anyone deserves to get messed up, she's at the top of the list."

Valla smiled, but before she could say anything, Tes called out from near the tent, "I saw the flames of your offering, Victor, and I see you mastered your new spell, Valla! I'm proud."

"Oh, look who finally made it home!" Victor grabbed Valla's shoulder and nudged her along as he started to walk back to Tes.

"Home?" Tes peered at Valla's tent and smirked. "I suppose in a very loose sense of the word . . ."

"Did you have fun?" Valla asked, hurrying over to the other woman.

"Oh, some. Cayle's wine was well fortified, and she and some of the other hunters played an entertaining game—until I started to win too much, and then they grew cross. Still, it was an amusing evening."

While Tes told them about some of her winnings and the irate reactions of the other players, Victor cooked breakfast, and Valla took down her tent. By the time they'd packed everything away and eaten a very hearty portion of eggs and sausages, the rest of the hunters were breaking camp, and word came around that Cayle wanted to hold a meeting at the head of the column.

Most of the others were starting to trickle into the meeting when the trio arrived, and they stood at the far right end of a big loose semicircle facing Cayle, where she stood atop a crate. The hunters milled about, laughing, joking, drinking hot mugs of coffee, and generally ignoring Victor and Valla. Some deference was given to Tes, though, and Victor learned, through her short greetings and conversations, the names of many of the hunters nearby.

He'd just decided to give in to his urge to ask one of the nearby hunters with coffee if he could bum a cup when Cayle shouted for everyone to be quiet.

"Listen up, you mongrels!" she called, chuckling with good humor. "Red just confirmed—he's in sight of the wyrm, and it's a big one! He claims it's the biggest adult he's laid eyes on, and you all know Red—he's been on many hunts." At those words, the hunters burst into excited babbling and cheering, and Cayle had to holler for them to quiet down again.

"What are we waiting for?" a huge Vesh with a single, enormous black horn jutting from his forehead called out.

"Calm yourself, Bricker!" Cayle said, smashing the butt of her enormous lance-like spear against the wood of her soapbox. "Listen! Red confirmed, visually, that his wyrm is a fire-blood! He saw the smoke as it breathed and the smoldering scrub in its wake. That means some of you might want to sit out this fight!" Curses, grousing, and general discontent drowned out her next sentence, and she had to shout for order again.

"Listen, you devils!" The hunters didn't listen, though, and continued to talk loudly and animatedly. Finally, a Degh hunter wearing darkly scaled armor walked up beside Cayle, looming over her, despite her elevated position, and turned to the crowd.

"Shut yer damned yaps!" he roared, and the words barreled over the noise, and almost everyone clamped their mouths shut.

"Thank you, Vormor," Cayle said, then turned to the crowd to continue. "As I said, it's a fire-blood, and you'll be wise to note the risk; with a wyrm this age, you're likely to see breath attacks and blood that will ignite materials short of epic. I won't stop any of you," she added, holding up her hand, "but you've been warned. If you don't have significant resistance to flames, you'd be wise to employ ranged attacks."

"And stay the fuck out of my way!" Vormor bellowed, and Victor's heart leapt in his chest—had that man just said fuck?

"Holy shit," he said, and Tes turned to him with a grin.

"I know what you're thinking," she said. "He didn't use the same word you're so fond of; it's an uncommon curse in the Vesh tongue, and the System translated it similarly to the one from your homeland."

"Ha! I don't care; it's nice to hear another foul mouth."

"Enough said; we'll leave the wagons and attendants here, and we hunters will move out in ten minutes!" Cayle called. Then she quickly added, "I'll be watching participation, and so will the other members of the Spears. No one has any looting rights until the battle is done and I've awarded merits!

Naturally, if you perish, your portion will be split among the survivors. There are no benefits paid to families on this hunt—use that information to inform your level of caution." With that, Cayle hopped down from her crate, and Tes turned to Victor and Valla.

"You'll stay by me, Valla. I know your Lightning Strike isn't your best attack yet, but you'll get some good hits in—I'll help you. Victor, I suggest you avoid the beast's maw, but I think your resistances will be sufficient to deal with the smoldering nature of its blood. Don't hold back."

"Doesn't he need to worry about the other hunters? Will they be using area attacks?"

"Naturally; stay on your toes, Victor."

"I will," he said, resting a hand on Lifedrinker, where she lay nestled against his side. Tes led them away from the main group of hunters up a rocky hillside on the south side of the gully that supposedly wound its way to where the wyrm was roaming.

"I can feel it," she said when they were away, standing high, back to the rising sun and facing down the meandering pathway through low stone and scrub-covered hills toward a distant rocky canyon. "He's old and angry, too big to ever sate his hunger in these lands. Stymied by his nature, he cannot find a way to progress. Wyrms aren't terribly clever, even old ones like him, and he'll respond with insane, frenzied attacks when he's set upon by the hunters. Victor, you should unleash everything you have near his midsection. Try to spill as much of his guts as you can. Lifedrinker will be able to part his lower scales, though you'll need to use all your might.

"Avoid the thick ridges on his back; if you thought the night brute prince's bones were hard, those would give you a new level of understanding of the word. Still, if you can do enough damage, those very scales will be a part of your prize; you can bet on it, and with them, I can help you craft armor that will eclipse what you lost two days ago."

"Shit!" Victor said, slapping a hand on his leather-clad chest. He was wearing one of the fringed and beaded vests Tellen's people had gifted him. "I was supposed to buy one of these Degh's old armor!" He gestured to the hunters below.

"Forget it." Tes waved a hand dismissively. "Nothing you could buy from these men and women would be much use against an ancient wyrm. Better to not let it bite you." She paused, considered for a moment, and added, "Or sting you with its tail."

"Sting me?" Victor groaned.

"Oh yes. This type of wyrm has a barbed tail with venom that will ignite your blood. Literally." While Victor let those words sink in, the other hunters began to ride, fly, and run forth, streaming over the hillsides with whoops, hollers, and jolts of Energy that lit up the gray shadows of early morning. "Let's go!" Tes said, and then she was running over the hilltops, suddenly much larger than before. Valla cloaked herself in lightning and wind and sped after her, and Victor grinned, watching them go.

He unslung Lifedrinker and held her up so the morning sun flashed along her silvery edge and said, "Time to go to work, beautiful. I'll be careful not to crack your handle again. I'll find a perfect spot to let you sink your teeth into this old bastard."

With that, he started to jog and gathered his Energy to cast Inspiring Presence. He whooped and laughed as the shadows fell away, and he saw the perfect path to run along. He checked his Sovereign Will boost to ensure it was still on his vitality and strength, where he'd kept it for days on end, no longer very fatigued or bothered by the constant use of the spell.

If he had to guess, he felt he was damn close to advancing the spell, so easy had it become for him to keep it going. Catching himself thinking that way, he wondered if his inspiration-attuned Energy was giving him the insight. He laughed and shrugged, shouting into the sky, "Does it matter if I'm right?"

Tes and Valla were small figures on the next hill, a solid mile ahead of him, and he decided it was time to quit messing around. He gathered up his rage and cast Berserk. When his body stretched and bunched with corded muscles, Victor roared, squatted his huge, powerful legs, and launched himself toward the next hill, soaring hundreds of feet over the blasted hillside to smash into the loose, dusty gravel on the next slope. Again, he laughed, turned to the bright, red-tinted sun, and howled, brandishing Lifedrinker at the baleful orb, seeking its blessing as he turned and charged up to the hill's crest.

Tes and Valla were no longer distant figures, and Victor, for the first time, managed to pass by Tes as he leapt again, soaring through the air to smash into the next hillside with a tremendous roar. The thrill of the chase didn't matter to him at the moment. He wasn't trying to catch Tes; he was rushing toward a mighty enemy, and there were weaklings ahead of him still, people bent on stealing his glory, and the glory he meant to win for his ancestors in the Ghost Lands.

32

A WYRM'S TALE

Victor tore through the loose, dry scree scattered about the hilltop, and with crimson rage tinting his vision, he surveyed the final slope that led down into the box canyon where his quarry awaited. Despite his efforts, several challengers had reached the canyon ahead of him, one riding on a twisting serpent mount, another atop the shoulders of a lumbering, giant, armadillo-like monstrosity, and a third soaring through the air, her massive, red-scaled wings allowing her to leave everyone else in the dust. Still, Victor saw her circling up there, perhaps afraid to initiate the fight with the terrible beast that lurked ahead.

Of the wyrm, Victor could only see its hindquarters—the rest of its enormous body wound out of sight beyond a steep bluff-like hill to the east. Still, enough could be seen to give even Victor's rage-soaked mind pause; this was a monster of legend, a creature large enough to swallow him whole or drive him into the soil with nothing but its great girth as a weapon.

"Great men aren't made by fleeing from danger," he said, pacing back and forth, clenching his fists and stoking his fury. He pumped his pathways full from the heat in his Core, focusing on the fact that he wasn't charging into battle. The thought made him angry, which further fueled his rage, and soon, his vision was such a deep shade of crimson that he could imagine he swam through air soaked in blood. He laughed and howled at the idea, and then he leapt off the hill, crashing to the hard, dusty floor of the canyon and racing toward the enormous black-scaled tail with its horrible, razor-edged barb.

"Ancestors!" he bellowed. "Witness our glory!"

Despite his fury and the urge to swing his axe, Victor forced himself to calmly utilize some of his other attuned Energy; he summoned his totemic bear using a surge of baleful purple-black Energy, and as an inky, dark, misty figure began to coalesce on the far side of the weaving, bobbing wyrm tail, he cast Channel Spirit, flooding Lifedrinker with inspiration. Before he gained enough ground to leap upon the mighty creature's tail, it began to thrash and surged forward—the other hunters must have engaged the beast's front end.

Undaunted, Victor bunched his legs into greater strides, charging forward, and that's when his bear fully materialized and roared so loudly that small rocks and dust began to cascade off the canyon walls. Victor howled at the sound, pleased, but then another sound burst through the air, one so vastly more tremendous that, at first, Victor's ears couldn't make sense of it. When it dawned on him that he wasn't hearing a volcanic eruption or a locomotive derailing but rather the roar of the wyrm, a mad exuberance filled him; here was a challenge worthy of demigods!

One more mighty stride and then an explosive leap that left a dust cloud in his wake, and Victor soared through the air to land atop that thrashing tail. He wrapped his powerful legs around it, just above where the lance-like stinger began. Before he could glance along the great length of scaled ridges that made up the wyrm's spine and perhaps grow discouraged, Victor began to lay into the bumpy, rough scales before him; he'd decided to try to manage this enormous beast one small piece at a time.

His first few hacks, aimed at the gaps between rough scales, were rebuffed by the tough hide of the ancient beast. Victor swung again, harder, and nearly unseated himself as the wyrm's tail lifted into the air. He bore down with his prodigious strength, squeezing the tail between his thighs and hooking his ankles together at the bottom. If he'd been less focused on his task and more aware of his situation, Victor might have laughed at the idea of riding a wyrm's tail as if it were the world's biggest bucking bronco.

Growling with determination, Victor gripped the ridge of a rough black scale and braced himself, hacking Lifedrinker into the crease between two scales over and over, his grip high on her handle so as not to apply enough force to damage the axe again. In his red-eyed fury, he could have lost himself to the effort, wholly given in to his berserking nature, heedless of Lifedrinker's safety, but his attachment to her was too great, his recollection of her previous wound too fresh in his mind.

Victor frequently glanced at her gleaming edge to ensure she was holding up, and when he saw nary a nick or scratch, he redoubled his efforts, grinning as the gap between the scales gradually widened. He was aware that he wasn't the only combatant on the field—he heard concussions, saw flashes of light, and heard screams. He knew he was flying through the air as the wyrm thrashed and brought its stinger to bear on its foes, but Victor was single-minded in his efforts, refusing to let go, to loosen his death grasp on the beast's whipping appendage.

When Lifedrinker's edge finally bit through the thick dark hide beneath those scales, hot blood like liquid fire spurted out, singing a hole through Victor's leather pants and scalding his arm. He knew if it weren't for his berserk healing and Flame-Touched feat, his flesh would have been rendered from his bones. As it was, the touch of that blood was painful and left pink welts on his skin, but they healed rapidly, and Lifedrinker didn't seem to mind it at all.

With the beast's flesh parted, Victor lifted Lifedrinker high and brought her down on the cut with all his might, driving her deep into the wyrm's meaty, muscular tail. Lifedrinker screamed with bloody intent as she tore into the wyrm, and Victor lifted his head into an ululating howl and screamed, with vicious bloodlust, "Dig in deep, *chica*! Drink!" Lifedrinker didn't need the encouragement; she shivered and throbbed, pulling herself deeper and deeper until only the very tip of her hammer spike was exposed.

Victor used her haft as a grip, better supporting himself as the wyrm writhed around the canyon, thrashing this way and that, trying to slay the swarm of attackers or dodge their more devastating attacks. He saw a spider-web of luminous orange Energy flowing through the scales of the beast into Lifedrinker. At that sight, he knew she would profit immensely from this battle, whether he survived or not, and the thought brought him comfort and amusement. "You'll get yours, won't you, beautiful? No matter what that little woman decides I've earned."

Watching his axe drain vast currents of Energy from the wyrm, Victor lifted his head to the sky again, howling. He jerked his gaze around, looking for his bear. Somewhat at the mercy of the wyrm and in what direction it chose to thrash and flip its tail, Victor had a hard time finding not only his bear but his sense of direction.

At one point, Victor hung upside down as the tail lifted into the air and curved as though to strike at someone. Hanging there, the battlefield below his head, Victor finally got a good look at the enormity of his foe. The wyrm stretched away from him for a hundred yards or more, and its long, twisting form was supported by no less than a dozen short, muscular legs.

That was when he saw his fearsome purple-black bear battling beside several Degh working to cut the tendons that operated one of the wyrm's legs on the right side. The one behind it was already hanging limp and bloody. "Good boy! Fuck him up!" Victor laughed, still clinging to the tail as it shot through the air and impaled an enormous, shaggy, mammoth-like mount, sending its Degh rider flying through the air to smash against a stone outcropping.

The hillock-sized mount wailed in agony as the wyrm lifted its stinger out and Victor with it. He watched, closer than he'd have liked, as the creature immolated from the inside out, gigantic gouts of flame shooting from its orifices. "*Chingado!*" Victor grunted, resolving not to let that stinger puncture his own flesh.

He wanted to do more, wanted to rip the wyrm to pieces, but even in his berserk state, as large as he was, he was small and weak compared to the monster. If he pulled Lifedrinker out and continued to hack away, he'd do some damage, sure. Maybe he could get the stinger off eventually, but Lifedrinker was probably doing more damage by drawing the creature's Energy, and if not, she was undoubtedly benefiting more. For the first time that he could remember, Victor wished he had another decent weapon, something capable of truly harming the ancient monster.

Somewhere, deep in the back of his rage-addled mind, Victor remembered the enormous black metal maul he'd taken from ap'Horrin's blackguard when he'd defeated his ambush in Gelica. Grinning madly, he summoned the huge maul, and in his mighty fist, it was simply an overlarge war hammer. The handle was metal, just as dark as the heavy metal hammerhead, and it all seemed to be one piece. "Perfect," Victor growled, inching his way up the tail, past Lifedrinker, and then bringing it down with a tremendous smash into the hard scales of the wyrm.

To the bones in his hands, it felt as if he'd just struck a great hunk of iron, and Victor's rage intensified as he was rebuffed so easily. "Piece of shit!" he roared at the hammer and tried again. This time the scale at the center of his blow cracked, but the hammer's haft bent. He screamed in fury and threw it to the side, heedless of its trajectory. Some ancient instinct took shape from deep within Victor, and he lifted his furious face to the sky and cried, "Ancestors!"

A sibilant voice came to him then, like a woman whispering in his ear. "*I am Citlalicue, and you have pleased me, child of the Quinametzin. Borrow my*

*grace and the touch of my whip. Make haste, though, for my power wanes quickly;
I offer you these boons knowing you'll repay me tenfold!"*

Before Victor could so much as whoop or laugh with delight at the contact with an ancestral spirit, he felt a surge of profound, rich Energy, heavy with the scent of rain and grass and the pulse of the verdant jungle. Suddenly a new understanding of movement came over him—the bucking and thrashing of the wyrm's tail was, to him, a gently swaying bough in the breeze. He released his hold on the knobby ridges of the wyrm's scales and leapt to his feet, running up the weaving, roiling spine of the creature as though it were a steady plank.

While he ran forward, Victor felt more Energy itching in his hand, and he lifted it above his head, and suddenly a twisting, luminous tendril of deep green Energy flared and snapped into the sky. "Feel this whip, beast!" he roared and brought the coil of powerful Energy down to crack against the wyrm's side. The whip snapped out and down, the torrent of Energy condensing at its tip like a miniature green sun, and when it tore through the wyrm's hide, the sound of the concussion was like a cannon going off.

That blow got the wyrm's attention; it bellowed another great roar that brought cascades of boulders and gravel down from the heights, and Victor laughed as he continued running along the thrashing beast, cracking that brilliant whip into its side over and over, blasting bloody, jagged holes in its flesh with each impact. Later, he might wonder just what his agility had been boosted to, but then, in the moment, all he could do was revel in his ancestor's power and bask in his foe's thrashing fury.

The ancient wyrm tried to unseat him by rolling to its side, but Victor nimbly hopped along the bucking, twisting surface of the monster, running over its ribs and cracking that terrible whip again and again. So desperate to remove him was the wyrm that as Victor danced toward the front part of its spine, the creature tried to impale him with its dripping, lance-like stinger. Victor adroitly leapt forward, though, landing some twenty feet farther toward its head, and the monster impaled itself.

Whatever fiery venom was in its barbed stinger didn't seem to bother it overmuch, as amusing as that would have been, and it pulled its stinger free just as a tremendous bolt of lightning, followed by a flaming boulder the size of a minivan, smashed into the center of its back. Victor made to leap away from the concussive explosion, but that's when his ancestor's gift dissipated, and he lost his footing on the rolling, flopping monster's spine.

As Victor fell toward the hard canyon floor, a great shadow followed him, and when he smashed into the dirt, the bulk of the wyrm's body rolled over him, pressing him down into the hardened ground. Had such a thing happened to him a few months ago, he would likely have had many of his bones reduced to shattered fragments and his guts pressed out of his mouth. Thankfully his body had undergone many improvements, and with his berserking rage still coursing through his pathways, the pressure of the great beast smashing him down like a rolling pin on dough was only briefly painful and unpleasant.

When the monster's bulk passed over him, he grunted and jerked himself up to his hands and knees, part of his mind mildly amused by the Victor-shaped impression in the dirt. At that moment, his rage began to fade, and he laboriously pushed himself to his feet, backpedaling from the still-thrashing, gigantic body not a dozen yards before him. To his more rational mind, it became apparent then that the higher-tier hunters had ramped up their attacks and were finishing the direly wounded creature.

Lances of light, lightning bolts, smoking orbs of fiery magma, and even a ball of something that looked like crackling plasma tore through the air, filling it with fumes, smoke, and steam, making it hard for even Victor's powerful lungs to breathe. He turned and hurried up the side of a newly-formed slope of scree, wanting to get above the haze of powerful magic to witness the wyrm's final death throes.

He clambered atop a boulder and turned, standing tall to watch as, borne on golden wings of Energy, Cayle streaked through the air to drive her lance-like, red-limned long spear into the rolling Wyrm's breast, burying ten feet of its shaft with an explosion of smoking, hissing wyrm blood. Then, the huge Degh, Vormor, ran forward with another long spear, this one crackling with white and blue electricity, and drove it directly through the wyrm's scaled hide, running forward to bury it six or eight feet into its flesh.

Similar actions played out all along the wyrm's length as Cayle's troop, the Spears of the Copper Sunset, earned its name, burying great spear after spear into the wyrm until its thrashing finally stilled and the surviving hunters screamed and whooped their triumph into the air. Victor joined in, of course, lifting his fists to the sky and howling. When his voice was lost in the clamor, he cast Titanic Aspect and redoubled his efforts, and this time his roars echoed out through the canyon with the best of them.

He leapt over several dead or gravely injured hunters to land near the wyrm's tail and sought out his wonderful axe, eager to see how she'd fared. As he reached for the tail, meaning to twist it so he could see Lifedrinker's haft, a rough hand gripped his arm near the elbow and pulled him back. "Hold up, off-worlder. We wait for Cayle to assign loot."

"I'm not going for loot," Victor growled, jerking his shoulder around to look at who spoke. It was the big Vesh with the enormous black horn jutting out of his forehead, Bricker. "My axe is stuck in the tail, and I'm going to pull her out." Victor reached his hand back toward the tail, but the guy jerked his arm again, and though Victor was titan-sized, the Vesh was stronger—much stronger—than he looked. "If you don't stop doing that . . ." he growled, feeling his rage begin to stoke, feeling it start to bleed into his pathways.

"What's the trouble here?" a cheerful feminine voice asked. Victor turned his head past Bricker to see Tes strolling forward. "The beast's last heart just stopped beating. Energy will be flowing soon; no need to quarrel, Bricker."

"I'm not quarreling; I'm just making sure this off-worlder doesn't get greedy."

"Nonsense! I can see his axe jutting out." She stepped past Victor and effortlessly lifted the enormous tail. "Just here. See it?" she asked, pointing to Lifedrinker's half-buried haft. As Bricker grumbled, Tes winked at Victor, and he reached forward to grab Lifedrinker and pulled with all his might to free her buried head.

"Gods," Tes breathed as Lifedrinker came free. She'd changed again—her blade was broader, the bearded part longer, and no trace of the dark ore that used to be mixed with her Heart Silver remained. More than that, she gleamed and pulsed with amber Energy. At first, Victor thought she was just slick with the wyrm's blood, but that had sizzled and drifted into the air as dark smoke the moment he'd pulled her free. No, this new fiery gleam was something new, an aspect she'd stolen from the great monster.

"*¡Que increíble!*" Victor hissed, gingerly reaching to touch Lifedrinker's head, noting how the dark, living wood handle had grown in girth as he held her one-handed. He hovered his fingers over the metal and was pleased not to feel any heat when he touched it, though he could feel the depths of the Energy beneath the surface, as though a lake of molten fire lurked in there.

"*Do I please you, Victor?*" her crystal voice asked in his mind, a new, smoky crackle lurking beneath the words.

"God, yes, *chica*. You're amazing!" Victor laughed and hefted her in his mighty fists, and then he was crushed by an avalanche of Energy that surged into him—his share of the ancient wyrm kill.

33

TROPHIES

When Victor came to his senses, he stood among more than two dozen other hunters who'd similarly gone through an incredible influx of Energy. Many stood, swaying on their feet, dazed like Victor. Others, perhaps having received less, laughed and cheered, slapping the hands of their neighbors and whooping, waiting for Cayle to make her post-battle announcements.

Victor ignored everyone, including Tes as she grinned at him expectantly, no doubt waiting for him to tell her about his gains. Instead, he carefully read through the System messages floating in the air before him:

*****Congratulations! You have achieved level 44 Titanic Herald and gained 12 strength, 22 vitality, 12 dexterity, 12 agility, 12 intelligence, and 12 will.*****

*****Congratulations! You have gained a Class feat: Titanic Presence.*****

*****Titanic Presence: The blood of mighty titans surges in your veins. Something buried deep in the primal instincts of other peoples and creatures recognizes your heritage and respects it. Your aura is heavier, and threat and danger are pervasive in its dense folds.*****

Smiling broadly, Victor looked at his altered attributes.

Energy Affinity:	3.1, Fear 9.4, Rage 9.1, Inspiration 7.4		Energy:	6554/6554
Strength:	159	Vitality:	244	

Dexterity:	64	Agility:	87
Intelligence:	56	Will:	437
Points Available:	0		
Titles & Feats:	Titanic Rage, Ancestral Bond, Flame-Touched, Titanic Constitution, Titanic Presence		

"Well?" Tes finally asked, reaching out to nudge Victor's shoulder. Victor glanced around and saw that the guy who'd been hassling him had wandered off and that everyone seemed preoccupied with their own situations.

"Where's Valla?" he asked rather than answer right away.

"She's up on yonder hill from which she tossed many a lightning bolt into this great old serpent." Tes gestured to the rocky slope a hundred yards or so behind and to the left of Victor. He thought he could see his diminutive blue friend up there, sitting cross-legged and staring into the sky.

"I hope she got a good amount of Energy from it." He grinned as Tes began to frown, staring at him pointedly. "Oh, all right—I gained two levels, a bunch of attribute points, and a new feat."

"Something to do with your aura?" Tes guessed.

"You can tell?"

"Yes, you're going to have to work harder to learn to control it. See how the hunters wander away, shifting subconsciously to be out of it? Your presence grows rather noticeable, and those with great power and pride might begin to take offense."

"Ah, damn. Yeah, I'll work on it." Victor shifted Lifedrinker in his grip and then lifted her to look at her broad blade and gleaming silver metal. The amber luster lurking beneath her surface was less visible now, but he knew it was still there. He smiled at her with pride, then slipped her into the harness Tes had crafted him. "Do you think I earned some trophies?"

"Oh yes! If Cayle doesn't recognize your contribution, I'll speak up on your behalf. She has a sharp eye, though. I think you'll be pleased. Look, here she comes." Tes gestured back toward the wyrm's corpse, and Victor saw Cayle's tall, lithe figure striding along the downed creature, hopping nimbly between the humps of knobby scales. When she drew closer to the densest pack of hunters near the wyrm's middle section, she lifted her arms, and everyone cheered.

"What a battle!" she howled. "Three cheers for the fallen; we lost seven brave souls today, but they'll be remembered! I'll mark their names on the memorial in Hunter's Hall myself!" Again the crowd cheered, and Victor joined in, loudly shouting with each of the three repetitions. When the noise died down, Cayle yelled, "I have my preliminary assessment, but I'll continue to analyze my memory stone"—she held up a perfectly round, bright blue sphere—"while the beast is butchered. After we've gathered the trophies, I'll award each of you your lots. Time to get to work!"

As the hunters began to draw carving knives and butcher blades, some bigger than Lifedrinker, Victor glanced at Tes, and she held out her hell blade with a grin. "Time to learn how to carve up a monster bigger than many people's homes. I'll give you a hint: take it one piece at a time!"

Victor chuckled and took the offered knife, and then he followed Tes to the tail, where she showed him how to carve off the stinger without severing the long, springy tubes that carried the venom from a gland deeper along the spine. "The hunters won't want us to spill the venom," she said, pulling on scales and holding them up so Victor could slice them out of the flesh. Once that was done, following her instructions, he cut along the tail until he'd removed the venom gland—a great, spongy orange organ the size of a five-gallon bucket.

Several times people came to observe his progress, perhaps intent on carving out the same organ, but they all left, seemingly satisfied with his work. Valla approached when he was halfway through, and Tes told her to help with the head—several people were needed to hold the jaw wide while teeth, horns, and other trophies were carved out.

Even with dozens of hunters and just as many retainers, it took the rest of the day and long into the night to finish harvesting the enormous body. It was hard work, even though many of the hunters had magical spells that could make the gathering of great stacks of wyrm meat, magically reinforced barrels full of wyrm blood, and piles and piles of wyrm ribs and vertebrae easier.

The more common items were piled on gigantic tarps, while other, more precious items like the seven wyrm hearts and other organs were stored in specially enchanted glass jars, some of which were the size of fifty-gallon drums. The teeth and claws were kept under guard, apparently so valuable that a hunter might risk ostracism to steal more than his or her share. In the end, when the work was done, nothing but scraps of cartilage, flesh, and stained desert soil remained as evidence of the great creature ever having existed.

When all the prizes were stacked and laid out with bright Energy lamps illuminating the scene, the hunters gathered up and broke open some casks of, apparently, fine ale. Some of the retainers and a few hunters took up instruments, kicking off an impromptu celebration. Victor worked hard to keep his aura in check, which prevented him from having much fun; it still took too much of his concentration to keep it from slipping free of the net he'd cast with his will.

"When do you think Cayle will announce the shares?" he heard a large Degh ask Valla as if she had any idea. His friend smiled and shrugged, drinking her ale with a lopsided grin.

"Not sure, but it won't matter to me; I'm sure my part will be small. I'm just happy I participated in the battle; I gained a level and improved a spell!"

"Well done, then, little miss." The Degh held out his enormous tankard of ale, and Valla clinked hers against it, sloshing out a shameful amount onto the ground. She didn't seem to care, laughing and looking away shyly, and Victor realized she might be drunk.

"You're doing well, Victor." Tes had walked up to him where he sat in the sand, feet extended and one hand holding his own mug. He was on the outskirts of the gathering but still within the light of the glow lamps. "Hard to have fun when you have to concentrate so much, isn't it?"

"Yeah, I guess, but I don't want to make enemies accidentally. I figure after Cayle speaks and we get our shares, I'll head off by myself to unwind." He took a sip of his ale, careful to drink slowly so his control didn't slip.

"You're making good decisions. Aren't you pleased with your growth on this hunt? I think it's been very good for you." Tes sat down in the sand next to him, and he saw that she held a red crystal goblet in one hand, the contents of which shimmered faintly in the glow lamp's glare. He'd seen a jar of mercury once in science class, and it had looked a lot like what she was drinking.

"That looks like a potent drink," he said.

"Oh, this? Yes—I'd offer you a taste, but I fear it would be a bit much. Perhaps when you've pushed your bloodline into the epic tier." She grinned and winked at him, and Victor admired how the light lit up the depths of her eyes. They glimmered like deep pools of honey with hidden turquoise stones in their depths.

"You're an interesting fellow, Victor. I'm sorry that this hunt is coming to a close; I've had more fun with you and Valla than all the rest of my time in this world."

"Well . . . I've had fun, too, Tes. I really appreciate all you've done for me. I imagine Valla and I will be in Coloss for several more weeks. Won't we see more of you there?"

"Surely!" She leaned closer, and he could smell something of her drink on her breath, something like whiskey and cinnamon, cloves and sugar, and underlying it all, the coppery tang of blood. His mouth began to water. "I'll visit you in the Warlord's citadel; how does that sound? I've more lessons for Valla, and you'll want more of that spell pattern once you've mastered the first part. No?"

"Yes! Definitely."

"Good!" She looked over her shoulder and said, "Here comes Cayle." Victor followed her gaze but didn't see Cayle for several seconds. Then she stepped around the pile of wyrm fangs, and the people who were drinking, singing, dancing, and carousing backed up, giving her room.

The instruments grew quiet, and Cayle produced her big crate, hopping atop it. Tes shifted so she could more easily watch the proceedings, sitting next to Victor, closer than she needed to, and he was very aware of her warmth as she leaned into his shoulder and whispered, "Some will argue at your share, but if they try to press the matter, let Cayle settle them down."

"You know my share?"

"I have a good inkling."

"Are you all ready to hear your shares of this amazing kill?" Cayle called, holding up a faintly glowing black slate. The crowd cheered in the affirmative, and Cayle smiled, gesturing around her to the piled wyrm trophies. "All of this represents one hundred shares. First, I'll award the tenth-shares.

"All of you retainers who didn't participate in the battle but aided us in our long journey and with the massive undertaking of cleaning our kill will be paid with a tenth-share. One hunter, Graga of Hot Rocks Spring, will also be paid in a tenth-share. I'm sorry you were knocked senseless so early, Graga, but be happy not to walk home with empty hands."

Victor saw a tall, lanky Vesh woman with a white mohawk laugh and bow as many of the hunters chuckled. Cayle smiled and continued, "Quarter-shares will be awarded to Thole, Furvett, Astor, Beysha, Cadric, Moon, Qanit, and Jasper." Victor shifted and smiled nervously at Tes. Neither he nor Valla had been called, and it seemed the shares were getting bigger.

Tes returned his smile, her bright teeth winking in the light, and, for the first time, he noticed she had a small gap between her two front teeth. He wondered if that was a choice or if her dragon body would reflect that tiny imperfection. He decided he quite liked it. So focused was he on Tes's smile that he almost missed it when Cayle called out Valla's name for a half-share.

"Nice!" he said, looking for his friend and waving at her. She was beaming, clearly pleased, and many nearby hunters raised their drinks to her.

Cayle continued to call out names, going from half-shares to full shares, and still, Victor hadn't heard his name. When she read off several names—members of her hunting company, who'd earned five full shares—he began to grow nervous. Victor looked at Tes and said, "Did I miss my name?"

"No, you silly oaf." She shook her head, a look of wonderment on her face, presumably at his goofiness.

Cayle continued to call out hunters, going more slowly now that people were winning larger and larger shares, allowing for some celebration. When she got to ten-share awards, she named herself, three other members of the Spears of the Copper Sunset, and then Victor. Cheering resounded for each name until she called out Victor, which was followed by some hisses and grumbling.

A few hunters, much higher rank than Victor, who'd been awarded a single share or less, started to argue loudly, and he could feel the angry glares coming his way. Victor remained seated, remained steady in the control of his aura, and tried to follow Tes's advice, waiting for Cayle to sort the matter out. When some of the louder, more powerful hunters began to walk toward him, and the grumbling crowd refused to listen to Cayle's shouts, he began to get nervous, preparing himself to leap to his feet.

He needn't have worried, though—when Cayle's shouts went unheeded, she seemed to lose patience and produced her enormous spear, smashing the haft against the crate, sending an explosive bolt of howling, brilliant Energy into the night sky. As the wasteland canyon lit up like noon on a bright day, people turned to see what their angry leader had to say.

"Before you try to undermine my tally, perhaps you'd all like to hear why Victor has won such a share, hmm? Do you all feel you can grant me that tiny bit of respect?" She didn't yell, but her voice was full of venom, and the grumbling malcontents looked away from Victor as Cayle began to list his accomplishments during the battle.

"How many of you were burned with the wyrm's magma breath?" She looked around, and when not one hunter spoke up, she continued, "That's because Victor planted his Heart Silver axe, Lifedrinker, directly into the great beast's primary Energy pathway! The axe never allowed it to build up the Energy necessary to pour forth a gout of terrible liquid magma!"

Some appreciative grumbles sounded around the gathered hunters, and Cayle continued, "How many of you witnessed a great dark spirit in the shape of a bear? Did you see how it tore out the tendons on not one but two of the wyrm's legs before it was destroyed? Victor summoned that bear!"

"Victor!" one of the Degh giants howled into the night, and a few others cheered along with his cry.

"How many of you saw Victor striding along the wyrm's back, tormenting it with a whip of powerful Energy that tore through its hide and caused it to thrash so madly that it gave us its belly?"

"Victor!" the Degh cried again, and this time others echoed his shout. "Victor! Victor!" Cayle nodded at the sound and raised her spear, looking over the heads of the gathered crowd to Victor, offering him a salute of sorts. He stood up, held a fist high, locked eyes with Cayle, and nodded back to her.

After that, it was just a matter of divvying up the goods, and Victor was glad to stand on the perimeter, waiting for the others to get their shares first. None of the hunters were hostile to him after Cayle's little speech describing his accomplishments, and Tes said he was probably safe to relax his hold on his aura for a while as the others picked up their shares.

Valla approached, though she grimaced as she drew near and said, "Could you make your aura any heavier? I don't quite feel enough of a strain!"

"Hey, I'm working on it! I held it in check all damn night."

"It's true." Tes smiled at Valla and walked over to give her a brief hug. "I'm proud of you, Valla! A half-share at your rank is nothing to be ashamed of."

"Thank you, Tes. A pity I can't compete with this lunatic, though! Still, all joking aside, I'm proud of you, Victor."

"Oh, man. Can't you insult me? I'm not used to people being nice." Victor chuckled, then added, "I'll share my rewards, don't worry. Though you'll have to wait and see if anything's left after I share with my ancestors . . ." Valla's mouth fell open, and her eyes widened, and Victor laughed, shaking his head. "I'm kidding. I mean, I will be sacrificing some of my share to them, but I'm sure there'll be plenty left over."

"Wise! Thanks to your ancestors, that battle went much better than it could have. People are stealing glances your way, Victor, and I see respect in their eyes." Tes stepped away from Valla and reached up to squeeze Victor's shoulder. "Your axe, Lifedrinker, she's going to be as famous as you, I think. I'm glad Cayle realized what she did—how you interrupted the flow of the wyrm's Energy. Its breath could have killed many more of the hunters."

"I, well, to be honest, I didn't know that would happen; I just wanted her to get a good long drink." Victor chuckled and gently patted Lifedrinker's haft hanging by his side. In an effort to get the attention off himself, he looked at Valla and asked, "Did you get your share?"

"Yes! A gallon of the wyrm's blood, a rib, five side scales, and two back scales."

"Shit! Not bad, I guess." Victor shrugged; he had no idea of the value of those trophies.

"Outstanding, Valla. Those back scales alone are worth a handsome sum." Tes, ever cheerful, smiled broadly at Valla as she congratulated her.

"Well, I can attest that they're hard as hell," Victor chuckled.

"People are clearing out, Victor. I think you can walk forward to claim your prize. Perhaps rein in your aura one more time tonight." Tes took his elbow and urged him back toward Cayle's big crate and the remaining wyrm trophies. Valla followed along, breathing a sigh of relief as Victor's aura receded.

"Victor," Cayle said as he approached. "I told you I was fair, didn't I?"

"Yes, Cayle, and you were true to your word."

"Well, you earned this." She turned and waved to the pile of wyrm parts on a large tarp. "A full ten shares." She walked around the tarp, pointing to each item as she listed them off, "Four fangs, twenty ribs, a hundred side and belly scales, forty back scales, a heart, fifty gallons of blood, a pint of magma venom, a quarter liver, seven pounds of the brain, five horns, two claws, and your option: the stinger or another heart?"

"*Chingado*," Victor breathed, looking at all the paper-wrapped and jarred wyrm parts. The barrel of blood looked like an oil drum he'd seen in vids back on Earth. He glanced at Tes and raised an eyebrow. "What should I take? The stinger or another heart—I mean, I know the obvious benefit of a heart, but . . ." His voice trailed off as he looked at the seven-foot length of hard black stinger. He supposed the venom tubes and gland had been severed so the hunters could divvy out the venom itself. Still, that stinger looked like something special to him.

"The stinger can be made into a powerful weapon," Cayle said before Tes could speak.

"Yes. The right smith could make a mighty spear or lance. Would Lifedrinker grow jealous, though?" Tes asked, gingerly reaching out to gently brush two fingers along the axe's haft.

Victor thought about her words—he doubted Lifedrinker would react that way, especially if the spear weren't intelligent and he kept it in a dimensional container. Besides, wouldn't it be nice to have a long, pointy weapon when Lifedrinker didn't quite suit the circumstance or when she was busy drinking the life from a foe? He chuckled and said, "She knows she's my favorite." As if to confirm it, he reached down to feel her silvery head, letting the heavy hammer spike at the back rest against his palm.

"What about it, *chica?* Do you care if I have a spear, too?"

"A spear is but a tool. I'm your weapon, your companion; your spirit and mine are bound. I care not."

"Well said, love, well said." Her words struck a chord within him, and Victor suddenly found the idea of using any other weapon rather unappealing, at least as long as he didn't have to. Why would he want to run around with some wyrm stinger when he had Lifedrinker? He looked at the three women standing nearby and their questioning expressions and said, "Lifedrinker doesn't care, but I'm not feeling it—I need to get my axe skill up to legendary anyway, right? I think I'll take another heart."

"It's settled then. Take your share, Victor. I hope you"—she turned to Valla—"and you, Valla, will consider hunting with us again. The Spears were impressed by you both."

34

THE HUNT RETURNS

The hunters' caravan traveled back to Coloss on the same route they'd used heading out, and the monsters of the waste seemed to be giving them a wide berth. Consequently, Tes didn't take Victor and Valla on more side hunts. That said, she did spend a lot of time on the return trip tutoring the two of them. In Victor's case, it was more that she gave him a peaceful place to keep working on his current projects: cultivating his Core, learning to control his aura, and studying the maddening, mind-boggling, utterly impossible spell pattern she'd given him.

He sat near the back of her floating travel platform and lost himself to the world each day. Victor started the day by making slow, steady progress with his Core in the morning hours. Then he'd break for a meal, and while he studied and tried to replicate the fragment of Tes's spell pattern, he'd dedicate part of his attention to wrestling with his aura.

During those early hours, while he worked through constructs of rage and fear and finished with an invigorating study of inspiration, Valla would hang behind the train with Tes, avoiding his aura and sparring with the dragon woman. Somehow Tes's platform trailed behind the monster hunters, always keeping him just far enough away so his aura didn't bother anyone, and by noon, Valla and Tes would race forward to join him as he ate his lunch.

When they hopped aboard the platform on the third day of leisurely travel—Cayle and her hunters seemed to be in no particular hurry to get back to Coloss—he grinned around a spoonful of bean and pork stew and proclaimed, "My Core just advanced to Improved Five."

"I sensed it!" Tes said, chuckling as she and Valla sat across from him on a pair of lovely teak armchairs. Victor sat on a rug, preferring to be on the "floor" when he cultivated. "Your friend here is getting ever so fast at alternating her sword forms with Energy attacks; I'm pleased with her progress!"

Victor looked at Valla, saw her pale blue cheeks darken as she blushed, and chuckled. "Good for you, Valla. If we get back to town tomorrow, what does that leave until your duel? Something more than two weeks, right?"

"That's right." Tes nodded. "Valla will use the Warlord's cultivation chamber while you're not in it, and I think with more sparring, she'll be more than ready to teach Reis a lesson in humility."

"I appreciate your confidence, Tes. Hopefully, I'll be able to afford some upgrades in town, as well."

"Oh, you certainly will." Tes glanced over her shoulder, and Victor saw that one of the hunters was approaching their platform. He was a tall, lanky Vesh with dark fur over most of his body, and he rode upon the back of a long-legged, pale creature that reminded Victor of a nearly hairless camel. "I don't think he intends trouble," Tes said quietly.

Victor swallowed his last bite of stew, stowed away the bowl, and watched as the man rode up beside their platform. "Hello," he said, his voice low and pleasant. Victor admired his armor—made from scales smaller and more supple than the ones he'd won from the ancient wyrm. It gleamed in the bright sunlight, clearly well-maintained and full of Energy. The scales varied in color from red to burnt orange and contrasted nicely with the man's fine turquoise riding cape.

"How fare you, Darnt?" Tes asked, and Victor shook his head, bemused— of course she knew his name.

"Well enough. My grief and anger fade." Those words got a reaction out of Valla, and she jerked her head up from where she'd been preparing a sandwich of sorts.

She opened her mouth to speak, but the newcomer beat her to it. "I'm not here for trouble, Tes. I feel I should speak to your charge, though, to put this chapter behind me."

Valla snapped her mouth shut and locked eyes with Victor. "Who is this man?" her expression clearly said.

Tes didn't speak, and the man turned his gaze to Victor, still riding alongside their platform. He had a lupine look about him, with long furry ears and big golden-yellow eyes. He nodded his head in greeting, and that's when it clicked. "Krista?" Victor asked as a rush of emotion he didn't know he'd been holding back flooded his chest, constricting his throat.

"You see her in me?" Darnt asked.

"Yeah." Victor offered a quick nod, his face solemn.

"I'm not here for vengeance; what would be the justice in that? She sought death in the arena, and you gave it to her. Still, I thought you should know you didn't kill a monster. You killed my little sister, and she was good and sweet once."

"I . . ." Victor struggled for words; the man's statement had left a mark. It was true—he had built Krista into a monster in his mind. That was how he'd managed to kill her without a second thought. He didn't want to think of her as a sweet little sister; what the fuck was this guy's problem? He began to frown, a scowl forming on his face, but before he could blurt out something he might regret, Tes reached forward to lay a hand on his forearm. Her calm, light touch stole his attention, and he looked away from Darnt to her ever-changing, sometimes golden-blue, sometimes honey-green eyes.

"Hear his words, Victor." She didn't say anything more, but Victor felt his anger cooling, and he had to wonder at its source. Was it logical? He almost laughed aloud at the thought—when was anger logical?

"Krista was angry at life, and she did some terrible things," Darnt continued, oblivious to the battle Victor had been having within himself. "She would have killed you in that battle had she been able to. You see, she'd been married and had a daughter—my niece. I won't take up your time with the tale of their demise, but they died a few years ago, and Krista was never the same—full of anger and hate, eager to see others suffer. I just wanted you to know, Victor, that though she wasn't a good person when you slew her, my sister was once a very kind, loving woman. I miss her."

Victor frowned again, feeling emotions making his throat thick—anger, guilt, sadness. "You know," he finally said, "I would have agreed to show mercy, but she insisted she would kill me. I'm not a monster." He nodded, setting his expression in firm resolve. "I'm not a monster," he said again, more softly.

"Well, who can blame you?" Darnt said, shaking his head. "I wanted to blame you. Wanted to be angry with you. When I saw your theatrics fighting the wyrm, I grew increasingly angry, but I spoke to Cayle and others, and they described what they saw in you, and I realized I saw through clouded eyes—what I took for grandstanding, others read as desperate valor, as courage and determination. So, I come to offer you peace, Victor. I ask for one thing in exchange. Will you try to think of my sister as I once knew her? As a loving mother with kind eyes and not a hate-fueled bully?"

"I'll try," Victor said, and, to his credit, he did. He pictured Krista for the first time since the arena. He thought of how she'd taunted him before their fight, how she'd angered him, and how he'd turned her into a monster in his mind to avoid dwelling on her death. Then he realized he'd done similar things with the other people he'd killed. He felt a welling wave of disgust and gripped his hands into tight fists. "Yeah," he nodded. "I'll try to remember she was a person, not a monster."

Tes nodded. "A hard truth that many of us must face."

"Aye," Valla said, her eyes distant and her face somber. Who was she thinking of, Victor wondered.

"That's all I ask," Darnt said, then holding up one hand in farewell, he clicked his tongue, and his long-legged, ugly mount began to trot, leaving the platform behind.

Victor sat in silence for a while, and so did Tes and Valla. When he finally spoke, he said, "I don't think I like arenas."

"Hmm?" Tes looked at him inquisitively, and Valla's far-off gaze refocused on his face.

"I know this world, well, this universe involves conflict. I know I'll have to fight again, but I don't like choosing to do so, not to the death. Not as a spectacle."

"You mean other people?" Valla asked.

At the same time, Tes asked, "Are you going to tell the Warlord?" Victor was surprised to see a glimmer of amusement in her eyes.

"I guess it wouldn't be right to keep using his chamber and whatnot if I weren't going to fight in the next tournament."

"What if you didn't fight to the death?" Valla offered.

"Well . . ." He licked his lips, searching for the right answer. "God, it's fucking tough! You guys don't know how much parts of me love it in there! The heat of the crowd's Energy, the brutal one-on-one competition—it all does something in here." He thumped a fist against his chest. "I'm made for it! I guess if I could be sure I go in with the intention not to kill for others' amusement, I could live with it. I don't even have to tell the Warlord, right? I mean, no rule in the next tournament says I have to kill my opponents." He looked at Tes for confirmation, and she nodded.

"What if you should accidentally end someone's life? Your dear axe is not a plaything, Victor." Tes spoke lightly, and something told Victor she already knew how he would answer.

"If someone makes me fight hard enough to let loose with Lifedrinker, then that's on them, but I'm going to give them every opportunity to yield before it gets to that."

"Such a heart in that big chest," Tes said, grinning. She glanced at Valla and said, "It makes me pity those who won't yield all the more."

"Well, I just hope he won't get himself killed. You can't hold back against someone forty levels above you, Victor."

"Yeah, I guess." He frowned and said, "I've got some time to think about it. Maybe I'll bail out before the tournament. I doubt the Warlord would chase us to Fanwath, would he?"

"Perhaps not, though I feel your future and his are more intertwined than you think." Tes glanced down at the pink gem on Victor's bracer, and he sighed, rubbing a thumb against the jewel.

"Yeah, probably."

"Enough dwelling on these topics, Victor. As you said, you've some weeks to think about things. For now, let me congratulate you on keeping your aura in check despite that unpleasant conversation."

"True!" Valla added. "I didn't feel it slip at all."

"How fares your progress with my spell pattern?" Tes asked, pressing the conversation further into the topic of Victor's studies.

"Slow and frustrating," Victor said, a variant of his usual response when Tes asked him about it. "I don't get how I'm supposed to replicate these lines." He pulled out the parchment Tes had given him, displaying the convoluted, multicolored, twisting, *writhing* pattern. He pointed to the lines that, in his eyes, seemed to move constantly. "I mean, they're never in the same place when I look at them. They're constantly shifting."

"Tell me, do they seem as shifting to you as when I first handed you the pattern?"

Victor thought about the question and tried to remember how he'd felt when he first looked at the spell as Tes had written it out. "No. Definitely not—the lines seemed to jump all over the place back then."

"And yet, I've not altered the pattern at all. You haven't somehow changed it on the page where I wrote it. Why do you think they seem less . . . shifting, as you put it?"

Victor wasn't stupid, so he sat there and thought about it for a minute, and then his face split into a grin as he replied, "Because I'm starting to wrap my brain around it. I just don't realize it's happening because it's slow and painful."

"Ha! Exactly, Victor. Keep working at it. Once you've mastered this portion, the next one will come to you even more quickly, especially if you continue to level and improve this." She reached forward and tapped her pointer finger on Victor's forehead, and the two women laughed.

"Love it when you two gang up on me," Victor grumbled, but he grinned beneath the bluster and turned back to the pattern, quite pleased to realize that he hadn't had to actively think about controlling his aura the whole while they'd been talking.

The next day, an hour or so before noon, Coloss came into view, and the hunters cheered, startling Victor out of his meditations. He stood up on the platform, admiring the enormous walls and tall towers of the city. As his gaze moved upward, seeking out the citadel atop King's Hill, he was once again awestruck by the enormity of the construction. The wall was one thing, but that towering edifice, lording over the tens of thousands of stone buildings, reminded him of just how awesome the place was, how far he had to go if he was ever going to challenge the status quo of this world and try to help Khul Bach.

"Quite a city, isn't it?" Valla asked, and Victor jerked his gaze around, surprised she'd approached so quietly. "When we first arrived, it was at night—it didn't seem so intimidating back then."

"Yeah." Victor nodded. "Where's Tes?"

"Talking to Cayle. She's finding out where the Spears will sell their trophies so we don't step on their toes while offloading ours."

"We don't trade them directly to the City Stone?"

"No. Apparently, there's quite a secondary market for prize tokens, and she thinks we'll be able to get a good deal if we're discerning."

"I've gotta swing by Shouza's place. The Alchemist." Victor gestured toward the city as if pointing to the woman's shop.

"Oh! Your arena prizes. Have you thought any more about the arena? I mean, about the next tournament? We didn't speak much last night, and you seemed troubled. Tes has a way of steering conversation where she wants it, and I wanted to ask you if you're feeling all right about things. I mean, while she's busy with Cayle . . ." Valla trailed off, clearly uncomfortable with the personal discussion but feeling as though she had to broach the subject.

"I've thought about it, and I think I'll keep my mind open about things. I liked your idea, Valla, about not going into contests with the intent of killing, at least unless my opponent is a truly evil asshole. Although I don't think I can make that judgment unless I really know them beforehand. You heard Krista's brother. She was tormented by grief!"

"Right. Just don't get yourself killed with that big heart, Victor." She turned, walking toward the front of the platform as it approached the enormous, wide-open city gates. "Here comes Tes." She pointed off to the side of the column of hunters, and Victor saw Tes jogging their way, pale blue ribbons trailing behind her breezy, knee-length, lavender skirt.

She hopped onto her platform and announced, "I have a lead on a few brokers for your monster parts. Have you decided what you'll keep as gifts to your ancestors, Victor?"

"I have, and it wasn't easy. When I look through the prizes, a few things stand out, and no matter how I try to balance the scales with other items, I feel guilt in my gut, and I know they won't be pleased if I hold back."

Valla frowned at his words, but Tes grinned and nodded. "Well?"

"I have to give them one of the hearts and two of the fangs. Nothing else seems to call to me, but I know those are probably some of the most valuable items I got." He frowned but shrugged, helpless to change how his instincts spoke to him.

"It's wise to listen to your intuition; it's part of who you are now." Tes nodded and gave Valla's shoulder a reassuring squeeze. "It leaves a great hoard of trophies for you to work with, don't worry."

"For Victor to work with," Valla agreed, apparently relieved that Victor wasn't burning up half his haul.

"With the night brute trophies and your shares from the wyrm, I think you'll both be rather pleased by what we can accrue. I'd like to offer you each a gift, as well." Tes stopped speaking for a moment as they passed through the tremendously thick wall, the long tunnel swallowing up the sun and pitching them into cool shade.

"A gift?" Valla prompted.

"Yes! If Victor is willing to hold back some of his scales, I'd like to craft you each some wyrm scale armor."

"Um, Fough showed me a wyrm scale vest he had for sale . . ."

"Bah! I was crafting better armor than Fough before I'd lost my egg horn."

"Egg horn?" Valla narrowed her eyes.

"It's an old saying from my world." Tes waved a hand dismissively and continued, "What say you, Victor? Let me hold back a few dozen scales, and you'll not be disappointed."

"Yeah, of course, Tes."

"Good! Here's what we'll do: I'll go and arrange for some brokers to visit the citadel, and you can make your trades there this evening. In the meantime, you should visit the Alchemist for your commissions. Valla, go with him and ask the shopkeeper about some acuity-boosting tinctures."

"Acuity-boosting?"

"Yes! Let's give your mental attributes a bit of an early jump as you embark on improving yourself."

"Oh." Valla nodded, though she looked a little embarrassed. "All right."

"Good! Hop off the platform, please," Tes said as they approached the end of the tunnel. "Time to pack it up. I'll meet you at the citadel later." Victor and Valla jumped off the platform's left side, hurriedly climbing onto the sidewalk near the busy gate road. Tes remained on her floating vehicle, waving to them as she disappeared around a street corner flowing with the quick-moving traffic of wagons and mounts.

"She just ditched us." Victor laughed.

"Do you know the way to the alchemy shop?" Valla asked, leaning back into the stones of the gatehouse, avoiding a stomping, grumbling Degh.

"Yeah, I think so." Victor nodded. "Follow me," he said and cast Titanic Aspect, grinning as his height stretched to the point where he could look down on most Degh. Then he reached down, holding out a hand, and Valla giggled, almost childlike, as she stretched her hand up to grasp his pointer finger. Victor chuckled, his deep voice rumbling in his chest, then pushed his way into the Degh lane of pedestrians and, Valla in tow, lightly jogging to keep up, he cleared the way for them as they hurried through the city toward Shouza's shop.

35

TINCTURES

Victor had to drop his Titanic Aspect in order to step into Shouza's shop, and even then, he had to duck under the lintel and take care not to knock over any racks of wares for sale. He saw Shouza deftly polishing some beakers with her tentacle arm behind the counter, and as Valla stepped in behind him, he called out, "Hey, Shouza."

"Ah, the arena champion returns!" She grinned as she looked up and met his gaze as though she hadn't seen him coming in through the door. "I was beginning to hope I'd get a chance to auction off your tinctures."

"Oh, how amusing, my dear lady!" Victor laughed, pleased with himself for his choice of words. He gestured to Valla, who'd come up beside him, and said, "This is my friend, Valla. She's in the market for a tincture or two as well."

"Pleased to meet you, Valla," Shouza said, leaning forward with an infectious smile, her eyes glittering beneath her white bangs. "Can I tell you, I've never seen someone with such beautiful coloring! I love your hair and the way it complements your eyes!"

"Oh?" Valla chuckled, perhaps a little nervously, and reached up to brush at some stray strands of minty-green hair. "Um, thank you."

Victor grinned and put a meaty hand between Valla's shoulder blades, urging her forward until the two of them stood before the counter. "Well? How'd things turn out?"

Shouza tossed down her cleaning rag and pushed her dirty beakers to the side, clearing some space on the counter between them while speaking,

"Really well, Victor. I had a class breakthrough while I made one of your tinctures, improving one of my skills, and I think I increased the efficacy of the end product. Oh, and I identified that vial of red liquid you left with me. Here." She produced, seemingly out of the air, the glass jar with the deep-red, thick fluid and set it on the counter. "Take a look. See this stamp in the bottom of the glass?"

Victor peered at the bottom of the jar as Shouza's nimble tentacle turned it upside down. Sure enough, indented into the bottom of the glass was a mark that looked kind of like an H or a partial hashtag. "Yeah, I see it."

"I found a reference to it in one of my texts. The mark is found on some System rewards, which led me to another reference manual, and after running a few tests, I found that it's a speed enhancement—permanent. Did the creature you had to kill to earn this reward have great speed? That's usually how the System does things."

"Um, yeah, he was a big-ass ghoul that moved really damn fast. So," Victor said, reaching for the jar, "a speed enhancement?"

"Yes, your dexterity, agility, or maybe both will improve with the consumption. I'd hold off on drinking it, though; you'll want to take this one first." Shouza handed him the jar but then produced a much smaller glass vial of sparkling silver liquid, stoppered with black wax. "This is your drake gall bladder tincture, the one I had the breakthrough on as I crafted it. You'll get more out of this than from that System prize."

"Oh!" Valla said. "It's really beautiful!"

"Yes! I was amazed at the Energy it absorbed in the crafting process." Shouza nodded, proudly smiling as she set the tincture on the countertop. "Finally, here's your magma horn tincture." Shouza put another vial next to the silvery one, this one slightly larger, more bulbous, and filled with a shimmering honey-like substance. She held her hand over them and grinned. "Just a minor matter of the payment. Three hundred beads, okay?"

"Oh, shit, Shouza. You deserve more than that." Victor pulled out one of his bags of beads and set it on the counter. "I mean, even though I provided the main ingredients, your skill clearly made a difference. Take five hundred out of here, please."

Shouza smiled and nodded, using her magical counting rod to lighten the bag's load. As it deflated slightly, Victor tucked it away, then he took his three tinctures or potions or whatever one might call them and safely stowed them away in one of his dimensional container rings. "I'll drink 'em back at the citadel."

"You'll want to save that Core breakthrough for when you reach stage nine in whatever tier you're working on. I'm fairly sure it'll push you through the threshold." Shouza nodded as though affirming her own words. "What can I help you with, Miss Valla?"

"Oh," Valla said, startled out of some contemplative thought, "I was looking to purchase some sort of acuity-boosting tincture. Mental acuity, that is."

"Oh?" Shouza looked Valla up and down and narrowed her eyes. "I thought you carried yourself like a swordfighter—you've got that easy grace and the posture of someone who's swung a lot of heavy metal around. Your shoulders are so straight, and the tendons in your arms . . . I was sure . . ."

"Can't a swordfighter want to improve their mental acuity?" Victor asked, wondering at Shouza's weird behavior.

"Yes, yes! Of course! I'm so sorry, Miss Valla." Shouza ducked her head several times. "Sometimes I think I'm more clever than I am!"

"You are clever, Shouza, don't worry. I am a Sword Dancer, and yes, I've spent more hours dancing around with my blade than I'd care to think about. I'm trying to clear up some deficits in my training, though, and that starts with the tincture I asked for."

"Of course!" Shouza said again, then she turned and disappeared among her rows of bottles, bags, vials, jars, boxes, and tins. Her voice came from behind the third row, calling out, "I have several options for you." Victor could hear the clinking of glass as the woman gathered up some of her products, and then she came back to the counter and set them all before Valla— nine different variously shaped bottles and vials.

As she arrayed them in groups of three, she looked at Valla and asked, "Are you familiar with how attribute-enhancing tinctures work? I mean, do you know about diminishing returns?"

"Yes, I've heard that if you take too many, they stop affecting you until you've gone through some racial or class evolutions."

"Correct—your system will build up a tolerance that only gets purged as great surges of Energy alter your body or your Core and pathways. That said, I have three different types of products here and three tiers of each." She gestured to the three separate groupings of vials and potion bottles. "I have mixtures that will improve your intelligence, mixtures that will improve your will, and then, more costly, mixtures that will improve both. The reason the mixtures that improve your overall acuity are more costly is that they'll boost both attributes before increasing your tolerance."

"I see." Valla nodded, looking over the colorful sealed glass containers.

"How much is the best one?" Victor asked, trying to get to the punchline.

Shouza let her tentacle hover over the bottles for a moment, moving from left to right, then selecting a black glass vial the size of Victor's thumb and stoppered with what looked like gold. She picked it up, held it aloft, and said, "This is a tincture made from the liquified and distilled brains of seven deep minds. I'll trade it for two Coloss prize tokens or one hundred thousand beads."

"What's a deep mind?" Victor asked.

At the same time, Valla said, "It will improve my will and intelligence?"

"Yes, to you, Valla. Likely a great deal." She turned to Victor and said, "A deep mind is a fantastical creature that dwells in the depths of Zaafor. They look much like a mushroom, though they're very different from the mushrooms you might put in a salad—they have a brain and work powerful Energy magics. It's quite lucrative and hazardous to harvest them."

"Wild . . ." Victor stared into the dark glass while his mind pictured huge mushrooms shaped like brains flinging fireballs through the darkness.

"I'll take it," Valla said with a curt nod.

"Shit!" Victor looked at Valla, startled. He'd expected her to settle on something cheaper.

"Wonderful!" Shouza said, carefully setting the black vial down and scooping up the other potions. "You'll see the most growth by far with that one."

Victor continued to stare at Valla, saw her pleased smile, and moved his suspicions that she had a lot of beads tucked away into the realm of confirmed facts. He thought about when she'd given him his arena earnings and said she'd done "similarly" with her bets. If she'd started with a bigger pot than his, she could have made a hell of a lot more. For all he knew, she was already sitting on a million beads. He almost asked her right then, in the middle of the store, but decided it wasn't really a cool question.

"I'll box it," Shouza said as Valla began to unload large leather sacks of beads onto the counter.

"Not necessary." Valla smiled. "I'll drink it later today."

"Of course, of course," Shouza said, tapping each bag with her rod, deflating them one by one until she got to the ninth one, and half of it remained. "All paid up, Miss Valla."

"Just Valla is fine," Valla replied, scooping up the gold-stoppered vial. She looked at Victor and said, "Anything else?"

He'd been watching, bemused, as Valla unloaded her sacks of beads and shook his head to bring himself back to the present. "Um, no, I think I'm good for now. We'll likely be back, though, Shouza. We have some monster trophies to trade away, and if things work out, we might need more tinctures or potions."

"Oh? I'm often interested in certain monster trophies." Shouza leaned forward, eyes eager.

"Well, we have a very knowledgeable friend handling the brokering of those for us. I'll tell her you're interested, though. That good with you?"

"Sure, Victor. I appreciate it!"

"Cool." He held out his hand and was amused and surprised when Shouza wrapped her tentacle around it and gave it a firm, warm squeeze. "Speak to you soon." He nudged Valla, and she smiled, waved, and followed him out of the shop. Outside, after the door closed, Victor looked at Valla and said, "You seem pleased."

"Oh, I am. I'd never find a tincture like that on Fanwath. Some of the top Alchemists in Tharcray claim to be able to improve an attribute permanently, but I know people who've spent a fortune to see a few points of improvement."

"Well, to be fair, we don't know how much these things will boost us."

"True, but I'll be surprised if it's not significant. Tes wouldn't have us waste our time and money. Well, me anyway—you earned yours in the arena."

"Right," Victor said, guiding them around a corner and up a steeply inclined street. One thing he knew about Coloss was that if they kept going uphill, they'd come to the citadel sooner or later. "You figure we'll get many prize tokens for our wyrm parts?"

"I hope so! I desperately want to get one of those stones for Blue Razor."

"What about the racial advancement items? Do you mind me asking? I mean, I'm curious how far you've advanced yourself."

"My race is improved, rank seven."

"That's not bad!" Victor said, a little surprised. He shifted around a parked wagon where some Vesh were unloading barrels and then hopped over a curb to turn left on a cross street, trying to avoid more of the jammed-up traffic. "I wasn't sure, but I thought you must have advanced it a few times 'cause you're taller than Thayla, and she was always a lot taller than the Ardeni we met."

"Well, Shadeni are generally more physically imposing than we Ardeni," Valla replied. "Though if I advance enough and unlock one of our bloodlines, I might gain some interesting traits. I saw an Ardeni with an advanced race who looked more cat than person."

"Shit, seriously?" Victor glanced down at her, eyebrows raised. She grinned and didn't respond, and he was left to wonder if she was messing with him. He sort of hoped she was telling the truth; a blue cat woman sounded kind of cool to him. "Well," he finally said, "I guess it makes sense—you have a lot of really sharp teeth."

"True!" Valla laughed and pulled back her lips, growling at him, exposing her pointy white teeth.

Victor laughed again, then said, "Rellia's gonna be proud of you when we get back. You've already made a ton of gains." Victor turned again, taking long strides up a nearly empty, upward sloping road.

"Yes, I believe she'll be pleased, but also with you. She never bargained on a titan leading her army into the Untamed Marches. Still, the stronger we are, the more difficult the System will likely make our resistance."

"You think so? I know the System will create a challenge for us, but wouldn't it take into consideration the average strength in the army? I mean, it wouldn't put a challenge against us that would be geared toward thousands of people like me, would it? If that's the case, Rellia would be better leaving me behind."

"No. The System is harsh and wishes to force growth through conflict, but it tends to be at least ostensibly fair. I think you're right. Perhaps the creatures or armies we'll face will simply have a champion or two for you to deal with." Valla chuckled, shaking her head. "The truth is, none of us know. It's been centuries since the Empire tried to push into unclaimed lands, and back when it was expanding, the world was new, and things were different— records don't reflect our current reality."

They walked in silence for a while after that, each of them lost in their thoughts. Victor was trying to picture what the Untamed Marches would look like. He envisioned mountains and jungles and then added in his wild fantasies of demonic, red-eyed, scythe-clawed enemies pouring out of portals or from deep caves to try to swallow up Rellia's army. His chipper mood and easy grin faded as his thoughts drifted deeper and deeper into the imagined scenario, and he was a little surprised when they finally crested the last upward-sloping road, and the citadel rose before them.

"Shit, that was fast," he said. He glanced down at Valla, and her scowling eyebrows relaxed a little, and she nodded.

"Yes. I was lost in thought."

"Yeah, me too. Where did Tes say to meet her?" Victor asked as they started over the expanse of open cobbles toward the great tunnel that led into the citadel.

"She didn't. Don't worry; she won't struggle to sniff us out."

"True," Victor chuckled, bemused by thoughts of Tes literally sniffing her way through the citadel. Then they approached the gate and the twenty guardsmen that perpetually stood outside it. Their heads swiveled toward the two of them, but none shouted out a challenge, and Victor took it for a good sign that they knew who he and Valla were and that the Warlord still considered them guests. "I wonder where Tronk is."

"Hopefully, he's decided the threats to our lives have died down enough to let us roam without an escort. Likely that's the case, or he'd have met us at the gate, don't you think?"

"Yeah, unless Bell sank her hooks into him." Victor chuckled.

"Bell?"

"I think she's his girlfriend. He acted really embarrassed around her. It was kinda hilarious. I mean, sweet, but hilarious."

"I'd like to see that." Valla laughed.

They were walking down the enormous central passage toward the gardens, and Victor wasn't sure if they should just head to their rooms or hang around and wait for Tes. He paused, about to ask Valla what she thought, when a tall Yazzian wearing pale-yellow robes approached them and cleared his throat. Yazzians weren't common in the citadel—it seemed the Warlord was far more likely to employ Vesh with the occasional Degh like Tronk. Victor looked into the Yazzian's hood, past its weird, lizard-snake snout to its rather expressive green eyes, and said, "Yes?"

The Yazzian had its delicate, yellow-scaled hands clasped before it and bowed its head, then said in a faintly masculine voice, "The Warlord welcomes you back. He asks if you'll be continuing your stay at the citadel."

"What might your name be, good sir?" Valla asked before Victor could form a response.

"I am Deargh, one of the Warlord's Ministers of City Affairs."

"We'd like to continue our stay in the citadel, yes." Victor took the opportunity to speak as Valla processed the Yazzian's title.

"Excellent. Your rooms remain ready for you, and the Warlord extends his earlier invitation to use his cultivation chamber. Victor, the mid-tier city champion, Yabbo, is eager to spar with you. Karnice has offered to tutor you both. Will you be available in the morning?"

"Karnice?"

"The arena champion," Valla supplied, apparently having paid more attention than Victor.

"Yes, the undefeated high-tier champion of the Coloss arena."

"Oh, cool." Victor nodded. "Yeah, I'll be around tomorrow morning. Where do I go?"

"I'll ensure that you have a guide waiting at your door. Would two hours past dawn be a good time?"

"Yeah . . ."

"Excellent. Lady Valla, War Captain Blue has requested an audience with you. He asks if you'd be willing to join him for dinner here in the citadel in one of the small parlors?"

"Oh," Valla said, holding one hand to her chest, just under her throat, apparently lost for words. An awkward moment passed, and then she said, "I think not, Minister Deargh. I have business with the Lady Tes this evening. Please inform War Captain Blue that I'll entertain his request in the near future should he wish to reschedule."

"Very well, Lady."

"Speaking of Tes, have you seen or heard from her, Deargh?" Victor asked.

"No, sir, I have not." He glanced up and down the grand, airy tunnel and then said, "I'll take my leave if that will be all. If you should need me, simply ask one of the servants stationed near your guest quarters."

"Thank you, Minister Deargh," Valla said, holding out a hand. The Yazzian unclasped his hands and delicately took Valla's hand, then he nodded, bowed, and quickly shuffled away.

"Interesting," Victor said. "Hey, I could meet with Tes, you know. You can have dinner with Blue if you want."

"I'm not sure I want to." Valla frowned at him, shaking her head slightly. "Strange that you want me to."

"I didn't say I want you to!" It was Victor's turn to frown, wondering what he'd done wrong this time. Valla folded her arms over her chest and scowled, and he sighed, saying, "Wanna take turns in the cultivation chamber while we wait for Tes? We could drink our tinctures."

That got Valla's frown to fade, and she nodded, surprising Victor by reaching up a fist and waiting for him to touch his knuckles to it. "That sounds like fun. Come." With that, she turned, and he followed her—a big, lumbering man trailing behind a small blue woman through the corridors and stairways of the citadel.

36

DESPERATION AND TRUST

When Victor and Valla stood before the huge bronze-colored door to the Warlord's cultivation chamber, she paused and looked at him with a raised eyebrow. "You think this will open for us? I hadn't thought about if we'd need an escort to get in there."

"One way to find out. Give it a try." Victor shrugged and leaned one shoulder against the wall, watching.

"Why me?"

"Are you afraid it'll zap you or something?"

"No . . . well, yes." Valla chuckled, then moving quickly as though to avoid any further doubts, she reached up and slapped her hand on the smooth metal pad Tronk had used to open the doors. She didn't cry out in pain or jerk her hand away, and after a second, a deep, resounding *click* sounded from the door, and it parted slightly from the other.

"Nice," Victor said, grinning. "Guess you're first."

"Are you sure?" Valla turned to look at him, eyes wide, as though suddenly filled with doubt about whether she should go into the chamber.

"Relax! If the Warlord cared, he wouldn't have set the chamber to open for you. Just cultivate for an hour or so and drink your tincture, and then I'll go. I'm sure Tes will be a little while anyway."

Valla nodded, her hair bobbing in its ponytail, and Victor realized, likely quite belatedly, that it had grown considerably since they'd begun traveling together. He opened his mouth to say something, then wondered if she'd be annoyed that he'd noticed, and before he had a chance, she'd slipped into the cultivation chamber, bathing him in a wash of potent Energy before closing the door behind her. "Huh." He shrugged and sat on one of the stone benches lining the chamber's entry.

Victor pulled out the two stat-boosting tinctures he intended to consume and looked at them. The first, the one he'd gotten long ago in the dungeon near Greatbone Mine, was about the size of a soda can, and he wondered if the liquid, which seemed far too much like blood to him, would taste better than it looked. "Hope so," he grunted, then held up the shimmering silver tincture that Shouza had made—one swallow, and it would be gone. "You're first."

He set them on the bench beside him and then settled in to wait. On a whim, he took Tes's partial spell pattern out of his ring and began to study it for the hundredth time. He was pleased to see the shifting lines, shapes, and angles seemed less random than the last time he'd examined the pattern, and that's when something clicked for him: the shifts were themselves part of the pattern. The more he watched them, the more he realized that Tes had created a spell pattern with multiple facets—it was like one of those old-school holograms that looked different if you altered your viewing angle.

"What the fuck?" he whispered, drawing out the curse softly as he watched the pattern change back and forth before his eyes. "I think I get it, *chica*," he said, resting a hand on Lifedrinker's warm metal. If he really concentrated, he found he could force the pattern to stay still, see the first version, and then allow it to shift and see the other. The more he did so, the more he began to understand how it worked; he saw the delicate lines Tes had made that created the extra dimension in the spell.

"Holy shit," he breathed again, thinking of how he could copy the design. Before he could lose the inspiration, he summoned one of his notebooks and then said, while laughing at his thought, "Inspiration!" Shaking his head, he cast Inspiring Presence and summoned a Globe of Insight, and then, in the light of true inspiration, he began to try to re-create the weird multidimensional spell pattern.

When Tes had drawn the original, Victor had watched with awe as she delicately scribed the complicated lines onto her parchment, and it had taken her more than ten minutes. His first, proper attempt at the pattern, sitting there before the closed door of the Warlord's cultivation chamber, stretched on and on, and when Valla pushed open the door and stepped out, he didn't notice her, so rapt with his efforts was he.

"Victor?" she asked, and when he didn't look up and she felt the inspiration of his spells, she nodded and turned to reenter the chamber. Quietly, over her shoulder, she said, "I'll check on you again in an hour." Then she stepped through the door, and it clicked shut behind her.

Victor was lost to the world, though, and if he'd noticed it at all, her presence didn't shake his attention. He could feel that he was on the right track; the bits of the pattern he'd finished were working. He could shift his attention and see both versions of it, and with each successful line and twist, he grew more confident and more determined to finish. By the time Valla stepped out of the chamber again, she could see the grin on his face and the light in his eyes, and when she spoke, he looked up to meet her gaze. "You figured it out?"

"Hell yes, I did!" he replied, holding up his notebook for her to see the wild, endlessly complex pattern. "I've been going over and over it—I can't find any mistakes! It looks just like Tes's."

"So . . . you can change your size now?" Valla leaned forward, trying to get another glimpse of the pattern, but he closed the notebook, sandwiching Tes's original inside. He laughed, stretched, and shook his head.

"Nah, this is only the first part of the spell. Now I get how it works, though, Valla!" He stood up and increased the intensity of his stretching, grunting with pleasure. "God! How long was I working on that thing?"

"Nearly two hours."

"Ha! So it's my turn in there, I'd say."

Valla nodded, sketching a silly bow, and stepped away from the door, gesturing for him to pass before her. "Be my guest! I'll wait out here. I imagine Tes will be here soon, don't you think?"

"Well, I guess. It's just now evening time, though, and she said 'tonight,' so who really knows." Victor laughed again, his mood beyond good thanks to his breakthrough with the spell pattern, and he walked up to the cultivation chamber door. Valla had left it open a crack, so he pulled it further open and walked in, savoring the richly dense Energy in the air. "Be out soon," he said as he pulled the door closed behind himself.

He turned and inhaled deeply, letting the Energy wash over him for a moment, acclimating himself, and then he climbed to the small circular platform at the chamber's center and sat, crossing his legs before himself. He clutched the tincture and potion in one of his hands, carefully set the blood-like jar in his lap, then held the silver mixture before himself. "Well, here we go," he muttered, running one of his thumbnails around the wax seal, loosening the outer edges so he could carefully pry the black lump from the mouth of the little glass tube.

As soon as the wax came out, Victor, still flooded with inspiration-attuned Energy, tilted it to his mouth, not wanting any of the potent fumes to escape. The glass must have been enchanted because not a single molecule of the mixture clung to it—every last bit of it slipped into his mouth, and he swallowed it in one gulp. It was surprisingly tasteless, almost like swallowing an oddly heavy mouthful of water. It didn't sit in his stomach like water, though.

Victor felt it bloom with Energy in his gut, and then, almost painfully, it surged out through his body in a powerful wave that sent tingles and shivers through every inch of his skin and made his muscles contract so that by the time he recovered, he found himself balled up, his muscles aching from the prolonged contraction. "Oof," he grunted, then, bleary-eyed, he studied the System message in his vision:

*****Congratulations! Your vitality and strength have each been permanently enhanced by 25 points.*****

"Damn," he said, surprised by the number. "Fifty stat points just like that?" He reached for his other potion and almost panicked when he found it had rolled to the side of the platform, knocked out of his lap by his convulsion. He snatched it up, glad it hadn't fallen off the raised dais to shatter on the stones below. He held it carefully in one hand while he stretched and arched his back, trying to get his blood flowing again.

Victor felt good, healthy, and strong, and he knew if he'd drunk that tincture when he was new to Fanwath, it would have been like shooting himself up with pure endorphins and PCP, but twenty-five points for him now were just a couple of percentage points or so of his strength and even less for his vitality. Still, it was good to see those numbers jump—twenty-five points in strength before casting Berserk was seventy-five after.

"Nothing to sneeze at," he said, grinning as he broke the seal on the cork stopper and carefully pulled it out of the jar. He wasn't surprised but wasn't exactly happy when his nose picked up the potion's coppery tang. It might be an alchemical mixture from the System, but it definitely had some kind of blood in it. Victor wasn't squeamish about a bit of blood, though. How could he be after all the raw hearts he'd consumed? Sure, he'd been berserk, but he'd be lying if he said he didn't remember the taste. "*Mierda,*" he grumbled, then, taking a deep breath so he didn't inhale while drinking, he tilted it to his mouth and gulped it down.

"Yep, blood!" He coughed, forcing his mouth closed so as not to lose any of the supposedly precious liquid. He breathed in and out several times, waiting to see what might happen, and he began to think he, or Shouza, he supposed, had been tricked. "Ack," he said again, sticking his tongue out, about to reach into his dimensional container for some cheb-cheb or wine to wash his mouth out, and then he felt a terrible cramp in his gut and gasped, doubling over and falling to his side on the stone platform.

The cramping continued, and it seemed to be spreading. With each convulsion, more of his muscles joined in the protest, his arms curling in, his legs painfully bending, and Victor struggled for breath, wanting to scream but unable to pull in a deep enough breath. "Jesu . . ." he managed to get out between two particularly brutal convulsions, and then, as quickly as it had begun, the cramping started to diminish. Within a minute or two, Victor found himself on his back, one arm sprawled out over the platform's edge, panting, blinking away the sweat that had run into his eyes.

"Holy shit," he gasped. "That was fucking brutal." He rubbed at his eyes and was relieved to see a System message—hopefully, he'd made some gains and not just survived a poisoning attempt.

*****Congratulations! You have gained a new feat: Desperate Grace.*****

*****Desperate Grace: When near death or suffering from severe blood loss, your body will rise to the occasion, allowing you to move with adroitness far beyond your usual means. When this effect is triggered, your current dexterity and agility will double for a short time.*****

"What the hell, Shouza?" Victor chuckled, relieved and surprised by the notification. Another part of him was dismayed that he'd sat on that potion for months. How many times might that feat have come in handy? Groaning, he struggled to his hands and knees and then laboriously to his feet. He felt weak, drained even, and decided that cultivating would have to wait. He stumble-walked to the door, slapped a hand on the metal plate, and then shouldered his way through as the door clicked open.

"Why am I not surprised to see you both sitting there," he said as he took in the sight of Valla and Tes, shoulder to shoulder on the stone bench, both carefully scrutinizing a textbook on Valla's knees.

"You look awful." Valla laughed.

"Ancient Gods!" Tes said, eyes widening, though her lips also twitched up at the corners.

"Yeah, that fucking Shouza!" Victor couldn't help it and laughed, too, shaking his head. "Nah, I'm good, but that old potion of mine didn't raise my stats. It twisted me into knots and gave me a feat."

"Oh?" Tes asked while Valla's eyes widened.

"You're the luckiest . . ." Valla trailed off, shaking her head, though her smile remained intact.

Victor shrugged. "Well, what can I say?"

"Tell us about the feat to begin with," Tes said, leaning back and crossing her legs. She wore the same brightly colored yellow skirts she'd worn on the early days of the hunt, and Victor admired how at ease she always seemed.

"It's called Desperate Grace, and it boosts my agility and dexterity when I'm about to die. I mean, I guess that's assuming I'm dying slowly." He laughed, thinking about how such a feat was essentially useless if he suffered some sort of catastrophic injury.

"The more powerful you become, the less likely you'll die suddenly. Battles between old . . ."—she winked at Victor and continued—"masters on my world sometimes last for days." He wondered if she had been about to say dragons, then chuckled at his naivety—of course she had; that's what the wink was about.

"What about you, Valla? I forgot to ask how your tincture worked?"

"Oh, wonderfully!" Valla beamed. "Shouza treated me well, Victor! I gained thirty intelligence and fifteen will!"

"Seriously? Damn! She makes good stuff, doesn't she?" Victor turned from Valla to Tes, then said, "Well, did Valla tell you?"

"Tell me what?" Tes asked, glancing sidelong at the Ardeni woman, who looked just as confused.

"About what I did before I went into the chamber?" Victor stared pointedly at Valla. When she still looked confused, he said, "Seriously, Valla? I finished your spell pattern, Tes!"

"You did?" Tes leapt to her feet and reached forward to squeeze Victor's shoulder. "I thought you'd be another week or two at it!"

"Well, it just clicked for me today; I figured out the double patt—"

"Tut-tut," Tes said, holding four delicate fingertips in front of Victor's mouth, "let's not advertise one of the secrets of my people's magic. I've agreed to share this one with you, at a bit of a risk to myself, but let's not speak about the details publicly."

Victor looked toward the closed cultivation chamber and down the long flight of stairs into the empty, vaulted corridor and shrugged. Either Tes didn't want Valla to hear about the spell's details, or she thought maybe others were listening or capable of listening to their conversation.

Victor didn't think it was the former—Tes hadn't asked him not to show her the pattern or anything like that.

He supposed it made sense that the Warlord might have some kind of magical ability to feel or sense what was going on in the citadel, his domain. Victor had no idea what a person with nearly a hundred and twenty levels under their belt was capable of. Glancing at Tes, he supposed he had an inkling, which made him wonder exactly what level she had reached. He almost asked, but then Valla stood up and spoke.

"Tes has a broker waiting for us in the garden."

"Oh?"

"Oh yes! I believe you'll be pleased; he's interested in wyrm trophies but has a particular interest in night brutes. Let's go and put your wares on display for him, hmm?" Tes stepped away from Victor and gestured toward the steps as though she wanted him to lead the way.

"Right." Victor nodded, stepping lithely down; he was already starting to feel better. With his near constant use of Sovereign Will these days, his vitality was almost always boosted, and with it now sitting at nearly four hundred, his aches and pains faded rapidly.

He wasn't an expert on the layout of the citadel yet, but he knew he had to get to the ground floor and had a general idea of the location of the major stairways. Equipped with such knowledge, Victor led them rapidly down and into the enormous central hallway, and from there, it was just a short jaunt to the central gardens. When they stepped into the artificial moonlight and the brightly lit lampposts that followed the main pathways through the thick foliage, Victor had to pause to marvel at the garden's beauty. It was great in the bright light of false daytime, but this nighttime version was even better.

Cloying perfumes from the myriad varieties of flowers filled the air, and the dim light made it easy to imagine that they weren't in the citadel, that they were outside in a wonderfully manicured little forest with shrubs and pathways, fountains burbling, and night birds singing. Glancing at Tes and Valla, Victor suddenly wished he were with someone else, someone closer. He imagined how much Chandri or Thayla would love the garden. Still, Valla had a bright grin on her face, and Tes, well, Tes was always fun to be around.

"He'll be near the western entrance," Tes said, steering them onto a pathway leading to Victor's right.

"It's beautiful at night," Valla said, echoing Victor's earlier thoughts, and he smiled down at her.

"Yeah, I was thinking that. Do you remember Deyni? The little Shadeni girl I gave my other vidanii to?"

"Of course. Thayla's daughter."

"Right! I wish I could show her this wonderful place."

"There are many wonders in the worlds, Victor." Tes turned to walk backward and smiled at him and then at Valla. "I think the two of you have many amazing places and things yet to experience. I hope I'll be able to see the marvel in your eyes as you behold some of them." She nodded quickly, then turned and hurried her steps. Victor glanced down at Valla again, saw her pleasant expression, and at that moment, he appreciated Tes even more. She was powerful enough to be a tyrant or a bully, but she seemed to enjoy helping people—he'd never seen her speak a cross word, only hardening her voice when it came to defending Victor a time or two.

Something tickled the back of his mind as he followed her springy steps through the garden; was anyone really that good? He knew she wanted a sample of his blood, but that would be easy enough to take; she didn't have to spend weeks or months helping him and Valla. Did she get a kind of vicarious thrill from helping people? If so, he wouldn't begrudge her—better that than enjoying other people's suffering. Besides, she'd trusted him with her spell pattern, and he'd never felt uneasy with her. His gut trusted her, and Victor trusted his gut.

"Here we are!" Tes called, hurrying her pace toward an opening in the cobbled path. Victor looked over her shoulder to see a strange, hirsute Vesh wearing a silky cream-colored vest and a black top hat. His bulging yellow eyes lurked behind thick, brass-wired spectacles, and his smile, though toothy, was warm as he raised a hand in greeting.

His voice was jovial and welcoming, rolling through the garden as he called out, "Wonderful! I look forward to seeing your wares!"

37

SENTIENCE

Victor watched as the ghostly white flames consumed his offering to his ancestors. He'd unloaded all his monster trophies from the hunt, piling them on two big tarps in the garden for Tes and the broker to comb through. While they worked on that and Valla watched, he'd taken one of the hearts and two fangs down a side path, stopping in front of a pleasant little fountain in the shape of three splashing fish, and then he'd cast Honor the Spirits.

The broker had been dismayed to see him walk off with the fangs; apparently, they were precious. Tes had quickly diverted the hairy Vesh's attention back to the trophies Victor had left behind. Valla, for her part, had simply smiled and waved as Victor walked away. He supposed it was good that they understood his need to give tribute to his ancestors. He barely understood it himself, but he had that feeling in his gut every time he looked at his loot and remembered Citlalicue's words about him repaying her tenfold—he owed her. If he didn't send offerings, he could forget ever getting his ancestors to intervene directly again.

After the last wisp of spirit smoke faded away, he returned to the larger trail where he'd left the others. Tes and the broker stood off to one side, conferring over a white, slightly luminous slate. Valla, who'd been listening to them, walked over to Victor.

"She's driving a hard bargain, but he seems pretty desperate for some of these parts. He got very agitated when he saw the night brute prince's bones."

"Really?" Victor looked at the large pile of dark, still-bloody bones that he and Tes had carved from the enormous corpse. "Did Tes keep back some scales to make our armor?"

"Yes, she made sure I was watching when she collected them into her storage . . . ring? I've never seen her storage device."

"Yeah. If she has jewelry on, I think she hides it with magic."

"She didn't take any of my scales. Are you sure it's all right that she makes armor for both of us from the scales you earned?"

"Yeah. I got a hell of a lot more than you." Victor sat on a bench and motioned for Valla to sit beside him. She complied, and they sat quietly for a few moments, watching Tes go back and forth with the Vesh, pointing at something on the glowing slate, then shaking her head. "I kinda feel sorry for the guy."

"You know, she annihilated that night brute prince. I'll wager the armor she's offering to craft us would sell for a fortune. I wonder—what's she getting out of helping us?" Valla's voice was soft, and she leaned forward, resting an elbow on her knee, holding her chin in one hand, staring at the subject of her speculation.

"I had similar thoughts earlier. I've decided it doesn't matter to me—she's powerful enough to take what she wants, but she's not doing that. She's helping us and seems to be having a damn good time doing it. How am I supposed to speculate on the motives of someone so powerful? Listen, on my homeworld, we had these things called video games. Imagine a dungeon, but contained in a magical box that you could explore with tiny avatars—bodies that weren't you but represented you. Do you follow?"

"Like a box that you could see into? And watch your 'avatars' fight monsters and solve puzzles?"

"Exactly!" Victor cleared his throat and tried to remember where he'd been going with the explanation. "Oh, right. So, imagine some people could get really good at the game. So good that the challenge of it became boring. Sometimes people like that would torment new players, making their lives difficult as a way to pass the time. Other people like that, though, would help the new players. They'd give their avatars equipment or help them kill monsters they couldn't handle on their own. I think Tes is like that."

"You think she's just bored and enjoying the 'game' through us?"

"Well, I'm probably oversimplifying things, but yeah, I guess that's what I'm saying."

"I think you're on the right track, but I wonder if it's more complicated, as you implied. Maybe she has challenging things to do, but she's stalling or taking a break. Maybe we're something of a diversion for . . ."

"Well," Tes said. Victor and Valla had been so intent on their whispered speculations that Tes had walked up completely unnoticed. Victor had no doubt that Tes could surprise them even if they'd had their eyes trained on her, though, so he just grinned at her and attempted to look sheepish. Valla slapped a hand over her mouth, eyes wide with shock. Tes, though, was smiling happily as she continued speaking. "If you're done trying to solve the mysteries of Tes, I have good news!"

"I'm sorry . . ." Valla said as Victor chuckled.

"You made us a good deal?" Victor looked around her to see the hirsute Vesh walking among the trophies, making them disappear into containers one after another.

"Indeed! Valla, for your share of the spider, night brute, and wyrm trophies, I've managed to collect a fee of four tokens!"

"Truly?" Valla stood and actually pranced in place with excitement. Victor didn't see what the big deal was—the item she wanted to buy was five tokens unless she wanted the better one, which was ten. She'd still need to earn more to teleport home . . .

Tes interrupted his thoughts. "Truly! Which means, Victor, your share of the trophies garnered a rather stunning thirty-seven tokens."

"Holy shit!" Victor said, suddenly understanding Valla's enthusiasm. Of course, she'd figured out that if she'd earned four with her smaller share, he'd have a huge haul, and, of course, she knew he'd share.

"Yes! Your pathway home is open, with plenty left over to purchase treasures. Or, if you want to take the time to bargain for other prizes, you might find some things more valuable than those on the Warlord's list." She paused as Victor's face grew contemplative and added, "I do hope you won't depart this very minute. If you have time, there's still much to learn here in Coloss. I'll also need a week or two to craft your armor."

"Tes, about what I was saying earlier," Valla said, but Tes waved her words away.

"Nonsense. You both have questions about me, and I'd love to answer them all, but I'm bound by promises to keep many aspects of myself to . . . myself. I'm the one who should apologize."

"Are you kidding, Tes?" Victor chuckled. "You've helped us so much; don't even think about apologizing."

"I agree wholeheartedly!" Valla said, reaching out to grasp Tes's hand with both of hers.

"All right, all right. Here you are." She produced two black velvety pouches, one noticeably more full than the other, and handed them to Valla and Victor. Victor produced his other four tokens and slipped them into the pouch with those Tes had bartered for him. He hefted the little bag, grinning at the weight of forty-one tokens, then placed it into his storage ring.

Valla also tucked hers away, then sat on the bench and motioned for Tes and Victor to sit with her. "Will you give us your advice, Tes? How should we spend these tokens?"

"Oh?" Tes sat on the bench next to Valla, and Victor sat next to her, though there wasn't enough room for him. Half his butt ended up hanging off the edge, and Tes laughed. "I'll give you the rest of my spell pattern so you can learn it while you're here, Victor."

As Victor grunted his thanks, she took a deep breath, and a small pulse of Energy surged out of her. Victor's ears popped, and then she said, "I can certainly advise the two of you with regard to those tokens. If you hadn't noticed, there are two markets in this town—the day-to-day market brokered in beads, and the secondary, less talked about market brokered in prize tokens."

"Yes." Valla nodded. "I paid a hundred thousand beads for my tincture, but I could have paid a couple of tokens instead."

"Thank you, Valla! This helps me to illustrate my next point: The Warlord's prize list is a good bargain for some things but a rather poor one for others. The alchemical ingredients are not a good value—your tincture contained two different 'epic' alchemical ingredients. Did you know that? To buy those ingredients from the Warlord's prize list would cost you, at a minimum, ten tokens. I say at a minimum because there's little chance you'd get the ingredients you wanted with the first selection."

"Ah." Valla nodded.

"Some items are exceedingly rare; thus, the Warlord's prices are better than you'll find in town. The epic racial boosts, for example. Generally, you won't find those for sale because they're so coveted."

"What about the stones of sentience and consciousness?"

"Rare, indeed, though I'd never pay for a Stone of Consciousness. If your weapon takes well to the Stone of Sentience, it will grow a conscious mind before too long."

"Oh?" Valla raised her eyebrows, excited at the idea.

"Yes, I think that would be a wonderful prize for your blade, Valla. That sword is powerful; granting it a spirit would be a wise investment."

"What about the legendary treasure?" Victor asked. "What kinds of things does the Warlord have for twenty tokens?"

"A good question, Victor. I've been on Zaafor, off and on, for nearly a decade and have yet to meet anyone who has purchased such a prize. The Warlord has a System-purchased vault tied to the Stone and its store. Even I cannot see within it."

"Would the racial boosts other than 'epic' be a waste of tokens?"

"For you, Victor, yes. The advanced boost would work nicely for Valla."

"Tes, what would you do with the tokens if you were in our shoes?" Valla asked.

Tes smiled and looked from Victor to Valla, then reached up to twist a strand of her golden hair around her forefinger as she contemplated. After a moment, she said, "I'd buy a few items from the Warlord's store, but then I'd purchase other things to bring home. Things that would make me a hero to my people—cultivation manuals, spell tomes, class advancement tabulations, alchemical recipes, enchantment glyphs, and dictionaries to understand them.

"Don't you see? Coloss is thousands of years beyond your world in experimentation with Energy and the System. It's clear to me that your world has yet to manage a connection to a significantly more advanced world, or if there's such a connection, the people in power on Fanwath are keeping it to themselves."

Victor sat back, blowing out a pent-up breath, and Valla said, "Ancestors!" as she processed Tes's words. "I hadn't thought of that! Are such things available for sale?"

"Oh, for the right price and from the right people, surely. I can help you find what you need."

"Rellia would like that," Victor said, directing his words to Valla.

"She's a ruler of Fanwath?"

"Oh, she's my adoptive mother and a noblewoman. She's gathering an army now so that Victor can lead them on a conquest of unclaimed lands."

"Ah, unclaimed lands. It's been a thousand years since any such existed on Zaafor. A hundred thousand on my homeworld. What a tumultuous time when the System finally grew strong enough to assert itself on Aradnue!"

"Aradnue's your homeworld, right?"

"Yes. Many of my people died fighting the System's . . . invasion." She sighed heavily, looked at Victor and then at Valla's wide eyes, and said, "It was long before my time. I'm not that old!"

"Whew," Victor laughed. He looked past Tes to Valla, the way she smiled and nodded along with Tes's words. He reached into his ring, took out his pouch of tokens, and said, "Hey, Valla, there's no reason to sit on these right now. I want you to get that sentience stone for your sword, and I want to make sure you've got three tokens for teleporting home in case something happens to me." She opened her mouth to say something, but he held up a hand to forestall objections.

Victor knew she wanted that stone badly, and he knew she was too proud to ask for the tokens. He counted out four from his pouch and handed them to her. "That gives you eight, right? Five for the stone and three to hold in reserve to get home. Maybe we'll earn some more while we're here, but if not, I'll make sure we talk to each other about what I spend the rest of them on."

Valla took the tokens and clasped both her hands around Victor's, awkwardly holding it in front of Tes, who still sat between them. "You're a good friend, Victor. I won't make an empty promise to repay you because I know you can earn these far more easily than I can. That said, when we get back to Fanwath, don't you dare ever try to split the bill at a restaurant or inn with me!" She squeezed Victor's hand one more time, then let go.

Victor glanced at Tes, saw the amusement in her eyes, then shrugged and said, "Well? Let's go get that stone."

"Yes!" Tes said, leaping to her feet. She turned to Victor and added, "You should buy at least one of the epic racial boosts if any are available."

"Right." Victor nodded, standing up. "Before the hunt, there were two."

"Much can change in a week."

"C'mon!" Valla said, hurrying down the path toward the center of the garden. Victor followed after her, walking beside Tes, happy to see his friend, once so reticent and taciturn, genuinely excited about something. Coloss had been good for her, he reflected. All except that *pendeja* who wanted to kill her for being blue.

"You worry about your friend?" Tes asked.

"Yeah."

"Don't. Reis felt her smaller aura, heard her speak of her level, and thought she was picking an easy fight. She'll come to regret that decision; I won't be surprised if she tries to back out of the duel in the next week or so. She'll likely make an excuse, saying she's learned about Valla's character and wants to allow her to live, which will put the onus on our friend. I'm sure Valla will let her back out, though it would be interesting if she didn't."

"You really think she'll do that? Reis, I mean?" Victor turned left, saw Valla hurrying up to the porcelain lady at the end of the path, and slowed his pace so Tes would have time to answer him.

"I do. Reis is no great duelist, and when she hears rumors about Valla's gains, her nerve will falter." She frowned and then shrugged. "That's my guess, in any case."

"Huh. I hope you're right, but I'm not so sure Valla will let her back down. She's different these days, but I've seen her be pretty hard on people—she was a captain in the Legion and, if I recall, one of the youngest to ever reach that rank."

"The Legion? This is the military from her homeland?"

"Oh, yeah." Victor nodded.

"Perhaps she'll press the duel or amend the stakes—third strike or first blood, maybe. *That* would be amusing to watch." Tes cleared her throat as they approached the gate, guarded by the two motionless knights and attended by the strange, fragile-looking woman on her stool. Valla stood waiting, a prize token in her hand, and Tes motioned for Victor to go ahead. "I'll wait here, you two."

Victor fished out one of his tokens, held it up to the porcelain lady, and said, "May I proceed?"

"Oh yes. Thank you for your politeness, young man," she replied, her strange lips curving into a smile, accompanied by a soft sound that made Victor imagine a damp stone sliding against another, bigger stone. "You may call me Gallia."

Tes caught her breath, and Victor glanced at her. She seemed almost shocked by the pale, diminutive woman's words. He hoped he'd remember to ask her why later, but there, in front of the porcelain woman, he didn't think it would be wise. Instead, he said, "Why thank you, Gallia. If you don't recall, I'm Victor. It's a pleasure."

"Thank you, Victor. Please proceed."

He nodded and followed Valla to the System's City Stone, and she was quick to place her hand on it. He figured he might as well check on available prizes, so he touched the stone and navigated to the Treasure Exchange menu, and then read through it:

Available Treasure Exchange

Elixir of Regeneration: 1 Prize Token

Racial Boost, Basic: 1 Prize Token

Racial Boost, Improved: 2 Prize Tokens

Alchemical Ingredient, Advanced: 2 Prize Tokens
Racial Boost, Advanced: 3 Prize Tokens
Cultivation Breakthrough: 3 Prize Tokens
Alchemical Ingredient, Epic: 5 Prize Tokens
Racial Boost, Epic: 5 Prize Tokens (1 Available)
Stone of Sentience: 5 Prize Tokens (1 Available)
Alchemical Ingredient, Legendary: 10 Prize Tokens
Stone of Consciousness: 10 Prize Tokens (2 Available)
Epic Light Weapon: 10 Prize Tokens
Epic Heavy Weapon: 10 Prize Tokens
Epic Ranged Weapon: 12 Prize Tokens
Epic Energy Focus: 12 Prize Tokens
Random Legendary Treasure: 20 Prize Tokens

"There are fewer available than last time," Valla said from beside him just as Victor drew the same conclusion.

"Only one epic racial boost," he said, then selected it, suddenly fearful that somehow someone else would beat him to it.

*****Tokens Received. Your prize will appear at your feet.*****

The sudden System message reminded him that this City Stone and the exchange within it were managed by the ubiquitous arbiter of Energy and classes and so much more. As he watched his purchase appear out of a cloud of bright yellow Energy, he wondered about Tes's earlier words. Her people had existed long before the System. They'd kept it out of their world for millennia, but when it grew bigger and stronger, it still forced itself on them. He wanted to ask her more about it and resolved to do so.

"If I can get her to talk," he grunted, leaning down and picking up the glimmering, heavy, silver flask. It felt like he was picking up an ingot of gold, so dense was the container or whatever was inside it. He slipped it into his storage ring, figuring he'd ask Khul Bach or Tes when it would be wise to advance his race again. He saw Valla straightening up beside him and that she cradled in her hands a shimmering silver-and-white egg-shaped object that emitted a soft, swirling mist of Energy.

"How do I use it?" she asked, her words a bare whisper as though she feared she might disturb the object in her grasp.

"Let's go ask Tes," Victor said, putting a hand on her shoulder and walking with her back through the gate. She moved slowly and carefully, and he almost laughed; she really did treat it like an egg.

"It looks like a magical chicken egg," Victor said as they approached Tes.

She stood from the wrought iron bench where she'd been waiting and looked at the beautiful object in Valla's hands. "It does, doesn't it? It's the most beautiful Stone of Sentience I've seen."

"They're not all the same?"

"No! That's the seed of a spirit, there, Victor. They can be as different as one person is from another." Victor's eyes opened wide at the idea, and he leaned closer as Tes said, "Valla, hold it in one hand and summon your blade."

"Just one moment," Valla said, carefully tilting her right hand so the stone rolled into her left, then she cupped it there and held out her free hand. A moment later, she held Blue Razor, the deep, dark blue blade aloft. The black leather-wrapped hilt, long enough for her to wield two-handed, jutted out below her fist. Victor took a good look at the sword, noting how lovely the silvery crossguard and pommel were, etched with vines and flowers. He knew it was heavy, having felt its weight in many sparring sessions, and he admired how effortlessly Valla held it.

"Now, Valla, this is important!" Tes said, moving to stand before the smaller woman so she could look her in the eyes. "Fill your mind with your intentions! Picture something that embodies a virtue you think is worthy, a virtue you'd like to see reflected in the spirit of your blade."

"A virtue," Valla said softly, then she closed her eyes, and when she reopened them, her gaze was far away and her face serene.

"Good, now, move your hand with the stone next to the blade; press it against it—not the pommel or hilt, only the blade."

Valla didn't speak, but she nodded in understanding, and she carefully moved her left hand over to the blade of her sword and pressed the Stone of Sentience against the deep blue metal. Victor watched as the stone seemed to melt and spread into it, and then the entire sword flared with blinding, silvery light. When the bloom faded from his vision and he saw the sword, now held aloft in both of Valla's hands, he gasped in awe at its beauty.

The sword's dark blue, almost black blade glittered with thousands of tiny motes of light that reminded Victor very much of the ones that lurked in Lifedrinker's haft. The blade's edges radiated faint, wispy-white Energy tendrils that faded to nothing almost immediately. Valla laughed and whipped the sword around in a few intricate practice forms, and when she stopped, she was practically glowing with excitement.

"I can feel it! Her! This sword is no longer Blue Razor! Her name is Midnight Hope, and she's wonderful!"

38

HINTS AND LESSONS

Victor opened his eyes and grinned hugely—his Core had just advanced to Improved Six, and he'd only spent a few hours in the Warlord's cultivation chamber. He pulled his little magical pocket watch out of his storage container and looked at it, noting the time was 11:34; Tes had helped him to get it set properly to Coloss time.

When he'd woken up and met with the servant outside his room, the young man had informed him that Yabbo and Karnice wouldn't be able to spar until "after lunch." Victor figured that was sometime around noon, so he'd spent the morning cultivating. He stood, stretched, popped his back a few times, and then walked toward the chamber door, reseating Lifedrinker in the harness under his arm. He pressed his hand to the plate on the door and, when it clicked, pushed it open.

"Well," a richly deep, friendly voice said from the left-hand bench when Victor stepped out. He turned to the sound and saw, for only the third time, the Warlord. He sat leaning back, his wings furled, his legs crossed, and a sly smile exposing sharp white teeth.

"Oh," Victor said, stopping short and sketching an awkward half bow. "Warlord."

"Indeed! I see you've made some good use of my chamber." The smile didn't falter, and the astute dark eyes beneath the weird feathery white brows reminded Victor of a hawk's.

"Yes! Thank you again for letting me, us, use it."

"Surely. You're doing me a favor, are you not? And your pretty blue friend is a welcome distraction around this place."

Victor didn't know how to take those words, but he knew he didn't like the sound of them. He frowned and straightened up, suddenly worried about Valla. Tes wouldn't let something happen to her, would she? Before he could voice a concern or another banality, the Warlord shifted and spoke again.

"I don't use the chamber much these days. My Core advances so slowly that I begin to wonder if there's a stage beyond the one I've reached. Rumor-mongers tell me I should travel to older worlds, face ancient challenges, and learn from the great wizards and warriors in those places. I'm not convinced they exist. Zaafor is old enough, is it not? I rule enough people, do I not? Why should I give up all that I've gained and earned for the pursuit of tiny, nebulous improvements?"

"Well, I don't know. I mean, I thought Fanwath was full of powerful people until I visited this world . . ."

"And I might find the same should I travel far enough abroad? Is that the line of your thinking?"

"I suppose." Victor frowned, then shrugged and asked what was on his mind. "What rank is your Core, or is that too personal a ques—"

"I've attained the last tier of epic, and I've ground away at it for nearly three hundred years."

"The chamber doesn't help?"

"Hardly. I heard an interesting rumor, Victor."

"Oh?"

"Is it true you were able to improve your Core by eating the heart of a vanquished foe?"

Victor's mouth fell open, and he stared blankly at the Warlord for a moment, his mind spasmodically traveling down multiple trains of thought—who had told him? Could he have heard him speaking to Valla or something? Was it a problem if the Warlord knew? Should he lie? Would he know it if he did?

"Are you dumbstruck?"

"Uh, no, Warlord, simply surprised. I wasn't aware anyone else knew of that. You see, that aspect of my bloodline is new to me, and I've only done it a couple of times. It doesn't always improve my Core, though. I think it depends upon the heart." Victor had decided that lying to this man about something he seemed to know already would be a mistake.

"Intriguing, Victor. Well, don't let me keep you any longer. I believe Karnice has a lesson for you. I'll be around, watching; I find you quite interesting."

"Well, thanks." Victor shrugged, uncomfortable with the strange praise. "Um, I was on my way to see Karnice, but I'm not sure how to get there. I was told to meet him in the "practice yard" outside the citadel—is that the big open space by the gate?"

"No, but close. Just walk around the citadel to the western side, and you'll see the practice yard; it's surrounded by a short wall and has a sand floor, perfect for soaking up blood." The Warlord laughed, then stood and motioned for the stairs leading down. "After you, young titan."

"Right, thanks again, Warlord." Victor nodded and hurried down the steps, and as he gained some distance from the powerful ruler, who'd stopped at the top of the steps and seemed to be watching him leave, he cast Titanic Aspect so he could move to the Degh side of the steps and double his pace. Something about the Warlord, though he was overtly polite and pleasant, bothered Victor.

He'd felt like a mouse being toyed with by an eagle, and he wasn't really surprised—the man had destroyed the Degh in a war thousands of years before Victor was born. The question about his heart eating had bothered him, not really because he was embarrassed about it, which he was, but because it had come so quickly after the Warlord admitted having been stuck with his own Core advancement. "He sure seemed pretty free with that tidbit of information, hmm, *chica?*"

"*Ware the old wolf, Victor, for he'd do much to cling to his power.*" Lifedrinker's sharp soprano, edged with a constant note of violence, surprised him; he spoke to her so often with no response that he'd grown accustomed to having a one-sided discussion.

"He makes you nervous, too?"

"*Oh yes! I yearn to taste his flesh, but we aren't ready yet. Can you not feel his strength? Be cautious, for his words are soaked in blood.*"

"I'll be cautious. Don't worry." Victor rubbed a thumb along the back of her metal head as he walked, and she hummed softly, apparently placated. The heat pulsing beneath her silvery surface gave him comfort, too, and when he stepped out of the citadel into the bright sunlight, he was in a better mood. He turned to the right, walking along the cobbled paths around the enormous edifice, passing by servants carrying baskets and buckets, pushing carts of linens and kitchen supplies.

Victor stepped to the side, making room for the servants, and that's when he realized there was another pathway on the other side of the row of planters, this one lined with sculptures of animals and birds, flowering plants, and succulent cacti. Well-dressed Vesh passed him occasionally on this path, and he reasoned that this was meant for the non-serving class that dwelled in the citadel.

Before he could spend much time speculating on the various types of people living in Coloss and their stations relative to one another, he came to a path to the left that opened into a large, depressed square. Victor walked that way and stood at the top of the steps, looking down on a "practice field" that would put many full-blown colosseums to shame. It might not have the stands of a colosseum, but rows of shady stone benches under pergolas lined the marble-block pit approximately the size of a football field. As the Warlord had said, the bottom of the pit was covered in fine white sand.

Victor could imagine hundreds of people practicing maneuvers out in that sand, but at that hour, only a few were scattered around the space, sparring with weapons and Energy. He watched a woman erupt with white, frosty Energy and perform a double backflip to avoid the fire-limned war hammer of her opponent as it smashed into the sand. As she leapt back into the fray, swinging her frosty bo staff, Victor started down the steps, looking around for a sign of his supposed trainer.

He was still wearing his Titanic Aspect, and so, when he reached the edge of the practice field, the first words he heard from Karnice were, "Gods! He's bigger than you said!"

"Are you berserk?" another voice asked, and Victor turned to see two Vesh eyeing him from a stone bench in the shade of the nearby clay-tiled pergola.

The one who'd spoken was shorter but broader than the other, with barrel-like shoulders covered in the same brown fur as his head and face—he looked more bear than man. He gazed at Victor through dark golden eyes and grinned, exposing canines too large for his mouth. He wore leather straps in lieu of a shirt and leather shorts that exposed the bottoms of his furry legs all the way down to the sharp black claws at the ends of his toes.

The Vesh sitting next to him was more akin to the Warlord than the beastlike man beside him. He was tall, bronze-skinned, and his red gleaming eyes glowered from beneath dark brows, a heavy weight of power emanating from them. He was a handsome man, and if it weren't for the double set of shoulders and four arms protruding from his green-scaled vest, Victor might have thought he was human. He'd combed back his black hair neatly and wore his beard in a sharp, well-oiled goatee.

After momentarily staring at the two Vesh, Victor replied, "No."

"Huh. I thought you were smaller when you weren't berserk. It seemed that way in the arena . . ." the bear-like man said.

"He's under the influence of a spell," the taller, four-armed man replied.

"Hey," Victor said. "Karnice and Yabbo?" Victor let his spell fade as he spoke and winced as the weird sensation of shrinking came over him. Even without his spell's boost, though, he was a good deal larger than the two Vesh, and if it weren't for the hints of Karnice's aura bleeding through his efforts to restrain it, he might not have been intimidated by them. As it was, when Karnice stood and approached him, Victor could feel the threat of his power, lurking like a viper in a decorative basket.

"Well met," Karnice said, holding out his top right hand, and Victor clasped it. "I'm Karnice, and I'll be helping you two to improve for the next couple of weeks. We want Coloss to win the tourney, yes?"

"Yes!" Yabbo said, bouncing to his hairy feet and rushing over to clap Victor on the shoulder. His hand was heavy and hard, like a frozen ham.

Victor grunted and said, "Sure we do."

"Let's get down there, then." Karnice released Victor's hand and then moved around the side of the practice arena until he came to a set of stone steps that led down to the sand. "Come, hurry. My time is valuable, whelps."

Victor hustled down, shoulder to shoulder with Yabbo, and when they stood on the sand, Karnice turned to face them, folding all four of his arms over his chest. "Well, I won't have you two playing flower flutters! Get your weapons out!"

Victor unsnapped Lifedrinker's sling and lifted her free, holding her crossways before him. Yabbo summoned a shield and a heavy-looking black hammer in his other hand. Karnice nodded and backed up, and suddenly an enormous silvery spear was in his hands, all four of them. "Good. I'll take your measure one at a time, weapon skills only. Give me everything you have—try to get past my spear and leave a mark on my flesh. No Energy abilities!"

Yabbo stepped forward, so Victor backed to the arena's edge to watch. While he stood there, he contemplated his Sovereign Will ability—at the moment, he was boosting his agility and vitality, and he changed it to agility and strength. The ability didn't cost him any Energy, so it was fair to use as far as he was concerned. As his muscles swelled and hardened, he watched Yabbo struggle to get close to Karnice.

It was evident that Yabbo was a powerful, fierce fighter. His shield was the size of a sled, round and brassy, with colorful red, black, and yellow runes flickering and glowing in the metal. He swung it as if it weighed nothing, but Victor could feel the air being displaced, could hear the way it crashed against Karnice's spear, and he didn't think it would feel good to be bashed by it. The bear-like man growled and charged, never seeming to tire as he swung that heavy hammer at Karnice, only to have the taller, lankier man dance out of reach.

Every so often, Karnice would go on the offensive, using his spear to feint, then smashing the shining, silvery haft into Yabbo's shoulder or shield or thigh, always with the result of Yabbo roaring in pain or frustration and flopping down into the sand, unable to withstand the force of the blow. The assessment bout went on like that for a long while—ten or fifteen minutes, which Victor knew all too well was a long time to be fighting all out.

When Karnice called a halt, he seemed perfectly at ease, not even breathing heavily, and Yabbo was heaving for breath with sand and sweat thick in his fur. "Not bad, Yabbo. Advanced skill with the hammer? Near epic with the shield?"

"Yeh . . ." Yabbo grunted between pants. "Not used to fighting without my skills," he added, still leaning with his thick, clawed hands on his furry knees.

"Well, let's have the off-worlder give it a go. You can get your wind back while you watch."

"Right," Victor said, stepping forward, Lifedrinker loose and ready in his grip.

"Come on, then!" Karnice growled, leveling the spear, apparently out of patience. Victor frowned at his change of demeanor; he could see he wasn't the favored student. With that thought, his Core surged, and red heat started to spill into his pathways, but Victor held it back, flexing his already taxed will—he'd been fighting his aura down all day. Still, he contained his fury and charged at Karnice, using the moves he'd learned from Polo Vosh and perfected through hours and hours of practice with Valla and alone, dancing with his shadow.

He immediately saw that he was faster than Yabbo, faster and stronger. Lifedrinker clanged against Karnice's spear, and sometimes clouds of black smoke and a splash of hot orange Energy would accompany her impact. The first time it happened, Karnice frowned but held his tongue. Victor could see he'd been about to yell at him for using Energy but realized it was Lifedrinker's doing.

The spear weathered Lifedrinker's blows, clearly a powerful weapon in its own right, though it lacked a mind. The first time Karnice went on the offensive and worked past Victor's guard, smashing the haft of his spear into Victor's hip, he looked a bit surprised when Victor hardly shifted. He nodded, though, and ramped up the offensive, twirling his spear like a staff, whipping the ends around, knocking Lifedrinker aside, and raking the razor-sharp edge over Victor's left pectoral, leaving a long, bloody rip in one of his better shirts.

Victor growled and pressed his offensive, trying to see the pattern in Karnice's evasions but never quite sussing them out—as soon as he thought he had an opening figured out, Karnice would surprise him with a new side step or feinting parry. The battle went on and on, and Victor ended up switching his Sovereign Will boost to vitality and agility. Once he'd done that, Victor never tired—he felt as if he could spar all day. By the time Karnice called a halt, Victor's shirt was ruined, and he had a dozen shallow gashes over his chest, stomach, shoulders, and back.

He stood beside Yabbo, his breath unlabored, and waited to hear Karnice's assessment. Yabbo, for his part, threw Victor sidelong glances, clearly surprised by how well he'd held up. While Karnice gathered his thoughts, he muttered into Victor's shoulder, behind one hairy fist, "I thought you were low tier."

"Well, close enough to mid." Victor shrugged.

"Well, off-worlder," Karnice said, leaning on his spear, the tip in the air, glinting red with Victor's blood. "If your axe mastery isn't epic, I'd say it's close, hmm?"

"Really? It's advanced, but I thought I had a long way to go before epic."

"Regardless, I can see you've lived the life of a warrior. You don't tire easily and are sturdy for a man of your rank. I'll wager your racial advancements and bloodline have helped you there, hmm?"

"I guess." Victor didn't feel like expounding—why did it feel like everyone was pumping him for information about his bloodline today? The question wasn't really out of the blue; it was a natural thing to wonder about, but following his chat with the Warlord, it triggered a little warning in his gut.

"Well, if I'm to teach you, I'll need to know more about you both. Choose one of your strongest abilities, and using only that ability, we'll repeat the assessment."

"Yes!" Yabbo said, stepping onto the sand. Victor watched as he held the metal disc of his shield up, gathering hot, acrid Energy. Victor could feel the caustic attunement, whatever it was, in his sinuses. Yabbo roared as his spell completed, and then his shield expanded, glowing green and dripping drops of acidic green liquid into the sand that crackled and sizzled.

The shield was large enough to cover most of Yabbo's body now, and Karnice had to work a little to get his blows past it. He didn't risk the health of his spear by striking it nakedly against that biting surface. Rather, he channeled his own red, scorching Energy along the length of the silvery shaft, coating it with a crackling aura that sizzled against Yabbo's shield, leaving charred lines on the metallic surface that only slowly faded and filled back in with Yabbo's green Energy.

Victor tried to pay attention to the "assessment," but he grew bored—it was much like the first time, and the two hardly did anything other than dance back and forth, circling each other. Karnice still managed to send Yabbo sprawling a few times, and after another ten minutes or so, he finally called a halt to the exercise. Yabbo let his spell drop, clearly exhausted, and walked back over to Victor.

"Well? Berserker? Will you show me your might?" Karnice asked, twirling his red-limned spear. Something about the question bothered Victor. Why did Karnice want him to cast Berserk? Was it truly to assess his strength? Victor almost refused, almost chose a different spell, like Inspiring Presence, but then he wondered if Karnice was just fishing, trying to see what else Victor could bring to the table. Everyone in Coloss knew he could berserk; what was the harm in using it now?

"I'm supposed to be practicing it anyway," he said, then, grinning like a madman, he formed the pattern for the spell and relaxed his will, letting his rage flood his pathways.

39

SECRETS AND OATHS

Victor smashed into Karnice's spear over and over, batting the length of dense, heavy metal aside with Lifedrinker or his fist and lunging at the tall, four-armed warrior. Each time, Karnice danced away, his agility so far beyond Victor's that the enraged titan-blood had trouble focusing on his form as it blurred into motion. Still, no matter Karnice's speed and no matter how he tried to punish Victor with his stabs and sweeps, the berserking giant kept advancing, shrugging off the weeping cuts and instantly fading welts.

Karnice couldn't move him with that spear, not even an inch, so he was forced to leap and dash to keep himself out of Lifedrinker's cutting arc. It began to grow evident that Victor's rage would outlast the champion's endurance—ten minutes into the sparring session, Karnice was drenched in a sheen of sweat, his face was flushed, and his lungs heaved like bellows. On the other hand, Victor continued to jump and rush toward him, swinging his great, silvery axe in liquid cleaves that ripped the air and left trails of black smoke in her wake.

Karnice finally seemed to have had enough and gathered a great surge of Energy. His body blazed with roiling red flames that rose up from his shoulders into a gigantic fiery double that leapt away from his sweat-drenched body and fell upon Victor with not one but four fiery replicas of his spear. Victor screamed in rage and pain as the spears stabbed into his flesh, cutting far more deeply than the physical version and leaving painful scorches that lined the puncture wounds.

Still, Victor fought. He hacked Lifedrinker through the fiery doppel-ganger, slashing her through its midsection, and she drank great torrents of its Energy with each hack. Victor's prodigious vitality and berserk healing closed the wounds almost as fast as the red nightmare could pull the spears out, leaving red welts where throbbing holes had been. His Flame-Touched feat was proving its worth; despite the burned flesh in the stab wounds, he healed cleanly.

The damage had been done, though; the pain and frustration of the clinging, fiery foe had driven Victor's fury to new heights, and he screamed and flailed, ripping his doppelganger to shreds but in the process burning off the last of his hot, red Energy. Karnice watched from a dozen feet away, lean-ing on the haft of his spear as Victor vanquished his gigantic, burning mirror image. As it faded away in a black wisp of smoke, Victor fell to his knees, his rage and Titanic Aspect gone. He heaved for breath, frowned, and growled, "Not really pulling your punches, were you?"

"I had to get your measure, and now I know." Karnice shrugged. "The wounds healed."

"And if they hadn't?" Victor touched one of the nearly twenty circular red welts, this one on his chest—his shirt was nothing but tatters clinging to his shoulders.

"Then you'd require some extra healing." Karnice looked at Yabbo and said, "You two will spend the next few hours sparring with axe and ham-mer. I'll devise some training strategies for tomorrow." With that, he turned, walked up the stairs leading out of the practice arena, and was gone.

"I don't think he expected you to press him so hard," Yabbo said, walking over to Victor and holding out a hand. Victor took the offered hand and let Yabbo hoist him to his feet.

"Eh, most old masters get a little surprised by my berserk state."

"I can see why. You have a heavy aura for someone not yet Tier Five."

"Thanks." Victor shrugged, not interested in banter. He was frustrated, and the pain of those fiery spears was still fresh in his mind, regardless of whether he had healed. "Come on, let's do some weapon work. I have some spells to help." He concentrated and cast Inspiring Presence and Globe of Inspiration, setting the bright orb ten feet over their heads.

"Oh!" Yabbo said, a smile brightening his eyes and exposing his too-full mouth of fangs. "I knew you were a Spirit Caster, but I didn't know you had more than one attunement! This is wonderful." He reached a hand toward the glowing orb of inspiration-attuned Energy and held it there as though trying to shield his eyes while peering at the sun. "Yes! I feel it; let's practice!"

"Right." Victor nodded, also feeling better now that he'd bathed himself in inspiration. He was always happy to train with someone, and Yabbo seemed like a decent guy. Karnice, on the other hand, was a bit of an asshole, in Victor's opinion. The four-armed champion was gone, though, so Victor decided to buckle down and get some real work in. He squared off with Yabbo and said, "Say seventy-five percent? Just spells that boost our weapon abilities? I mean, I want to get some good work in and not beat each other up."

"Yes, sounds good to me. Do you mind putting on a helmet? This hammer is heavy . . ."

"Sure," Victor said, then he set Lifedrinker down and produced his Kethian juggernaut helm from his storage ring. Arms straining at the weight, he slipped it onto his head and grinned as he felt it distribute its weight through his frame. "Should be good now." Victor picked up Lifedrinker and said, "Okay, *chica*, we're just practicing; don't murder him."

Yabbo eyed him speculatively. "The axe understands? I don't want to have to regrow any limbs . . ."

"I'll be careful, and yeah, she understands." Victor backed up a step and bowed to Yabbo, who grinned and bowed back, and then the two of them began to train. They fell into an easy rhythm and, as they grew increasingly comfortable with each other's style, picked up the tempo until a casual observer might think they were fighting in earnest.

Neither of them sustained a serious injury, though Yabbo had to drink a healing draught twice to staunch badly bleeding gashes, one on his shoulder and one just under his ribs. Victor received many a bruising blow from Yabbo's shield or hammer, but his vitality and titanic heritage allowed him to heal such wounds within minutes. He didn't doubt that Yabbo was pulling his blows, but so was he.

One thing that he appreciated about Yabbo was his stamina; he kept up the intensity longer than things usually went with Valla. In fact, the sun was sinking toward the eastern horizon when they finally decided to call an end to their work. Neither of them had improved the ranks of any skills or spells, but Victor felt he was close to some breakthroughs. "A few more days of practice like that will do me well," he said, shaking Yabbo's thick, paw-like hand.

"Indeed! I hope Karnice doesn't simply torture us tomorrow; I'd like to make some gains." Yabbo rubbed at a new scar along his forearm, his breath still a bit ragged from the exertion.

"Yeah. Here's hoping . . ."

"Hello, gentlemen," a cheerful, feminine voice called from the covered benches at the side of the sand pit. Victor recognized Tes's voice instantly and turned to wave. He felt a strange sense of relief when he saw Valla sitting beside her.

"Hello," Yabbo said, ducking his head, touching his thickly furred head with his free hand—some sort of show of respect, Victor figured.

"Hey, Tes." Victor turned to Valla, caught her eye, and said, "Hey, Valla."

"Victor, I brought you a present," Tes said, holding up a rolled-up piece of parchment.

"I should get going," Yabbo said, clapping Victor's shoulder. "Ladies." He ducked his head again and then hurried up the steps.

"What time tomorrow?" Victor called after him.

Yabbo stopped, turned back, then shrugged and said, "I say we meet here at noon again. Karnice will let us know if he wants something different."

"Right." Victor nodded, and Yabbo turned and was gone, walking around the corner and up toward the citadel. Victor climbed the short steps out of the sand to sit on the bench beside Tes, looked at the parchment in her hand, and asked, "The rest of your spell pattern?"

"Just so! Take your time; you'll find that the entirety of the spell is a bit more perplexing than the section you've learned so far."

"Thanks, Tes." Victor took the parchment, surprised by its weight, and suddenly dreaded unrolling it—the pattern had to be pretty damn long. He tucked it safely into one of his storage rings and asked, "So, what've you ladies been up to today?"

"Cultivating and practicing my spells. I made a rank with my Core, but you look like you had a much harder day. What happened to your shirt?" Tes leaned back, allowing Victor to look at Valla while she spoke. She was clean, her hair neatly coiffed—more so than during the hunt—and she'd put on one of her signature uniform-style shirts with the high, buttoned collar.

"Karnice happened." Victor shrugged.

"He was hard on you?" Tes raised an eyebrow.

"I think I pissed him off 'cause I wouldn't go down easy when he was 'getting my measure.'"

"He's a dangerous one—deep-fire attunement."

"Deep-fire?"

"A kind of elemental affinity, but it has a different Energy signature than fire; you can find it naturally in the deeper parts of worlds like this. A few people in such worlds are born with an affinity for it. It's hotter and more volatile than typical fire-attuned Energy."

"Yeah, I felt it." Victor pointed to some of the pink circles on his chest and arms, though they'd already faded noticeably.

"Reckless of him. He didn't know you'd heal so easily." Tes frowned and held one of her long, slender fingers over a mark on Victor's nearest shoulder. She let it hang there as if debating whether she should touch him, but she ended up curling it into her fist and shaking her head. "Be careful of Karnice and accept his aid with a guarded mind."

"Speaking of being guarded when accepting aid," Victor said, glancing over his shoulder toward the hulking, colossal edifice of the citadel. Tes shook her head and held up a finger.

A moment later, Victor's ears popped, and Tes said, "I can shield our discussion out here, but within the citadel, the Warlord's seat of power, even I must be wary of his prying ears."

"Well," Victor said, considering his words, "he kind of gave me the creeps earlier. He was waiting for me when I came out of the cultivation chamber and seemed to be fishing for information about my bloodline, specifically my ability to improve my Core by eating hearts."

"That man should indeed worry you," Tes nodded. "You know how the Vesh came to be, yes?"

Victor looked past Tes to Valla, and she shrugged, clearly as clueless as he was. "No."

"Oh, goodness. Well, the Vesh, a few millennia ago, were actually a clan of Degh."

"What the hell? Seriously?"

"Oh yes. They were always the smallest of their kind, though they were once quite a lot larger than they are now. There used to be many other peoples here on Zaafor. You should know it took me some time to uncover this history." Tes paused and stared into the sky, clearly savoring some memory or another. "I spent years poring through texts in libraries—many of the old histories were destroyed, but I found enough. I even found some of the old cities of the dead races."

"Dead races?" Valla asked, clearly engulfed by her words as Tes laid bare the mystery.

"Yes, the Vesh, once a rather weak clan of Degh, learned that they could steal the bloodlines from other peoples. You might guess the people subjected to their method didn't survive the process. As the Vesh gained new powers and became greedy for more, they slaughtered, wholesale, some of the less populous races on Zaafor, doing enough damage to wipe many of them out."

"Holy shit! Is that why Khul Bach called them mutants?"

"Oh yes. The Vesh you see in Coloss are largely in the early or, in a few cases, middling stages of digging out the many stolen bloodlines buried in their people's dark history. You'll note the higher-tier individuals, such as the Warlord and Karnice, are a bit more refined, less animalistic; they've unlocked a complementary set of bloodlines that give them true advantages in this violent world."

"He wants Victor's bloodline," Valla said, echoing a fear that had begun to form in Victor's mind.

"Undoubtedly. The lazy, fearful tyrant has been looking for a way to improve his Core without traveling abroad for centuries."

"How does he . . ." Victor thought about his question, then continued, "How does he keep his power? I mean, how has no one from a stronger world come and kicked his ass?"

"He controls the City Stones—and refuses connections from other stones. It keeps this world obscure—one of the reasons I was here, studying its history. I've learned much, but I'll be moving on soon."

"But powerful people can open portals, right?"

"A portal for an army? It could be done, though the effort would be great. Why, though? I'm here to study, but others like me would find this world a dead end. They've stagnated."

"So, um, you knew the Warlord was going to try to get my bloodline?"

"I know he wants to. I don't know that he'll try anytime soon. I imagine he'll need to study you for a while. I think, though, that it might be wise to seek an alternate route back to your world—I wouldn't be surprised if you tried to purchase teleportation from his City Stone and it didn't work."

"Do other Vesh know how to steal bloodlines?" Valla asked, her light blue skin suddenly paler than usual.

"Oh, many. The powerful, older ones."

"Tes, how are we going to get out of here?" Victor asked.

"Don't fret, Victor. Keep learning while you can. I've a lead on someone that may be able to help you. Didn't you tell me the wizard whose portal you used was named Boaegh?"

"That's right," Valla quickly answered.

"He had students; did you know that?" Tes grinned and added, "I'm going to visit one of them tonight."

"Seriously?"

"Oh, very seriously. In the meantime, keep your guard up, as you have been, and I'll also be watching. We must time your exit well."

"Were you always going to help us with this?" Valla asked.

"I . . ." Tes paused and pursed her lips, clearly trying to decide how to answer. Finally, she said, "I think I must be honest with you. How strange!" She turned to include Victor in her words and then continued, "I was sure I wanted to help you, but I was also curious about the Warlord and what he might do."

She turned back to Valla and reached out to clasp her hand in hers, then holding it tight, their fingers intertwined, she said, "I thought, at first, to help you prepare for the duel and to help Victor prepare for the arena. What a spectacle, I thought! I was curious how the Warlord and Blue would respond to your successes."

Valla's eyes had grown dark, and as she listened to Tes, Victor saw her growing tense, perhaps pulling on her hand, still in Tes's grasp. Victor, for his part, wasn't surprised at all. He could feel it early on when he'd met with Tes; she'd seemed almost to be toying with him. She continued, "As I grew to know you both, though, I grew fond of you. I do want you both to succeed, and I've surprised myself by realizing that I can't stomach the idea of the Warlord and his minions defiling either of you, stealing your bloodlines, or worse."

"So the idea was to fatten us up, let us entertain these savages, and then observe the Warlord's methodology as he killed us for our bloodlines?"

"Well, Victor's bloodline for certain, though Blue has been quite interested in trying to attain your natural coloring . . ." Tes knew she'd gone too far with that; she clamped her mouth shut, and as Valla jerked her hand, she relaxed her grip, letting her pull it away.

"That's pretty fucked up, Tes," Victor said.

"I'm a scholar, and I was trying to respect the culture of these people." Tes sighed, clearly upset, worried that she'd alienated Valla, who was leaning forward on her knees, head cradled in her hands. "Valla, for what it's worth, I'd decided by the second day I knew you, the day we watched Victor in the arena, that I wouldn't let the Warlord harm you." She turned to Victor, adding, "The same for you, Victor. I knew, speaking with you during Blue's dinner, that I was probably going to violate my oath and help you."

That got Valla's attention, and she lifted her head, eyeing Tes with moist eyes. "Oath?"

"Oh yes!" Tes nodded with a chagrined look that clearly indicated she'd forgotten to mention something important. "I'm a member of a league of scholars from a world much closer to my home—an ancient world with people who have ten times, nay a hundred times, more power and influence than I. I'm not supposed to interfere with the people in the worlds we study. I'm supposed to observe and report; sometimes, our order will vote to interfere with the progress in a stagnant world like this, and sometimes they'll choose to leave it for a while.

"I'm violating my oath by even telling you this, but I see a loophole; you didn't intend to travel here. My oath wasn't sworn with your world, Fanwath, in mind; I don't think that world has more than a single summary sentence in our index; it's too young. I think my advocate will help me avoid repudiation if I explain your situation."

"You're breaking your oath for us?" Valla asked, the tears now freely flowing down her cheeks.

"I am! I promise, Valla; I do care about you both!" Tes softly chuckled as Valla pulled her into an embrace, burying her face in Tes's blouse, just under her chin. Tes tucked her chin against Valla's head, pulling her tight, and smiled at Victor. He looked at her, wondering if he should feel tricked or betrayed, but he was unable to find any hurt feelings. He knew Valla had grown close to Tes, fond of her in the way Victor might have followed around a pro baseball player who'd decided to hang out with him one summer and teach him how to pitch.

Victor also liked Tes and had decided she was a good person; in his opinion, her explanation and confession had only solidified that assessment. She'd been honest with them, almost to a fault. Would she really get in trouble for helping them? He met Tes's eyes and smiled, and he was infinitely relieved when he saw moisture gather in those deep, honey-green orbs—a genuine display of emotion that made it easy to forget he was dealing with a dragon.

40

❧

IRON

After that first day of practice with Yabbo and Karnice, Victor's day-to-day life fell into a kind of uneasy, watchful routine. At the start of each day, he'd go to the Warlord's cultivation chamber, where he'd work on his Core, slowly pushing it closer and closer to rank nine of the "improved" tier. After that, he'd spar with Yabbo with Karnice's rather gruff and violent guidance. Then, he'd sit with Tes and Valla in their suite and study his spell pattern in the evenings, usually exhausted with dozens of new, rapidly fading scars.

The cultivation was going well; each rank was like a deeper trench in the ocean of Energy than the one before it, but he knew nine would be a sheer cliff the size of a mountain, and he hoped the tincture he'd gotten from the arena would be enough to push him through it. Still, his gains were huge with each cycle of his drill in the profound, rich Energy of the chamber, and it only took Victor four days to go from rank six to rank eight; he could feel that he was on the verge of nine.

The sparring was another matter. Each day Karnice tried to egg Victor into using a different set of skills, trying to push him into pulling from his different affinities. Knowing what he did about the Vesh, especially the powerful ones like Karnice and the Warlord, Victor was reluctant to put his talents on display. He'd stubbornly refuse to use anything other than his Berserk and weapon skills with the deadly spearman, despite punishing lessons that left him bleeding and battered. Karnice typically stormed off after losing his temper, and Victor would be left to spar with Yabbo, which he much preferred in any case.

Tes and Valla kept him sane during those days—he'd come back to their suite to the scent of great feasts, and they'd drink and eat, laughing and telling stories for hours before Victor and Valla pulled out their studies. Tes helped them, Valla with her new spells and Victor with the singular, impossibly complicated pattern that spanned more than a meter of rolled-up parchment. Still, he made progress, and with each section he memorized, Tes celebrated with him as though he'd done something inconceivable.

On the morning of their fifth day of this routine, Victor broke through to the ninth rank with his Core and was surprised when a System message appeared before him:

*****Congratulations! You have achieved level 45 Titanic Herald and gained 6 strength, 11 vitality, 6 dexterity, 6 agility, 6 intelligence, and 6 will.*****

"Nice!" he grunted, the word echoing in the circular stone chamber. He sat there contemplating for a moment, his immediate thoughts drawn to the Core breakthrough tincture. Should he drink it right away? He could wait until later and ask Tes about it, or he could ask Khul Bach now. "Or I could just drink it."

Setting aside the thought for the moment, he considered the other things he had yet to consume—the epic racial boost he'd bought with tokens and the various monster hearts still lingering in his storage containers, including the one from the ancient wyrm. Tes had said to save the racial boost until he'd gone through the other improvements he was working toward, and he knew she'd meant specifically his Core.

Victor pulled out his watch, saw it was nearing noon, and sighed. He was getting damn sick of Karnice—sick of taking his beatings and sick of holding back his talents. He wanted nothing more than to surprise that asshole with a sound thrashing, but he knew he wasn't up for it, not yet. "Well, if I'm going to go get my ass kicked, I might as well pump up my Core first." Victor rubbed his thumb along Lifedrinker's warm, pulsing axe-head, steadying his nerves, and then he pulled Shouza's bulbous, honey-colored tincture from his storage ring.

He could feel the Energy pulsing within, and when he pulled out the cork stopper, a scent like the richest, sweetest syrup imaginable hit his nose, and his mouth filled with saliva. With a great effort of will, he steadied his hand and forced himself to drain the concoction calmly. When it touched his tongue, his taste buds burst to life, tingling with ecstasy, and though Victor tried to savor the taste, he found his throat reflexively gulping, and soon the mouthful of blissfully sweet syrup was in his stomach.

In the back of his throat, he felt the deep notes of herbs and spices, and he coughed a little, feeling a weird rawness in the wake of the tincture's passage. He sat for a moment, wondering if he should be feeling something, wondering if he'd done something wrong. Was he supposed to just drink it? It was for his Core—should he have tried to cultivate from it?

Before his thoughts could spiral out of control, something happened in his gut. A tiny spark seemed to have ignited in there—a single hot spot in the center of his stomach, at first warm and pleasant, as you might feel after drinking a strong shot of liquor on a cold day. Then the spot of warmth became an ember, became a hot coal, became a scorching lump of magma. Victor doubled over in pain and, not knowing what else to do, turned his gaze inward to his Core.

Sure enough, he saw the dense, rapidly pulsing orbs of his affinities, and nearby, bleeding out of reality and into his inward vision, he saw the scorching sun of the ball of Energy that had to be the result of the tincture. Victor instinctively reached out with his will and began pulling threads out of that white-hot orb of Energy into his three attunement orbs. The Energy was malleable and easy to tug, and soon three wide ribbons were flowing, one each, into his fear, inspiration, and rage affinities. As the Energy flowed, the burning in his gut faded, and Victor knew he was on the right track.

The ball of hot, vibrant Energy seemed to be incredibly dense. Victor had to tug strands of Energy out of it for a very long time before it seemed to dim slightly. Meanwhile, his affinity orbs were pulsing and swelling, brighter than he'd ever seen them. Still, he kept pulling on those threads, kept pushing them into his Core, and as some inner sense screamed at him that his Core was ready to burst, he pushed and pulled even more.

"Let's go!" he roared, somewhere between discomfort and pain but feeling as if a bomb were getting ready to go off in his gut. Still, his Core pulsed and stretched, each of his affinity orbs blindingly bright, even the dark, purple-black fear attunement—when he looked at it, everything else was obscured by its violent pulses.

The ball of Energy from the tincture was still flaring brightly, and Victor knew there was more he was supposed to do. Finally, in desperation, he began to channel the threads of Energy through his pathways, running the full circuit around his body, filling them to bursting before he let them feed into his Core. Finally, that seemed to do something. The ball of Energy from the tincture was gone. Just the Energy in his pathways was left, and as it began to feed into his Core, he felt as though he'd tipped some sort of scale, and suddenly he didn't have to push or pull on the Energy—it rushed into his Core as if it were falling down a drainpipe.

Victor's Core pulsed violently. Each of his blazing attunements seemed to stretch, pushing outward into one another, bleeding together into a great ball of dark, shimmering Energy that expanded outward, flooding his pathways, burning them, stretching them, growing them. It felt as though someone had filled his veins with magma, and Victor lifted his head and screamed as the process spread outward, through his chest and stomach, into his arms and legs, and up into his head.

It felt slow and agonizing, but before Victor could even contemplate allowing his conscious mind to slip away into oblivion, it was over. The Energy suddenly snapped back to his Core, and his three affinities contracted into tight, incredibly dense, slowly pulsing, calmly orbiting balls of attuned Energy. Gasping and sweating, Victor watched his Core for a long moment, admiring how the Energy seemed more solid than before.

The orbs used to look as though they were mostly light, wispy, and bright, but now they seemed more solid—truly weighty with their potential. Victor knew he'd have to cultivate for a long time, gaining levels and consuming treasures to make those newly dense orbs strain to hold what he fed them. "It's gonna take a while to get to epic." He chuckled, wiping sweat from his brow. He started to turn away from his Core, and that's when he noticed his pathways.

They were easily twice as broad as before; his one-lane road for Energy had become a divided highway. "Was this what Tes meant? Can I manage more than one powerful spell now? Can I go berserk and still cast Inspiring Presence?" Victor knew the answer—of course that's what she'd meant. "Hell yeah," he grunted, struggling to his feet. He picked up Lifedrinker and added, "Let's go see if we can cut that asshole, hmm?"

As he walked through the citadel, Victor reached into his storage ring and pulled out an item he'd been holding onto for quite some time. He held up the belt he'd gotten so long ago from the creepy alien who'd been hunting Tellen and his men and, as he channeled a bit of Energy into it, reread the System message.

*****Dragonsteel Belt of Energy Absorption. Prerequisite for use: Advanced tier Core or higher. This belt will absorb Energy attacks aimed at the wearer.**

It will absorb a total of 4500 points of Energy before it needs to process the absorbed Energy and reset, becoming inert for up to twelve hours.***

Considering Victor now had just a bit more than 7900 Energy, he figured being able to absorb 4500 Energy worth of attacks was a pretty big deal. If someone comparable to himself were attacking him, he could ignore half of their Energy abilities. "Am I thinking of that correctly?" he wondered aloud. He supposed the belt couldn't absorb physical abilities that cost someone Energy to perform, like a special weapon attack. Still, it should be able to absorb pure Energy—things like lightning bolts or fireballs.

He shrugged, unhooking his old belt and weaving the beautiful, shimmering, silvery-blue metallic belt through the loops on his pants. He'd taken on his Titanic Aspect and so made good time through the Citadel. As he strode down the steps toward the practice yard, Victor contemplated what he'd already taken for granted—he now had over 7900 total Energy.

He knew part of the reason for his increase was, obviously, the leveling of his Core, but he also was cognizant of the enormous boost he was getting with each level thanks to the forced increase of his intelligence. The more he realized how valuable his other attributes were, the more he appreciated his new class; it was nice not having to deliberate what points to put where—having every attribute improve was a nice change of pace.

"Victor, you're late." Karnice's voice was a harsh growl, and Victor didn't respond as he lightly jogged down the steps into the sand.

Yabbo was waiting for him with a raised fist, and Victor punched his hairy knuckles with a grin. "Yabbo."

"Victor."

"Now that the pups have greeted each other, are you ready for some work?" Karnice snarled, stepping closer and leaning on his spear. "I've already taught Yabbo a few new techniques. Do you know why, Victor?" When Victor just shrugged, he said, "Because he doesn't hold back! Are you ready to push yourself today? Are you ready to show me what you can do?"

Victor had heard the speech before, and yet again, he tried to explain, "I'm trying to improve my Berserk and axe skills. You're a good whetstone."

Karnice growled, clearly not pleased by being called a tool. "Go ahead and Berserk, but show me more! Damn it, Victor! We all saw you use a dozen other skills and spells in the arena. Why are you hiding what you can do?"

"My ancestors want me to keep working on this ability." Victor grinned, pleased at his dodge. It sounded like something Thayla might say, and who could argue with the desires of someone's ancestors?

"So. Another beating, hmm?" Karnice's spear ignited with red, baleful Energy, and he beckoned for Victor to approach.

Victor sighed, lifted Lifedrinker, and cast Berserk. As his vision tinted with red and his form expanded in size, his muscles straining against his simple shirt as it hurriedly expanded, he noticed something strange. His mind felt clear, and he saw a message from the System:

*****Congratulations! Your spell, Berserk, has morphed!*****

*****Congratulations! You have learned a new spell: Iron Berserk, Epic.*****

*****Iron Berserk, Epic. Prerequisites: Affinity Rage, One of Several Elder Bloodlines, Epic Will Attribute. You double your strength and speed for a short while, losing yourself in the glory of combat. Your body becomes more resilient, and you benefit from rapid regeneration throughout the duration. With this variant of the Berserk ability, your powerful will and experience with rage have allowed you to retain your sense of self and rational thought, and your body's resilience is peerless. Energy Cost: Minimum 500, scalable. Cooldown: Medium.*****

Victor laughed as he read the words and wiped the message away. He laughed again when a hundred balls of deep purple Energy burst into being around him and rushed toward his chest, flooding his pathways with the influx. Still, even euphoric and amused, he remained berserk. He could feel the rage simmering in his pathways, feel it causing his heart to thud passionately. He could taste the lust for battle and desire to see his enemies ground to paste.

Despite those influences, Victor was still himself. He grinned at Karnice and stepped sideways further into the sand, hefting Lifedrinker before himself, slapping her haft into his other hand, and holding her sideways. On a whim, he cast Inspiring Presence, considering Yabbo his ally and Karnice his foe, and sure enough, the spell surged through his pathways, finding space alongside his rage.

Victor grinned, his vision growing brighter, though still tinted with a haze of pink. Everything seemed more clear—Karnice was angry but intrigued. The way he held his spear made it evident he'd be sweeping it from left to right, attempting to take Victor off balance and strike him with the haft as he charged in. It was so obvious that Victor had to laugh again.

"Quit laughing like a fool and let's dance," Karnice spat, literally chasing the words with a gob of thick saliva into the sand.

Victor didn't need another invitation. He charged, lifting Lifedrinker but only feinting with her. Just as he'd envisioned, Karnice brought his spear around in a sweep, but Victor was ready; he raised his left foot, stomped down on the haft, and then, fast as he could, he brought Lifedrinker down toward Karnice's topmost left shoulder. Victor had been boosting his agility and vitality with Sovereign Will, and with Iron Berserk increasing his speed and Inspiring Presence helping his timing, Lifedrinker cut the air like a thunderbolt.

Karnice, off balance because of Victor's stomp to his spear, surprised by his accuracy and speed, cast some sort of Energy spell, causing his body to shimmer with red heat and flash back over the sand, abandoning his weapon. Still, the furthest edge of Lifedrinker's blade sliced a straight, razor-clean gash in his shoulder as he retreated.

Victor stood atop Karnice's spear, turned his axe so he could see the tiny, bloody smear on her gleaming edge, and lifted his head to the sky and howled. Karnice was furious. He rubbed at his shoulder, smirked at the tiny wound, then spat into the sand again. Then he did what usually took ten or fifteen minutes to provoke—he swelled himself with Energy, created his giant, fiery doppelganger, and proceeded to try to beat the hell out of Victor.

It was different this time, though. Victor was rational and clever—inspired, you might say. More than that, he was exceptionally resilient. Karnice and his double pushed him back, driving him away from his spear, but it wasn't easy, and Victor saw the strain on Karnice's face as he bent to retrieve his weapon. With his spear in hand, his fiery double suddenly sprouted four spears, as usual, and attacked Victor with speed and a vengeance.

The spears bit into him, but unlike before, when they left painful, deep, throbbing holes that ate up Victor's rage to heal, this time, they hardly sank into his flesh. The fire's touch was more a singe than a burn, healing almost instantly. Karnice roared in frustration and redoubled his efforts, summoning spells that Victor hadn't yet seen.

A sheet of fiery Energy blasted out of the sand, engulfing Victor, burning his clothes, and reddening his skin. He rolled out of it, angry at having yet another pair of pants ruined, but otherwise hardly hurt. Karnice looked fit to burst, and Victor felt the full weight of his aura and his prodigious store of Energy when he lifted his spear above his head, screamed, and cast a spell that darkened the sky with red clouds. Suddenly lances of bright, burning, crimson Energy shot down in their hundreds, peppering Victor and the sand around him with tiny magmatic explosions.

Victor dove and flipped, sweeping his axe left and right, and finally, as a few of the spears made contact, driving deep lances of Energy into his flesh, he simply turned toward the citadel and used Titanic Leap. He exploded out of the pit in a shower of sand, flying out of the dark, red cloud's area of influence and landing with a concussive thud on the top steps, some fifty yards away from where they'd been "sparring."

Victor could hear his belt hissing and ticking, and he knew it had eaten some of those fiery lances for him. He patted the hot metal thankfully, then looked at Karnice, standing in the pit, fury writ on his face. Victor lifted Lifedrinker in a mocking salute, then he turned to Yabbo and shouted, "Catch up with you later, Yabbo. I'm done with these lessons."

41

BLOOD FOR BLOOD

Victor sat on the stone railing of the balcony adjoining his and Valla's suite, staring at the strange and beautiful yellow, green, and red striations streaking through the sunset sky. Coloss and the wasteland around it were harsh, but they held deep beauty and mystery that reminded Victor of the size and age of the place. People had been living and dying in these lands for thousands of years, long before even the Warlord had come to power. If you listened to Tes, there used to be many civilizations, rich forests, and fertile valleys filling the tens of thousands of miles swallowed by the wastes.

He wondered how Zaafor had changed so much. Was it all due to war and conflict using vast quantities of Energy? He knew the Degh were downtrodden, but had they been innocent? They had titan blood and had performed strange rituals to gain power, and they'd clearly not all been at peace with each other. Would the Vesh have resorted to the theft of bloodlines and genocide of entire species if they hadn't been desperate? Victor snorted—why was he trying to make excuses for those people? He couldn't deny an interest in the history of this strange world, and he wondered at that; he'd never been able to pay attention in history class before.

Was it a sign of maturity, or just that he was more invested in what was happening there on Zaafor? "Wars, stealing bloodlines, an ancient spirit asking me to save his people—I guess that makes things a little more interesting." Victor stole a glance over his shoulder, something he'd been doing more and more of late. He'd made an enemy of Karnice, one of the most dangerous fighters in Coloss, and he'd spent the last few days dreading what he felt was an inevitable reprisal.

He wasn't fool enough to think Karnice couldn't hurt him; sure, he'd gotten out of their latest little scuffle relatively unscathed, but Karnice hadn't dumped everything he had. He'd started off slow and tried to hector Victor into doing something interesting. If he went all out, using the full extent of what had to be a prodigious Energy pool and high-level spells, Victor wasn't so sure he'd be able to escape as easily.

Valla hadn't looked exactly pleased when she'd heard about his behavior on the practice field, but Tes had been amused. She'd encouraged Victor to keep sparring with Yabbo and to keep using the Warlord's cultivation chamber as much as possible. She seemed to think Karnice would leave him alone as long as the Warlord still expected him to fight in the next tournament. Victor counted on his hand, thinking about that, and came up with two days until Valla's duel and five days until the tournament. He still wasn't sure if he'd stick around—it felt very much like a trap.

"How's the spell coming?" Tes asked from behind him, and he jerked his head around, frowning.

"Damn! How do you do that? I *just* looked at that door, and it was closed."

"I have a lot of tricks. So? The spell?"

"It's getting easier and easier. I think my last level helped a bit—amazing how I don't feel any smarter, but I seem able to concentrate longer and hold more in my head. I can almost write the whole pattern out in one sitting. It takes me a couple of hours, but last night I only had to check for a hint a few times."

"Intelligence is a tricky attribute; it tends to sneak up on you. After a big boost, you'll still feel like yourself, but you'll find you might deliberate more about decisions, acting a bit less impulsively. You might find yourself interested in things you used to simply shrug off. For instance, as I improved my intelligence, I became more and more interested in crafting." She grinned and winked. After Victor stared at her blankly for a moment, she added, "I was trying to hint at . . ."

"Our armor?" Victor turned and hopped off the railing.

"Yes! Valla is waiting inside; let's go in, and I'll show you both what I've crafted." Tes, her face beaming with amused excitement, went inside, and Victor was hot on her heels. Valla was sitting on one of the two couches that faced each other just inside the balcony doors, and Tes walked straight to the long coffee table between them, pushing it away off the plush, decorative rug and onto the dark hardwood. "Making space," she said as Victor sat down next to Valla.

"Tes, how can we ever repay all that . . ."

"Hush, Valla," Tes said, waving a hand dismissively. "I don't do things I don't want to do, at least not on this world. Now, Valla, your armor was much quicker to make; thankfully, you don't tend to grow into the size of a giant at the drop of a hat. That doesn't mean it's not well made or durable, mind you, and if you ever had the opportunity to increase your size, it would weather the abuse quite well.

"Without further ado, I give you"—she held out her hands, and a shimmering blue-scaled hauberk appeared, hanging between them—"a lightning-forged, wyrm-scaled hauberk of alacrity."

Victor sucked in his breath when he took in the armor; it was on another level compared to the one Fough had tried to sell him. Somehow, Tes had cut the scales into uniform shapes, much smaller than one of the elder wyrm's scales they'd harvested. He figured she must have carved five of the little perfectly matched scales for each original. More than that, they shimmered with Energy, their sheen vibrant and colorful, clearly having absorbed some sort of magic during the crafting process.

The scales were sewn into a supple, dark hide, and Victor asked, "What's that leather?"

"Why, flesh from the wyrm you slew. I claimed enough from Cayle for your armor, and she didn't object."

"Ancestors, Tes!" Valla said, standing to lean close to the armor, blowing out a pent-up breath. "It's so beautiful!"

"Watch," Tes said, holding the hauberk aloft with one hand and gently running her hand down the center of it. As her hand passed lightly over the scales, they parted, opening as a jacket might if you unzipped it. "Once you bond with it, you'll be able to do the same." Tes held it open and added, "Come, let's see it on you."

Valla didn't object; she took off her sword belt, resting Midnight Hope on the couch, and then turned to slip each of her arms into the leather-lined sleeves of the hauberk. "It already feels perfect!"

"Wait until you bond with it." Tes grinned, turning Valla and tugging on the high collar of the hauberk, pulling it close around her throat. "Go ahead."

"How'd you get the scales to have that blue sheen?" Victor asked, watching as Valla rested a palm on the scaled hauberk and concentrated. Suddenly it flared with bright white light and shimmered as a wave of crackling electrical Energy ran through it. When the current faded, Valla stood with the biggest smile Victor had ever seen on her face, her eyes moist with tears. The hauberk had closed up and hugged her snuggly, and Victor couldn't deny that it looked perfect for her—it was the most beautiful armor he'd ever seen.

"I've quite a few artificing skills, Victor. It wasn't hard to imbue those scales with a blue luster." As Tes replied, Valla turned and threw her arms around her, pulling her into a tight embrace.

"I love it, Tes!"

"Good!" Tes chuckled. "I used your old enemy Boaegh's workshop. His apprentices were happy to accommodate me after I gave them news of their master's fate. Don't worry," she added, looking over Valla's head to make eye contact with Victor. "I told them he met his doom in an unfortunate run-in with a wyrm when he stepped out of his portal."

"They believed you?" Valla asked, stepping back from Tes's arms. "Why didn't you tell us you'd found his apprentices?"

"I can be quite convincing when I want to. As to why I didn't tell you, there wasn't a need, and you two have had plenty on your minds. Now, tell Victor about your hauberk."

Valla walked over to Victor so he could see it more clearly and said, "It's enchanted to make me faster. It uses air-attuned Energy from my own Core."

"That's right! Of course, it's also incredibly durable, can self-repair, and will shrug off most lightning-based attacks." Tes beamed proudly.

"It's so comfortable!" Valla said, stretching at the waist, rotating her torso, and flexing her arms.

"I'm pleased that you're happy. You've been a wonderful student, and I'm delighted to give you this gift." Tes surprised Victor, and perhaps Valla, by stepping close to her and gently cupping her face in her hands. She leaned down and kissed her on the forehead. Victor knew the two of them had been spending a lot of time together, but he didn't think he'd quite realized how close they'd become. "Well?" Tes asked, stepping back from a moist-eyed Valla. "Victor? Are you ready?"

"Hell yeah," he said, leaning forward on the couch, his hands resting on his knees.

"I cleared this space because I crafted your armor to fit your titanic frame. As you know, that will ensure it doesn't lose any of its strength and potency as you increase your own size." Tes stepped to the edge of the rug between the two couches and gestured with one hand. Victor's armor appeared on the floor with a loud *thud* and a rattle of scales. It was the size of a blanket, and unlike Valla's full hauberk, this garment was a sleeveless vest. Had Tes known that's what he wanted? Victor couldn't remember if he'd described the armor Fough had shown him.

The scales were much larger than on Valla's finely crafted hauberk. Victor guessed they were nearly the full size of the back scales on the elder wyrm, almost four inches from side to side. Still, they were shaped differently, more regular in size—Tes had clearly done some work to refine them. More than that, they were all dark in color, a beautiful blend of near-black that faded to a deep, almost burgundy red at their tips. Just like Valla's armor, Victor could see the lining of his wyrm scale vest was darkly stained, supple wyrm hide.

"Wonderful!" Valla breathed.

Victor grunted, nodding in approval, and approached the enormous garment. "Should I grow to put it on?"

"No, it's fine. Just touch it and bond." Tes was still grinning ear to ear—had been ever since she'd produced Valla's hauberk. Victor found her good mood contagious, and he quickly leaned forward, rested a palm against the warm, hard wyrm scales, and trickled some Energy into the vest. A message appeared in his vision, and he remembered what he'd learned a long time ago from someone he couldn't remember—had it been Gorz? Whoever it was had told him that sometimes an Artificer would create a description for the magical items they made and that the System would incorporate it into its . . . system.

*****Wyrm Scale Vest of Resilience: This artifact, crafted by the master Artisan, Tesia'liveen'ashalah, has been constructed from the hardest, oldest back scales of an ancient wyrm. Each scale has been imbued with a drop of dragon blood and will be nearly impervious to damage from fire or acid. Additionally, the vest will rapidly regenerate if it suffers physical damage. Finally, the vest imbues its wearer with a fraction of its resilience, providing a ten percent boost to vitality.*****

"Holy shit, Tes," Victor breathed, so stunned by the description that he hadn't noticed the vest rapidly contracting to a size he could wear in his present form.

"Put it on, Victor!" Valla said, but Victor had other thoughts. Tes had made him this incredible armor, had put her own blood into it, and he'd done nothing for her. He knew he couldn't train her, couldn't fight for her, couldn't reward her with trophies or wealth, but he knew one thing she wanted.

"Hang on. Tes, do you have an empty, uh, jar or vial or something?"

"Hmm?"

"You know, an empty glass container with a cork or screwtop."

"Well, of course," Tes frowned, a slightly puzzled expression on her face as she perused her storage containers and produced a crystal bottle, maybe big enough to hold four or five ounces. It had a stopper made of a material that appeared too dark and pliable to be cork. Victor wondered if it was some kind of rubber. She passed it his way, and he nodded, walking out to the balcony, leaving his new armor glimmering faintly on the ground.

Valla and Tes gave each other puzzled looks, but as Victor unsnapped Lifedrinker's harness and leaned over to whisper to the blade, Tes's eyes narrowed, and she nodded. "I see," she said, smiling at Valla.

Victor, for his part, lifted Lifedrinker a few inches out of her harness and quickly ran his palm along the top edge of her blade. She sliced into the meat of his palm, and he hardly felt it. He squeezed his fist, pulled the stopper from the vial, and held it under his bleeding palm so the blood dripping from it began to gather inside the crystal container. While he did that, he felt a warm hand grip his shoulder, and Tes came to stand beside him.

"I didn't expect anything in return for the gift I made you."

"You bled for that armor. It's the least I can do." He shrugged.

"I swear to you, Victor, I have no ill intent for you. I'll never let this blood fall into the hands of your enemies."

Victor almost spilled some of his blood onto the polished marble tiles on the balcony when he turned his gaze to her. It was his turn to frown, for he hadn't considered how the blood might be used other than to open a passageway to Earth. "What sorts of things could my enemies do with my blood?"

"Those with the knowledge could make a poison more effective against you. They could use it to create a binding ritual. It could be used to send terrors to you in your sleep. I could list a hundred, nay, a thousand ways a powerful Ritualist could harm you with your own blood."

Victor opened his hand and squeezed his fist again—his cut was already half healed, and the flow had slowed significantly, but the bottle was nearly full. "How much do you need?"

"That's enough." Tes held out a hand, and Victor passed the little crystal vial to her, then handed her the stopper. "Thank you for trusting me, Victor. Though, to be honest, I could have scraped enough blood from the night brute lair to accomplish what I needed." She saw Victor's widened eyes and declared, "But I didn't!"

The crystal vial of his blood winked out of existence, and Victor heaved a deep breath and moved back inside. Valla sat where they'd left her, and it was clear from her expression that she'd figured out what Victor was doing. She pointed at his new armor and said again, "Put it on."

"Right, right." Victor chuckled, unslinging Lifedrinker's harness and resting her on the couch. He leaned over to pick up the wyrm-scale vest and staggered under its unexpected weight. "Sheesh!" He laughed, making a show of struggling to lift it.

"The enchantments added some density to the already heavy scales. Let's not forget that it's reduced in size at the moment!" Tes nudged Valla and added, "I hope it's not too heavy for him."

"Hey, now!" Victor said, then lifted it and started to try to pull it over his head.

"Wait!" Tes laughed. "You can open it like Valla's armor. Run your palm over the center, starting at the neck, and think about what you want."

"Aha!" Victor pulled the armor off his head, followed her instructions, and found that he could feel, like a line of invisible Energy, the seam at the front of the armor. He pulled his hand down over it, and the scale vest parted. "Much better," he said, shrugging one arm and then the other into it. He held his hand over the opening and brought it up, sealing himself into the suddenly light, incredibly comfortable piece of armor.

"Very dashing!" Valla said.

"Indeed!" Tes nodded, walking around him in a slow circle. "Exactly as I imagined it. Fine work, if I do say so myself." Victor turned left and right, stretching his waist to try to look at himself. His vest fit him differently from how Valla's hauberk hugged her. Where hers fell almost to her thighs, clinging tightly to her form, easily resting under her sword belt, his vest was shorter and not as tight around his waist. It rested over his metallic dragon-steel belt, ending just beneath it.

"Did you make it to hang over my belt? Should I take off the belt and put it on over the top, like Valla's?"

"That wouldn't look right, Victor," Valla said.

Tes nodded along with Valla's words, "Your belt is remarkable, but this vest is a hundred times more durable. Let it protect your body, belt, and whatever you might tie to it."

"Did you run out of scales for his arms?" Victor couldn't tell if Valla was trying to tease him.

"No, but he told me about his favorite armor, a chain vest he lost when he was much smaller."

"I like having my arms free." Victor shrugged.

"I'm afraid we need to change topics, you two," Tes said, clearing her throat and moving to stand where she could see them both. A moment later, a popping sounded in his ears, and Victor knew Tes was trying to keep their conversation private. "Please sit down. I have much to discuss with you, and it begins with news of a portal to Fanwath."

"A portal?" Valla echoed, sitting down. Victor followed her lead and sat opposite her on the other couch.

"Yes. I mentioned I was using Boaegh's workshop to make this armor. Well, you know the reason I went to his tower was that I was following a lead, a rumor that he had an apprentice who could work most of the same spells as that rather nefarious wizard." She frowned, then clicked her tongue, and Victor saw an expression he hadn't seen on her face before—anger. Her eyes grew dark, and she hissed, baring surprisingly sharp white teeth.

"What is it?" Valla asked, standing up, reaching for Midnight.

Tes tapped her ear with one delicate-looking, blue-polished nail and gestured at the air around them. "Come, you two. Let's take a walk. I'd like to hear about Valla's practice for her duel and Victor's preparations for the tournament."

Victor nodded and stood. He knew the Warlord had power, more so in his citadel than outside it, but it still chilled his heart to think that Tes was worried about him. "Right," he said, "I've got a few strategies I'd like to ask you about."

"Yes." Valla nodded and added, "Tes, can we talk about what sorts of weapons are typically allowed in duels?"

Tes grinned at them both like a proud teacher and beckoned toward the door. "Wonderful. A bite to eat while we're out?" As Valla and Victor both professed their hunger, the trio hurried out, down the stairs, and toward the exit of the Warlord's citadel. Despite their forced enthusiasm to be out and about, the three of them felt a shadow of dread hanging over them, as though a favorite book had been closed and another, gloomier one had been opened.

42

LOFTY GOALS

Victor walked with Tes and Valla through the evening streets of Coloss until they'd meandered down toward the western wall of the city, far from the Warlord's citadel and his center of power. When Tes led them into a single-story, tan stone building, its doorway hung with colorful beads and the scent of roasting meat thick in the air, Victor's mouth began to water.

The restaurant wasn't sized for Degh, and Victor struggled with the low doorway and crowded dining room. Still, the proprietor—a cheerful, small man with a bald head and pink-red tentacles rather than arms—showed them to a quiet corner where an oversized chair sat snugly against a big wooden table. "I have a Degh friend who comes to drink with me once a week; this is his chair. You should find it roomy."

"Thank you, Gurt," Tes said. "Please bring us your best wine and a sample of your meats; I'm sure my friends are going to love your food."

"Right you are, Miss Tes. I'll get right on it." With that, the little man scurried away, and Victor shifted around the table to sit in the oversized leather chair. It was too large for him, but he'd rather that than one too small. Tes and Valla sat on either side of him, and once again, Victor heard the strange *pop* and knew Tes was making their conversation private.

"He can't pierce my veil this far from his chamber," Tes said.

"You have more news for us, Tes?" Valla asked, leaning forward, arms resting on the tabletop.

"Oh, I do. I do, indeed. First, I've convinced one of Boaegh's apprentices to open a portal to Fanwath. His name is Hark, Geomancer Hark, and he's not a bad fellow. He's been sort of running Boaegh's business in his absence, enchanting objects for a fee and training the more junior apprentices. When I explained Boaegh's fate, Hark was rather pleased, if I know how to read a man's face—and I do, Victor, I do."Tes chuckled and paused as Gurt returned with a carafe of dark wine and three glasses.

"Give me ten minutes or so for the food, please. Anything I can do for you while you wait?"

"No, thank you, Gurt." He shuffled off, and Tes continued, "As I was saying, Hark is pleased to be the new master at Boaegh's little coven. He knew exactly where Boaegh had been, the ritual used to open his original gateway was still in place, and he says he'll happily do me the favor of opening it again."

"That's wonderful, Tes!" Valla said.

"Hell yeah." Victor nodded. "Saves us six tokens!"

Tes chuckled and said, "That's the least of the benefits. More importantly, you're no longer under the Warlord's thumb; your transport away from this place is no longer in his control." Tes lifted the carafe and poured generous servings of wine for each of them. She pushed their glasses toward them and said, "Now the question is, how long should you stay?"

"This Hark, can he create the portal at any time? Now?" Valla sipped at her wine after she asked the question.

"He can." Tes nodded. "There's the matter of your duel in two days' time. I was sure Reis would back out, but she's done something even more interesting. Blue wanted to pass this information to you, but I insisted that we already had plans for the evening; Reis would like to alter the duel to one of skill and with nonlethal consequences—weapon abilities only, three wounds that draw blood."

Valla smiled, the wine staining her teeth a faint shade of purple, and Victor thought he could see the tension flowing out of her shoulders. "Truly?"

"Yes. When Blue approached me with the offer earlier today, I almost burst into laughter; you're a far better swordswoman than she. She thinks to have an advantage because of her rapier—an epic weapon Blue won for her in a very deep dungeon. She doesn't know about Midnight." Tes gestured toward Valla's sword, leaning against the side of her chair. "Nor does she know about your martial background."

"So what's in it for Valla to take the offer?" Victor asked, drinking a gulp of wine, frowning when he saw he'd nearly emptied the delicate glass.

"Excellent question. Reis has sweetened the deal by putting five of the Warlord's tokens on the line."

"And what does she expect me to put into the pot?"

"She expects you to sign a binding contract—should you lose the duel, you will serve in Blue's household for one year."

"Nah, fuck that." Victor snorted, reaching for the carafe to refill his glass. "Let's just bail out right now."

"Victor, I can beat her."

"And then what? We're in a nest of snakes here, Valla. If you win . . ."

"*When* I win, I'll have some more tokens. We can buy something valuable and depart that same day."

Victor frowned, not really agreeing with Valla's assessment. Somehow he didn't think Reis or Blue were stupid. No, in his opinion, they'd have some sort of trick or trap set up, some way to guarantee Valla lost. Rather than press the issue at that moment, though, he changed his angle of attack. "Well, I'm not going to stick around for the tournament. It feels very shady to me. I'm confident the Warlord is devising some scheme to cause me trouble or to get me somehow bound to him. You know what Tes said—he wants my bloodline, Valla. Blue's the Warlord's right-hand man."

"So you think there will be foul play at my duel?" Valla frowned.

"Undoubtedly," Tes agreed, drinking her wine. They all sat in silence for a few moments, and then their conversation was further put on hold when Gurt approached their table with a huge wooden platter. Moist, smoked, roasted, and grilled meats were sliced and piled high on one side, and two large wooden bowls, one filled with a mixture of beans and herbs and the other with sticky seasoned rice, occupied the rest of the space. Gurt placed them on their table, and one of his servers brought over wide, shallow bowls and silverware for the three of them.

"Enjoy!" Gurt said, grinning and nodding as though he knew they would. If so, he was right. Victor dug into the meat, and it reminded him a great deal of something he might find at a barbecue restaurant back on Earth. The beans were tangy with a bit of spiciness, and when he added them to the rice, mixed in some of the cut meats, and began to wolf everything down, Valla and Tes weren't far behind.

"This is good stuff, Tes," Victor said around a bite, leaning forward over the too-small table from the too-large chair. He didn't care about his comfort, though; the pleasure in his mouth and the warm glow in his stomach more than made up for it.

"It is good, but wouldn't a cold ale go with it better than this wine?" Valla asked.

"Hush." Tes chuckled. "I like wine." Victor watched her chew a bite of meat, licking the salty grease from her lips and then chasing it with a drink from her wine glass. She caught him watching and narrowed her eyes, offering him a half smile as she cleared her throat and said, "Valla, I've gathered some texts for you to take home to your family. They're a collection of some of the types of books and tomes I suggested you and Victor should gather. I know you've both been busy training these last weeks, and I wanted to offer them to you as a gift."

"Tes, you've already given me so much . . ."

"True! But this is nothing; just a little time spent exploring old shops and family libraries, which I rather enjoy anyway. By the way, if Black asks about some missing books, you don't know anything about it." She laughed, winking at Valla. "I only ask one thing in return."

"Oh?" Valla asked, wiping her mouth with a napkin.

"Yes. I'd like you to go through with the duel, even though it's not the smartest move." She glanced at Victor, ducking her head apologetically.

"Why, Tes?" he asked.

"Because I've spied some of the preparations Blue is making for, in his opinion, the inevitability of you joining his household. I've seen some strange deliveries make their way to his estate, and I'm curious about what else he intends to do. This is rather valuable for my research, you see; if they intend to try to steal some part of your heritage, I might learn a great deal from watching their actions."

"C'mon, Tes," Victor said. "We're not going to have you using Valla as bait."

"No. Allow me to observe them for another day or two, and I promise you that, I will thwart whatever they intend to do to ensure Valla's loss. She'll never have to go to his estate."

"If you want me to do this, then I will," Valla said, setting her mouth into a firm line and nodding her head.

"I don't like it," Victor growled.

"Do you trust me?" Tes asked, and it was clear the question was for both of them.

"I do," Valla said.

Victor frowned, glancing down at the beautiful scale armor he wore, made from Tes's own blood and hard work. He thought of how she'd guided him out on the monster hunt and helped him to understand so much of his potential. Rather than answer her immediately, though, he said, "Tes, I know you don't want much from us—not right now. What about in the long term? I feel like you're planning something . . ."

"Is that your answer? When I ask a simple question of trust, you frown and glower and then ask me what my plans are for you. I thought I'd earned more respect than that." Tes didn't look angry, she didn't yell, she didn't even raise her voice, but she stood from the table and said, "I need some air." Then she turned and walked through the restaurant, out the rear door, where, presumably, Gurt offered outside dining.

"Sheesh," Victor sighed, blowing out a breath.

"You don't trust her? After everything she's done? She's spent months of her life with us, and it's cost her far more than she's gained. You heard what she said about breaking her oath! She'll likely be in some trouble when she heads home . . ."

"Easy, Valla. Chill." Victor held up a hand. "I didn't think my question was going to piss her off, and yeah, if she'd given me a chance, I would have come around to the point that I do trust her. I guess I'm just used to her being a lot more easygoing than that!" He jerked his thumb toward the balcony.

"I should go and talk to her." Valla started to slide her chair back, but Victor stood up first.

"Wait! This is my fault. Let me speak to her." Victor tried to look reassuringly into Valla's troubled eyes, but she continued to scowl toward the patio where Tes had gone. He sighed and carefully wended his way through the tables and ducked out through the balcony doors, straightening in the cool evening air, thick with the scent of cloying night blooms. A few people were having dinner on the cobbled patio, and a path led away from it, down through a flowering garden, so he walked that way.

Energy lamps here and there shed diffuse light on the garden path, and the moon, strange and green-tinted, hung nearly full in the sky, so he could see quite well as he followed the little pathway toward the sound of a tinkling fountain. When he came around the corner and saw Tes standing in the moonlight, looking into a little pond where he could hear fish playing in the clear water, he froze for a second, not for the first time struck dumb by her beauty. She had an effortless grace, and there in the moonlight, she seemed otherworldly to him.

He shook his head, remembering she was the very definition of otherworldly. "Hey," he said, clearly trying to impress with his vernacular.

Tes looked at him and frowned. "I could hear you coming. I almost departed."

"Why'd my question piss you off so much?" Victor asked, getting right to the point, still not really sure why she'd been so short-tempered.

"Half the reason I came out here is that I was surprised at my own vehemence. I'm not sure why, but it hurt when I saw I hadn't earned your immediate trust. I've sacrificed much, you know, choosing to help you avoid the Warlord's clutches. My . . . organization is going to put me under review, at the very least. I'll likely have to return to journeyman status and follow a master to the next world I study." She sighed, frowned, and rubbed her brow as though trying to soothe a headache.

"I'm . . ."

"I know that doesn't sound like such a big problem, especially when your very lives are on the line, and that's why I chose to help. I can sacrifice a few decades of freedom to see you and Valla live . . ."

"Decades?" Victor blurted.

She waved a hand as though dismissing the idea. "If I choose to stay with them. It's a prestigious guild, but there are others. My uncle, Yek'nakkara'ma'shohon, thinks I waste my time with them. Perhaps he's correct." When she said her uncle's name, the word rolled out of her throat like a growl, and Victor had to give her a double take, making sure she hadn't assumed her dragon form.

"Your uncle?"

"Yes, Victor. Dragons have families, too." She sighed and then pointed at the pond. "I like that one, the white one with the orange and blue spots."

Victor stepped closer to her so he could look more closely into the water, and then he saw the fish she'd described. He watched it flitting among the colorful decorative rocks and crystals at the bottom of the clear pool, and when it passed close to another fish, one with black and yellow scales, he said, "That's a pretty one."

"Aye," she sighed. "They all are, aren't they? In their own way." Tes looked up from her study of the pond and stared at Victor, and he found it a little unnerving that her expression didn't change when she went from admiring the fish to looking at his face. "I can see the look on your face, Victor, and no, you aren't just another pretty fish for me to watch. I see so much in you. I wish . . ." She sighed and shook her head, looking away.

"You wish?" Victor pressed.

"I wish I weren't ten times your age and so far beyond your . . . potency. It's not right to have the feelings I have." She looked away, and the words were so softly spoken that he doubted he'd have heard them if not for his exceptional hearing and the quiet of the little garden.

"Really, Tes?" Victor said, his turn to speak softly. "I mean, I have a massive crush on you, but I thought that was a hopeless cause." His lips turned up as he spoke, and he allowed a little humor into his voice.

"Is my heart something you'd mock?" Tes asked, jerking her head back toward him.

"I'm not mocking you." Victor chuckled. "I'm trying to make you feel better. I'm sorry, but I'm a clown that way—I try to relieve tension by teasing others or making fun of myself. Tes, I'm hopeless when it comes to you. You're so damn beautiful and smart and capable. I wish I could be a match for you, but you don't want someone you have to babysit following you around like that. Wouldn't you get bored and start to resent me after you had to hold my hand for the ten thousandth time?"

She turned to face him more directly and reached out one of her hands to rest her palm on his chest. It was warm, and it made his skin tingle and awoke a desire that he'd held down for the very reasons he'd just listed—Victor didn't want to be babysat by the woman he was attracted to. Still, the electricity in her touch was undeniable, and it stung a little when she said, "You're right, Victor."

She gently moved her hand sideways until it rested over his heart, and she stood there for a moment as though memorizing the feel of its beat. "You're right, but let's remember this feeling, because if I'm in control of my fate at all, we will meet again, and I have great confidence that you'll continue to surprise everyone with your accomplishments."

"Anyway," Victor said, his voice husky and thick with emotion, "the answer is yes."

"Yes?" Tes looked confused.

"Yes, I trust you."

That got a smile out of her, and she nodded, her blonde curls bouncing with the movement. "Good! You should!" She laughed, then, giving his chest one more pat with her hand, she turned and said, "Let's go join Valla. I care about her a lot, you know. I wouldn't ask her to duel that woman if I weren't going to be there to watch over her."

"I get it, Tes." He followed her back through the garden, breathing in the rich, sweet air and wondering about his feelings for the strange, incredible woman. He'd badly wanted to kiss her back by the fish pond but knew he wasn't ready for that; she was brilliant and quick-witted, clever and funny. She was kind and always ready to help others. He felt a certain way when he was with her; it was as if some of her confidence and good intentions brushed off on him, making him better. He knew he'd forever be comparing other women to her and coming up short.

Those thoughts and feelings in his mind while they walked, he thought about how he'd find his way back to Tes someday. He wondered how much he'd need to change for her to take him seriously. Would it be enough to conquer the Untamed Marches? Would he need to explore other worlds? Conquer other lands? How many dungeons would he have to delve into and plunder? When he'd returned to Zaafor and crushed the Warlord, would that be enough? He grinned, shaking his head at himself, amused that nothing sounded too daunting. As far as he was concerned, it was good to have goals, and getting a kiss or more from Tes was definitely a worthy goal.

43

❦

DUEL

Victor sat on the couch in the parlor where Blue's staff had directed him, and he watched Tes quietly as she helped Valla prepare for the duel that was due to start in the next few minutes. Valla stood, back straight, eyes closed, Midnight Hope held before her with its—her—point resting on the carpet. She wore one of her Legion uniform shirts, the ones she usually wore under her half-coat uniform blazers. The shirt was white, perfectly form-fitting, with a high collar and not a single wrinkle to be seen. Her black pants were trim, close-fitting, and tucked into knee-high black boots polished to a mirror sheen.

As always, Valla's hair was perfectly coiffed, held close to her scalp with silver barrettes. Victor thought she looked exceptionally pretty and vulnerable, and he began to worry in earnest for her safety. Objectively, he knew there was nothing new that should be making him worry more; he'd just seen her standing there, face serene, eyes closed, concentrating as she listened to Tes, and some instinct in him wanted to protect her. Still, he wished he were the one getting ready to fight; how hard it was to watch someone else do it for a change!

The announcement had gone out the day before that the duel would be one of weapon skill alone. Each combatant was allowed her chosen tool of battle but no armor. The rules were simple; the first to yield or be struck three blows that drew blood would lose. Should one of those blows prove fatal, that was the nature of combat—there was always some risk. Tes was confident in

Valla, though, and she said she'd figure out what Blue was up to, why he was sure Reis would win. She hadn't gone into details, but she'd insisted to Victor and Valla the night before that she was sure she could counter anything they might do to interfere.

Victor had complained that a year of servitude was worth far more than five measly tokens. Tes had agreed but pointed out that Blue was acting as though Reis was giving Valla a gift by changing the terms of combat; without using Energy-based spells, much of her higher-level advantage went away. Victor had seen the wisdom in going along with the change, even with the disparity in wagers, especially when Valla insisted she wanted to fight.

"Do you see it? Can you picture how you're going to strike her? She'll be fast, and that sword of hers is meant for dueling, but she doesn't know you're a Sword Dancer. She doesn't know about Midnight and your epic-level skill. You'll have a counter for all her strikes; just believe in yourself." Tes had her hands on Valla's shoulders, gently squeezing them and speaking softly into her ear, and Victor knew that if he hadn't been included in her privacy spell, he wouldn't be able to hear what she said.

"I'm ready, Tes." Valla nodded.

"Good. I want you to take this now; I'm not sure how things will play out over the next few days, and I don't want to forget." Tes reached over to her left hand and began to twist a tiny, silvery ring off her pinky. Victor could have sworn her fingers hadn't had any jewelry on them, but there it was. She handed Valla the ring and said, "The books, scrolls, and tomes I promised you. If you and Victor are successful in your conquest back home, these will help you build a truly remarkable society."

"Tes, I . . ." Valla took the ring, slipped it onto her own pinky, and then turned to hug Tes, putting her chin on her shoulder. "Thank you."

"You're welcome. Now, focus. You're going to be . . ."

"It's time," a blue-liveried servant announced, poking his head through the door. "They want her out front; everyone's gathered on the carriage lane."

"We'll be right behind you, Valla," Tes said.

"Kick her ass," Victor added, standing up. He walked over to Valla and, because he'd always appreciated simple gestures before a fight, he held out his fist and grinned as Valla bumped his knuckles with hers.

"This way," the servant badgered.

"Right. See you soon," Valla said, offering Victor a bright smile. As he nodded his encouragement, she hefted Midnight Hope, resting the dark star-speckled blade on her shoulder, and followed the servant out the door.

"I have something for you as well, Victor," Tes said.

"Huh? You already gave me my armor; it's enough. C'mon, this day is about Valla."

"There's likely to be a bit of an upheaval around here when Valla wins, Victor. Let me give you this; I've been holding it for a while." Tes held out her hand, and a gallon-sized jar appeared in it. It was dark, and Victor thought the glass was tinted, but then he realized the contents were black, and the jar was full to the brim, the contents held in place by a rune-etched, silvery lid.

"What is it?" he asked, reaching out to receive the gift. As Tes set the jar in his hands, he felt it—deep, powerful Energy and a taste of something familiar, a lick of Energy that sang to his fear attunement.

"This is the night brute prince's heart. Take it, Victor; hold onto it until you've gained more strength; eat your ancient wyrm heart before consuming this one."

"Oh shit," Victor said, hefting the jar, savoring the depth of its power. "I didn't know you got this . . ."

"I wasn't sure I'd give it to you back then. Now I am. Come, put that away, and let's go watch our friend." Tes turned and walked out the door, and Victor followed after her after, tucking the heart away with his others. They'd only walked a few yards down the hallway when Tes paused, though, and Victor saw her sniffing the air. She said, "I don't like the Energy in the air, Victor. Something is afoot, perhaps more than I bargained for. Should we grow separated, do you know where to find Boaegh's tower?"

"No, you never told us . . ."

"Right," Tes sighed, shaking her head. "It's near the southwestern corner of the city. An open-air bazaar borders it on one side and a large abattoir on the other. It's squat, only three stories high, with yellow pennants hanging from the grasping claws of ugly, pot-bellied stone gargoyles. You'll find it easily. Should the time arise when you must flee this city, tell Geomancer Hark that his debt will be wiped clean if he opens the portal for you."

"Debt? I thought he was happy to help . . ."

"Not now, Victor. Do you understand my directions?"

"Yeah, I get it."

"Good, let's make haste now." Tes continued down the corridor, and Victor, somewhat at a loss, followed her.

Blue's place was a little different in the early morning hours than during a nighttime party. Still, everything was still blue, and Victor found himself starting to hate the color as he associated it with the smug War Captain. "Nah, that's not right," he grunted, contemplating Valla and her pale blue skin. He liked the color just fine; it was the asshole that had to put so much of it everywhere that he didn't like.

When they stepped outside the front door, a crowd confronted them; hundreds of Vesh nobles were present to watch the spectacle, all gathered on the big, curving, cobbled drive that ran in a loop at the front of Blue's estate. In the center of the loop, as though built for just such an event, was a circular patch of grass about twenty yards in diameter. Valla stood to the right side of the circle of grass, and her opponent, Reis, stood on the other.

Reis was six inches or so taller than Valla, and she held her glittering, black-scaled wings partially open, making her seem like more than a match for Valla; her physical presence was formidable compared to the neat, lithe figure Valla cut, once again leaning on the pommel of Midnight Hope, the glittering, dark blade's point in the grass. Reis, by comparison, whipped her long, flickering red rapier left and right, the weapon hissing through the air, leaving a trail of glittering sparks in its wake.

Valla's challenger wore a silky black jumper that clung to the pale flesh of her torso and legs while leaving her slender, muscular arms free. She'd painted her face with sharp, contrasting lines of black and white makeup that reminded Victor of images he'd seen of ancient Celtic warriors. Tes grasped his wrist and pulled him close to the circle, effortlessly pushing past much larger Vesh, who seemed suddenly eager to move out of her way as she lightly touched their shoulders. When they took a position at the edge of the circle of grass, Tes frowned and said, "Something feels off."

"What?" Victor asked, suddenly quite concerned. Tes held up her hand, though, frowning as she concentrated.

"Here we are!" Blue's voice boomed out from the far side of the ring. He stepped forward onto the grass, and Victor saw that he'd dressed to impress in a fine blue suit, complete with an absurd-looking tophat designed to allow his black horns to poke through the brim. Still, Blue looked as though he was rather impressed with himself and his style, and he turned and bowed at the waist so deeply that his fingers brushed the grass in a flourish. The object of his obeisance was the Warlord who stood on the edge of the grass almost directly opposite Tes. "Thank you for attending this little affair, Warlord. You grace my estate with your presence."

"By all means, War Captain Blue. How could I not attend when the Lady Tes foresaw such a thing?"

Tes's gaze had gone distant, but she refocused on reality at the mention of her name. She nodded to the Warlord coquettishly and performed a slight curtsy, lifting her pale red skirts. Blue chuckled and cleared his throat. "Wonderful. We have quite a spectacle in store today! For anyone who lives with their head in the sands of the waste and doesn't know the stakes—Lady Reis has put up five Coloss prize tokens, and *Captain* Valla has agreed to indenture herself to me, Blue, for a year, should she lose." Victor didn't appreciate how Blue sneered when he said "Captain."

"Three blood strikes or a yield is what we're looking for. No armor or magical devices are allowed. Healing potions will signal your intent to yield. No one outside the match may interfere. Does anyone have a question or objection?" Blue spoke in a booming voice and looked around the circle, and when his eyes fell on Victor, he tilted his long black horns toward him and grinned, exposing bright white canines. Victor felt the heat in his Core begin to fan to life as that taunting expression stirred his rage. He frowned, though, crossing his arms over his chest, and simply stared. It was Blue who looked away first.

"I'll take this silence as a sign that we're all ready for things to begin!" Blue howled, and it was true; the crowd was so quiet that Victor could hear their hushed breaths of anticipation. At Blue's declaration, though, some scattered applause and a few hoots broke out, and the War Captain's smile widened. He stepped back to the edge of the circle of grass and said, "Ladies, you may commence."

Valla glided onto the grass, Midnight Hope held in a high, aggressive guard, and Reis stepped forward lightly, circling Valla, exceptionally light on her feet. Victor nodded, confident as he watched Valla move; she was a dancer, a gymnast, a woman of exceptional skill with that sword, and it showed—anyone who'd done any fighting or made a practice of watching others do so would know that she outclassed Reis.

As they circled each other, though, Victor was surprised not to see confident determination on Valla's face. She didn't have that ready, severe expression she always wore when they sparred. Her eyes were wide, and lines of stress were evident on her brow. "Something's wrong," he growled.

"Yes," Tes said, but she reached out a hand to grasp his wrist, and it felt like a band of iron, reminding him of the time she'd restrained him at Blue's dinner. Victor didn't have time to object before the first explosive interchange between the two duelists rang through the yard. Reis darted forward, lifting slightly off the ground as she clapped her wings, and she feinted and jabbed with her rapier in a series of rapid blows. Valla batted them aside, dodging like a feather before a breeze, sliding over the grass, and when they parted, not one of Reis's blows had landed.

Reis frowned, growling and circling, and Valla did the same. Victor knew Valla, knew she'd be taking Reis's measure, deciding how best to slip her guard and land a blow, but when he looked at her, his heart began to hammer in his chest. Valla's pale skin had lost a shade of blue, and a sheen of sweat stood out on her forehead and cheeks; her breaths looked ragged and forced. Again Victor growled, "Something's fucking wrong, Tes."

In response, Tes squeezed his wrist, but he saw that her eyes were closed and her brow was drawn sharply down; she was concentrating on something. At the sound of another clash of metal on metal, Victor jerked his gaze back to the duel and saw the two women exchange a flurry of blows and parries, and to his eye, one well-experienced watching Valla, she looked sluggish. When the two women parted this time, a red bloom of blood was spreading on Valla's white shirt, just above her left breast.

"One for the Lady Reis!" Blue crowed.

Valla, no longer a picture of perfect grace, tried to circle Reis, but her legs looked leaden, and her breaths were coming in ragged gasps, her face sheeting with sweat. Victor took in a breath, ready to roar a protest, but again, Tes squeezed his wrist, and this time she muttered, "One moment, Victor. I almost have it."

Victor jerked his gaze back to the fight in time to see Reis dart forward, quick and nimble, and then Valla gasped in pain as that bright, sparking rapier tore through the air and pierced the top of her thigh. Reis barked a savage, short laugh and backpedaled long before Valla could sluggishly cleave downward with Midnight Hope.

"Two for Reis!" Blue announced, lifting his arms, signaling the crowd to cheer. Most of them did, but Victor wasn't the only one who could see something was wrong. Some muttering sounded among the observers, and Blue frowned. Victor could see he was debating whether he should exhort them to silence after he'd just encouraged them to cheer.

Suddenly Tes released Victor's wrist, and she strode into the circle. Her voice rang out, "A moment, dear War Captain Blue. I fear there's been a mistake." Valla stood to Tes's left and leaned forward, resting her hands on her legs—the front of her white shirt was entirely red now, and Victor knew her leg was bleeding just as severely.

Reis danced from side to side on the other side of Tes and shrieked with blood lust, "What's this? Forfeit!"

"What is this indeed, Lady Tes? Do you seek to intervene for your young companion?" Blue asked, stepping into the circle. "Warlord, don't you think this is grounds for forfeiture?"

"Perhaps so. What's the matter, Lady Tes?" The Warlord kept his position on the edge of the circle, a look of slight amusement in his eyes.

"Oh, I think when you see the issue, you might agree to allow Captain Valla to continue with the duel. Here, observe, Warlord and War *Captain*." This time it was Tes's turn to sneer as she spat the honorific. She held her hand out over the center of the grassy circle, and, with a slight rumble and the squelch of damp soil and grass, a long, rune-carved, circular rod of stone lifted from the ground.

"Isn't this strange?" she asked, a savage grin on her face. She lifted the yard-long stone rod and held it over her head. "Can you feel it now?" She strode forward, closer to the Warlord and War Captain, holding the stone rod over her head as though it were a broomstick. "How odd to find a siphoning stone here, one meant to drain away air- and earth-attuned Energies. Why, what a strange coincidence—the very affinities within Captain Valla's Core."

"What's this?" the Warlord asked, staring pointedly at Blue.

"I have no idea! A scandal! Lady Tes, did you place that there to discredit me?"

Tes snorted, and suddenly the rod winked out of existence, presumably sent into one of Tes's storage devices. Valla immediately sighed with relief and began to breathe more regularly. "Oh no, War Captain. I wouldn't do such a thing, and the Warlord knows it. It's no matter, though. I'm sure Captain Valla will understand that this must be a mistake or an act of sabotage by some disgruntled lackey of yours. Give her a moment to catch her wind, and she'll continue the duel."

"Nonsense," the Warlord said. "Surely we should reschedule; the Captain has two wounds already."

"I'll be fine," Valla said, taking a slow, steady breath through her nose and out through her mouth and then spitting a wad of bloody saliva into the grass.

The crowd had gone quiet at first when Tes pulled the rod from the damp soil, but now people were muttering and cursing, and the loud buzz of conversations began to make it difficult to hear anyone speaking other than Tes. A tall, lanky woman with golden scales on her arms and forehead shouted, "She should get a healing draught!"

"What?" Reis howled. "I didn't know about that rod! I scored my blows with fair skill!"

Tes held up her hand and turned in a slow circle, making eye contact with many people in the crowd. Slowly the buzz of outrage diminished, and when things were quiet again, she looked to Valla and said, "Well, Captain? Do you require healing?"

"No." Valla stood and whipped Midnight Hope in a complicated pattern, and her blade sang in the air. "Let's finish this."

"I'm of the opinion that Reis should have to forfeit," the Warlord said. He looked long and hard at Blue, and Victor saw something pass between them as though Blue were outraged. Had the Warlord been in on this scam of a fight? Was he throwing Blue under the bus, so to speak? Perhaps even the Warlord was worried about public perception. He turned away from Blue to Valla and said, "Are you certain you wish to continue? I will award you the prize right now if you wish."

"I'm sure," Valla growled, her eyes locked on Reis's face. The crowd cheered, and Victor felt a hot lance of pride in his chest. In his mind, at that moment, Valla was truly amazing—beautiful and brave with an undauntable spirit.

Tes backed out of the circle and said, "You heard her. Restart the fight at your discretion, dear Blue."

As Valla and Reis squared off again, Blue bellowed, "Begin!" The crowd fell silent again, and then Valla charged. Reis tried to meet her head-on, but Valla was back to her usual, graceful, brilliant self. She slapped Reis's rapier aside, and in a combination that was difficult to track, Victor saw her work Midnight Hope in a series of feints, slashes, and thrusts. Reis valiantly whipped her blade in response, trying to parry, dodge and duck Valla's quick blows.

As Victor struggled to track the sword strokes, a scream cut through the clash of metal, and Valla backed away from Reis, a grim smile spreading her lips. The tall, black-clad woman fell to the grass, writhing in agony, one of her glittering, scaled wings twitching in the grass, severed from her body. "I yield!" Reis moaned, desperately scrabbling at the grass where she fumbled a healing draught she'd summoned from a storage container.

44

BEST LAID PLANS

et up, you wretch!" Blue shrieked at Reis, stepping forward onto the grass. His face was livid with fury, and spittle flecked his lips. Valla ignored him, as did the crowd of Vesh—most of them were applauding her by now, some even cheering in the face of Blue's outrage. Valla whipped her sword with such snapping force that Reis's blood splattered off the blade into the grass. She smoothly sheathed the dark star-speckled blade and strode over the grass toward Tes and Victor, outwardly unbothered by the wounds she'd earlier suffered.

"Hell yes, Valla!" Victor cheered, reaching out to grasp her shoulder. "That was fast! I've never seen you move quite like that."

"Rage is a good motivator," Valla growled. "I learned from the best," she added, giving him a wink.

"Good"—Tes chuckled—"but we should make haste from here. Too much heat is in the air." Victor nodded and, still holding Valla's shoulder, began to guide her back through the crowd, but the Warlord's voice cut through the noise, and the buzzing crowd grew still at his words.

"Captain Valla, hold, please!"

Tes stiffened but stopped moving and turned back to the grass circle. Victor noted how the crowd that had begun to fill in around them gave way, revealing the Warlord standing over the still sobbing Reis. He grinned when Valla turned his way and then gestured to Reis and her healed but still short-ened wing. "I believe Lady Reis owes you something."

"The Captain can collect another time," Tes said and started to move again.

"Tut, Lady Tes. Now's the time, I think." The Warlord nudged Reis's shoulder with the toe of his shiny black boot. "Come, Reis, pull forth your wager."

"Yes, Warlord," Reis said through swollen red lips. Victor hadn't gotten a good look at her after Valla's winning blow, but he could now see the woman hadn't been ready to suffer such an injury; her eyes were bloodshot and her face streaked with tears. Seeing her like that, he had to wonder if she'd ever been prepared to conduct a fair fight—had Blue set this whole thing in motion from the start?

Valla turned, brushed past him, and started back to the green. Meanwhile, Reis held out her palm, and a pile of silvery tokens appeared in it. "Good; a debt well settled," the Warlord said, his words laced with patronizing barbs. Valla walked forward, and Victor could see Blue at the far edge of the circle, red-faced, furious, hands clenching and unclenching. The Warlord, meanwhile, looked amused, watching Valla approach with sharp eyes beneath white-feathered brows. Something tickled in Victor's gut, warning him much as a hound might sense pending misconduct in a stranger. Something wasn't right.

He felt Tes pushing past him through the crowd, following after Valla. Victor, too, started forward, but the Vesh nobles seemed to contract in front of him, making progress difficult. Still, Victor was head and shoulders taller than most of them, and he could see Valla stoop to scoop the tokens from Reis's palm. As she straightened, though, the Warlord rested a hand on her shoulder, his black-taloned, long fingers grasping the bloodstained fabric of her shirt.

"A moment, Captain Valla. I believe I'd enjoy it if you joined *my* Captains and me for brunch. Surely that's not too much to ask? A meal with the champion? I'd love to hear more about your sword skills and where you learned such feats of martial prowess."

"Yes! A lovely idea!" Blue said, his glower suddenly replaced by cheerful enthusiasm. Victor wanted to push through the crowd and knock that stupid blue hat off his head. Instead, he let go of his aura, something he hadn't fully done since returning to Coloss. The people around him instantly began to press outward. Some of them probably realized what they were doing, but Victor could tell it was involuntary for many. These sycophantic noble Vesh were mostly mid-tier, and their wills, their own auras, were like tide pools to the ocean of Victor's rage.

As a wide passage through the crowd opened and he started forward, he was surprised to see that Tes was already striding onto the grass. "I'm sorry, dear Warlord, but I've made plans with my young friend here. Perhaps she could join you later?"

"Oh?" the Warlord said, though his voice was difficult for Victor to hear over the suddenly outraged, murmuring crowd that had grown aware of the source of its discomfort. A few insults were hurled his way, though no one came forward to impose on him physically, and soon Victor was on the grass, and he could hear the rest of the Warlord's statement. "I'm sorry, Tes, but you'll need to reschedule. Yes, I think I'm quite in the mood for brunch, and my Captains and I are eager to get better acquainted with this fierce young woman."

"Yes, we are, Warlord," Blue said, stepping forward.

"I don't even see your other Captains, Warlord. I'm surprised they didn't attend the duel."

"Oh, they're about. Never fear." Victor's rage intensified at the smug words, and he began to let his fury seep out of his Core and into his pathways. It was all too easy as he watched Valla strain against the taloned grip of the tall, white-winged Warlord.

"Well then, since I already had plans with Captain Valla, perhaps I'll join you," Tes pressed, now only five feet or so from the two. Victor noticed that Reis had been scrabbling over the grass and was now near the edge of the crowd, clutching her dismembered wing in her lap.

"Tes, tut. How impolite, inviting yourself to a private affair."

"I'll have to insist; otherwise, Captain Valla and I will be departing."

Suddenly the Warlord's demeanor changed; his faux humor melted away, and his eyes grew dark and charged with metallic, glimmering Energy. He seemed to grow in stature, though physically, he remained the same size. Still, Victor suddenly felt as though the Warlord towered over him, over everyone, and his authority came crashing down as he boomed, "You dare? You dare to think you can insist on anything? In *my city*? On *my world*? Begone, witch! I have matters to attend!" Suddenly Valla screamed as the Warlord tightened his grip and cracked open his wings.

Victor knew what was coming—he'd seen how fast the Warlord could fly. He was about to launch himself into the air with Valla in tow, and Victor would never see her again. He wanted to go berserk, wanted to leap at the Warlord and break his arm, rip it off, even smash him to bits with the stump. He couldn't, though. He could barely move under the weight of the Warlord's aura. He growled and furiously tried to rally his will, lifting his head to watch, which was more than most of the Vesh could manage—they'd all fallen to their knees or onto their bellies, completely prostrate before the Warlord's show of strength.

Not Tes, though. Tes stood before the Warlord's fury, her pale red skirts billowing behind her, her soft blonde curls bouncing before his outburst, but her face serene and unbothered. As the Warlord's wings unfurled, but before he could snap them down and launch into the air, Tes twirled her fingers, and a coil of electricity, much like a crackling lasso, snapped through the air to wrap itself around Valla. With a flick of her wrist, Tes yanked Valla free of the Warlord's talon, but not without paying a toll of flesh and blood—the Warlord's grasping fingers left long, deep furrows in Valla's skin, and she screamed as the rope of lightning pulled her away.

"You dare!" the Warlord roared.

"I do," Tes replied, still calm. She propelled Valla into Victor's arms and said, "You know where to go." Then she shifted to the left, like a flickering hologram, as the Warlord cleaved a mighty silver blade into the grass where she'd been standing. He screamed his outrage, a look of disbelief on his face as the gleaming, straight-edged, seven-foot blade tore a smoldering trench into the grass. Again, his furious aura pulsed forth, and the Vesh, even Blue, were driven further into obeisance, faces pressed to the ground. Valla moaned and collapsed, but Victor struggled against the wave of force and held her up, stumbling backward toward Blue's villa.

Tes was like a mighty oak standing tall in the face of hurricane-force winds, and she sidestepped to put herself between the Warlord and Victor again. "Go," she said, and though her voice was calm, Victor could feel the urgency in the command. Somehow she was absorbing the ferocity of the Warlord's aura, keeping most of it from Victor and, as if by instinct, he cast Berserk. When the rage filled his vision and flooded his mind and pathways, when the haughty fury of his ancestors sang in his blood, he straightened enough to lift Valla into his arms, then turned and stumbled away, propelled by a deep instinct to flee that terrible aura.

Tes wasn't pleased. Everything had gone sideways, and now she was well and truly in over her head. This Warlord, the leader of the greatest nation in this world, wanted to kill her. She'd utterly blown her cover, completely exposed herself, and for what? To save a diminutive woman from a backwater world? How many innocents had she seen slain during her travels around Zaafor?

How many had she watched kill each other in their arena? Why was she ruining her reputation to help these two hopelessly trouble-prone strangers?

"Because they're not strangers," she muttered as she dodged the Warlord's blade yet again. It was true; she had to admit, she'd grown fond of them both. Perhaps taking on a mentor's role with them had been a mistake; she felt responsible for them now. She laughed at the thought—would Yek'nakkara'ma'shohon believe it? His niece's maternal instincts had come to life at last! Yes, she certainly felt a bond with Valla, something she'd never managed with another pupil. Perhaps that was because Tes had refused to take on any of her younger cousins as apprentices. Perhaps that was because they were scheming, power-hungry little bitches.

The Warlord was working himself into a frenzy, and Tes knew she'd need to try to defuse the situation before he began to call on his deeper powers. If she didn't, she might not be able to escape his fury without harming him. "Warlord, calm yourself," she said, Surge Stepping away from his blade again. "I can pay recompense for what you've lost today."

"What I've lost? You dare? I've lost nothing! Nothing other than my temper, but your blood will satisfy that!" Suddenly the Warlord's aura flared again, and this time Tes could feel him touching the rather impressive pool of Energy at his Core. She pulled forth more of her own Energy as a tremendous wave of steel-laced force rolled out of the Warlord, accompanied by a thunderous "Kiai!"

As he shouted, he'd swung his great, legendary sword, Scale Song, in an arc, and a wave of force, cutting just like the edge of his sword, poured forth. It would have bisected Tes if not for her shield of Energy. Still, the concussion of the blow, accompanied by the flare of lightning from her barrier, devastated many of the unwilling spectators lying prone in the nearby grass. Tes almost found humor in the thought that many openings in the Vesh noble lines of succession would need to be filled.

The Warlord's cutting wave of force didn't discriminate—several Vesh were cleaved in two, their innards watering the green grass. Still more were burned and blasted by the shockwave of electricity that rolled away from Tes's shield. "Look what you've done!" Tes cried, her reputation as a member of the Celestial Envoys cratering with each death. Suddenly her reputation became a lesser concern as she realized that War Captain Blue was no longer on his knees behind the Warlord. A tingle in her gut told her to move, and she did so, flickering through the air, fast as lightning, as the ground on which she'd been standing exploded with red magma.

"Now, Green!" the Warlord yelled, and then a geyser of caustic liquid exploded under her feet, bathing her in its terrible, destructive acid-attuned Energy.

Tes screamed and launched into the air, riding a surge of electricity out of the acid, but not before she felt its painful caress. So, Green and Red had joined the fray. She hissed in fury as her perfect, soft pale flesh peeled and warped, revealing red sinew and pulsing veins. With a surge of Energy, though, she mended her body, painting over the damage with new skin. Suddenly more angry than concerned about her reputation, Tes released some of the tight bindings that held her form in its minuscule prison.

She kept her human shape, but she allowed her mass to expand, and she crashed to the ground with an enormous concussion, suddenly a thousand times heavier than she should be. She had to spread the impact with a surge of elemental air-attuned Energy, or she might have sunk into the ground. Still, her landing rocked the courtyard, sending a ripple of earth out from the point of impact and flinging the nearby Vesh like ragdolls.

The Warlord cracked his wings and took flight, hanging in the air nearby, and Tes could see his three War Captains moving to surround her; they'd fared better than the sycophantic nobility, and it made sense—not one of them was beneath Tier Nine. "So," the Warlord called, "you begin to show your true colors. Is she not a better prize? Did I not tell you, men? *Fist!*"

As he screamed the final word, Tes felt the first hint of panic she'd experienced in a very long while, for suddenly, ten powerful auras bloomed into being, and she saw, evenly spread out around the walled enclosure of Blue's front courtyard, the Warlord's most potent fighters shrugging out of dark, thick cloaks that had held them concealed, even from her. A trap? Could it be that she'd been so blind? While she'd worried about her two young charges and schemed to keep them safe, she'd been the target all along?

Victor held Valla to his chest, and he ran. He didn't slow when he saw the gate to Blue's estate but rather bunched his thighs and jumped, flying through the air as he activated Titanic Leap. When he crashed down onto the cobbles of the street, he glanced over his shoulder, saw the blue-plated guards scrambling, and continued to run. They were Vesh, and he was bigger than most Degh—they couldn't keep up as he ran and jumped.

Valla squirmed in his grasp and said, "Victor, I'm okay now. I can run."

In his red haze of fury and singular purpose, only one thing was on his mind: Tes's command to "go." Victor grunted in response but kept Valla tight to his chest while he charged down the street, leaping wagons or crowds, smashing through gathered weaklings who didn't move quickly enough. He could feel something happening behind him, a distant surge of auras and great pulses of Energy—they sang to his blood, reminding him of battles he'd never seen but somehow remembered.

Visions of great winged serpents in the air, gigantic men and women in chariots driven on lightning-streaked clouds, and the tremendous concussions of elemental Energies exploding with the primal force of volcanoes or tidal waves ran through his mind as Victor raced through the streets of Coloss. Part of him wanted to stop, wanted to turn and watch whatever was happening. Part of him wanted to drop Valla and charge back toward Blue's estate—his friend might need his help. Still, a bigger part of him wanted to get Valla to safety and knew that Tes wanted him to do so; she'd told him. Her last word had been "go," and Victor had felt the force behind it. She'd be furious if he returned.

"Victor," Valla tried again, still held tightly to his enormous, heaving chest, "Tes might need us!"

"She said go!" Victor roared, and his words were thick and guttural, loudly echoing through the street. He'd been making good time, blasting through the light traffic, turning down long, straight roads, and he knew he was nearing his destination. He could see the convergence of the great city walls, indicating he was coming up on the southwestern corner of Coloss.

"Victor! What if she dies? What if the Warlord takes her?" Valla tried, but Victor had felt the command in Tes's voice, had felt the certainty and the need for him to obey. She wanted him and Valla to leave, and that was that.

"We can't help with that," Victor growled. His worry for Tes, his momentary doubt, and the sharp knife of cowardice in his heart dampened his rage, so he forced out a furious roar, stoking the flames of fury back up. He leapt an enormous flatbed wagon being pulled by two great, gray-skinned, double-humped animals—something like a cross between elephants and camels. He was at the apex of his leap, sailing for the cobbles of the street, when a lancing pain tore through his lower back, and he tumbled in the air, careening toward the street headfirst.

Victor never forgot about his charge, though, and he tucked himself into a ball, holding Valla safe in his arms as his shoulders smashed into the roadway. He rolled three times and flopped onto his back before he let go of her. Something kept him from lying flat; an uncomfortable lance of pain from his stomach radiated with each move he made. Grumbling with fury as Valla scurried out of his grasp and stood on the street beside him, he looked down and saw a long, silvery spear jutting out of his guts. The only thought that came to him when he saw it was one of surprise—it must be a good spear, indeed, to pierce the wonderful armor Tes had given him.

"Going somewhere, whelp?" The voice came from where he'd last jumped, and Victor, sitting in a growing pool of blood, watched as Karnice made his way around the big wagon. He gave a Degh, still holding the reins of a panicking mount, a shove, and the man abandoned the beast and ran off. Dimly, Victor saw that the street had cleared, though citizens peered out from doorways, windows, and around corners. Karnice smiled broadly, his body clad in thick bronze-colored, rune-etched plates. He held his four arms aloft and said, "You seem to have my spear. Mind if I take it back?"

45

❊

STANDOFFS

Tes cloaked herself in lightning, streaking through the courtyard, intent on leaving her would-be ambushers far behind. She'd been quite well surrounded, and whatever direction she chose, she'd have to deal with at least one of the members of the Warlord's Fist. With that in mind, she decided to fly toward Bambori, a squat little fellow who was exceedingly tough but sluggish in both action and wit. Just as she'd hoped, he was slow to intercept her, and she flew past, quicker than a thought—and slammed into a barrier that had no business being there.

"What have you done?" she cried at the terrible impact.

"Now! Hurry! Contain her!" the Warlord cried, thrilled excitement lifting his voice into a near shriek. While Tes reeled, stunned by the collision with the wall of force—she'd been traveling at speeds too great to track with the naked eye, and her mass was prodigious—the Warlord, his Captains, and his Fist closed in, laying layer upon layer of binding Energies upon her. She felt the weight of those spells, those weavings designed with a singular purpose—containing Tes and her particular Energy signature.

"You've been planning this for some time, haven't you?" she asked, folding under the weight of the bindings. She didn't speak loudly, and though the air crackled with the hum of the spells, and Vesh nobles cried and groaned, whimpering with pain as they tried to distance themselves from the battle, her voice still rang out through the courtyard.

"Oh indeed, dear Tes," the Warlord crowed, moving close as his ambush party pressed in, their eyes focused, their brows beading with sweat at the effort of the complex binding weave. "For years now, in fact. Fough, that clever bastard, had the idea; it took us all months to master this weave. He's not here to see our skillful implementation, but never worry; he's preparing your bath."

Tes crouched in the grass, feeling out the net of Energies that the fifteen most powerful people in Coloss had woven around her. It was true; the web was well constructed, matching the signature of her Energy, absorbing and reflecting it back at her, squeezing the magical threads tighter and tighter the harder she struggled. "So . . . you used my charges as bait? My curiosity as the tripwire?" Rather than fight fruitlessly, she sat in the grass, smoothing her skirts against her thighs and looking up at the Warlord as he stalked closer. His comrades had stopped some ten yards away from her, their faces strained with concentration, their mouths silently working as they toiled to maintain and reinforce the bindings.

"Yes. Why would I care for some blue flesh when I can delve into your blood, Tes? You flaunted your power one too many times, and I began to understand that you were so bold with your words because you held no fear or respect for me. That will change."

"Ah," Tes said, nodding along with his words as she looked around the circle of his lackeys. She began to worry he wasn't present, but then, as she looked over her left shoulder, she locked eyes with him, War Captain Ardek—Black. His face was sweaty, his brow furrowed, but when he met her eyes, she saw what she'd been hoping for. Deep in the depths of those big gleaming orbs, colored like red-tinted amber, she read what she'd hoped to find: a streak of rebellion. Tes lifted an eyebrow as if to ask, "Well?"

Karnice's voice rang out over the abandoned street. "You seem to have my spear. Mind if I take it back?"

Victor put one hand out onto the cobbles, pressing his knuckles into the hard surface as he leveraged himself to his knees, the great, silvery length of Karnice's spear jutting out before and behind him. "This spear?" he asked. He felt Valla behind him, felt her press a hand to his shoulder in support, fear, or comfort. He didn't know which and didn't care; it was enough to know she was close. He reached down, grasped the blood-soaked metallic shaft of the spear, and began to pull it through, his fury climbing to new heights as the weapon kept his flesh apart, kept it from knitting, and the wound flared with new pain as each inch slid through his guts.

"Oh? You'll hand it back to me? What a good lad," Karnice said, continuing to stride down the cobbles, closing the distance from a hundred yards to seventy to fifty. By then, Victor had pulled the now-bloody length of silver from his guts, and he grinned as he felt his flesh knit. He lifted the spear, holding it aloft and admiring its long, gleaming blade as it winked in the sunlight.

"You want it back? I'll leave it here for you," he growled, and then, with every ounce of his mass, muscle, fury, and frustration, he grasped the spear with both hands and drove it down into the street. The blade slipped between two cobbles, and with a shriek of tearing, melting stone, the shaft sank into the street, all the way to where Victor grasped the shaft. When he straightened, only four feet of silvery metal stood out from the ground, and Karnice had stopped walking.

"Annoying, but not my only spear, boy." He held out the two hands on his right side, and suddenly a thick, black, metallic spear appeared in them. To call that spear black was a gross understatement—it was a spear-shaped tear in reality, an absence of light. It confounded Victor's attempts to gaze upon it, and he almost felt mesmerized by its strange, inky stain on the colors of bright daylight. "Do you like this little beauty? She's going to leave more of a mark than that elegant lady you so callously drove into the ground."

"Victor, do we run?" Valla asked from behind him, and he knew she was standing there to keep out of Karnice's line of sight. Was she planning a surprise attack, or was she simply afraid? Afraid . . . The word echoed strangely in Victor's mind. Was he fearful of Karnice? As the thought raced through his mind, he watched the tall, powerful, four-armed warrior approach and found he couldn't find a trace of fear for the man. Did that mean he could beat him? Victor chuckled, shaking his head ruefully, and the laugh only deepened as he saw Karnice's puzzled expression and hesitant step.

"Is your friend mad, little blue?" Karnice asked, apparently well aware that Valla was hunched behind him. Valla didn't answer him, but Victor wouldn't have noticed if she had; his mind was too busy analyzing the crack he'd found in Karnice's formidable strength. Victor knew he couldn't beat the warrior in a straight fight, but it didn't seem that Karnice felt so confident. Was that fear lurking behind those smug laugh lines? If Victor could give him pause with a chuckle, how would he fare against some true terror?

"Valla, I promise you," Victor said, his voice low, rumbling out of his enormous chest, "I won't harm you."

"What?" Valla asked, and he felt her touch on his back lighten as though she were preparing to pull back.

Victor's pathways were aflame, filled to the brim with fury, and if not for his Iron Berserk upgrade, he knew he'd be flinging himself at Karnice at that second. As his mind raced, and he thought of the consequences of his arguably insane idea, Karnice shrugged at Valla's lack of response and continued his swaggering approach, twirling the void-black spear as he grinned, exposing his long canines.

Logically, Victor knew he'd changed a great deal since he'd last tried out his Aspect of Terror. He had more will, more Energy, and a stronger tie to his bloodline, but more important than all of that, he knew he could maintain his Iron Berserk while he did it; wouldn't his rage, his fury, help him cope with that overwhelming desire to feast on fear? While his mind raced, he felt another enormous surge of Energy across the city from where he and Valla had just fled. Back where Tes was dealing with far more dangerous foes than this spear-twirling *pendejo*. If now wasn't the time to pull out the stops, when would it be?

Tes smiled as she felt a thread fray in the weave of the Warlord's trap. Black was pulling back his Energy, but he was being sly about it; she knew he was risking a brutal death at the Warlord's hands for this betrayal. Still, the fraying thread of Energy was all she needed. Tes reached out with a thought and a knife of primal wind Energy, and she pulled apart the weave, stretching a wide hole through it. As the Warlord's Fist screamed in unison, their carefully woven trap snapping back, flaying their pathways, Tes reclaimed the enormous mountain of Energy she'd put into her current form, holding herself tightly bound to this diminutive, if pretty, shape.

As her Core flared with power, and her body elongated, widened, and shimmered to life with blue metallic scales, Tes looked down at the Warlord, who'd stumbled to a halt, glancing from left to right at his fallen Fist. She growled, running a long, pink tongue over sword-like fangs, "I think you brought a net too small for this catch."

"Kill it!" he screamed, then snapped his wings, lifting himself into the air. He held his blade before himself, and Tes was impressed; her dragon aura was no small burden to bear, but he was holding up well. Several of his Fist, too, were struggling to their feet around her, staggering backward, their shields and weapons clutched in white-knuckled fists. The courtyard had become a much smaller space than when she'd been a petite human-shaped woman.

"It?" she purred, her rich voice pouring like liquid silver from her throat. "How rude, Warlord. Desist now, before I have to alter the history of this world by slaying you and your cohort."

"We can glean what we need from her blood and bones!" Suddenly the Warlord surged with power, and great metallic echoes of his white-feathered wings stretched out behind him. He screeched as he exploded into flight, his enormous, silvery sword held down at a cutting angle as he tore through the air at Tes.

Tes was sure she could shrug off the Warlord's attack and knock him aside with one muscular foreleg and its scythe-like talons. In fact, she had half a mind to snap him out of the air with her jaw, swallowing the insufferable tyrant whole. Still, he moved quickly, and her first instinct was to dodge, so she did, rolling on waves of wind and electricity that coursed through her body, just as thick, just as much a part of her as the blood in her veins.

The maneuver was devastating to the members of the Warlord's Fist on her left side, along with War Captain Red. Her bulk alone was enough to cause terrible harm, but the surging electricity that allowed her to move faster than most eyes could track compounded the damage as she flattened those four powerful men, sending them scattering, tumbling through the courtyard to smash through trees, shrubs, and ornamental statues. Tes uprooted a tree, and her great tail, whipped without a thought to aid her balance, smashed through the wall, blasting a twenty-foot hole in the stones.

The Warlord's streaking attack was fruitless, his blade carving a deep furrow in the cobbles of Blue's drive, and when he flew in an arc to turn and try to assess how he'd missed, his eyes were troubled. Tes snarled and glanced around, choosing an example. Her gaze settled on Green, and she remembered the brief pain of his acidic deluge. She inhaled and coughed out a fork of lightning, thick, blue, and so bright that anyone—even the nigh-immortal Warlord—who witnessed it would struggle to see anything but its afterimage for many minutes.

The streak of lightning entered Green at the chest. His body and even his armor turned black and then burst, with a clap of thunder, into a cloud of charred ash. The Warlord cried out; the surviving members of his Fist, Blue and Black, fell back, their hands instinctively going to their eyes or ears as they struggled to recover from the concussive blast of light and thunder.

Tes hadn't held back; the Energy for that attack had come from her Breath Core, nurtured there for many long months. It felt good to release it, like letting go of a sneeze held too long. Still, she couldn't muster such a burst of electricity again, not anytime soon, but the Warlord didn't know that. She'd meant to give him pause, and it worked. He flapped his wings, rising higher into the air, and she saw him trying to peer around his fingers, looking for an avenue of escape.

"I can fly faster than thee, Warlord," Tes rumbled, her words and the cadence of her speech slipping back into the rhythm of her homeland. "Lower yourself before me. I'll have words with you and yours. Move with alacrity, and I'll consider mercy."

The Warlord, still blind and dumbstruck by her show of power, seemed to resign himself, awkwardly descending, clearly unsure how far away the ground was. Tes watched him and stretched out her senses, feeling for Victor, wondering if he'd managed to find Boaegh's tower. She'd barely begun to explore the city with her prodigious perception when she felt something startling—a surge of Energy with a familiar taste, but one she'd only seen hints of before; Victor had unleashed his fear affinity.

Karnice was a tall Vesh, but he still had to look up as he approached Victor. He slowed when he grew near, confirming Victor's suspicion—the Warlord wanted him alive. He knew how fast Karnice was, knew he could have been upon him in seconds from the instant he'd crashed into the cobbles with that spear in his guts. Two things were holding Karnice back: his desire to get Victor back to the Warlord in one piece and something else, something Victor had seen lurking behind those gleaming red eyes—he was struggling with fear.

"So? You don't pick up your axe, and you don't flee. Are you coming with me back to the citadel?"

Victor felt Valla stir behind him and knew she was wondering why he wasn't doing anything. She didn't speak, though, and he admired her willingness to steadfastly delve into depths of danger with him rather than run for her life. Perhaps she simply knew Karnice could catch them again if he'd done so once. "I don't think so, Karnice. I'm curious—what makes you fear me? Is it that I shrugged off your attacks the other day? Is it my aura?"

"Ha!" Karnice growled, hefting his spear, this time with one left and one right arm, leveling the point so that it was trained on Victor's chest, just three or four short feet away. "I don't fear you, boy."

"Oh?" Victor growled, and though his voice was deep and rumbling as it came out of his great chest, something shrill chased the word, something that sent a shiver down the spines of anyone who'd been listening. Valla inhaled with a trembling lip and stepped back as she heard that note. Karnice frowned, and his nervous tongue flicked out, licking at his lips as he braced himself.

For a moment, it seemed as if the sun was going behind a cloud, but then the new shadows shifted and began to writhe as they wrapped themselves around Victor. They multiplied, building on each other until he was dressed in a cocoon of clinging, sliding, snake-like shadows. Cracks, grunts, and deep, hoarse gasps escaped the shadows, and Karnice yelled, "What are you doing! Lie down, fool! Let me take you back to the citadel!" Panic tinged his words, and as he cried the last word, he desperately drove his spear into the darkness cloaking Victor's enormous form.

Victor felt the spear as it bit into his shoulder, felt it slide off the bones and slash away some of the shadow flesh cloaking them. He chuckled—not a bit of pain had accompanied the blow. What did hurt was the way his body was stretching, cracking, and bursting apart. It wasn't as bad as the first time; he was still berserk, and his body was far more durable than before. More than that, he knew what was happening—the fear-attuned Energy was coursing through his pathways, sharing the wide channels with hot rage.

As he shifted and stretched, his flesh fell away to be replaced with shadows, and his fingers elongated into bony talons. He screeched, roared, and bellowed, the noises echoing off the stone-faced buildings nearby. Karnice stabbed him repeatedly, then he began to launch Energy attacks, trying to stun or disable him, trying to interrupt whatever process Victor was going through.

Victor's belt did its work, though, absorbing those red spears of Energy, those grasping claws of fiery magma that rose from the ground. His armor deflected blow after glancing blow from that spear. Valla, pale and sweaty with fear of her own, also did her part to buy him time. She danced around from behind his huge, shadowy cocoon and lashed out with Midnight, trying to distract Karnice.

The Vesh champion was initially annoyed, allowing himself to be distracted by her attacks. She scored several blows, hacking a deep cut in his leg and stabbing Midnight Hope into his ribs, only to have her sword caught short by his thick metallic armor.

"I don't need you alive, bitch," Karnice growled, and then he turned from his assault on Victor to launch an all-out attack on Valla, his spear dancing and weaving, stabbing and slashing. She put up her barrier of wind and electricity, the one Tes had taught her, and she backpedaled, parrying with a skill beyond her tier. Karnice pursued her, his fury redirected, momentarily forgetting Victor.

All of this Victor was aware of. While he lurked in his cloak of shadows, painfully changing as he underwent the transformation of his Aspect of Terror, he kept himself cognizant of his inner self with the fury of his rage-attuned Energy. Each time he started to slip into fantasies of feasting on the bright spirits around him, he refocused himself with the rage he felt at Karnice. He watched as the Coloss champion blasted him with spells; he watched as Karnice bullied Valla, and he worked to force his heart to share the dual facets of the Energy coursing through him. His fury toward Karnice allowed for only one target in his hunger for terror.

In the gray, colorless expanse of Coloss, where countless bright spirits lingered behind stones and watched from a distance, he observed the nearby blazing spirit as it battered and bullied the smaller, bright, silvery spirit. He knew that spirit. He'd tasted it before, and while he'd love to taste it again, he knew he couldn't. No, his fury would allow only one feast today. He refocused on the more formidable target and saw the dark terror-attuned spear that it swung about, trying to tear the Energy out of the small one.

Time to put a stop to this, Victor decided. He stretched out of his cocoon of shadows, allowing them to ripple and flow along his lengthy limbs and terrible, lupine form. He was huge, bigger than when he'd transformed before, bigger than when he'd simply taken on the aspect of a Quinametzin.

Victor was a nightmare made of shadow and bone, and strangely, the shadows that once clung to him like black flowing fur now coated his great body like dark feathers. His snout was long and ended in a hooked beak. The blazing red, rage-filled eyes in his terrible skull glowered like menacing lanterns as he lifted his head and howled such an awful sound that Karnice fell to one knee and ducked his head before he mustered the strength of will to turn toward the sound.

Victor felt nothing but hunger and fury, and when he saw his target fall to the ground, he leapt upon him, grasping him by the shoulders with razored talons and bearing him down to the cobbles with the weight of his massive form. The spirit was bright, full of vibrant Energy, and as the terror bloomed within it, Victor feasted, pulling it in, growing stronger, despite its thrashing, despite its desperate attempts to harm him. With each heaving pull, Victor grew more potent, and the spirit grew weaker, more feeble.

More than that, Victor could feel the waves of fear from those lurking nearby. He could feel them making him stronger, feeding his hunger, and he began to contemplate feasting upon more than just the spirit beneath him. As it grew weaker and his desire never diminished, Victor felt his rage fading; why had he even been enraged? What was the point of anger when he was so hungry? He glanced up from his feeble, twitching prey and saw the bright, silvery spirit still lurking nearby, still exuding soft waves of fear. It watched him, and he felt his hunger intensify. "No," he grunted. "She. Not it. Valla."

With a roar and a gasp, Victor pushed more of his rage into his pathways. Then he started to clamp down on the fear-attuned Energy that had surged so powerfully into him, flooding his pathways and Core, driving the dark, purple-black orb to new surging heights, nearly overshadowing his other affinities. He pulled it back, pushed it down, and as the fear left his pathways, his rage surged hot, and he regained himself.

The shadows fell away from Victor's body, and the strange fear-monster aspect with them. He hunched over Karnice, the man's face ghost white, his spear rolling over the cobbles, fallen from his listless, twitching fingers. Victor looked up at Valla, crouched behind a nearby overturned wagon, and felt an uncomfortable surge of guilt; he hated that he'd made her afraid again.

He lurched to his feet, still struggling with the duality of his mind, then lifted Lifedrinker from her harness and, not trusting Karnice to stay down, he stepped to the side and brought her down with a terrible wet crunch onto the brassy, rune-etched plate on Karnice's chest.

Lifedrinker's edge bit into the metal but didn't penetrate it. Still, with Victor's enormous strength and her sturdy, heavy axehead, he'd bent the metal into a concave shape. Karnice gasped and sputtered a bloody cough, and Victor lifted Lifedrinker again, smashing the dense metal further into the man's chest. Again crunching, wet sounds erupted from the blow, and Karnice, already nearly drained into a coma, stopped coughing, and his eyes grew glassy.

"Let's go," Victor growled, motioning for Valla to follow him.

46

"HOME"

Wait!" Valla called from behind Victor. He slowed, a little frustrated; his impulse, his instinct, was to hurry, to get to Boaegh's tower and get off this world. He didn't want to look back at Valla, didn't want to see what he'd done. It wasn't that he regretted killing Karnice; it was a nebulous guilty feeling deep in his gut as though he'd done something wrong, even though he was pretty sure he'd only attacked the champion spearman.

He turned, though, and looked at Valla, saw her wide, imploring eyes, and though some haunting fear still lurked behind them, they were bright. "What?"

"Take his spears! Take his rings! He was wealthy in this world!" She walked from around the wagon toward Karnice's corpse, and Victor had the presence of mind to wonder why no Energy was gathering around it.

"Is he dead?" He started back toward the body and the scene of his transformation and battle.

"Yes." Valla picked up the dark spear, the one that seemed like a dark stain in the air. "This spear . . . I'm amazed you didn't die."

Victor looked around, saw the deserted street, not even a hint of activity behind windows or doors, and the nature of his guilt hit home. He'd drained some Energy from the people watching the fight. Though he didn't think he'd killed or even hurt anyone overmuch with it, they'd been collateral damage and were probably still shaken by the nature of his Aspect of Terror.

He reached out for the spear. Valla released it with a shudder, and he felt the dark pulse of a kindred attunement. Entwined with the weapon's metal were deep, dense threads of dark Energy, darker than the fear in his Core; this spear was steeped in dread. "He tried to kill me with dread—a cousin to my fear. I didn't even feel it."

Victor slipped the spear into his ring, then walked over to grasp the haft of the silvery spear he'd driven into the road. Again, he sent it into his dimensional container and chuckled, wondering why Karnice hadn't thought of that. Maybe he hadn't cared; maybe he'd thought the dark spear was a better weapon with which to kill him.

"He has two rings; we can study them later. Here." Valla tossed the rings to him, and Victor nodded, stuffing them into his pocket. Then, impulsively, he reached down, took Valla's hand, and began to jog toward the nearby southwestern corner of the city wall. Valla didn't resist but clutched his fingers with her small hand and ran along with him. "I don't know how you killed him, Victor. He had to be more than Tier Eight."

"I don't know. His will was weak. When he walked toward me, I saw fear in his eyes and knew I had him."

"Thank you," Valla said, squeezing his hand again. When he glanced at her, a puzzled look in his eyes, she added, "For warning me. For telling me you wouldn't harm me. I almost ran, but I believed you." She paused, looking around, then said, "The streets are empty. I don't think it's because of your fight with Karnice. Something big is happening back at Blue's estate."

"Yep." Victor turned around a corner and was hit with the stench of charnel as the abattoir Tes had told him about came into view. It was a long, wooden, warehouse-like building with stinking, fly-coated drainage canals that ran from its interior toward grates in the cobbled street. Victor held a sleeve to his face as he ran past, straight toward the squat, square building with the pennant-grasping gargoyles. They'd made it to Boaegh's tower.

"You lackeys may flee. The Warlord and I will conduct some small business, and then I'll be gone, and he will be free." Tes's words rumbled out of her massive maw, and she watched as Blue, Black, and the remaining members of the Warlord's Fist glanced at the defeated, crestfallen man. He stood stoically, staring at the ground, his great silver sword still clutched in his white-knuckled hands. When he didn't say anything, they fled, taking his lack of protest as confirmation enough.

Still enormous and still coated in shimmering, electrified blue scales, Tes leaned her great head down so her hot breaths ruffled the Warlord's disarrayed, dirty feathers. Her scythe-like teeth, slick with saliva, slid against each other as she said, "Come, Warlord. Let us visit your citadel. Before I leave this place, I'll have the mixture your court Artificer has devised. I'll know how you and your ilk have been stealing bloodlines all these many years."

The Warlord frowned, but he didn't speak. Tes chuckled, then lurched upward, shifting her weight onto her enormous rear legs. She snatched the white-feathered man up in her foreclaw, and with a great surge of Energy and physical power, she flexed her silver-blue wings and burst into the air, scattering the corpses of those who'd died assaulting her.

Ten seconds later, she was gliding toward the vast courtyard before the citadel, and when she landed, Tes didn't bother trying to be gentle. She tore up a hundred cobbles with diamond-hard claws as she slid to a stop. The guards who stood watch at the gigantic gateway looked terrified, leveling their spears her way, so Tes gave them a true roar, unleashing her full aura. As the terrible sound split the air and they felt her power, the men panicked and ran, not a single one able to resist enough to even think of closing the gates.

Tes set the Warlord down, and as he stumbled, shaken from the quick journey and her rough treatment, she growled, "I'll revert to my less formidable form. Do not think of returning to your previous hostilities. My mercy has run its course."

A great roar split the air of the city as Victor and Valla approached the door to the tower. "Tes," Victor said.

"Really?"

"Yes. She lives, and she's giving the Warlord hell." His voice carried his relief, and Valla, still clutching his hand, looked up at him with moist eyes.

"I felt so guilty running from that fight. I was so worried about her. Should we go back?"

Victor shook his head. "She's fine. I hope she can find us again, but we can't hang around here, Valla. As much as I want to try to help her, if she's still fighting with the Warlord or his Captains . . ." Victor sighed and slipped Lifedrinker into her harness, then rubbed at his head, staring at the tower. "No, they're on a different level, and I can't expect to get lucky with them as I did with Karnice. She wanted us to get away. The whole reason she's fighting is so we can get out."

"I know you're right, but running still feels wrong." Valla glanced over her shoulder, and her eyes widened. She yelled, "Get ready!"

"What?" Victor whirled, reaching for his axe, but then he saw what she meant. A thick wave of silvery, purple Energy was rushing toward them, and before he could so much as take a deep breath, it smashed into his chest. As he was lifted into the air in a paroxysm of euphoria, he saw Valla, too, lifted up. The Energy coursed through him, replenishing, restoring, and improving him, and when he fell back to his feet, still standing on the stoop of Boaegh's tower, the System had left him several messages:

Congratulations! You have achieved level 47 Titanic Herald and gained 12 strength, 22 vitality, 12 dexterity, 12 agility, 12 intelligence, and 12 will.

Congratulations! You have learned the spell: Aspect of Terror, Improved.

Aspect of Terror, Improved. Prerequisite: Affinity, Fear or related affinity. You change your appearance to represent something terrifying. While you wear this illusion, you will passively harvest and cultivate fear-attuned Energy emanating from those who perceive you and cannot resist your will. You begin to understand the nature of fear, recognizing it in others and mastering it within yourself. Energy Cost: Minimum 100, scalable. Cooldown: Long.

Congratulations! You have gained a new feat: Challenger.

Challenger: Time and time again, you have faced those with power that outweighs your own, and you have prevailed. Your unique abilities, affinities, and personal determination have made you a formidable foe. Henceforth, your aura will carry extra weight, and those who suffer its full impact will have to work hard to resist nagging doubts and fears. Effect: Your enemies, especially those of greater level and power, will find their resistance to fear reduced.

"Two levels!" Valla announced.

"Hell yeah! Nice one, Valla."

"I don't know why, though; you did most of the work against Karnice . . ."

"Because the System saw how important you were in that fight. You kept him off me while I figured out my Aspect of Terror. Anyway, c'mon." Victor walked up to the door and slammed his fist against the wood. It opened almost immediately, and a brown-robed man stood before them, his reptilian face deep in the folds of the hood.

"I wondered how long you'd stand out there." His voice was sibilant, more so than the other Yazzians Victor had met.

"Are you Hark?" He pressed forward, pulling Valla with him into the tower.

"I am . . ."

"Time to open the portal. Tes says your debt will be repaid as soon as we get through it."

Hark backed up a few steps and peered through the still open door. Victor, meanwhile, examined the dim stone antechamber. Hallways led away to the left and right, and a circular stairway led upward. "She said that? My debt will be forgiven?"

"Yes. What do you owe her, anyway?" Victor moved past him and slammed the heavy wooden door closed.

"If you don't know, then it's not my place to say. Come. The ritual is prepared; I simply need to activate it." He started for the stairs, and Victor and Valla followed.

Tes followed the Warlord through his citadel, walking a pace or two behind, her body relaxed but her mind sharp and ready. He was a dangerous man, this Warlord, especially here in his seat of power. Still, she'd thoroughly humiliated him and crushed his strongest retainers. She didn't think he'd be foolish enough to try her again.

Before she'd constrained herself, binding her flesh with ropes of powerful Energy, she'd reached out with her senses and found that Blue and Black were lurking together in a deep cellar beneath Blue's estate. The Fist was similarly scattered—all but the big oaf, Tronk, whom she'd felt in the southern part of the city.

Tes grinned, imagining the big, likable fellow drinking away the memory of his part in her attempted abduction. She could forgive him, for she'd felt little resistance as she tore apart his portion of the net, and he was in league with Black. Someday he might come to Victor's aid when the titan-blood returned to set this world on a new course.

Victor and Valla had been safe when she reached out; she'd felt them both hale and full of Energy near Boaegh's tower. Tes's biggest regret when it came to those two was the lack of a proper goodbye; she'd have loved to go with them to see their world briefly before returning home to face her judgment. If she wasn't wrong, Victor's rapid growth and potential for disruption would likely see the System sending a tribulation or two his way.

She sighed, shaking her head; the poor thing had been through so much already! She certainly wished she could have spent a bit more time with him.

Still, Victor had nearly mastered one of her spells, a true dragon working, and if he learned from that experience, there was no telling what he might accomplish. Some of his spells were quite powerful—with the proper alterations and enhancements . . . "Ah-ah, dear Warlord. Please don't step too far ahead. Isn't the tunnel to your Artificer's lair just ahead?"

"Yes," the man snarled, having found his voice and a touch of courage again when Tes took up her human aspect. "You know," he said, over his shoulder as he ducked into the narrow tunnel, "Karnice was set on watch to wrangle that boy of yours should he run free. The man's not gentle . . ."

"Oh, I'm sorry, Warlord. Your prizefighter has been slain."

The Warlord stumbled to a stop, reaching out a hand to the tunnel wall, and he barked a short laugh. "Impossible! Wait! Did you slay him?"

"No, no, that was all Victor."

"But Karnice was a champion, high tier at that!" The Warlord began to stumble forward again, shaking his head. "Who helped him?"

"None, save perhaps his lady friend, Valla. Karnice was a bad match for Victor, Warlord. The man had a pitiful will. His skillset was lovely when it came to arranged fights against his noble friends—men and women he'd studied exhaustively. Against a true killer, though? A man built for destruction? An iron-willed juggernaut of terror? Ha, he likely collapsed and suffered an ignoble fate. A pity we couldn't have put the battle on display for the city in the arena. Still, I imagine some witnessed the fight, and the tale will travel."

The Warlord was silent as they continued through the tunnels, and even when they stepped through the doorway into Fough's laboratory, he didn't speak. Tes wasn't surprised to find Fough on his knees waiting for them— the man knew better than to flee her. With a surge of her aura and whip of pure, primal wind Energy, she pushed the Warlord to the ground beside him. She announced, allowing some of her draconic pride and cruelty to taint her voice, "If you are quick to provide me the materials and design documentation for the ritual meant to steal my bloodline, I will leave you with only a small reminder of my wrath."

The top room of Boaegh's tower was a bare, square, stone-walled room. High, narrow windows allowed diffuse light to fall on the marble floor, illuminating an interwoven spiral pattern laid out in black and red sand, punctuated with glowing amber gems at the intersections of lines. Hark stopped short of stepping into the pattern, pausing near the top of the stairway. He said, "Are you sure you're ready? I won't hold the portal open long, for the Warlord has forbidden such magic."

"Yeah, and don't worry about the Warlord. I'm pretty sure he has his hands full." Victor stepped to the edge of the lines of sand and said, "I just wish we could've spent these dumb prize tokens."

"Well," Valla said, "if you actually come back someday, we can spend them with merchants in this city or others. They're highly valued."

"We?" Victor grinned at Valla.

"I . . . well, maybe!" Valla shrugged.

"It's true about the tokens," Hark added, unbidden. "If you don't mind me asking, how many do you have?"

"Between the two of us? Like forty."

"Ah! A true fortune. You're right, though—such wealth will be useful should you ever return to this world. You could raise an army with that many. A small one, at least."

Victor felt an urgency in his gut, and while Hark spoke, he began to pace back and forth. Finally, he said, "Right. Sorry, Hark, but we're in a hurry. I feel like we need to get going. Can you open the portal?"

"Of course. The sooner, the better—I don't want the Warlord or his Captains to learn of my involvement. As I said, I'll be closing the portal right behind you." Hark moved forward and gingerly reached down to touch one of the black sand lines with his left hand, and then he gently placed his right hand onto a red sand line. Victor felt a surge of Energy pour out of him, and then, at the center of the pattern, an oval rip in the universe appeared, wreathed in crackling orange flames.

It was about seven feet high and three feet wide at the center, and Victor shivered at the idea of stepping into it—something about the empty darkness beyond it reminded him of open space. "Is it safe?" he asked, belatedly wondering if he could trust this Geomancer, a one-time student of the arch-asshole Boaegh.

"Certainly!"

Valla reached up, took Victor's hand in hers, and said to Hark, "Tes will kill you if this portal is anything other than what you've promised."

"It is not a trick!" Hark wailed, apparently quite fearful at the mention of Tes's wrath. "This is the doorway Boaegh used to venture to your world."

"Okay. Make sure you destroy this pattern. Don't tell anyone you know how to open it." Victor squeezed Valla's fingers, then stepped toward the portal. "Ready?" he asked, pausing before it.

"Yes. Let's go home." She licked her lips nervously and looked up at him, mustering a brave smile. The choker at her neck glinted in the portal's light, and Victor was once again struck by how pretty she was. He smiled, squeezed her hand, and stepped into the shimmering gateway.

Status			
Name:	Victor Sandoval		
Race:	Human (Quinametzin Bloodline): Advanced 2		
Class:	Titanic Herald: Legendary		
Level:	47		
Core:	Spirit Class: Advanced 2		
Energy Affinity:	3.1, Fear 9.4, Rage 9.1, Inspiration 7.4	Energy:	9274/9274
Strength:	202	Vitality:	302 (332)
Dexterity:	82	Agility:	105
Intelligence:	74	Will:	455
Points Available:	0		
Titles & Feats:	Titanic Rage, Ancestral Bond, Flame-Touched, Titanic Constitution, Titanic Presence, Desperate Grace, Challenger		
Skills:			
System Language Integration		Not Upgradeable	
Spirit Core Cultivation Drill		Basic	
Cooking		Basic	
Animal Taming		Basic	
Unarmed Combat		Basic	
Knife Mastery		Basic	
Spear Mastery		Basic	
Bludgeon Mastery		Improved	
Axe Mastery		Advanced	

Grappling	Advanced
Sovereign Will	Advanced
Titanic Leap	Basic
Spells:	
Iron Berserk	Epic
Channel Spirit	Improved
Inspiring Presence	Basic
Enraging Orb	Basic
Globe of Insight	Improved
Project Spirit	Improved
Dauntless Radiance	Basic
Heroic Heart	Basic
Spirit Walk	Basic
Tether Spirit	Basic
Manifest Spirit	Improved
Shape Spirit	Improved
Harsh Light of Justice	Improved
The Inevitable Huntsman	Improved
Aspect of Terror	Improved
Imbue Spirit	Basic
Honor the Spirits	Improved
Titanic Aspect	Basic

ABOUT THE AUTHOR

Plum Parrot is the pen name of author Miles Gallup, who grew up in Southern Arizona and spent much of his youth wandering around the Sonoran Desert, hunting imaginary monsters and building forts. He studied creative writing at the University of Arizona and, for a number of years, attempted to teach middle schoolers to love literature and write their own stories. If he's not spending time with his dog, you can find Gallup writing, reading his favorite authors, or playing *D&D* with friends and family.